CAPSCOVIL

Complimentary

{ Capscovil and their authors support several non-profit organisations with selected books. For further information please visit:
www.capscovil.com }

Acknowledgements

This book would never have come about without the help of others.

Above all, I would like to thank my beloved partner, who has accompanied me on every step of this journey with endless patience, leading me from the depths of despair back towards the light.

Particular thanks are due to my family:

My father who has always urged me to go my own, unconventional way and believe in myself.

My mother who, despite her grave illness, never had grown tired of offering encouragement and motivation.

My "little" sister, whose loving support ensured time and time again that I did not lose sight of the important things in life.

My aunt for her creative input that she supplied, in ample quantities, at the most unusual times.

I am also extremely grateful to my loved ones all around the globe for their unflinching candour and honest advice and, most of all, their abiding friendship.

My profound thanks go to Niall Sellar for translating and Helen Veitch for editing and proofreading. Both have done an exceptional job, exceeding expectations constantly along the road. It has been a great pleasure to work with them.

About the Author

Alice N. York was born in southern Germany. Before writing her first novel she has been working in several sales and marketing positions in technological and global industries.

Alongside her business life Alice supports, often with a focus on cancer, several non-profit organisations.

GAME

FAINT SIGNALS

ALICE N. YORK

Translated by Niall Sellar

A CAPSCOVIL BOOK | GLONN | GERMANY

Original edition „Richtungswechsel" published by Capscovil Verlag, Glonn, Germany, April 2010

*

First Imprint English Edition
Perfect Paperback
Copyright © Alice N. York, 2011
Published by Capscovil Verlag, Glonn, Germany, May 2011
ISBN Print 978-3-942358-08-8

All rights reserved. No part of this book may be used or reproduced in any manner whatsoever without written permission, except in the case of brief quotations embodied in critical articles and reviews. For information address Capscovil Verlag (info@capscovil.com)

Cover design: MusiDesign, Glueckstadt, Germany
Design: Capscovil Verlag, Glonn, Germany
Editor: Helen Veitch
Printed by: Lightning Source

Additional electronic versions of this edition available
ISBN 978-3-942358-09-5 - First edition ebook (epub)
ISBN 978-3-942358-10-1 - First edition textunes-App
ISBN 978-3-942358-11-8 - First edition iBooks

www.capscovil.com

Attention: Organizations and Corporations

For information on special quantity discounts for bulk purchases for sales promotions, premiums or fund-raising, please write to:

game@capscovil.com

For Mom

In loving memory

Chapter 1

January

Before Alex entered the PsoraCom building through the automatic double doors, she turned once more to Sandro. He sat in his slightly dented, red Hyundai and blew her a good luck kiss.

"In bocca al lupo!" he cried in Italian, wishing her luck in the would-be lion's den. "Crepi!" came the obligatory, smiling response – although of course she didn't seriously hope he would die.

She squared her shoulders and made her way confidently to the reception, asking politely for Thomas. For her first day at work she had decided on a plain black suit with a white blouse and flat, black patent leather lace-ups. She always felt good in this outfit because it was classic: not too feminine, but rather business-like and professional. Besides, black contrasted nicely with her copper-red hair, and Alex had never been that into skirts. Even as a child she had loved lederhosen and jeans because whenever she cycled, climbed trees or played football, dresses had just got in the way.

In her professional life she had encountered some women who displayed their feminine charms provocatively in order to achieve their goals. Alex had never understood the logic behind this. Despite being only five foot five she almost never wore heels, even though she thought they looked really good with suits. Unfortunately she couldn't walk in them for very long.

While she attached her visitor badge and waited, she marvelled once more at the imposing, modern lobby, which seemed to be made completely of glass. Actually the exterior consisted entirely of solar modules, the electricity generated from which was fed into the company's own energy network. "Building-integrated photovoltaics" was the name of this concept, she remembered. The solar modules were part of the building itself. The reception area was oval shaped, a good 1000 square feet, with a counter in the centre underneath a dome-like cupola. PsoraCom's fir-green company colours stood in direct contrast to the breezy transparency of the glass. Three women dressed elegantly in green uniforms attended to visitors. Some distance to the right of the counter, surrounded by an oasis of palms, were a few dark-green wing chairs and small plain chrome tables. Behind the counter, in front of the passage through to the building, there was a biometric scanner similar to those at airport security. To the left stood high bistro tables, amply spaced. Only these weren't just tables, but highly developed pieces of computer furniture whose entire surfaces doubled as touch-sensitive screens. Visitors could surf the net while they waited, or watch the latest updates from PsoraCom as they hovered in holographic 3D above the tables.

Thomas, her new boss, picked her up from reception. He was a good head taller than her and looked as though he had sprung straight from the glossy catalogue of a luxury gentlemen's outfitter. She guessed that he was probably in his mid-forties although there was not a single strand of grey in his black hair. He was sportily elegant and dressed in a classic double-breasted suit with a white shirt and grey pullover. Calmly, he came towards her.

"Good morning. I trust you had a good journey."

Despite the polite greeting, she found him just as impenetrable as she had at her interview a few months before. He was the type of person who was difficult to read. Not that he looked at her in an unfriendly way, just seriously and without any discernible emotion.

"Good morning. Yes, thanks. I didn't have far to go."

The biometric scanner briefly flashed green as Thomas led her through into the hallway, which forked a little further on into two double-storey corridors. Just as in the lobby, everything was solar-glazed and very bright. They took the left-hand corridor past the bright meeting rooms that Alex already knew from her first visit.

At the end of the corridor, past the glass elevator to the upper storey, they reached an enormous open-plan office. All the outer walls were made of pale-coloured solar modules and the approximately 25-foot-high ceiling furnished the room with sufficient air. A good hundred workstations had been set up in a circular arrangement, like a honeycomb in a hive, separated only by head-high walls of tinted glass that offered a little privacy from one's neighbour. While Thomas took Alex to his cubicle, she noticed that there was an outer and an inner circle, both of which were broken in four places by a gangway, dividing the room into eight segments in total. At each crossing there was a sign with the names of the people who sat in that particular segment. In the middle of the inner circle there was a colossal sculpture that looked like the pointed apex of a cone.

"Inside are encapsulated rooms for secret strategy meetings," explained her boss as they walked past.

There was a free space opposite his cubicle which she could use for the time being. Alex wouldn't be allocated a desk in the office; she would work from home. This was not at all unusual: indeed many companies saw cost benefits in staff working from home. Field managers were with clients most of the time anyway – at least, that's what was expected of them. All the members of her team worked from home; only Thomas, as group leader, preferred a designated desk in the office building.

Alex put her bag down and Thomas led her back to a small room next to the elevator. There were coffee and drinks machines, as well as a few tables with ashtrays on them. It was highly unusual for an American company to have a smokers' room. Nevertheless, the tables were equipped with mushroom-shaped suction units, which ensured that there was no lingering smell of cold smoke. Coffee of all kinds, from espresso to latte macchiato, as well as tea and non-alcoholic drinks, were available to employees free of cost. The company probably hoped this would encourage them to work longer hours. After both of them had taken what they wanted, he accompanied her to the IT department.

"This is where new employees get their laptop and an IT systems briefing," he said. "Everyone is on first name terms here by the way," he added. "Come back to me when you're finished and I'll give you a tour of the office."

He turned round abruptly and seemed almost happy to be rid of her for a while.

After an hour she went back to Thomas. He led her through the entire office on the ground floor and explained where Sales and Marketing and New Businesses were located. Whenever they met a colleague, he introduced Alex immediately. As time went on, she found it increasingly difficult to remember all the names, let alone their positions. On the first floor they found the design and development, book-keeping and legal departments. After the tour there was still enough time for Alex to collect her company car and home office equipment.

"Let's meet in the canteen for lunch," said Thomas, after he had left her with the relevant colleague.

The facility manager was in her early fifties and told Alex that she had previously worked as a self-employed office clerk.

"I always took care of whatever my clients asked of me and became the go-to girl for everything, so to speak. PsoraCom was one of my first clients and after the company's explosive growth they made me a very generous takeover offer. The good thing about the job is that I can afford to work just half days."

That explained the state of her desk, perhaps: it was overflowing with all sorts of different papers, and she seemed to be a genius in chaos.

"Do you need a mobile?" she asked.

"Yes," replied Alex. "But I'd like a Zeus68. Since I work in New Businesses, I should have the latest kind of netphone."

"No problem," said the facility manager. "I'll order you one. It should be here by tomorrow."

Alex loved new gadgets and would have bought one for herself anyway. Currently the Zeus68 was the only netphone with integrated thin-film solar cells.

Next they put together Alex's employee ID. Unlike the temporary visitor badges, this wasn't just a piece of plastic. PsoraCom highly valued the use of the latest technology and new employees were given a corporate accessory pack comprising a watch, bracelet, necklace and earrings. Each of these objects was a combination of plain but high-grade leather with beaded gold or silver, and included an integrated microchip containing all personal and biometric details. If lost, the items could not be misused. The microchip generated its electricity using body heat, or rather by using a thermo-generator, which exploited the differences between ambient and body temperature. If you took your watch off, the chip was deactivated; it could only be reactivated by an integrated voice sensor. If you lost it, it would be of no use to anybody else, other than as a nice piece of jewellery.

In order to programme the sensor, they needed to record Alex's voice. Being somewhat vain, it took her three attempts. But that was nothing compared with some of her other colleagues, the facility manager smiled kindly.

Afterwards it was time for lunch and together they made their way back to the reception area, taking the right-hand corridor at the V-shaped fork, which also led into a big, round room. The canteen took up the front quarter, with the research department in a cordoned section further back. Work there was top secret and only certain people were allowed access to this area.

"Hey, listen, I know your surname from somewhere," began her colleague unexpectedly. "You're not related to Franz Ruby are you? I worked for him before I became self-employed."

"Yes, Franz is my father," replied Alex, astounded. "Do you still remember him?"

"Of course I do, we worked together for a few years in an office by the station."

"I can still remember that office," Alex smiled. "My dad used to take me there occasionally during the school holidays. I must have been eleven or twelve. The thing I remember most is the big fridge with lots of coke cans. They were for clients, of course, but you could always take a few, and since we didn't have coke at home I didn't hold back."

"I wish I had such fond memories," laughed her colleague. "I remember one time when a colleague of Franz's had a rip in his trouser seam just before a client meeting. Very unprofessionally, we used a stapler to mend it. After the meeting he came and told us that the whole time he had felt like a fakir."

Thomas came into the canteen shortly afterwards and explained that the food was subsidised. There were various round counters with wooden roofs located on the left-hand side. Each counter offered different dishes, ranging from Asian, Italian and American, right through to vegetarian and traditional fare or just fresh salad.

There was no fixed seating plan so they sat down at a long table. Several people had already taken their place. All of them worked in Sales and Marketing. However, none of them were from Alex's team. They greeted her pleasantly and some of them asked what she was responsible for at PsoraCom.

"I've been hired as part of the new Vabilmo team to work as a consultant for a select group of solar plant manufacturers. I've been in the power plant and energy sector for a long time and I'm really looking forward to viewing everything from the perspective of the solar industry."

Her colleagues nodded appreciatively.

"That sounds very exciting – best of luck," said one of them.

PsoraCom were the market leader for solar cells. Originally their photovoltaic cells were made from pure silicon. In company factories, solar cells were still made from big silicon chips, also known as wafers, and then used by PsoraCom's customers to build larger solar modules. In turn, plant manufacturers combined many electrically connected solar modules to build power plants.

However, the manufacture of crystalline silicon solar cells was expensive and used up too much energy; alternative products were therefore being sought. Alongside thin-film, concentrator and dye-sensitised solar cells, there was now Vabilmo: a new sector that aimed to be more cost effective and energy efficient when it came to mass production. Here, solar cells were processed using organic solutions. The cells were razor-thin and as flexible as film, enabling the assembly of completely new configurations, which, together with the reduction in weight, would result in considerable savings.

In the first instance, PsoraCom saw two principal markets for these polymer cells. There were the traditional solar plant manufacturers, who built both grid-connected plants and off-grid systems; and then there were the companies who made robots. These robots ranged from complex machines in the production industry to machines built for specific tasks, and even simple household robots that could cook, iron or mow the lawn.

Based on these twin approaches, their basic aims were to increase the efficiency of solar power plants and to reduce robot energy requirements, thus lowering cost. Once the polymer cells were market-ready, contracts needed to be won from suitable clients because the implementation stage would take one to three years, depending on the size and nature of the project. Only if the new solar cells were widely used in the industry could appreciable savings be made.

For this kind of product launch, PsoraCom adopted a two-fold strategy. First there was direct sales – the classic approach, which allowed the company to speak to solar module manufacturers. In order to generate revenue, they had to be steered away from the currently employed solar cells and convinced to use the polymer cells (internally code-named "Vabilmo"). Second, PsoraCom also had an indirect sales unit made up of consultants whose objective it was to influence new market trends. The consultants worked together with end customers - that is, plant and robot manufacturers -, analysed processes, delivered strategy recommendations and assisted in the transfer of knowledge.

Their job was to make sure end customers would buy from module manufacturers who used PsoraCom's polymer cells.

In the past few years Alex had learned everything there was to know about power stations. It was her long-standing knowledge and experience that had got her the job. At least that's what Thomas had said.

The task of the Vabilmo team was to concentrate exclusively on the potential market for polymer-based solar cells. Aside from Alex, the team consisted of an additional consultant, a colleague from direct sales and a developer who worked on new concepts for the configuration of the solar modules. As yet, Alex had only met Brian – the other consultant – at the interview. She was scheduled to have a joint strategy meeting with him and Thomas in the afternoon. The meeting would also serve as a training session on existing activities of the Vabilmo team.

Lunch went by in a flash. Alex was delighted by the warm welcome and the keen interest her new colleagues had shown in her. Somehow, she immediately felt as if she belonged. After lunch she accompanied Thomas to one of the conference rooms on the ground floor, which was elegantly furnished with black gloss marble tiles, a large, round polished wood table and high-backed, fir-green leather chairs. Everything in the room could be controlled by a touch screen device which stood on the table. Besides the obligatory air-conditioning, telephone system and Bonsai data projector, the device also boasted the controls for a large plasma screen with an integrated webcam for video conferences.

Brian followed closely behind and greeted them both with a jovial "Hello". At five foot nine, he was not only smaller than Thomas; his whole appearance stood in stark contrast to him. His ash-blond hair, bound untidily in a ponytail, was immediately noticeable, as was his goatee beard. Not to mention his very casual attire. He wore his striped shirt nonchalantly over a pair of faded jeans, from the back pocket of which hung a long key chain. Nevertheless, he pulled a black trolley behind him in a business-like manner. Its plastic surface was covered in all kinds of stickers, some of which Alex recognised as belonging to famous surf schools. He took out his laptop and hooked it up to the touch screen device using a cordless connection.

"I've put together a few slides on our strategic approach," he said as he turned the plasma screen on.

They sat down at the table like three points of an invisible triangle so that they could all see the presentation on the screen. The title page announced in bold letters: "VABILMO STRATEGIC OVERVIEW – BRIAN, SENIOR CONSULTANT, VABILMO TEAM EUROPE, NEW BUSINESSES, STRATEGIC DIVISION."

Brian scrolled to the next page and began to explain the table illustrated there step by step. Thanks to the eight-point font the text was both barely legible and, as the table took up the whole page, extremely confusing. It referred mainly to plant manufacturers and their activities. He spoke very deliberately and paused regularly for dramatic effect. The way he chose to express himself seemed to contradict his external appearance. Occasionally, however, his search for the appropriate expression was unsuccessful, and a protracted "um" crept into his speech. Nevertheless he seemed nice and good-tempered, and he smiled openly at Alex.

While he spoke she had time to take a closer look. His sun-tanned face had already begun to display a few wrinkles, even though he was only thirty-five. Judging by his collection of surf-stickers, she put this down to too much sun and salt-water. The goatee corresponded to the surfer-snowboarder cliché, but it was a little unkempt and needed trimming. Working with him promised to be interesting.

Brian was self-confident. He had casually rested his arm on the back of the nearest chair and seemed to enjoy talking. She had already noticed this at the interview– but it was almost certainly linked to his wealth of experience. For the whole afternoon they went through projects and existing contacts to potential end customers. A major development contract had already been signed with a plant manufacturer, and Brian went into detail about this project. It sounded exciting and very promising. They paused once for a short break, after about two hours. For most of the time Alex only listened. She spoke merely when asked for her opinion or if something was unclear. Thomas said very little, simply letting Brian speak. Four hours later, he concluded the presentation with his take on the future.

"I thought that for the first few months Alex and I could deal with solar plant manufacturers in Europe, planning and designing all steps together. During this time I can teach her everything and familiarise her with the most important issues. At the same time I'll show her the best-known methods, which I devised specifically for the development contract with Roffarm, and which have already paid off on several occasions. After that she can take on some end customers of her own. I'll look for other manufacturers, and additionally try to establish myself in Asia so we can move things forward there strategically. I've got a few ideas already."

Thomas nodded. "Sure, why not."

"Of course, sounds good!" Alex agreed.

Her probationary period was set at three months, during which time she was guaranteed her full salary – including the variable component. Thereafter the latter was based on her own performance and the percentage to which she achieved her objectives. She had collected over ten years' experience selling complex products and solutions and was used to having a defined sphere of responsibility. For her, work was neither duty nor habit, but a challenging game that brought enormous pleasure.

They decided to call it a day. Alex had received so much new information that trying to remember everything had made her head swirl. Even after the drive home, a normally relaxing thirty-minute journey on a country road past small villages, meadows and woodland, she was still buzzing.

Back at home, Sandro was already waiting and greeted her with a passionate embrace.

"So, how was your first day?" He had just made dinner.

"Great, but totally exhausting," she called from the bedroom, while she changed her suit for a more comfortable pair of jeans. Once she was back in the kitchen, she sat down at the counter and began to tell him about it.

"The building is really impressive. There are solar cells fitted to every window; or rather all the windows have been made into solar modules. It's a power station in itself, with the latest technology everywhere. You only have to look at my new employee ID."

Proudly she showed off her new necklace; he, however, used the opportunity to kiss her an inch lower.

"Do you want to know how it was?" she asked with mock indignation. "Or do you want something else."

"Something else," he grinned mischievously. "But I'll listen first if I have to."

She smiled. "Good, then listen! There are so many people buzzing around in the office, it's like being in a beehive. I couldn't begin to remember all of their names. In the afternoon we went over some of the projects. There's a lot going on already, but I've still got so much to learn."

"So you got a good impression, then?" Sandro stirred in the pot, while it all came gushing out of her.

"Absolutely. Everything is so new and exciting. It's going to be really interesting. So, what are we eating?"

"Pasta Pomodoro." As usual when he had cooked he stood there grinning mischievously, like a child expecting to be praised. He had already set the table and lit the candles. She couldn't resist that look.

"You're such a sweetheart!"

"You can show me after dinner," he gave her a conspiratorial wink. "But let's eat first, the linguini are al dente."

Her parents didn't call until Alex was getting dressed again; it was as if they had known what would happen after dinner.

"And how are your new boss and colleagues?" her father asked with interest.

"So far I've only met Brian. He made a good impression, even though he likes the sound of his own voice. A real surfer-type, but he seems OK otherwise. I can't work out my boss at all. He's so quiet and hardly says a thing. He probably just needs to thaw out."

In the meantime Sandro had collected their glasses from the kitchen and topped them up with wine. After the phone call they lay snuggled on the sofa, each happily lost in their own thoughts. Alex remembered how they had first met.

It had been in their previous company; she was in Sales and Sandro had been a freelancer in Research and Development. He had aborted his medical studies and turned his hobby of developing software components into a career; concentrating on programming different sensors. When implantable sensors used to regulate and control blood pressure and pulse came on to the market, he took his chance. They had first met each other four years ago in the small canteen, where she had gone to get a lunchtime salad.

"That looks delicious," Sandro had said to her.

"You look delicious too," Alex had thought to herself as she admired his Mediterranean looks, with his almost-black eyes and hair.

His muscular arms had been the icing on the cake. But it had been something else that attracted her to him. To begin with she had pigeonholed him as a macho Italian, although he later turned out to be very shy. That was precisely one of the reasons she had fallen in love with him and ignored reservations about their cultural differences. He had, it was true, been born and brought up in Germany. Nevertheless, in his thirty-six years he had never lost touch with his Sicilian relatives – even if he seldom visited them.

Just now she realised again how attractive he was. A head taller than her, his stature was reminiscent of Michelangelo's David. He still had chin-length hair, tamed with a little gel. Alex was certain that Sandro was the man with whom she would start a family, build a home and grow old. The thought felt very good, prompting a small sigh.

"How was your day, anyway?" she asked him finally.

"Oh, same as usual. The project's been going well ever since I took it on - it's almost like a permanent position. But my boss can be very narrow-minded sometimes. I can't shake the feeling that he undervalues my work."

"From what you've been saying, that really does seem to be the case," she agreed. "Companies often don't treat external staff very well: frequently their motto seems to be no-one is irreplaceable."

"That's true," Sandro nodded. "I have to renegotiate every additional cost – he's a real bean counter."

"He seems like a very hard-nosed client," responded Alex. "Unfortunately, nothing comes for free in the working world. You have to prove yourself the whole time. Only then are you in a position to make demands."

However, in order to make demands one needed to have a healthy degree of self-confidence, and that seemed to be where Sandro's weakness lay. She often tried to share her experiences with him, but knew at the same time that these could never simply be transferred from one person to another.

"But enough about work," she added, drinking the last drop of wine.

"You're absolutely right. There are considerably more enjoyable things we could be doing."

There it was again, that wicked grin she found impossible to resist.

The next few days Alex left early so that she could be in the office shortly before eight. That meant she could start the day in peace with a bowl of muesli or fresh fruit from the canteen. She almost always took the desk next to her boss as most of her colleagues didn't arrive until at least nine. Things seemed to be done differently at PsoraCom. Thomas generally arrived an hour after her, surprised to find her sitting there already. She devoted her first half hour to looking at the Financial Times website and different RSS feeds. Then she went through her emails. Even on her first day she had received more than twenty mails. Colleagues and team assistants from different departments had been informed the previous year that they would have a new co-worker. In addition, for certain topics, such as general project updates, internal meetings and mandatory training, there was a fixed mailing list in which she had likewise been included. You had to give PsoraCom one thing: their IT department was highly organised.

Most of the mails were not yet directly addressed to her; rather, she had been copied in for information. That was good though – she had always liked learning things by reading. It didn't matter if it was presentations for clients or project plans; development transactions or white papers; product descriptions or general information about PsoraCom's far-reaching organisation: the more she could obtain, the happier she felt. When it came to knowledge, she was like a dry sponge greedily soaking up water. Even when she didn't require it, she liked to know the details in order to improve her understanding. Her studies, a mixture of electronics and mechanics with a little business management and marketing, meant she didn't shy away from technical descriptions. She always tried to expand her horizons, even if it meant tackling the limits of her comprehension.

Thomas mailed her some information and then referred her to other people. "Ask Brian when he comes. He has more material."

There it was again, the feeling that her boss just wanted to be left in peace. But Alex didn't dwell too hard on it. Even if she enjoyed discussing current topics and projects with other people, she would only ask him when it was absolutely necessary. The rest she would find out herself. She had never been particularly shy. Brian provided her with different links and intranet addresses later. With that she had enough material to keep herself busy for the time being.

There was only one more issue: she was expected to answer a few emails about an event in February.

"That's our yearly planning conference," he explained. "Employees are flown in to Florida from all over the world. During the day there are product training sessions and in the evening our directors hold presentations. The whole team is going to be there."

Her pulse quickened with excitement. Finally she was going to America again. To Florida! She had received an email about every little detail – flights, airport transfers and the hotel.

"Which sessions should I pick?"

"Just choose the same ones as me," said Thomas without any further explanation, handing her a print-out.

After finishing her booking she returned the paper with a silent nod. Alex would get used to the way he dealt with employees. Printing out her agenda - Hard Rock Hotel booking included - she felt a tingle in her stomach. The last time she had been in Florida was eighteen years ago. If the agenda was anything to go by, she wouldn't have much time for herself, but she would still enjoy warm summer weather in February. It also meant realising a long-standing dream of hers: staying in one of the Hard Rock Cafe chain's hip casino hotels. Excitedly she went to get a coffee, bumping into Christopher on the way. He had also attended her interview, having been in charge of the Vabilmo team at the time. A month later he had swapped with Thomas and taken over as head of Consumer Retail. Job rotation was common at PsoraCom. The company recommended it to both managers and employees after two or three years so that they could remain flexible. Alex had found Christopher very agreeable.

"Ah, the new member of the Vabilmo team," he hollered. "It's great to see you - welcome to PsoraCom." His broad grin underscored the friendly greeting. His wavy blond hair looked a little tousled, although it suited his casual, neat style nonetheless.

"Thank you, thank you," replied Alex, instinctively adapting to his open manner, which seemed to have been shaped by an upbringing in the countryside.

Alex spent the next few days reading through various intranet sites to gain an overview of PsoraCom's company structure. The headquarters were in California, in Oakland to be precise, on the other side of the Bay of San Francisco. Like so many other technology companies, they worked closely with Berkeley University because the company founder had completed his degree in the energy and resource faculty there. He had acquired a plot of land in the hills above a cemetery a few years ago. It was flanked by a country club and measured the equivalent of fifty American football fields; in America, that was enough to get started. Thus, Human Resources were only about three miles as the crow flies from trainees, PhD students and future co-workers. A great number of management staff came from Berkeley.

Despite its relatively brief existence, the company had a complex structure. New sites had already been launched around the Bay Area. Explosive increases in revenue had led to the hiring of thousands of new employees and the establishment of offices all over the world; meanwhile a bulk of new purchases made to serve the solar heat market had necessitated a complete reorganisation of the company's ten-thousand-strong workforce six months ago.

Everything had been converted into a matrix structure. Verticals were responsible for the development of solar cells for certain markets and purposes. Each of their departments had a specific area of expertise, whether it was the use of solar cells for big power plants or smaller house-installations, for building components, or for appliances such as machines and robots. Horizontals comprised cross-divisional functions such as the sales and marketing, research, finance and legal departments.

The Vabilmo team was situated in the first of these and would be working mainly with specialist departments of two different verticals to receive both technical and product marketing support. One of these departments concentrated on traditional solar plants, the other on appliances, robots and machines. The organisational network was complicated by the fact that there were colleagues in Sales who already dealt with companies from different sectors using the traditional amorphous silicon cells. The Vabilmo team would therefore advise these colleagues internally, while at the same time jointly calling on clients until a contract was signed. Alex needed time to let it all sink in. That's how she knew she was part of a big company, not a simply structured medium-sized company.

Initially she spoke very little with Thomas. Only when she went for coffee or headed to lunch with a colleague did she ask him if he wanted to come. He accompanied her more and more often and Alex quickly began to feel happier. All of her colleagues in the office were very kind and had made her feel like one of them from the start. It didn't matter whether you met in the corridor or at the coffee machine, everyone said hello, and at lunchtime conversation came easily.

Apart from Brian, she still hadn't met anyone from her own team since they all worked from home. The first joint team meeting had been scheduled for the next week. Otherwise the days passed quite uneventfully. She, like her boss, stayed at the office until just after six. At home she cooked with Sandro and they talked about their days, just as all couples did in the evening.

Her first discussion with an external company took place before the team meeting. Brian had set up a meeting with a retailer. In principle, retailers were dealt with by a member of Christopher's team. Most of these companies sold solar modules to private home owners, with whom PsoraCom had no direct dealings. Nevertheless, some retailers offered machines and robots to end consumers, and were therefore of potential interest to the Vabilmo team as an additional sales channel.

Brian came straight to the meeting room from his home office. Although dressed in a black suit and checked shirt, he wore no tie. His hair was neatly combed and bound in a ponytail. Thomas was also present, dressed elegantly as always. Owing to the energy sector's extreme conservatism Alex had adopted an unobtrusive, somewhat muted, almost gender-neutral style over the years and wore a dark-grey suit with an apricot-coloured pullover. Apart from mascara and rouge, she wore no make-up. She wanted to be valued for her knowledge and personality, rather than for wearing the right colour of lipstick.

During the very informal discussion Brian presented the Vabilmo strategy. In the end, both parties agreed to remain in loose contact and to keep each other up-to-date. Afterwards Brian returned straight home to his office. A meeting where no tangible arrangements were made was a completely new experience for her.

The weekend passed without noticeable incident. On Saturday morning they went shopping, did their washing and cleaned the house. Later Sandro played tennis for a few hours as usual. He was almost addicted to it, and would spend almost every free minute on court. In the evening they cooked, made themselves comfortable on the sofa and watched a movie. Alex studied the rental properties in the local newspaper at the same time.

"The landlord doesn't lift a finger anymore," she vented her anger. "It's about time we got out of here. He's never really shown any interest in the house, and in the last few years it's only got worse."

"That's true," Sandro agreed.

"There's even mould on the neighbours' walls," Alex continued. "A three- or four-room flat with at least 900 square feet would be ideal. We'd be able to fit everything in there." She needed a lot of space for furniture, books and her extensive Harley Davidson collection.

"It would be pretty nice to have all my stuff in one place," Sandro admitted. "Like the trophies that are still at my parents' place."

Alex nodded. "I'd like a flat with a garden next time. In the summer, it's like having an extra room. And I'd love a mountain view. But I know they're hard to come by in this area. Also I don't want to be much further away from the airport than we are at the moment."

"That wouldn't make much difference to me."

"But you don't fly as often as I do, and PsoraCom's not going to be any different from my previous companies."

"If you say so," he murmured to himself.

There was nothing in rental properties. Sandro continued to watch TV, even though it was he who had been pressing for the move. Alex leafed through to properties for sale.

"We could almost buy a house with the rent we'd be paying for these flats."

"We'd need capital for that," he replied, "and you know I don't have much."

"But I have some, perhaps it would be enough." She had already been saving up for this dream.

But she wanted it to be a detached house. Not one of these prefabricated townhouses that were once again being talked up in the area like cheap wine. With them, you didn't know who would be living next door, and the garden often was nothing more than a 200-square-foot, street-facing speck of land. The advertisements didn't yield much and the few places that were of interest were all too expensive. She didn't have that much capital. In frustration, she put the paper down.

Sunday began pleasantly and they both enjoyed a long, peaceful sleep. After a leisurely breakfast, Alex stretched out on the sofa reading and Sandro went to play tennis. In the evening they spoke to friends and family on the phone. The weekend had come and gone.

In the following days, Alex continued to bury herself in product descriptions, company presentations and intranet sites. When something was unclear, she searched the internet, referring to wikis for an explanation. With time, she would understand the specialist terminology. She smiled as she remembered what her father always used to say: "Slow and steady wins the race."

The inaugural team meeting took place in the second week in one of the sculpture's four rooms. Besides the usual technical gadgetry, the room was fully soundproof. Lamps helped to create an atmosphere akin to daylight, while foliage plants around the room and on the ceiling made it feel almost homely. The setting was supposed to boost creative thinking.

A man with short peroxide-blond hair and a sun-tanned face almost completely devoid of wrinkles pierced her with his gaze as soon as she entered the room. He was wearing a violet suit and yellow shirt, from the collar of which emerged a dark-blue neck scarf. Thomas and he were roughly the same age but they couldn't have been more different. One looked like an elegantly reserved Englishman; the other like his more colourful relative.

"Well, hello," said the latter. "You must be Alex. I'm George."

While he spoke he repeatedly drew breath, which, although barely audible, made his speech sound rather clipped. His laptop was open in front of him and he was holding a netphone in his hand. In an instant he was looking at it.

"This thing is an absolute piece of shit," he said, turning back towards her. But it didn't stop him from fumbling around on it with his little pen.

Alex secretly agreed with him. The phone had been on the market for over a year now but various teething problems had still not been solved. It bore no comparison to her Zeus68. Brian strolled in shortly afterwards, trolley in tow, and gave everyone a nod. As always, he looked as though he had come straight from the beach.

"Hugo is using the bridge," Thomas explained to them, shutting the door.

"Internal network bridge number five, verification: Vabilmo." He spoke into the equipment on the table, activating the system. Voice recognition software enabled PsoraCom employees to dial into a conference call.

After Thomas had welcomed them rather stiffly to the first official Vabilmo team meeting, they started going through Brian's strategy presentation. Brian began with his report, at times speaking so slowly that he began to drawl.

"But Brian, we still need to identify a suitable inverter manufacturer for Roffarm and…" George broke in.

"Yes George, I know. We've discussed it a few times now," Brian cut him short before returning to his report, only to be interrupted on several more occasions.

Alex sensed a slight tension developing but Thomas didn't intervene. He just sat there and looked at the slides on the wall, completely devoid of emotion. It was almost as though George was a fox waiting for the rabbit to emerge from its burrow. He longed for any opportunity to pass comment, before finally tasting relief in the form of Brian's final slide.

Conversation turned to PsoraCom's direct clients, the solar module manufacturers for whom George was responsible. At last he was able to take the helm and inform them about current project statuses. This he did at length and in great technical detail, with the result that Alex was unable to follow in places. She noted all the catchwords he used to look up later. His unusual breathing patterns made his pace seem increasingly frantic – almost as if he were afraid time would run out before he'd had the chance to convey all the thoughts racing through his mind. He said a huge amount, but that didn't bother Alex because she was in "sponge-mode" and greedily absorbed all the information that came her way.

Information was something George had plenty of, as he'd been in solar energy with PsoraCom for many years and had a lot of experience. Every so often Brian now interrupted George to ask a question: it was as if the two of them were engaged in a competition only they knew about. But George's staccato continued undeterred, pausing only to allow comments from the light Swiss accent that came from the loudspeakers.

The comments supplemented what had just been said and were likewise very technical. They had to pay special attention because Hugo spoke very quickly and his accent was difficult to understand over the phone. At some point Thomas interrupted George in mid-flow to say that the meeting would end in five minutes. Two hours had gone by in a flash and it was agreed that no concrete decisions would be taken. Project work would continue as before. Ultimately, they were only just getting started and needed more experience.

"By the way," Brian addressed Alex unexpectedly, "there's a kick-off meeting with Roffarm next Monday. It would be good for you to be there. I'll mail you the invitation, but pencil it in."

"It will be too much if Alex is there as well," said George.

"What do you mean?" Brian objected instantly. "The more people there from PsoraCom, the more the client will see how important this is for us."

Thomas just shrugged his shoulders. "I'm okay with that. It's just round the corner so there'll be no additional travel costs."

Although Alex had found George's comment rather impolite, she didn't want to draw any hasty conclusions. Perhaps he was all right, despite having made a bad first impression.

She spent much of the next few days reading up on the flagship project with Roffarm, although she wouldn't be greatly involved in the discussion on Monday. Nevertheless she wanted to have enough background knowledge to follow proceedings mentally.

Away from her research, she got to know more and more colleagues from different departments at lunch or over coffee. Alex would never have any direct contact with the majority of them. Still, all of them were kind and interested in what she was doing. Of her team colleagues, she saw neither Brian nor George; Hugo she would meet for the first time at Roffarm. She was excited about that because he was the technical lynchpin of the team and they would be working closely on various projects.

Thomas seemed to be thawing slowly. Perhaps he felt bad about Alex obviously leaving him in peace. Although thrilled that he was loosening up, she tried not to show her pleasure for fear that he might retreat back into his shell.

At the weekend Alex and Sandro were invited to the birthday party of one of his tennis friends. It was held at the clubhouse and clearly a great deal of money had been spent: bistro tables had been set up with leather bar stools and the food came from an exclusive local catering service.

The evening proceeded as expected until Sandro moved on to do shots with the boys.

"Come and have a drink with us," he said as he came by again to give her a quick peck on the cheek. He was already a little tipsy from various rounds of schnapps.

"You know that I have to drive," she responded.

Disappointed, he returned to his friends to find the next round already waiting. After a further two hours Alex had had enough. Most of the people were good-natured but drawn-out conversations about the latest fashions and must-see events were simply not her thing. She turned to Sandro.

"Hey, I'm pretty tired. Let's go home."

"What, now?" he asked, a little annoyed. "But it's just getting going here."

"It's already quite late and I'd really like to go."

"Mamma mia!" His irritation showed clearly in his face and the drive home was anything but pleasant.

"Why are you being such a kill-joy today?" he continued in the car. "The atmosphere there was fantastic."

"I'm just tired," she repeated, "and you've had quite enough to drink. You know what happens when you drink too much."

"I'haven't had that much to drink. Just a few shots."

"You've been downing them one after the other," she countered, before realising straightaway that further discussion would be pointless. It was impossible to argue with people when they were drunk.

In the meantime, she had been forced to leave the motorway and stop the car because Sandro had taken a turn. It was exactly this situation she had wanted to prevent. He had to vomit. Now they could stop every ten minutes and take the back road home. There was nothing for it but to try and suppress her fatigue by chewing gum. Back home, Sandro went to bed at once and fell into an exhausted sleep.

As always, he apologised the next morning.

"I'm really sorry. I shouldn't have been drinking so much yesterday."

He put on his most convincing innocent smile and crawled playfully over to her side of the bed. It achieved the desired effect but later, however, it left Alex with a strange feeling and a few nagging doubts began to appear. Were they just too different? Was their lack of common interests more important than she cared to admit? And what about their supposedly shared desire to start a family?

Alex met the last of her colleagues on the day of the big kick-off meeting with Roffarm. At six foot three, Hugo was a giant in comparison with her, and in his formal brown suit he looked like a young student thrust into an unfamiliar second skin. His pale, round face was framed by black curls that made him look younger than he probably was. As he shook her hand with a shy smile, powerful muscles showed through the sleeves of his jacket. Then he nodded a brief hello to Brian and greeted George warmly. In person, his lisp was even more noticeable. But it could have been down to a combination of his Swiss accent and occasionally swallowed consonants.

After they had all registered by fingerprint, Roffarm's project leader took them into a big meeting room high above the roofs of the city.

As was so often the case, Alex was the only woman. There weren't many women in the energy sector full stop. During the introductions she outlined both her previous industry involvement and her current remit. Otherwise she let her colleagues take the lead as they had been dealing with this particular end customer so far.

Roffarm planned and built new solar plants every three to five years, depending on their size and location. Until now they had used crystalline thin-film cells, but attached great importance to being perceived as a technical innovator within the industry. They had already proved this in the past and wanted to strengthen this position in the future. That was the reason they had decided to test PsoraCom's polymer-based solar cells. If the deal was successfully completed, Roffarm would be the first company to use these cells in a new power plant. A corresponding clause in the contract, which Brian had negotiated, was set to serve as a guarantee.

Although the discussions in the meeting were mainly of a technical nature, Alex was happy to be taking part. She watched her colleagues in admiration as work packages were outlined and demands adapted to the project goal. George and Hugo were the most active members of the team and clearly the two with the most know-how. Brian seemed to be more au fait with contractual matters. These were keenly argued, particularly when it came to the formation of the project team and the question of how much both parties were expected to contribute. By the end Alex was exhausted, but happy nonetheless. She had obtained lots of new information. Brian and Hugo were unanimous in their opinion that Alex's attendance had been more than worthwhile. Even George, dead against her presence originally, joined in the congenial post-meeting atmosphere. Her colleagues were certainly a colourful bunch, but all of them seemed competent in their own way. Alex was convinced that she could learn a lot from them.

In the following weeks, she continued to read up on the material and began to take on small projects that Brian had given her. These projects were a good exercise and could be taken care of over the phone. Most of the time, it was simply a question of passing on details about polymer-based cells or discussing possible methods of cooperation with different companies.

Of greater importance, however, was the monthly meeting she had been invited to attend by Brian. It was an internal conference call with product managers from the vertical division specialising in power plants. Although for the most part working on the project with Roffarm, they were also considering other avenues. The meeting was supposed to serve as a mutual information exchange so that everyone could be kept up-to-date.

Privately, everything was going fine, leaving aside the little quarrels that were normal for any long-term relationship. Only the flat hunt continued to frustrate her. There didn't seem to be any great willingness on Sandro's part to commit to buying a house together, let alone discuss topics such as marriage and children. Despite her impatience, she probably just needed to give him more time.

Still, having to pay so much rent to such an ignorant, unfriendly landlord pained her more than she cared to admit. Alex covered the rent because for the time being Sandro had only one client and wasn't earning very much. To make up for it, he paid for all household costs, which was fair in her opinion. She had never taken the trouble to count everything up, convinced that things balanced themselves out in other ways. How could he take her out to dinner or the cinema when high maintenance costs meant he had no money left at the end of the month? These little gestures were more important to her. He could have quit the tennis club, as the monthly fees there were exorbitant. But Alex knew that tennis provided a counterbalance to his work – just as jogging or reading did for her. Besides, almost all his friends were from the club and she could never ask that he give them up. Life was full of compromises; this was one she'd just have to live with.

2

February

She could more than live with her first pay check, which represented a cool step up from her previous job. If things carried on like this, they would soon be able to afford a little house after all. It doesn't get any better than this, Alex thought to herself. She worked in a respected firm with nice colleagues. The job gave her enormous pleasure and allowed her to travel all over the world. That called for a celebration. She invited some friends and neighbours round to dinner on the spur of the moment. A few bottles of wine and Prosecco, as well as antipasti and other Italian treats were soon purchased from the delicatessen. Alex paid the bill, almost the equivalent of a one-week holiday, without so much as batting an eyelid. Given her current bank balance, she could easily afford it.

Her young neighbour Moritz, who had lived in the flat below for six years now, was the first to arrive with his sister, Renata. He was always good for a surprise; and their carnival costumes immediately got everyone in the right mood.

"Hey babe, tonight we're really going to whoop it up," he said, swinging the hips of his raffia skirt. A pair of fish-net stockings concealed his muscular legs.

Moritz worked shifts in a factory, and when he wasn't out partying spent every waking moment in the mountains. He went skiing in winter and spent the rest of the year on his mountain bike. He was an absolute breath of fresh air and always good to have around. His sister was in charge of the fitness and wellness centre of a major hotel.

"Hey girl, so why are we celebrating?" Renata asked as she hugged Alex.

"Hey girl," Alex laughed. "Does there have to be a reason?"

"You're serving up some real treats – these could almost come from our hotel," Renata noted amazed.

"Then dig in. Like my grandma always said: Everything must go."

"No second invitation required," her friend grinned back.

Renata was a bon viveur just like Alex, needing physical activity but only in strictly measured doses. She was very close to her brother and they often went on holiday together, mostly when neither was in a serious relationship. Moritz still needed to sow his wild oats, while a life in the hotel business had made Renata into a committed single. This often surprised Alex, but both of them seemed happy enough.

Sandro and Moritz also got on like a house on fire as they both shared two passions: sport and partying.

"Hey, fish-face," her friend Anna burst in between them. "Good to see you." Anna often spent time working abroad and was just back in the country. You could always rely upon her for a party or a good night out, and that's what Alex liked about her. She didn't take herself too seriously and had enough humour for three.

Alex countered with her standard greeting: "Hi, pudding chops, come here and give me a hug." Jokily, she added: "See that you don't eat everything, now babe: leave some for the others." Her friend tended to live off coffee rather than real food.

Slowly the neighbours from across the street appeared and began to take over the living room and kitchen. Since almost everyone knew each other, there was soon so much chatter that the windows began to steam up. The racket would have done credit to a flock of geese. Wine and Prosecco were consumed in ample quantity and no-one turned their noses up at the finger food. Alex was always happy when her guests were having a good time. 80s classics and cool rock music from Pink made the loudspeakers tremble.

Suddenly Moritz grabbed Alex and spun her around wildly on the living room's makeshift dance floor until she felt faintly dizzy. Sandro, who to Alex's eternal disappointment had never been much of a dancer, stood watching from the door. Her neighbours didn't need much encouragement to take on the next round of dancing. With the first beats of "Get the party started" Renata and Anna began to sing along at top of their voices, barely able to control their laughter. Moritz made as if to seek refuge with Sandro. Luckily, none of the neighbours could complain about the noise since they were all there, merrily contributing to the party atmosphere. It was well after midnight when everybody left and Alex fell exhausted into bed, where Sandro was already soundly asleep.

When she woke the next morning she felt quite sad, without knowing where this feeling came from. It was probably just that the schnapps had temporarily made off with the brain cells she needed for thinking clearly. Sandro was still sleeping peacefully next to her. Without any great desire to get up, she turned over again and pulled the bedcovers tightly to her chin. Besides, it was pouring it down with rain. The world would feel like a completely different place later.

The next week they made the final preparations for the planning event in Florida. Nobu, a colleague from South Korea, had arranged a meeting with developers from Natioba for the last afternoon. The company was a market leader in the solar energy industry but had specialised in off-grid systems and was therefore only an indirect competitor of Roffarm's. Nobu invited Alex along at short notice after Brian had mentioned that she would be responsible for Natioba. Although actually an Italian company, Natioba had one of the most up-to-date development labs in Seoul. Many different companies had labs there as the majority of new industry trends originated in South Korea. With the help of the International Monetary Fund, service departments for research and development had been promoted and generously supported there in the last decade.

All those participating in the conference were scheduled to arrive in Florida on the Saturday. However, a small group from Sales was flying out two days before to visit a big solar plant near Miami. George and Hugo had campaigned with Thomas for Alex to take the earlier flight. In their opinion a visit to the plant would be good training for her.

"Let's get some breakfast first," George decided, as they met at the airport early in the morning.

Like a true gentleman, he refused to let her pay for anything. He even pulled out her chair as they sat down. At nine in the morning, they made for such an odd couple that people passing stared at them. In his dinner jacket, white shirt and Bordeaux-coloured waistcoat George looked more like he was on his way to the opera. Alex, meanwhile, had gone for business casual, combining a pair of faded modern jeans with a dark-blue jacket and copper-red roll neck. That way she'd be able to make herself comfortable on the plane without freezing.

"So, tell me George, how do things like expenses and budget work at PsoraCom? Is there anything I should look out for?"

Her colleague didn't have to be asked twice.

"Expenses are really easy. Just use your receipts to calculate how much you've spent. PsoraCom is extremely generous there. As long as you don't take advantage. Our team doesn't have a budget yet. If you need anything, just ask me."

"I'll do that," she thanked him. "And since we're sitting here so cushy why don't you tell me about Vabilmo's beginnings."

It was as if George had been waiting for just this opportunity. He began to reel off facts, thereby proving himself to be something of a walking encyclopaedia.

"Originally solar cells were manufactured as thick-film cells using mono-crystalline silicon. Man-sized silicon cones were cut into lots of thin slices – so-called wafers. Even though they were fingernail-thin, that was still very thick in comparison with other materials. Different machinery was then used to plane their surface and prepare them for conversion into solar cells. The bulk material of the wafers was treated with a special gas and thus positively doped. Now the minus pole had to be established in order to generate an electric current."

George took a quick sip of coffee before getting back to his explanation.

"This was brought about by a series of different processes. The surface of the upper side was treated with chemicals and gases to make it light-sensitive; then it was doped with another gas, thus establishing the negative pole. An electrically conductive grid pattern was printed on the upper side to provide the electrical contact. Finally, the underside was coated with a conductive material.."

Alex could picture it all very clearly as George continued.

"But manufacturing solar cells using crystalline silicon was extremely expensive and energy inefficient. In addition, a lot of dust accumulated during cutting, which could not be used again. Put simply, we're talking high production costs. This minimised the advantage gained by the low cost of generating electricity and the solar cells' relatively high efficiency. Also, despite enormous resources of quartz, silicon was needed in other sectors, such as the electronics industry. They manufacture processors for computers, cell phones and electronic control units for cars."

George illustrated the point by taking his netphone from his jacket pocket.

"In the long run all this only exacerbated the existing supply shortfall, forcing research to begin on alternative methods of solar cell production. And research was always PsoraCom's forte. Our company holds various patents that ensure our market leadership. Traditionally we've always been one of the first companies to branch out into new areas in order to generate more revenue."

Alex had already heard this from other sources. PsoraCom were known for their high-risk strategy, when it came to launching new products. But more often than not the risks were accompanied by the chance of great rewards.

George went on.

"Vabilmo represents such a new product. Here, solar cells are processed using organic solutions. The key to all this is a special kind of electrically conductive polymer. Polymers have been used in different ways for years. In polymer electronics, light can be produced as a result of a discharge of electrons. Very early on, PsoraCom began investigating whether it was possible to reverse this process. The goal was to create electric energy by exposing polymers to sunlight. About two years ago we made the breakthrough with polymer samples that were different to all the ones before. The patent has been filed and published and we expect it to be granted later this year."

"Do you have the patent specification?" Alex asked. "I'd really like to read it." Even if she wasn't able to understand everything, it would still be interesting.

"I must have it somewhere," said George, before picking up the story again. "Since then, the research department has been working feverishly to standardise production methods, as there are still a few reliability issues cropping up during mass production. At the moment the scrap rate is just under 50%. But enormous strides have been made here too. We should reach our target of 20% sometime this year. Although that still sounds relatively high, it would be something of a revolution in the industry. The mass production of polymer-based solar cells can help us make considerable savings, both energy and cost-wise. With efficiencies of 45% and counting, these solar cells are more than twice as effective as traditional cells."

In his obvious enthusiasm for the topic, he almost got carried away.

"There's still enormous room for improvement. The physical properties of these cells are equally decisive. They are razor-thin and flexible as film. The reduced weight will result not only in enormous savings but also in completely new designs."

When he spoke about Vabilmo and who had come up with ideas for the new designs, Alex again perceived that invisible tension between George and Brian. She couldn't shake the feeling that the two of them were secretly on bad terms. On the face of it, they were two alpha males trying to mark out their territory. Alex smiled at the thought.

They met Hugo, likewise very casually dressed, during the stop-over in London. As Hugo would be in overall charge of the project with Roffarm, the discussion became more concrete. He seemed to highly value George's opinion, while at the same time interspersing his own knowledge into the conversation. Again and again she noticed the admiration in Hugo's eyes when George spoke. He listened with a keen smile and bent down so that the two could make eye-contact. George not only radiated knowledge but behaved very chivalrously towards Alex, which she found flattering. There weren't too many gentlemen left in the industry – it was almost as if good manners were regarded as some sort of weakness.

Having landed in Miami, she broke out in a sweat. It must have been close to 80 degrees in the shade and the humidity was unusually high. Before the shuttle left for the hotel she basked for a moment in the warmth of the sun. Shortly afterwards they were on their way to an up-scale restaurant that looked out onto the Art Deco District and the sea. The plant developer had invited them to dinner with his project team. Conversation flowed freely, and business cards, still in use even in this high-tech era, were keenly exchanged. Alex was sitting at a table with Hugo and very soon engaged in an animated discussion. Her colleague had completed his PhD the previous year, having focused on alternative forms of solar module design. Some of the others were also civil engineers and greatly interested in what he had to say. The atmosphere was fantastic, but they returned to the hotel soon after the meal, as everyone was tired from the long journey.

Alex slept soundly and felt completely rested when her alarm went off the next morning. After a long shower she called Sandro quickly to let him know everything was fine. He was already on his way to Heidelberg for a tennis match. It was snowing heavily back home.

The day was packed full with tours of different labs and production sites, where solar modules were being assembled into large elements. A visit to the first section of the plant rounded things off.

With her two colleagues, Alex had bagged a place at the front of a large convoy of solar vehicles that looked like golf buggies. From there she gazed in wonder at the biggest plant in the world currently under construction. She didn't know many people who had the chance to experience something like that.

There were no more activities planned for the evening so George assumed the role of tour guide. Alex and Hugo had swapped their suits for jeans and light sweaters; George, on the other hand, looked spick and span in a stylish Prada outfit and had doused himself liberally with a delicate sweet scent. They met a few colleagues in Coral Gables, at a Mexican restaurant with a mural depicting the nearby Venetian Pool.

"Does anyone fancy coming along to have a look at the pool?" Alex asked the group. The hotel brochure had said it was gorgeous.

A few people mumbled that they had been already. The rest were unmoved, preferring to stick to their margaritas.

"And they say that chivalry is dead," said George incensed. "You can't let a beautiful woman like this wander the streets of Miami alone." He grinned at the group mischievously and indicated to Hugo that he should join them.

"Don't let Crockett and Tubbs here lead you astray, Alex," someone called jauntily after them.

They got there just before closing. Alex held her breath at the sight of the green pool shimmering like an emerald in the evening sun. There were no swimmers to mar the immaculate view. At one point rivulets cascaded into the pool from the waterfall above. A little further back grottos opened up. Opposite, a Venetian style Rialto Bridge made of pure stone led across to an island. Huge palm trees were everywhere, existing in peaceful harmony with the surrounding buildings.

"The pool was created in the 1920s from an old coral rock quarry," George explained readily. "During the planning stage, the architects were inspired by the charm of Venice's bridges and lagoons. Originally only the cream of society was allowed to use the pool but after the Second World War it was opened to the public."

"You really are a walking encyclopaedia," remarked Alex surprised.

"Only when it comes to exclusive places and objects, isn't that right Hugo?" George teased his colleague.

The security guard indicated with a friendly nod that it was closing time. Although it had only been for a few minutes, Alex felt as if it had been a holiday for the senses. Its languorous silence stood in stark contrast to the relentless flurries of the day. Indeed, for a while as they made their way back to the restaurant it seemed that Hugo too had been caught up in its spell.

Everyone was a little tired on the flight to Tampa the next day. Alex dozed and listened to Eros Ramazzotti on her iPod. On landing, George assumed the role of guide again, because he, the old hand, knew where the shuttle buses departed from. There was a great deal of commotion as employees from all over the world greeted each other excitedly. Around a thousand people had been split up into four different hotels, which the bus called at, one after the other. They never put everyone in the same hotel for security reasons.

With the enormous guitar in front of the entrance the Hard Rock Hotel was visible from miles away. In the bright, spacious reception area there were pictures of famous musicians and their instruments. Right next to the counter Alex spied a well-equipped fitness room. The obligatory souvenir shop offered all kinds of T-shirts, jackets and other desirable objects. The hotel was moderately sized by American standards, with only 250 rooms spread across twelve different floors. From her room on the eleventh floor she had an excellent view of the pool. Perhaps she would have the chance to swim a few lengths herself. Her room, still a fair size despite the two queen-sized beds, was bright and modern. There were two guitar-shaped chocolates on her pillow. Somehow it was cheesy and charming at the same time. After finishing the room inspection she opened her laptop, read the latest news about the conference and called George.

"What's the plan for later?" she asked.

"No idea. I've just got to write a few mails quickly and then we could go and get a bite to eat."

"Do you know what the others are doing?"

"No, but we could rent a car and drive to Clearwater or St. Petersburg. Call Hugo and find out if he can be ready in an hour."

After she had spoken to her colleague, she called George again.

"OK by him. Let's meet at the elevator in an hour."

"Agreed."

That gave Alex enough time to unpack her things and take a shower. Exactly an hour later she met a sportily clad Hugo, whose tight-fit shirt highlighted his muscular upper body. George was wearing black gloss trousers and a pink shirt, with one too many buttons undone for Alex's liking. He had already taken care of the car and took no notice of her protests even though he couldn't claim the cost back on expenses. On the way to the car they met another colleague who decided to join them spontaneously. Henry worked in Marketing as company spokesperson and was also pretty much right-hand man to Wolfgang - the managing director of the German office. Alex had seen Henry in the office from time to time but hadn't really had the chance to speak to him.

George called Brian. They hadn't heard a thing from him since arrival. As it turned out, he had gone to Clearwater straight from the airport with another colleague and spent the whole afternoon there. Clearly the surfer was drawn to the sea like a moth to the flame. They would meet later in the casino perhaps. Brian didn't seem to think that doing something with his fellow team members was particularly important. There had been no word from Thomas either, but he was almost certainly out and about with other top managers.

It was already dark when they arrived in Clearwater. Restaurants and bars with flashing neon-signs were populated by smiling people dressed in summer clothing, while the streets bustled cheerfully to the murmur of the jet-black sea. Alex was overcome by a holiday feeling.

After a brief search, they found a table in a sports bar where it was colder inside than out. That was one of the things that really annoyed Alex about America. She was glad of her warm sweater.

During the meal she chatted with Henry, who had been at PsoraCom since the beginning.

"It's pretty cool, this stuff with the new solar cells," he began. "Are you working on the Roffarm project too?"

Alex shook her head. "No, I'm going to be dealing with other plant manufacturers. After the conference here we've got an initial meeting with Natioba for instance. They're one of the biggest off-grid-systems manufacturers in the world."

"We're always on the lookout for new things. Just come to me if there are any specific projects you want us to mention."

"Sure, I'll remember that," Alex promised.

All the while George and Hugo had been talking shop about possible Vabilmo designs. Alex nodded at her older colleague gratefully when he asked for the bill. Despite her turtle-neck sweater she was frozen stiff. Clearly concerned about her health, George switched off the air-conditioning in the car as they drove back, opening a window instead.

"Just say if there's a draught and I'll shut it again," he called behind him.

"Most kind of you sir," she thanked him, delighted.

It was only nine thirty when they got back to Tampa.

"Hey, what do you think?" their driver called. "Should we take a trip to Ybor City? It's Tampa's Latin Quarter."

George didn't seem ready to go back to the hotel yet.

"I'll go with the majority," said Henry.

Hugo gave a nod and turned inquiringly towards Alex.

"Sounds good. The night is still young – and it's pretty mild." With that she had made the decision.

They took a leisurely stroll down 7th Avenue, keeping a lookout for a nice bar. There was live music coming from every direction and the sweet smell of Cuban cigars hung pleasantly in the air. 7th Avenue reminded Alex of Key West in places. Inviting-looking benches stood at irregular intervals under the subdued light of round lanterns. The high palms lining the street swayed softly in the gentle breeze.

An upstairs bar with a wrought-iron balcony looked particularly appealing. A table up there was still free, as if earmarked for them. The house specialty was a harmless-tasting cocktail called Hurricane.

"Hey guys," Alex spurred them on. "Let's try one of these. You won't make me drink alone will you?"

George played along immediately. "Of course not, we're not that mean are we boys?" he called to Hugo and Henry as he ordered himself a Cohiba cigar.

Their glasses were soon empty and a second cocktail ordered. As the rum slowly took effect, even George's cruder puns seemed to cause great amusement. One of the jokes gave Hugo his cue, and he began to tell the others about the book he was reading. It was about a Japanese businessman who experiences all sorts of weird and wonderful things in Tokyo with his European client. It was called Men's Business or something like that.

"One evening the two of them go with their business partners to the back room of a restaurant," Hugo described a scene from the book. "After dinner, ten women come in and the Japanese man glances quizzically at his client. The European is surprised, but shakes his head. A little while later ten different women are shown into the room. The client shrugs his shoulders again and shakes his head. When another ten women enter a third time, an awkward silence descends. Slowly it dawns on the European that his business partner is offering him an escort for the evening, possibly even the night."

After a brief pause Hugo picked up the story again. "The Japanese had thought that none of the women were to the European's liking. The idea that his client simply wasn't interested would never have occurred to him."

Henry nodded, as if something similar had happened to him.

"Yeah, on business trips you need an SNDA sometimes," George interjected.

Alex gave him a questioning look.

"A sexual non-disclosure agreement," he whispered conspiratorially, "so that the parties involved keep quiet about whatever went on."

The third round of Hurricanes had arrived and, because of the alcohol-induced merriment, Alex didn't attach any great importance to what had just been said. Nevertheless, she did notice that Hugo was staring constantly at George, almost as if waiting for a reaction. But George just drew blissfully on his cigar.

"In Asian hotels you just have to ring reception and ask for a second pillow. Then they know straightaway that you're looking for company," Hugo grinned. He seemed to really like the book.

The juicy direction the conversation had taken didn't bother Alex. After enough alcohol, most men started talking like this. She didn't mind as long as the innuendo wasn't below the belt; being neither a prude, nor the kind of woman who immediately cried sexual harassment. It was just how men were. Alex had grown up mainly around boys. She had chosen a field of study, and then a profession, that had always been dominated by men. The harmless teasing and flirting helped to ease the mood, and the few conversation partners who had crossed the line had been quick to notice her discomfort.

Back at the hotel, George wanted to take a trip to the casino to see if he could meet up with a few colleagues. Hugo was undecided, but Alex said her goodbyes and went to bed.

The next morning, George and Hugo appeared just as Alex was about to finish a leisurely breakfast of fresh fruit and scrambled eggs. They both looked shattered and had dark circles under their eyes.

"What are your plans for the morning?" George uttered wearily.

"The Harley shop. Fancy coming along?" Alex asked with a mischievous smile. "My collection could always do with a few more accessories. You don't have to, though – I can take a cab."

Hugo sipped on his coffee, it seemed to take effect.

"Why not? What do you think, George?"

He nodded. "I don't have any special plans. There's no point going to the beach today."

The first official meeting, a talk on the "Dig Deep" strategy, to which Nobu had invited around thirty people from all over the world, was scheduled straight after lunch. That was still about three hours away and so it was agreed. They had a car after all, and Alex knew the address.

"No problem," said George as they got into the car. "We'll find it with my netphone navigator."

Alex let Hugo and his long legs take the front seat. When, after half an hour, the streets became more and more narrow and their names could no longer be deciphered, George stopped the car.

"Give the netphone to me," he said to Hugo. "The GPS isn't even switched on. No wonder it's not working."

He began tapping on it wildly with his pen. "If it works then at least we'll know where we are."

Alex would have asked a passer-by but she didn't want to spoil the boys' fun.

"Damn!" George exclaimed. "The GPS has no signal. I'll have to drive a little further."

This happened a few more times, before he eventually got a signal after about fifteen minutes. He gave the netphone back to Hugo. They had taken the wrong turn at a big intersection a few miles back.

"Let's go back," George said. "It's almost noon already. We might not make it otherwise."

But Alex didn't want to give up when they were so close to their destination.

"Come on, I promise I'll be quick," Alex coaxed. She couldn't resist taking a playful little swipe. "If you guys hadn't spent so long messing around on that netphone we'd have been there ages ago."

Half an hour later, Alex came out of the Harley shop, bags full and eyes gleaming like a child in a sweetshop. Besides T-shirts, socks and signet ring, the piece de resistance was a great chalkboard mirror with a wooden frame. It had cost less than a decent evening meal.

"Take a look at what I found," she said, proudly displaying her purchases. "It's almost like Christmas."

"Women and shopping," George and Hugo grinned in unison.

At the start of the afternoon meeting, George personally introduced Alex to their colleague from South Korea. Nobu was responsible for marketing in Asia. He was more than interested in Vabilmo and wanted to support the idea locally. After a brief introduction Nobu passed things on to Brian. Visibly tanned, the latter began to talk about his success with Roffarm. He outlined in detail how much he had achieved thanks to the Dig Deep method.

"Roffarm were a real challenge when I took the company on as a client a few years ago," he started. "There was absolutely nothing there! No contracts, no contact network! They didn't use a single one of our products. Naturally, the first thing I did was to arrange a meeting with the board of directors."

There were some appreciative nods. Meetings with the board of directors weren't exactly easy to come by. Everyone in Sales knew that.

"The best method is the top-down approach," Brian continued. "You have to secure the support of those at the highest level right from the start so that the board of directors can tell their employees what's what."

He paused dramatically in order to let what he had said sink in.

"Then I built up my network to all key executives and spoke to everyone I possibly could. Within a few months I had more than a hundred new contacts."

Things continued in this vein for the remainder of the hour.

Alex wasn't really sure what was meant by "Dig Deep". Some of the others seemed equally uncertain.

Back at the front of the room, Brian was concluding his presentation. "If you need any more advice about how best to employ my methods, just ask. I'll explain exactly how it all works."

At the end, all those present received a book from Nobu outlining the Dig Deep method. Most of the participants disappeared extremely quickly. Only one of them approached Brian.

There was still some time before the chief executive's speech that evening. Alex had spoken to Sandro shortly after the meeting. He had returned from his tennis tournament completely exhausted only to find eighteen inches of snow to shovel. Alex had decided not to go into raptures about the weather or her trip to the sea the previous day. After the call, she decided to spend the warm late afternoon by the pool and swim a few lengths. Hugo seemed happier lifting weights in the air-conditioned fitness centre, while George preferred to sit in front of his PC. As agreed, they met for dinner an hour before the speech.

"Hey Alex, did they not have your new Harley shirt in attractive?" joked George, although his gaze conveyed exactly the opposite.

"Don't listen to the old man," Hugo called to her. "You look great. I think the sporty look really suits you."

That was music to her ears. She didn't receive too many compliments at home anymore.

After a cold beer in the warm evening sun, where the lively atmosphere had made it feel more like a holiday than ever, they joined up with the scores of PsoraCom co-workers chattering away contentedly. Their uniform chains and bracelets made them all instantly recognisable as they streamed into the great ballroom with its theatre-style seating. Alex had never been to such a big work event before. Wood-panelled walling adorned by giant screens and a thick carpet helped reduce the chatter to a gentle murmur. Awestruck, she saw countless casually dressed people all around her from the most different backgrounds. The average age was below forty. The doors were shut and Alex felt a growing sense of anticipation go through the rows.

Suddenly the green company logo appeared on the screens and the distinctive tones of Lenny Kravitz's classic "Are you gonna go my way" boomed from the loudspeakers. Together with the music the loud applause from the first rows sent a shiver through her, bringing out goose-bumps. The last murmurs were abruptly silenced as a middle-aged man with a headset entered smartly through the side door. Once on stage, the founder of PsoraCom surveyed his audience like a prize bullfighter before loudly welcoming them to this year's conference. Renewed applause and isolated heckles rang out.

"We have achieved much in the last year," he began. "And you made this possible! You all deserve medals!"

Clapping and enthusiastic cheers sounded once more, predominantly from the front rows. Different graphs and diagrams appeared on the screens. They illustrated the development of sales and earnings, as well as the total market share and the market share of each individual sector.

"You are the best sales team in the world! But it's still not enough for the investment analysts. You have to get better! You have to sell more products, at higher prices! Our interest margin must be increased further!"

Slogans like "our competitors are not sleeping" were followed by a comparison with rival products, some of which were superior to those of PsoraCom.

"Nevertheless, we are the better company," proclaimed the chief executive. "We will use all means at our disposal to regain the lost market share. You will accomplish this! We will accomplish this! We are a magnificent team. The best there is!"

The chief executive had dangled the carrot once more.

"Bring me sales! Bring me profit!"

Shouts of enthusiasm erupted from the front rows, followed by frenetic applause. Some leaped from their seats while others stamped their feet on the floor. More and more colleagues jumped up and began applauding. Individual cries of approval drowned out the stamping. The atmosphere was electric and Alex could hardly contain her elation. Next to her Hugo and George seemed less impressed. They had experienced it all before. To the renewed pounding of Lenny Kravitz, the chief executive left the room, clapping his hands as he went. The rear doors opened simultaneously.

The night was still young and the mild weather drove everyone out of the air-conditioned ballroom into the fresh air. It took a good ten minutes for the threesome to make their way outside. They had seen Brian from afar, but then lost him again in the crowd. At the exit they met Thomas for the first time since their arrival but couldn't persuade him to share a night-cap in Ybor City. So they set off alone, ending up in the same place as the night before. The first round of Hurricanes promptly arrived and straightaway George began to pick holes in what they had just heard.

"Every year the same. The product comparisons with the competition are totally misleading."

"You're right there," nodded Hugo in agreement. "It doesn't matter what criteria you base it on, one way or another they just don't stack up."

Alex was still completely psyched by the whole thing. It was hard to say whether it was because of the music or the enthusiastic applause.

"For me it was pretty exciting actually. I've never experienced anything like that before. The man's got charisma and he knows how to get a crowd going."

However, after the first cocktail the speech was already forgotten, and George began to talk shop with Hugo about the technical possibilities offered by Vabilmo. As the evening went on, the latter seemed to display his admiration for his older colleague more and more openly. But Alex could have been mistaken.

There was only a small window for breakfast the next morning between seven and seven thirty. Alex met her colleagues in the ballroom, along with hundreds of hungry, scrambled-egg-loving, vegetarian, fruit-eating, sausage-devouring people of every nationality, all of whom were amply catered for. After absorbing large quantities of vitamins and cholesterol to reduce the still-elevated blood-alcohol levels, a voice from a loudspeaker politely invited them to make their way to the training sessions. Nothing here was left to chance.

On their way they realised that Alex was not booked onto all the same ones.

"That doesn't make much sense. It's probably best if you just come with us," said an utterly exhausted George.

As proof of their attendance, the barcodes on their badges were scanned as they entered the room, just like goods at a supermarket checkout. A warning tone sounded upon Alex's entry to the sessions she hadn't registered for. She wouldn't receive any credits but she could square that later with her boss.

The sessions lasted for an hour each and went on until the late afternoon. Short restroom breaks were scheduled every now and again. There were lunchboxes prepared for the half-hour midday break to give employees as much time as possible to check their mails. Nobody could escape the company network. Even at mandatory company events, they still had to carry out their everyday work. Fortunately, Alex didn't receive many mails yet and was able to get away from the fridge-like climate during the short breaks. The newly cut grass in front of the hotel and the colourful flowers in bloom exuded a sweet, fresh scent, while the rustle of the palm trees completed the feeling of summer. Too late it suddenly occurred to her that she should have called Sandro. Amid all the hustle and bustle there was little time for her private life. She sent him an apologetic mail, using exactly those words.

After the training sessions, things continued apace as no-one wanted to miss dinner before the mandatory evening event. This time the entire pool area of the Hard Rock Hotel had been booked out. Buffets on both sides of the pool provided the hungry with all manner of delicacies. The ornate bistro tables on the lawn and the fairy-lit palm stems created a wonderful atmosphere.

The ensuing presentation, held by the technical chairman, paled in comparison to the day before, especially in terms of the atmosphere. Alongside existing developments to core technology, the audience's enthusiasm was only aroused by the mention of a special project. The basis for the research was the Japanese art of origami. A film demonstrated vividly how the thinnest sheets of half-metal could be made into spherically shaped solar cells. The evaporation process was employed to alter the surface tension of the moistened material, helping to create a new design. A few stray individuals leaped to their feet, applauded and allowed themselves to become carried away with cries of appreciation. Alex slowly began to understand what George had meant the previous evening.

After the presentation an internal exhibition took place where different product groups provided information about the latest applications and developments. There were even freebies, just like at tradefairs, each item engraved with the product or department name. All electronic giveaways were of course solar-cell powered and ranged from wireless hard drives and netphone chargers to backpacks and T-shirts. The clear favourite, however, was a solar-cell-powered cool bag. Alex sped off excitedly to snatch one up. A little later she saw her boss with an enticing-looking beer in his hand. The pool buffet had been converted into a bar.

"How do you like it so far?" Thomas asked abruptly after they had topped themselves up.

"Very much!" she replied instantly. "The presentations are all interesting. Still, I need to warn you, George and Hugo took me to a few sessions I wasn't registered for. Just in case it looks as if I haven't been attending."

But that didn't seem to interest her boss particularly. "That's fine. I'm sure you wouldn't be playing hooky."

Thomas drained his beer and said his goodbyes. He was tired and at the most would have a nightcap at the hotel bar.

Alex took up conversation with a few other colleagues. George and Hugo had gone off somewhere, and Brian had been nowhere to be seen the whole day. Shortly before midnight she went to the casino. She hadn't found time for it since her arrival and wanted to take a quick look inside. The ringing of the fruit machines stood in stark contrast to the rock music emanating from the loudspeakers. Alex inserted a handful of coins here and there, winning a few dollars. She recognised a few stray faces behind the machines but soon the din became too much for her.

Moving on to the poker tables, all of which were completely occupied, she watched a hand or two of Texas hold'em. At one of the back tables, Alex spied George sitting down with Hugo leaning forward behind him, a drink in hand. From a distance it looked as though he had his arm around George, but she wasn't certain. Neither of them saw her. They were both looking at George's cards in fixed concentration, as if they needed to win back a month's salary. She decided to go to bed.

After a refreshing shower the next morning, Alex spoke with Sandro for a few minutes. Everything at home was fine but there had been a lot of snow. Hopefully the roof would be able to cope. Last winter there had been a lot of water damage due to ancient and leaking roof tiles.

She met her two team colleagues at breakfast; both of them looked completely washed out and had dark circles under their eyes.

The second presentation was the most interesting of the entire event. The machine and robotics department introduced new solar modules that had been developed in conjunction with a select group of module manufacturers. Previously, solar modules had been flat and rectangular. But advances had been made and thin-film cells could now be fabricated on metal substrates. Thanks to the flexibility of the carrier material the cells could be used not only to create linear designs but, up to a certain degree, concave and convex ones too.

The 3-D modules would be available in selected shapes. Just like Lego blocks, standardised interfaces could be used to create all kinds of designs. This would yield countless potential combinations that could be individually tailored for specific purposes. The biggest stir was caused by a prototype shaped like a large globe, which somehow evoked images of a 1980s dance club. A second item had been fashioned into the shape of a wave. It was possible that these so-called bend-modules could represent a significant development for Vabilmo.

Hugo was absolutely enthused and immediately began to play out different possible scenarios. With him at least, the coffee seemed to have taken effect; George, however, was still staring absent-mindedly into space.

The sales chief finished off the conference by going over the figures for the previous financial year again, as well as the revenue and profit forecasts for the coming year. He concluded his speech with a solemn expression and invited all those present to swear an oath. The majority stood up. He put his hand on his heart and began reading a text out loud for everyone to repeat. Alex remained seated and was relieved to see her colleagues had likewise refused to join in the theatre. After a few tense moments it was all over and all she wanted was to get out into the fresh air.

"That was pathetic," George muttered indignantly behind her. "In my long years, even I have never seen anything like it."

"The Yanks always like to put on a show, but for me that went too far," Hugo agreed.

"It's like being in a cult," Alex heard someone else grumble behind her.

There were still a few hours to go until the meeting with Natioba. George wanted to check his mails and perhaps catch up on some sleep as well. The hotel lobby was bustling with activity and outside the main entrance the shuttle buses were ready to leave for the airport. Unless there was a very good reason, the company requested everyone to depart as quickly as possible so that normal routines could be resumed the next day. Hugo suggested that they take a few sandwiches to the poolside.

There wasn't a lot going on, just two couples and a blonde lolling in the sun. Hugo pushed two deck chairs closer together under the shade of the tall palm trees. A gentle breeze almost made the holiday feeling complete. It only needed a bottle of sun cream and a pina colada.

"So, what do you do when you're not working then?" said Alex first.

"I build model cars," he began proudly. "I've got over a hundred already. From vintage cars and Ferraris right through to Ford Mustangs, pretty much everything is there."

"A civil engineer who builds cars, not houses. That's an interesting combination. How did you end up working for PsoraCom?"

"I did a lot of work with the research and development department here during my PhD. About a year ago they made me an offer I couldn't refuse."

He spoke openly about his first few weeks and how George had taken him under his wing. Not much has changed there then, Alex thought to herself.

The blonde opposite surveyed Hugo curiously. He didn't look unattractive, what with his dark curls and muscular upper body clearly visible under a skin-tight sports shirt. He allowed his gaze to pass admiringly over her barely concealed curves. Her body could not disguise the effects of the cool breeze in the shade.

The meeting was scheduled to begin in two hours and Alex took this as a sign to make her exit. She decided to go to the fitness studio and leave Hugo to his fate by the pool.

The ballroom of the Hard Rock Hotel had been completely reorganised since the closing speeches and transformed into eight different rooms of equal size, two of which Nobu had reserved for the meeting. While he was opening the meeting and outlining the agenda, Alex stood up and shut the door.

"We don't want Mick Jagger to suddenly appear, do we."

"But Pink, on the other hand…" a developer from Natioba smiled at her kindly.

Alongside the conventional solar cells, the main focuses were the Vabilmo technology and the bend-modules. A non-disclosure agreement with Natioba existed so some details could be shared. When a member of the robotics team introduced the new spherical prototype, made out of the latest bend-modules, he aroused an unmistakeable curiosity.

Suddenly Alex had an idea and turned to George next to her. An information session was all very well, but why not go a step further.

"Why don't we run a pilot project with the client?" she whispered. "We could fit a small off-grid system with the polymer-based solar cells."

George thought about it.

"Or better still," Alex continued her train of thought, "why don't we equip the new bend-modules with the polymer-based solar cells? That would be the icing on the cake!"

He wrinkled his forehead before eventually nodding in agreement. "That should be no problem from a technical point of view."

During a short drinks break she spoke to Hugo and Brian, the latter looking even more tanned since their last meeting. The two of them also endorsed the idea.

After the break Alex put her suggestion to the clients, who willingly agreed. They spent the next two hours in intense discussions and by the end had worked out a rough plan.

Despite the air-conditioning, the excitement had made her sweat. She wasn't the only one for whom this was the first face-to-face meeting with Natioba. Coming away from discussions with a green light was no bad result at all. Admittedly, it was only a pilot project but she knew from experience that to expect anything more at this stage would have been unrealistic. Nearly always, pre-development work had to be carried out. No-one could deny that it would be a steep learning curve for both sides. But she needed to control herself if she didn't want to fall off her chair. It was just a question of keeping a poker-face and not making the client feel as if PsoraCom were desperate for the project. They weren't. Nevertheless, the attention such a project could attract, both internally and externally, couldn't be ignored. Natioba was one of the big shots in its market sector. Very few companies in the world built more off-grid systems, even though there had been a dramatic rise in the last few years.

During dinner, the tense working atmosphere dissolved slowly into small talk. Alex briefly turned the conversation back to business and the possibility of presenting the pilot project to a suitable audience. The developers from Natioba didn't seem averse. They agreed to head for a date in the summer and make a decision after putting together a realistic project plan. That was more than she could have hoped for. Chris, the young developer next to her, had worked in the development lab in Seoul for a few years. Since he often had to deal with headquarters, he was learning Italian in his spare time. Alex had managed to pick up a few smatterings through Sandro so they tried to converse in Italian for a few minutes until they laughed and admitted defeat.

"To be honest, I'm not really sure if the project makes sense," George began suddenly in his staccato voice after their clients had left. "They're just amateurs who spend their days playing in sand pits and building castles in the sky. They're not much use to us."

Alex couldn't believe her ears.

"But you just agreed to the idea. What's caused this change of heart? Have I missed something?" She was angry but refused to let herself get too worked up.

"It was on my mind earlier – but you were all talking so animatedly. It's no big deal. We'll just call it off."

"And how do you suppose we do that, George?" she shook her head. "It's not so easy in my opinion. How would it look to the client? First we suggest something they agree to and then it's a big nothing?" She took a deep breath. "Besides, I still think the project is an excellent way to gain a little experience. I mean, we do want to win Natioba as a client after all."

"I have to say Alex is right," Brian joined in the conversation. "We could all learn a lot from this project, so we need to pull this off – Natioba are really important for us."

He had strolled over to them and taken Alex's side, both literally and figuratively. Relieved, she looked back at George, who yielded hesitantly.

"Yeah, well we can talk about it in more detail another time, but I'm not convinced."

Hugo stood next to him and maintained a diplomatic silence.

"Let's celebrate. That was a quality meeting and Alex did a tremendous job." Brian rescued the situation.

They strolled into the lobby bar. Maybe they were all just a little overtired. It was only supposed to be a quiet beer but in the end it became four pints of Samuel Adams. Before she went to bed, Alex bought a hoodie and a shot glass from the shop. She couldn't help herself. At the elevator she spied George and Hugo from the corner of her eye, heading towards the casino. Brian stood at the bar with a new beer in his hand. A sun-kissed beauty, similar to the one by the pool that afternoon, stood next to him with a Cosmopolitan.

Only a few hours later the alarm clock abruptly put an end to her dreamless sleep. She put the light shakes down to a combination of lack of sleep and excess alcohol; even the floor seemed to sway beneath her as she walked. A few days off would definitely do her some good. To make up for it she traded some of her air miles for an upgrade to business class. Shortly after take-off she reclined her seat, reached for the face mask and ear plugs, and promptly fell asleep.

Sandro picked her up from the airport. She hadn't given him much thought in the US. There had always been something going on and the time difference hadn't exactly helped. But now she was glad to see him again. Even though he soon needed to leave for work, a quick glance was enough to persuade him to give her a proper welcome home. For some things, there was always time.

Jet lag and lack of sleep meant that she spent the next few days like someone who'd just crossed the Bay of Biscay in a force-nine gale. She felt the floor shaking continuously beneath her. It took her almost a week to fully recover.

The following weekend Alex went to Lindau. Her mother Ricka had been on a health cure there for a few weeks to recover from a liver operation. After the initial shock of the diagnosis two months ago, Alex was feeling a bit more relaxed about things. Although her mother was still weak, she was becoming steadier on her feet. They sat on the heated terrace of a café near the promenade, drinking lattes and soaking up the sun.

"Do the doctors know the root cause?" Alex asked.

Her mother shook her head. "They suspect that I contracted hepatitis B at some point. It was left undiagnosed and might ultimately have led to the tumour. Perhaps it was when your father and I were in China for three months."

"Have you got back the results of your tissue sample yet?" Alex probed further.

"Yes. Fortunately, nothing was found. That's why they're considering the partial resection of the liver a success."

That there were no guarantees was something they both left unsaid. Everything had gone well up to now and optimism was still the best form of therapy.

As they were walking through the winter countryside, Ricka listened to her daughter's account of her time in the US.

"The solar plant we visited in Miami was really impressive," Alex gushed. "It's difficult to say how big the plant will be when it's completed. But we needed almost half an hour just to drive around the first section."

Ricka had worked as a technical designer for a few years and nodded in appreciation.

"Tampa was something else," Alex continued. "Absolutely nothing like events at my previous companies – definitely an experience."

She responded to her mother's queries with a detailed description of the conference, not forgetting to mention her successful bid for the pilot project.

On the way home that evening she was overcome by a feeling of melancholy, something that happened almost every time she visited her parents. Where it came from, she couldn't say. Her parents had always taken good care of her and made sure she enjoyed an excellent education. They were her closest consultants. No matter the problem, Alex could always count on their support. Exactly the same was true of her twin sister, Jenny. Although they had often quarrelled as children, once their wild years were over they had grown increasingly close. Now they were not just sisters but best of friends, and Alex had the impression that their connection was only getting stronger. Even in times when they didn't have much contact – Jenny was always away somewhere – both knew the other would be there if needed. Alex could talk to her about anything. Except music, that is.

The next few weeks flew by. Alex took part in different meetings, mostly organised by either George or Hugo. The majority were discussions with companies from the ecosystem, who were being sounded out on the subject of Vabilmo. The ecosystem, she had learned, comprised all companies with a significant influence on solar technology. She continued to gather all the relevant data on the companies she would be responsible for. Brian had even pleaded for her to assume sole charge of these earlier than planned so that he could focus on additional clients and taking Vabilmo international. That was fine by Alex, who was feeling more and more comfortable in her role.

Although still in the office a lot, she was beginning to work single days from home.

Despite the regular team meetings once a week, she talked on the phone with George and Brian almost every day. More with George, it had to be said, as Brian was difficult to get hold of and rarely checked his voice messages. Hugo preferred communicating via chat, providing Alex with daily updates on Roffarm. As an outsider, it didn't always look like progress was being made. It seemed as if both sides were deliberating over details for hours without finding a way forward. In some areas there was simply no precedent; perhaps that's why discussions were so extensive.

For Alex, actions spoke louder than words. Sometimes you just needed to try something out, to take a risk. At such times she suggested that Hugo go into "Nike mode" and "just do it." In her opinion, there was no such thing as a wrong decision because decisions were judgement calls based on the information available at the time in question. A decision might have undesirable consequences, but then you had to adapt and revise. Occasionally, when a project decision on certain issues was pending, she got the distinct impression that Hugo was asking for her opinion. Naturally she enjoyed this feeling.

"Can you stand in for me at a client meeting?" Brian called her one day. "It's a high-level meeting with Roffarm. Their senior manager is meeting with Bill, one of our vice presidents."

"Of course I will," Alex replied.

"Bill is responsible for the power plant and off-grid systems vertical. He's fully behind Vabilmo."

Brian had another meeting. Besides, he knew both people already. In team meetings he had often discussed whether Alex should take on Roffarm and oversee the implementation of the contract. She wasn't especially keen on this because it would have meant restricting herself to a single client; she preferred working with a variety of companies. Nevertheless, she was happy to take part in a single meeting. It was an opportunity to obtain more information and, at the same time, integrate management staff into her ever-expanding internal network.

Bill turned out to be very amiable and seemed well acquainted with the whys and wherefores of the market - the secret codes and handshakes, so to speak. The first thing she noticed about him were his steel-blue eyes. Along with the silver streaks in his hair, he was somehow reminiscent of Paul Newman. His wiry appearance made him seem disciplined, yet despite his penetrating gaze he had an air of peaceful harmony about him. A typical American business uniform of beige Dockers and dark-blue jacket slightly concealed his slim figure. During the meeting he was calm and level-headed, giving friendly answers to all his client's questions.

The contract between PsoraCom and Roffarm formed the basis of the discussion. It contained an exclusivity clause that was being more tightly interpreted than had been envisaged. The divisional director had flown into a rage and was complaining bitterly about Brian, who, in his opinion, had already violated the clause. Bill calmed the client down, intent on reaching an agreement and safeguarding PsoraCom's interests. It was difficult for Alex to judge whether the client had overreacted, or whether Brian really had gone too far. The latter was perfectly possible. On a few occasions she had already noticed how openly Brian would speak about Vabilmo projects in public places such as airports and train stations. She was always extremely careful because one never knew who might be listening. One of her very first employers had drilled into her the importance of treating confidential material with a caution bordering on paranoia, and she had found no reason to do otherwise since.

After everything seemed to have been smoothed over, Bill concluded the meeting with a few to-do items and some that still needed further clarification. On the way out he asked Alex about her professional background.

"You only started with us last month?" he expressed his surprise. "Judging by your knowledge of polymer-based solar cells, I would have said you'd been here for a year at least."

Alex was visibly flattered, even if she had registered the deliberate exaggeration.

"After the conference in Tampa, we won a pilot project with Natioba," she added in a whisper, although there was no-one else around.

"Excellent," he responded, his voice lowered likewise. "Keep me posted on any developments."

"OK," she assured him. "At the moment Robotics are responsible for the project."

Revenue-wise, that meant they were in competition with Bill's division.

"Things can change quickly," said Bill. "In the long run it probably makes more sense to integrate all applications with polymer-based cells into my division."

"I can arrange a meeting for you with my end customers the next time you're here," Alex offered.

"Sounds great," he bid her farewell, as he climbed into the taxi.

The issue of Brian's alleged contract violation was naturally the focus of the next team meeting. Bill had asked Thomas to clarify the matter and copied Alex in to the mail discussion. Now Brian, George and Alex were sitting together with their boss in the meeting room. For reasons unknown, Hugo had decided to join by conference call. Perhaps he had spent the weekend in Switzerland again and was working from there.

"He's a sandwich short of a picnic," Brian rejected the accusation vehemently. "I told them from the start that we would be talking to other players in the industry. And of course we don't tell the one what the other's doing, unless it's already public knowledge. The guy's always had a hot temper. The slightest thing sets him off."

"I'm not interested in whose fault it is," Thomas tried to calm him. "I'm more concerned about the meaning of the contract and the interpretation of the exclusivity clause."

The first warning lights went on in Alex's head. "We need to sort this out quickly," she broke in. "Otherwise it could endanger our project with Natioba. It could also lead to all our work with other manufacturers being indefinitely suspended. If the wording can be interpreted as they claim, then we can't implement any projects with other plant manufacturers without Roffarm's say-so. Our hands would be tied because since we already have non-disclosure agreements with the other companies we wouldn't be able to pass any information on to Roffarm. That would be a real catch-22."

"You're right, Alex," her boss agreed. "But nothing is decided yet. Until Legal has had a good look at it, we continue as before. Business as usual, those were Wolfgang's exact words." Thomas had almost certainly discussed the issue with his boss beforehand. After all, it was Wolfgang who had to justify the contract implementation internally to US management.

"Can you send me an electronic copy of the contract?" Alex asked. "I'd like to read it."

Not that she thought she knew more than the legal experts. But Alex wanted to assess the situation for herself. Besides, it couldn't do any harm to have the information.

"I also think it's a serious cause for concern," George joined in. "Good idea, Alex! Let's all read the contract. Thomas, send me a copy as well. I want to have a look at it. The question of exclusivity has to be fully clarified so that we can work freely with clients."

"The guy's completely overshot the mark," began Brian again. "There was never any question of an exclusivity clause. I should know: I'm the one who negotiated the contract. I'll have to have a word with the old biddy who translated what I said into contract-speak."

"Brian's right," Hugo came to his aid. "I don't know anything about it either. The project with Roffarm is extremely important for us. They're going to be the first ones to build a plant using polymer-based solar cells. Perhaps it's enough if we stall the other end customers for a bit."

"Exactly. The project with Natioba is a joke anyway," George started again.

"Don't talk crap," Brian thwarted him straightaway. "We've been through this hundreds of times already. Natioba are at least as high a priority as Roffarm. If Mr Angry carries on like this, the Italians and South Koreans will overtake him on the inside lane."

"Ah, Brian, they're just boys playing in sandpits. They'll spend ages tinkering with something that will never make it and then discard it anyway." George made no secret of his contempt.

"I've already done a heap of overtime for Roffarm," Hugo complained. "We've got to keep going there. There are so many things that are still unclear. That will also become apparent to Natioba once they start development properly."

"Of course we have to continue working with Roffarm," Brian appeased his nervous colleague. "But in order to create a market standard, we need other manufacturers. It can't happen with Roffarm alone, simply because of the size and number of their plants. Natioba has much greater potential than Roffarm there; that's why both companies are so important to us."

At times it seemed as if everyone except Thomas and Alex was talking over each other. She wasn't a great fan of interrupting someone purely for the sake of expressing her own opinion. But after a while it was clear that they were going round in circles.

"Let's wait and see what Legal says," she suggested. "At the moment we're just groping in the dark."

Thomas didn't say anything, but nodded at her and slowly looked towards the others. She took his restraint as a sign that he approved of her intervention. Alex studied the contract, the exclusivity clause in particular. At first glance it looked as if Roffarm would be able to insist upon their narrow interpretation, which would severely restrict the work of the team. Surprised, she wondered who had chosen such a wording. Speaking against the narrow interpretation was the description provided of the Vabilmo project, which was no longer current. It was all a bit of a mess.

"We'll have to get it looked at very quickly," Alex said to her boss again after the meeting. "We need to know what repercussions the contract has. It makes no sense to spend money on projects with Natioba or other end customers if contractual stipulations don't allow it."

A little frustrated, she added: "Starting a project only to call it off later doesn't go down well with clients."

The contract seemed to have been hastily cobbled together. Thomas promised to take care of it.

"And one more thing: perhaps it would be better if you intervened sometimes."

"Why?" Thomas asked. "You do it so well."

"Thank you," Alex replied. "But at the end of the day you are the boss and I'm just a co-worker. I don't want to put anyone out."

"It was okay," he waved her aside. "You did nothing wrong. You should do exactly the same again next time. They need someone to bring them into line."

A few days later, Thomas arranged a meeting with a colleague from Legal and took Alex along. After a quick glance at the contract, Emily was equally concerned.

"We'll have to examine this clause very carefully. I wasn't at the contract negotiations. I'm only filling in for a colleague on maternity leave. But I'll go through it with our US colleagues today – they're the ones who negotiated the clauses. Let me talk to Brian again to find out what the original purpose of the contract was."

Alex liked Emily straightaway. She seemed very professional, although this impression was offset by her short mini-skirt and long, blonde curls. People outside of the company would probably suspect she was a wannabe model or an it-girl on the lookout for the next party. Alex learned that Emily had started working for PsoraCom two years ago after completing her law degree, and that she was currently writing her PhD thesis. Ambitious and career-driven though she was, she didn't seem dogged in the slightest. Emily promised to get in touch as soon as she knew more.

To Alex's frustration, there still wasn't much happening on the house market. She didn't need a lot of space to work but using the desk in the living room annoyed her. She found herself confronted by work even during her free time, making it very hard to switch off. It didn't seem to bother Sandro much because he never looked at the ads without prompting. Only now and then did he remark how nice it would be to have all his things in the same place. Two bigger flats they had looked at in the area hadn't been suitable. In one of them, the main road seemed to pass straight through the kitchen; in the other, shoppers at the local supermarket could have applied lotion to Alex's back while she was sunbathing on the balcony. Perhaps she was being too demanding, but she didn't want to give up hope.

3

March

In the morning she made her way anxiously to reception to pick up her new team colleague. There was a guy with a moustache standing by the window. He was in his early thirties, small and thickset, and dressed in a drab catalogue suit. He carried a worn attaché case in his right hand, while beady, salesman's eyes grinned at her expectantly behind thick lenses. With his experience in the machine and robotics industry, Carl would complete the Vabilmo team - though he wouldn't have much to do with solar plant manufacturers. Alex led him into the bright open-plan office, as Thomas had done with her. They visited all the necessary departments so that Carl could get his car, laptop and employee ID. Then they spent the rest of the day in one of the meeting rooms, where Alex outlined what she had learned so far herself.

"I've always been in the machine industry," Carl told her over lunch. "In my last job I played a key role establishing the robotics division. We were one of the first companies to develop and sell kitchen robots."

"Not bad," Alex replied. "I haven't had much to do with robots yet so I'm sure I could learn a thing or two from you."

"I'd be happy to help in any way I can. We've been using one at home since we had our little pumpkins. It takes care of the cooking and cleaning, which means I can concentrate on the girls in the evening. I learn something new from them every day. Kids are just so special."

"So, how old are your little pumpkins?" Alex asked.

"The youngest is one and a half, and our five-year-old already comes to church choir with me and my wife," his eyes gleaming proudly as he added: "she's going to be an opera singer one day."

It didn't surprise Alex that he sang in a church choir. It suited him somehow. But he was a nice guy and they got along straightaway.

Carl would also work from home, only coming into the office if need be. He lived near the Baltic Sea. She made sure she gave him all the electronic information, presentations and links so that he could read up on everything in detail. For the moment the Vabilmo team was complete.

There was Brian, the laid-back surfer. He saw himself as a strategic visionary and never missed an opportunity to highlight his own achievements; he might have shied away from detail but he was happy to take people under his wing. For Brian, free time was just as important as success.

George was the peroxide-blond dandy. With his experience in the solar industry, he was a walking encyclopaedia. He shared his knowledge about clients and products willingly, although he had plenty of misgivings about both. These appeared to be the driving force behind his private dispute with Brian. During discussions he lay in wait for an opportunity to express his opinion like a fox stalking its prey – making sure he looked damned good in the process.

Then there was Hugo, fitness model and doctor fresh out of college. Up until now theory had been his thing: now it was time for practice. He was electrifying when it came to technical architecture, and treated it like a jigsaw puzzle. His brain seemed to function quicker than his Swiss accent could follow. Taking decisions was the exception: if in doubt, Hugo preferred safety first and sided with George.

Thomas was the elegant introvert. He observed this colourful hotchpotch from afar with his impenetrable gaze. He'd never had anything to do with solar plants directly - even though he'd been with the company for years. As the boss of this troupe he maintained a stoical silence, intervening only to prevent the occurrence of collateral damage.

Carl was the kindly, thickset sales type from the church choir. He knew a lot about machines and robots and was understandably keen to remain in the background for now. He listened attentively at work and at home, but would never neglect his family for the sake of his job.

And finally there was Alex, token red-head with a thirst for knowledge. For her, work was a game; she didn't shy away from expressing an opinion, even if it made her unpopular. She preferred decisions to lengthy discussion. She had no respect for seniority or hierarchy, rating instead ability and knowledge. Alex, whose first impressions told her she had found her dream job.

Hugo and George had been working hard to arrange meetings for the world's leading solar trade show in Barcelona, at which only part of the team would be present. Thomas didn't think it important to attend and neither, strangely, did George. Carl was still too new to it all, but if necessary he could fly over for the day. Alex had booked three rooms.

They met in the airport lounge on the day of departure. Brian was already indulging in his third beer, in deep discussion with Hugo about Roffarm. He wasn't even whispering. He waved aside Alex's concerns with the argument that anyone listening would have no idea what they were talking about. After his fourth beer he had talked himself into such a rage that even Hugo agreed with her, and put an end to the discussion. Something seemed to be bothering Brian about the project.

Having checked in, they went downtown straightaway. There were no evening meetings scheduled. Although it was already dark, the mild spring air made for a pleasant stroll through the city centre as they searched for a restaurant.

They struck lucky not far from La Barceloneta. During the typical local meal the reason for Brian's ill humour became apparent.

"Wolfgang has lost the plot," Brian vented his anger. "I used to admire him but he's been so strange in the last few months. He's gone completely crazy."

"What happened?" Hugo asked.

"Oh, it's total bullshit. He can't be trusted anymore. When I started here he was a top guy. But now he's just a joke. I worked my arse off for the Roffarm contract and this is how he repays me."

Brian didn't reveal the exact details of his conversation with Wolfgang, but the anger was clearly etched upon his face. The continuous beer-drinking only seemed to intensify his rage. Alex began to feel very uncomfortable and a glance across to Hugo confirmed he did too. Without further delay they pressed for the bill, but Brian didn't want to go back to the hotel. He was still too agitated and wanted to go to the nearby beach. Relieved, they went their separate ways.

"Finally we can get to the enjoyable part of the evening, eh Alex?" Hugo joked, as they used the stroll home to work off their evening meal.

"You can say that again," Alex replied. "I've got no idea why Brian was so worked up."

"He didn't really want to come out with it, you're right. I haven't seen him like that before. Must have been a really unpleasant conversation. I'd rather have been alone with you."

Although Hugo's last remark could have been construed as flirting, Alex enjoyed what was to her just a harmless compliment.

The next day was packed full with meetings. Both plant manufacturers and solar module companies showed interest in the Vabilmo technology. Only in the late afternoon was a quick tour of the exhibition halls possible. There was no indication that other solar cell manufacturers were pursuing similar projects.

Dinner with Hugo and Brian was just a question of taking on fuel and was soon over. No-one seemed interested in continuing the previous evening's debate, least of all Alex, who detested internal backbiting.

The meetings on the next day also went very well. An initial, informal meeting with the power plant manufacturer Premve, arranged by Alex, even produced a wave of euphoria among the three. They learned that Premve was currently carrying out internal investigations. Division heads from different departments had been asked to form a committee, which was to decide both on the location of future solar plants and what technology they would use. Premve's contact offered to set up a meeting with his boss, who was responsible for submitting logistics reports to the division head. The latter was part of the committee. Time was short at the end, so they arranged for a more detailed follow-up to take place in the next few weeks. Premve, like Natioba, would be handled directly by Alex.

Brian and Alex sat next to each other on the flight home.

"You know, Alex, our job's a lot like surfing. You have to wait for the right moment to catch the perfect wave. It requires a lot of patience, believe me. I know that better than anyone. I was only so successful with Roffarm because I set up countless meetings with anyone I could. Dinner here, coffee there. You have to be present the whole time. Each week I sent all my contacts a newsletter I had put together myself. I kept them up-to-date with everything, even if it wasn't directly relevant. That way they could see how innovative we were, and that they would have to work with us if they wanted to retain their market position."

Alex nodded, barely able to suppress a yawn.

"You have to stay tuned the whole time. The first thing they think of when they get up in the morning has to be you."

Preferably not, Alex thought to herself.

"When you surf you have to keep on it too, it's exactly the same. I paddle in the water for hours until the right wave comes along and then I ride it through to the end. It was just crazy in Tahiti."

It was like listening to a broken record. After two long, tiring days at the trade show, she had no desire to listen any longer. Luckily she had her iPod with her.

"It's been a long day," she said, yawning for the second time. "I'm going to take a little nap. We're going skiing with friends tomorrow and I need to leave early."

She untangled her headphones slowly so as not to appear impolite, then closed her eyes to Bryan Adams and his acoustic guitar.

Arriving home at last, she realised that Sandro hadn't lifted as much as a finger before he went to bed. She would have dearly loved to drag him from his peaceful sleep. Furiously, she packed a few necessities and then set the alarm for half an hour early. The last thing she wanted was to pick up her friends late because Sandro had failed to get his act together again. The morning didn't exactly begin well after such a short night.

"You could've at least packed a few things," Alex began her tirade. She was still pissed off and fatigue took care of the rest.

"How am I supposed to know what we need?" he responded. "Besides, we've still got enough time." His reaction just made her blood boil even more.

"If I hadn't set the alarm last night, we'd still be in bed. You knew I was coming home late. It might have occurred to you to help me out a little: you must have known I'd be tired."

Sandro acted aggrieved as usual and retreated into his shell. It annoyed Alex when he behaved like a spoiled child and assumed he didn't have to take care of anything. During the trip she tried not to let it show to their friends. Sandro did likewise, pretending nothing had happened. The snow was good and luckily neither of her friends wanted to stay up all night partying like normal. Back at home Alex unpacked her things and went straight to bed. She was still angry because Sandro had not attempted a reconciliation. But maybe she was just being obstinate.

Alex built up more contacts with the end customers she had been allocated and used former contacts to help her gain a picture of the industry's potential. It was clear to her that a lot could be achieved. But in order to be not only efficient but effective, it was necessary to set some priorities. It was easy to think that there was no difference between "efficient" and "effective", and indeed the two words were often used interchangeably. It was possible to work efficiently and carry out one's tasks quickly, without using too much energy. However, so long as these tasks served no specific aim, they were not effective.

Phone calls with George were a good example. They were effective because Alex learned a lot about PsoraCom's production methods and which clients had bought what products so far. She got the feeling that George was being increasingly open with her. But perhaps it was because she was genuinely interested in what he had to offer and he liked this. Nevertheless Alex had to take care that their conversations didn't get out of hand. George could get carried away in the blink of an eye, and often a whole hour could be lost. But since Alex was still learning, she was happy to take the time to listen – just not for several hours at once. Because that would not have been very efficient.

Brian and George also sent her a lot of information, mostly articles from the internet.

"Alex, can you take a look at this?" they usually said. She read the information and stored it away. But she urged Thomas to arrange a longer meeting so that the whole team could set its priorities. Without a team strategy with clear responsibilities for each individual, they would row in opposite directions. The topic was so new and exciting that the whole industry seemed to be jumping on it. That's why they needed to determine which companies offered the greatest chance of success. Each one of them had only limited resources and they needed to be used selectively.

Thomas shared her opinion and arranged for a two-day get-together to take place off company premises. She gladly accepted his request for help with preparations. The good thing was that Vabilmo seemed to be a completely new subject for both of them, so they were able to think in more abstract terms. Nevertheless, Alex had more experience in the energy sector than Thomas, something he was only too glad to fall back on. She got the feeling that he too was steadily opening up. Now and again he smiled at one of her little jokes when things were getting too serious. Sometimes he even made a joke himself, taking Alex completely by surprise. Thomas' ability to view things as almost completely detached yet somehow broadly interconnected was extremely instructive. Their discussions soon made it clear that some of his questions carried far greater implications than Alex had initially suspected. Now and again, however, she could contest his strategy by referring to her own knowledge. It was a symbiotic relationship, their collaboration.

In contrast to her colleagues, Alex regularly came into the office. As well as her meetings with Thomas, she also enjoyed getting to know people from different departments over lunch or coffee. That way she learned about things potentially of interest for Vabilmo. Equally, many of her colleagues were eager to learn about Vabilmo's progress.

She had often seen Wolfgang in the office. He sat two cubicles away from Thomas, right by the glass facade. She hadn't said anything more than a simple "good morning" to him yet. When she arrived shortly after eight he was mostly sitting at his wheelchair-accessible desk already, his face serious but not unfriendly. He used one of the visitor's chairs as a wardrobe. A few ties and simple but elegant jackets were neatly arranged over it. There was an air of authority about him.

Their typical conversation consisted of his question: "Everything OK?" to which Alex would reply with a brief: "Yes, everything's fine thanks." It was difficult to know whether he was really interested in her work or whether he was just being polite. He did seem like an executive who wanted to be close to his employees. She decided to only say more when she had something important to report. The project with Natioba might be suitable at a later date.

Quite often she ran into Christopher. In contrast to Wolfgang, he always had a little joke handy. She liked his sense of humour.

"Well, if it isn't our apprentice for Germany's Next Big Business," he teased her. „No dough without Vabilmo, right Alex?"

"Sure, what"s baking – ehm, shaking," she countered immediately. "By the way did you hear about our pilot project with Natioba? We're just beginning the planning phase."

"I'm instinctively suspicious of any plan I haven't cooked up myself," he laughed.

"Oh, you'd like nothing better than to be our head chef again," Alex joshed. "There just isn't the same potential bill of fare in consumer retail, is there?"

"Heaven forbid! Wild horses couldn't persuade me to take that flea circus back!"

The off-site meeting took place at the end of the month as agreed. Its goal was to define the team strategy and approach as well as the roles and responsibilities of each team member. After they had waited for Brian in vain for twenty minutes, Thomas declared the meeting open.

"Welcome to the inaugural Vabilmo strategy meeting. Alex and I have spent the last two weeks preparing a few things, which I suggest we go through now together."

Just as George was raising a freshly plucked eyebrow, Brian burst in through the door, hair blowing behind him. The door crashed against his trolley before clicking shut. Thomas continued undeterred.

"What is it that we really want from the next few years? When will our team have achieved its goal? Which end customers and direct clients need to be won before we hand things over to Sales?"

An animated discussion began. Alex took a back seat. She had talked about this a lot with Thomas beforehand. Now it was the others' turn to put forward their suggestions. As usual, a number of different viewpoints came to light.

"We have to adopt a pull strategy," Brian joined the discussion immediately. "That's quite clear – and my extensive contract with Roffarm shows it's the right course of action. The end customers have the industry whip hand; they're the ones who set the tone."

He turned abruptly towards Alex. "Just so you know, Alex, a pull strategy begins at the top of the value chain. We need to convince plant manufacturers and operators about polymer-based solar cells so that they ask their suppliers to use Vabilmo technology in their solar modules. It's exactly what I managed to do with Roffarm; it's the best approach and we should use it with everyone else."

Alex nodded silently. She was well versed with different market approaches.

"If we don't include our direct clients, we won't sell a single new cell," George contradicted him loudly. "There's no way round a push strategy. The plant manufacturers don't buy from us. We're completely dependent on how module manufacturers price their goods. We need to speak with them one way or another. We need to assist them in their price calculations so that the whole thing becomes financially viable for plant manufacturers and operators. We need to push up from below."

Brian wouldn't let go. "The plant manufacturers can make enormous savings with Vabilmo because efficiency is higher than other thin-film cells. If we can get that message across, they'll be convinced straightaway."

Such a generalisation seemed to come at just the right moment for George and he prepared for retaliation. "The polymer-based Vabilmo cells have an efficiency of 45% in comparison with the 20% of our other thin-film cells. Purely theoretically, if both modules were the same size, the Vabilmo cells would generate 100% more solar energy. But you can't just calculate price using a simple 1:1 ratio, as the integration costs are different. A further sticking point lies in adjusting the inverters so that a direct current can be converted into an alternating current. Only an alternating current can be fed into the general electricity supply. If we don't take these variables and dependencies into account together with solar module manufacturers, there'll be no plant prepared to give us a look-in."

"The payback period stands at between twelve and eighteen months post plant inauguration, that's right isn't it, George?" Alex had made a rough estimate using the data at hand. She looked at her colleague enquiringly.

The answer wasn't long in coming. "Yes. Any theoretical savings made by the increased production of energy are cancelled out by the cost of developing new module designs and adapting the inverters. After this period, however, solar power plants could – just on the basis of figures – have an efficiency of between 35% and 40%. We won't have any precise data until the first Vabilmo plant has been established."

"By using Vabilmo technology, our direct clients could set themselves apart from other module manufacturers by virtue of their increased energy production," Alex summarised. "However, other equipment is also required, new inverters for example. Would it make sense to push for standardised inverters to go with the modules?"

George turned his head to the side thoughtfully. "That's a good question, Alex. Only a few module manufacturers develop inverters as well. Normally they work together with a bunch of inverter manufacturers with no standard in place. Nevertheless, standardisation would be of enormous benefit to us and greatly simplify our work. As long as the standard specifies the use of polymer-based solar cells, that is. That would be another constant in our calculations. The price is really a decisive factor."

George looked around and summarised his practical explanation, leaving no-one in doubt as to his viewpoint.

"All this shows why we have to choose a push strategy! We have to develop the modules together with our clients and then present them to the plant manufacturers. Besides, I know all the relevant solar module manufacturers, as well as their possible motivations for switching to Vabilmo. In addition, Hugo and I have a clear perspective on the technical challenges to be overcome."

Brian, who had followed the practical explanation in silence, wouldn't let up. "It is perfectly clear to me, George, that implementing the new technology in existing power plants won't be a walk in the park. That's why PsoraCom has assembled an elite team of consultants like us. If we can't convince the plant manufacturers about the Vabilmo cells, then we may as well give up now. We've seen how to do it already with Roffarm."

But it wasn't quite so clear to George – and so he indulged in his favourite hobby: contradicting Brian.

"Nevertheless! There are still lots of things to be adjusted, 75% of which are not currently being taken into consideration by developers. That's why we need to increase our co-operation with the development sectors of our direct clients. We've cleared an important hurdle with Hursoc. They're one of the world's biggest module manufacturers. Just a few weeks ago they issued a press release stating that they'd be working with the Vabilmo technology. They're the only other company apart from Roffarm to have gone public on this."

"Yes, George," Brian responded impatiently. "We've all read the article, but until now not a great deal has come of it. You've been working on them for as long as I have on Roffarm, if not longer."

The tension between the two was obvious. Initially, they had tried to use objective arguments. But the more different their viewpoints became, the more it seemed like they were two prize fighters engaged in a fight to the death. Brian adopted a visionary pose, his statements underscored by a patronising tone. George countered in staccato with a welter of specialist terminology from his box of magic tricks. Despite being interrupted on several occasions by the attention-seeking ringtones of his netphone, he began to develop inverters and other components that didn't even exist. Hugo tried to make the odd comment now and then, but had to wait before George provided him with a speaker's slot.

"I agree with George," he said finally. "We should increase our activities with direct clients such as Hursoc. At the same time we shouldn't forget about Roffarm, as the pull strategy worked very well there."

George disagreed straightaway. "Roffarm haven't brought in any module manufacturers yet. We're a far cry from our goal there."

But Brian was having none of it. "If we'd tried to get to Roffarm via Hursoc, we'd still be groping around in the dark."

All the while Carl sat in silence, observing the verbal exchange. He'd been hired specially to advise potential robot manufacturers, and for the moment they were not part of the discussion. Besides, he didn't know much about solar power plants. His time would come later.

Alex had grown impatient. Of course, there was a lot to discuss and everybody's opinion needed to be heard. Nevertheless, some of the points being made had gone too far off topic. After exchanging an enquiring look with her boss, she tried to steer the discussion back on course.

"I think," she began, "that our strategy is not simply black and white. In my opinion, both approaches are equally valid and should be adopted in parallel."

"That's my view too," Thomas agreed. "Good. Now that we've heard the different positions, let's go for some lunch. We'll resume in an hour."

The arbiter had spoken.

During lunch there was no sign of friction, perhaps because Brian and George were at opposite ends of the table.

The afternoon began with the second focus of the day: robots and machines. Carl now became increasingly involved, acting as a buffer between Brian and George in the process. Both of them had a lot to say on this topic as well. Alex listened and made notes, as she knew little about robots. She only contributed to the discussion when general or strategic questions were raised.

"Not all robots are the same," Carl responded to her questioning gaze. "And definitions can vary immensely. In engineering, the term refers to industrial robots used to manoeuvre and operate materials. These can be programmed to function autonomously in different axes. In Asia, however, there are several kinds of robots. They range from simple manipulators, controlled by humans, to highly intelligent, almost entirely self-governing machines. That's why a number of separate categories have been created to describe each kind of robot. We mainly differentiate between autonomous mobile robots, industry, service and household robots, as well as between humanoid, toy and military robots."

"That's correct. But still, fitting all appliances with solar cells isn't necessarily sensible. Especially, of course, where there is little sunlight available. Please excuse the interruption, Carl."

"No problem, George. I know very little about solar requirements. I'm grateful for any support you can provide."

Brian immediately interpreted this as an invitation. "To begin with, I think you should examine the major players and conduct a market analysis. We know who the players are already. Feel free to consult me whenever you have any questions. I'd be happy to show you my methods, which have proven themselves many times over the years."

The discussion proceeded far more peacefully than in the morning and there was noticeably less strain between Brian and George. Carl shared his knowledge readily, without reinforcing any specific opinions. Over the course of the afternoon, Thomas drew up a list of companies that could potentially help establish Vabilmo and generate revenue for PsoraCom. He took on a much more prominent role than in the morning, raising queries and putting an end to aimless digressions. He also encouraged them to think not only about end customers and direct clients, but to consider companies that might contribute to a comprehensive platform solution.

Companies that generated no revenue but were nevertheless vital for the strategy as a whole were generally extremely important to PsoraCom as partners. Working with them could help make a decisive contribution to increasing solar power plant efficiency or lowering energy consumption in robots. Consultants and developers were required to work with companies from the so-called ecosystem, now seen as an indispensable part of the industry. PsoraCom's goal was to use this channel to wield the greatest possible influence over solar cell applications. This sphere of influence would be widened by cooperation with power supply operators; developers and manufacturers of inverters; software companies; engineering firms; contractors and architects.

The Vabilmo team's field of activity could have provided a hundred people with jobs. But the team had only five members. As team leader, Thomas was responsible more for the administrative side of things, and would only provide support now and again at important meetings where a senior presence was required. Thus, a clear line of approach needed to be established and their focus directed towards the most successful companies.

By the late afternoon, they had drawn up an extensive list of potential companies they might have to deal with. The list included solar power plant manufacturers (end customers), solar module manufacturers (direct clients), buyers (end customers) and robot manufacturers (direct clients), as well as companies from the ecosystem, such as inverter manufacturers. Only the peripheral issue of contractors had been neglected.

"Good work, let's stop there," Thomas wanted to conclude the meeting for the day. Everyone was wiped out after concentrating so hard and looked at him gratefully. Everyone except Alex.

"We could cover the last point quickly," she suggested. "It'll only take half an hour. Then tomorrow we can focus entirely on evaluating the different companies and establishing our priorities."

She wanted to get all the screening done so that they didn't have to start back at square one the next day.

"Fine," Thomas agreed with a sigh.

Pointless discussions were avoided and after half an hour they were really finished. Thomas smiled appreciatively at Alex, and she nodded back, satisfied. Now the fun part of the evening could begin. Work-related topics were almost completely ignored during dinner. They talked about hobbies, interests, places they had visited and good wine. Alex sat next to Thomas, who even allowed himself a joke, describing Alex as a little terrier. Opposite, Carl was talking about his trip to Zurich with the church choir. For Hugo it was like all his Christmases had come at once - he knew the city like the back of his hand. The muscular model and the sales-type: the contrast made her smile. While she listened in, she occasionally had the impression that Hugo was looking at her expectantly. Although what he was expecting she wasn't so sure.

"The meeting was very well organised," he turned to her directly. "But that was never in any doubt. I noticed it with Roffarm. They thought you were very professional – you could see it in their faces. I was watching their people and they didn't view you as a woman, but as an expert."

It was always nice to hear things like that. After dessert, Alex couldn't shake the feeling that Hugo had something on his mind. As usual her instincts didn't let her down: Hugo wanted to speak to her because she was the only woman.

"I feel like I'm stuck in a rut," he began after everyone else had left. "I'm really unhappy and I feel torn."

"In what sense?" Alex probed. "Professionally or privately?"

"Privately. My girlfriend lives in Zurich and she doesn't want to move. She's always pressuring me but I'm not even sure if I want to be with her anymore. I've met someone else."

Alex had seen it all before. It was usually men who came to talk to her about stuff like this. Why it always had to be her, she hadn't yet discovered.

"But the team doesn't have to know," he added, frantically looking over his shoulder.

"They won't hear a word from me," Alex promised.

"Our relationship has stalled over the past few years. It's always about children – children and marriage. I can't listen to it anymore. I don't want children! Besides, I almost dread the sex. Luckily it doesn't happen very often anymore. And then the endless travelling to Zurich, I only do it for the sake of my friends. With the other person I've met, who lives here, doesn't want children and just wants to enjoy life together, it would be so much easier."

She listened attentively, hardly surprised at all by his candour. The alcohol had almost certainly loosened his tongue. She had heard it so many times before. It was always the same. The million dollar question: is the grass really greener on the other side?

"At first, whatever's new or different seems better or more desirable," she replied. "But most of the time it's just a question of perspective. Change position and all of a sudden what you had will appear more attractive. The important thing is to think about what you want from life. There are compromises in every relationship. Irrespective of whether you stay with what you've got or swap it for something new. You never get 100%."

She was shocked by how much of a know-it-all she sounded. Nevertheless, she knew from experience that she was right.

"I can't tell you what to do," she continued, "because I don't know what it's like in your shoes. Only you can know what's right for you and what you want. If you feel you can no longer live with your girlfriend, then make sure you end it before you start anything new. Two-timing her just isn't fair. But before you make a decision, consider what you like about her and what you stand to lose. Contrast that with what you stand to gain with the new person. There'll almost certainly be a couple of unknown factors in the equation as well. At the end of the day, though, it's your decision and no-one can make it for you."

It probably wasn't what he wanted to hear but it was the truth. Decisions weren't always easy and you had to be able to live with the consequences. You couldn't hold anyone else responsible and that was precisely the problem. Some people preferred to maintain the status quo, even if they were unhappy, so they didn't have to live with the potentially tragic repercussions of a decision. Others couldn't summon the courage to make a decision in the first place, because this normally triggered a whole slew of actions, reactions and additional decisions. People were basically driven by pleasure or pain. They wanted to maximise their pleasure and minimise, or even eliminate, their pain.

On the way home, Alex thought about the conversation some more. Perhaps Hugo wasn't torn at all. Perhaps he simply couldn't deal with the fall-out from a decision. Was he too comfortable and just hoped the whole thing would vanish into thin air? That someone else would make the decision for him?

The next morning, Thomas opened the discussion purposefully with the list from the previous day. The others needed no encouragement, with opinions emerging thick and fast as soon as the first slide had been projected onto the wall. Once more the central question was whether they should focus on plant manufacturers or those who made solar modules. Astonishingly, this wasn't an issue in the robotics department.

"We have to adopt a joint push and pull strategy," Thomas made his view clear. "We need both so that we can penetrate the market from different sides."

There were a few basic criteria according to which priorities needed to be set; how big a company was, its global market share and in which sector it operated. There were solar plant manufacturers in both the grid-connected and off-grid-systems sectors. Generally innovations in grid-connected plants received more funding, as the number of solar modules per plant dictated that the ROI was higher. Most of the profit was invested in development to boost energy yield, increase sustainability and distinguish them from the competition.

Off-grid systems were usually set up in remote areas or in places where their energy requirements could be closely monitored by the consumer. Although the ROI on a single off-grid system wasn't particularly high, it was the total number of them that made the difference. The demand for small-scale independent plants had risen dramatically in recent times. Here the important factor wasn't the increase in energy yield but the reduced development times made possible by the Vabilmo technology. Even unusual designs could result in significant financial savings.

In order to ensure that polymer-based solar cells were widely used, tackling both of these markets was a necessity. Alex was soon in agreement with Brian. She would assume sole responsibility for Premve and Luxumi (from the grid-connected sector), as well as Natioba – one of the biggest manufacturers of off-grid systems – immediately. Brian could target other plant manufacturers in Europe and assist with Roffarm if need be. Thomas informed everyone that owing to the complexity of the contract with Roffarm, a separate team had been formed and placed directly under Wolfgang's control. Technical resources – that is, Hugo – would be shared between both teams for consultation and project work. The chance to lead the team had been offered to Brian no doubt, although it seemed he had turned it down. A colleague from Sales would assume the role in a few days, with Brian serving as a link between him and the Vabilmo team.

It was also decided that they would initially concentrate on Europe, following a directive from the US to factor out China for the time being due to patent restrictions. They didn't have the capacity to deal directly with companies based in the US or other parts of Asia. If they needed something done there, they'd have to bring in local colleagues; just as they had involved Nobu in the pilot project with Natioba. Brian raised strong objections here. In his opinion the time was right to try and tackle the Asian market. But Thomas had settled this with Wolfgang before the meeting. For now there was no budget available for trips to Asia, although this might change in the next quarter.

Brian had to grudgingly admit defeat and take on responsibility for two companies that successfully manufactured off-grid systems. As a compromise, however, he was to consolidate his contact-base in Asia and familiarise them with Vabilmo, so that they could approach companies there directly. The sword of Damocles was still hanging over their heads thanks to the unresolved issue of the Roffarm contract. Again, Thomas underlined his view that work should be „business as usual".

Prioritising their direct clients was a little trickier. In addition to the handful of market leaders that George had dealt with for years, there were also a vast number of potential customers. Alex had come across a few of these companies in her previous job and would be able to provide some assistance. After they had been ranked from "important" to "irrelevant", Thomas decided that George would assume responsibility for this sector as before. Alex could deal with other prospective customers that were viewed as important, as long as it didn't harm her work with end customers. Additionally she was to check out potential contractors in the next quarter and propose the best way forward. Carl was tasked with conducting a market analysis of the machine and robotics industry and presenting his findings, objectives included, in one of the next team meetings. George promised to assist him, as the different industries overlapped to some extent.

Finally, they discussed the issue of technical support. 50% of Hugo's time would be allocated to the Roffarm project. Everyone agreed that the contract made this a priority. Still, it was very clear that at some point a greater level of technical assistance would be required. For that reason, everyone agreed that Thomas should ask management for additional technical support. For the time being, however, the team would have to cope with just Hugo, whose brief also included evaluating partner companies in the inverter business. George promised to lend his experience here too.

With that, all issues had been clarified.

"One more thing before we all disappear," Thomas said. "As far as I know, until now everyone has been attending almost every client meeting. In future, I would ask you to consider carefully whether you are needed or not. We've got a lot of work to get through and we need to pool our resources sensibly."

Everyone nodded. Except Brian.

"But Thomas, the reason the whole team goes to these meetings is for our clients to see how serious we are. They have to know that Vabilmo isn't just a one-man show."

Naturally, George had a different opinion.

"Everyone must be able to explain the technology to clients up to a certain point. There should be no need for Hugo or myself to be present at initial meetings."

After a brief pause, he added: "Still, the fact we've all been there has meant it's been a steep learning curve. I find Hugo's technical abstractions during his sales pitch very convincing."

There he was again: the admiring father figure, who could completely contradict himself within the space of two sentences. Out of the corner of her eye, Alex saw that even Thomas was struggling to suppress a grin.

Instead, he replied: "I only want you to be reasonable about who needs to attend meetings. It's a simple question of expenses."

Now that all responsibilities and clients had been assigned accordingly, Alex could really get going. Team priorities had been identified and these were to serve as guidelines to help define activities regarding the individual client accounts. She asked herself what she wanted to achieve with each end customer and by when. She drew up blank documents for each individual company, filling them in turn with her experiences and insights. She started by incorporating all the information she had gathered thus far into these so-called account plans. This included everything from organisational and decision-making structures to development activities and new products, right through to contacts with suppliers and other companies. Later she realised that all her end customers employed robots, especially those in the service industry.

She would proceed together with Carl to see if they could unearth any further potential for Vabilmo. However, they still needed to clarify who held the main responsibility. Was it with Robotics or would Carl be assisting her? Maybe she was being too meticulous – ultimately it would be a member of the Vabilmo team handling the client, after all. Still, in her experience it made more sense to map things out clearly from the start. It would help avoid misunderstandings later, and clients always wanted to know who their designated point of contact was. She decided to mention the issue at the next team meeting.

Things had calmed down between Sandro and Alex since their skiing weekend. Everything was back to normal. During the week they came home late and unwound in their own ways. For Alex that meant a quick hour's work-out. While it got dark early, she worked out in the flat; otherwise she went jogging. Afterwards she relaxed on the sofa, alternating between novels from the best-seller lists and specialist books for her own personal development. The latter was an interest her father had awoken in her years before.

Sandro went straight to the tennis club after work or sat at home in front of the PC, tinkering with software for new sensors. If there was a good thriller or comedy on TV, they'd watch it together. Sometimes Alex wondered whether they did too little as a couple. Her repeated suggestions that they should train together had so far proved fruitless – for Sandro, sport meant tennis. Alex had played tennis for a few years as a teenager but she wasn't particularly good at it, and Sandro didn't have the patience to coach her. Also Alex didn't really get on with the people from the tennis club. Their interests were simply too different, as the last party had proved once again.

At the weekends they ate out or invited friends round to cook, which they both greatly enjoyed. From time to time they went to the movies, or played backgammon at home. But the feeling persisted that they could be doing more together. It was probably just the time of year. When it got dark early, people locked themselves away at home and did whatever they liked doing best. For Alex that meant sport and reading; for Sandro it was the tennis club and programming. Some of their friends did even less together. A few of them didn't even live in the same flat. Things weren't quite so bad between her and Sandro in comparison, were they?

4

April

The project with Natioba was slowly beginning to take shape and it was now a question of finding the relevant internal resources. Alex was in email or phone contact with Nobu at least once a week. Her marketing colleague had obtained the bend-module samples for Natioba; their standardised interfaces, which paved the way for a number of different design forms, had ensured their enthusiastic reception. The marketing and development of the new products was overseen by Robotics at PsoraCom USA.

One of the product managers there had tested whether the bend-modules could be equipped with polymer-based solar cells instead of thin-film cells on metal substrate. Without exception, the results had been positive. It had taken Nobu no time at all to convince him of the project and secure his services as project leader. The fact that the products could be tested for the first time with a global corporation such as Natioba had spoken for itself.

During a telephone conference arranged by Nobu, Alex discussed the primary objectives of the project with said product manager, Hank. In addition, they agreed to a weekly telephone conference, to which members of the Vabilmo team, as well as any other colleagues of Hank's, were invited. After all, there were many potential projects in this area and they needed to consolidate information and experience. Alex promised to post details of the meeting on the internal calendar programme.

She included Thomas on the mailing list as well, as he wanted to be kept informed even if he wouldn't necessarily be participating. The advantage of the calendar programme was that it allowed you to organise meetings with several people, as well as having an automatic reminder function that enabled employees to dial straight into the network bridge. Almost all meetings at PsoraCom were arranged over this system. However, sometimes it seemed as if it prevented spontaneous phone calls. Everyone could use the calendar system to see when someone else had an appointment, although they couldn't see what kind it was.

Alex had already observed that a number of colleagues "blocked" the calendar in order to work on something specific in peace. Even for normal calls between two people, it seemed common practice to arrange an appointment which was then entered into the calendar with a minimum duration of half an hour. It wasn't possible to arrange a shorter call. Alex still needed to adjust to this system, as she was used to simply picking up the phone and dialling.

As far as her meetings with Hank were concerned, she was fortunate that Nobu was the only person taking part from Asia. Trying to factor in all three major time zones for a weekly meeting was like trying to juggling five balls in one hand. However, since Nobu was something of an early bird a suitable time was soon found. She sent the details to Brian, George, Hugo, Carl and Thomas, as well as the colleagues Hank had mentioned to her.

Next Alex turned her attention to the follow-up meeting with Premve, which she had arranged at the trade show in Barcelona. In principle, this end customer was handled by Marco, a sales colleague from the crystalline solar cells division. He always seemed friendly and laughed a lot during phone calls. It was often said that portly people were cheery souls, and Marco's stature dictated that he conformed unmistakeably to type. Maybe that was the reason he always wore a suit – so that his girth could be lightly concealed by a jacket. The few times they had spoken, Marco had seemed very interested in Vabilmo.

She decided to go to him directly.

"Hey Marco, how's it going? When would be a good time to talk about Premve? We had an initial meeting with them in Barcelona and I'm keen to push things forward."

"I've got half an hour now if you like," he replied straightaway.

"Great," Alex was delighted. "That suits me perfectly. I thought I'd have to look for a time in your calendar."

"No, no. If I can take care of something immediately, then I just get it done.."

Most likely, this set him apart somewhat from other colleagues.

"So," she began. "In Barcelona I met with a contact from the purchasing department, who gave me the following information. Premve are currently examining when, where and how their next solar power plant should be built. An internal committee has been formed comprising different division chiefs, among them the head of logistics, who is also in overall charge of purchasing. The next step is to arrange an appointment with the head of purchasing at Premve. With his help, my aim is to approach the committee, introduce the subject of Vabilmo and start a joint project."

"Sounds great," exclaimed Marco. "Count me in."

"If I have understood correctly," Alex continued, "they are planning to build their next major grid-connected plant in about three years. In my view, we don't have a realistic chance of getting the contract unless we initiate a trial or development project."

"OK," Marco interrupted her only briefly to signal his agreement.

"I just can't imagine that any plant manufacturer is going to risk equipping an entire plant with new technology without testing it first. There's always a pre-development stage."

"My point of view exactly," he concurred. "I'll call the head of purchasing's secretary straightaway, she'll get us an appointment."

Five minutes later, it was arranged.

"That was quick," Alex said delighted. "I'll tell Brian, we should bring him along too."

"If you say so. I don't think Brian needs to be there, but I'll leave the decision up to you. Still, why don't we prepare the slides together, then you can clear them with your contact at Premve. Will you give the presentation? You're the one responsible for Premve after all."

"Right, I'll give the presentation. We decided just recently that I would assume sole responsibility for these clients. Nevertheless, it would make sense for Brian to come too; he knows the back-story."

Marco's comment flagged up the question of how well he and Brian got along.

In the next few days, Alex got down to the preparation. Her training period was over and she needed to get things going. During the first three months she had received 100% variable pay, as agreed. From now on new objectives would be set each quarter, so-called MBOs, or "Management by Objectives". It was still too early to set sales targets in terms of dollars (everything was calculated in dollars at PsoraCom); that wouldn't happen for another two years. Until then, each member of the Vabilmo team had their MBOs, defined together with Thomas.

As Alex had learned at a mandatory training session during the first few weeks, all PsoraCom employees were obliged to schedule regular meetings with their boss. She was to meet Thomas on the last Monday of each month.

Alex had tried to keep Mondays and Fridays as free as possible in her previous jobs too. Mondays were especially suitable for internal meetings and preparing for appointments; Fridays were ideal for call reports and turning in expenses.

According to the Pareto principcle, you only needed 20% of the time available to carry out 80% of your workload if you were disciplined. Alex stuck to the 80/20 rule on her office days, leaving plenty of time to deal with unforeseen matters. You couldn't always get hold of contacts; colleagues sometimes requested assistance or information; and clients, of course, didn't inform you weeks in advance when they'd call.

Alex's father had put all this to her years ago, but as usual theory and practice diverged - sometimes more often than Alex would have liked. Nevertheless, it was a useful point of orientation.

Maybe that's why she could get impatient in meetings from time to time, particularly whenever she had the feeling that discussions were getting out of hand, or that valuable time was being wasted. However, perhaps even in these situations she wasn't aware of the bigger picture, and was unable to appreciate that in fact exactly the right issues were being discussed. Who was ever in a position to know? There was often a political element too, of course, even if it wasn't immediately obvious to everyone. Still, for her a well-structured meeting with clear goals and corresponding outcomes was always preferable to a debate with no tangible results.

For this reason, she found the monthly meetings with Thomas exactly to her liking. Each time, they went through all the companies one by one. Alex gave the latest status and outlined the next possible steps, which she and Thomas then finalised together. In their first meeting about quarterly MBOs, Thomas explained the procedure.

A maximum of five main objectives were to be set, derived from the account strategies. What was going to be achieved with which company, when and how. There was overachievement and underachievement. A performance level system, starting at 50%, was standard company policy.

For instance, one objective could be a successful project bid. If the agreement of several company hierarchy levels was needed, then securing the approval of the lowest level would amount to a 50% achievement. If the project had been given a formal go-ahead at a higher level and a procedure had been roughly outlined, then that might constitute a 150% or even 200% achievement.

The value of each of the five objectives was judged according to its overall importance to the team or company aims. Thus if an important objective had only been achieved to 50%, it could be offset, if necessary, by achieving a less important objective to 150%. All in all, it seemed a fair system. If achievements exceeded the overall threshold of 100%, then variable pay would be adjusted accordingly: a financial incentive for high achievers.

It turned out that Thomas wasn't prepared simply to present her with a set of objectives. Instead, he asked her about her own targets and what objectives she would set for herself.

"For Natioba I imagined the following," she began. "By the end of the quarter I'd like to have written confirmation of our joint project from Seoul – and to know its scope. At the moment we only have their oral consent. It still hasn't been decided what kind of off-grid system will be fitted with the Vabilmo technology."

"That's how I see it too," said her boss. "Natioba has priority. How would you grade this objective?"

"I see 50% as achieved when we have written confirmation that they want to do the project. 100% when the scope is confirmed and a time-line established. 150% once the project has been started and 200% if the project is completed this quarter. In terms of overall priority, I'd put the project at 40%."

It was highly unlikely that the project would be completed by the end of June. Things might drag a little at the beginning as well, unless an agreement was soon made on its scope.

"Exactly which factors does your timeline take into account?" Thomas probed. "The most important thing is the official presentation of the project. We can work out the stages in between from that."

"Not necessarily," he countered, "unless the project is already complete when you do the presentation."

"Of course; to me that's self-explanatory. Before that our hands will be tied by the non-disclosure agreement – unless Natioba want to make it public earlier, which I doubt."

"OK, fine. I can live with that, but let's establish the priority of each of your individual objectives. What are your other four tasks?"

"I can't ignore Natioba headquarters. I'd like to do a project with them too if possible. First, I'll plan a workshop to synchronise our strategies for the new technology. We need to know what their plans are. Then I want to get the go-ahead for a joint collaboration, or, best-case scenario, a new project."

"How will the project be different from the one in Seoul?"

"Well, I can easily imagine that the Seoul project will be geared towards future international needs, and will result in the creation of a new kind of off-grid system. Headquarters, in contrast, will be more interested in looking after its main products and hybrid systems. Here we could take classic off-grid power generators and fit them with Vabilmo."

Thomas nodded, and so they went on, going through her objectives one by one.

"All my clients use robots for different tasks such as service and repairs. That's another potential area for us. How does that fit in with Carl's objectives?"

"There are areas that overlap, of course," her boss admitted. "But his priority is consumer industry robots. We'll discuss any conflicts as and when they arise."

After two hours, they had established all her objectives for the coming quarter with corresponding performance level percentages. Basically they were counting on each end customer to agree to a collaboration on an initial pilot project. Finally, they determined the priority of her objectives. With projects planned in Seoul and Italy, Natioba was accorded highest priority, followed by Premve and Luxumi. If she still had time, Alex could check out additional solar module manufacturers not already in contact with George.

If everyone had such high objectives – and these were met – the team would make rapid headway. And that's what it was all about.

She would need seed units for her end customers, that much was clear. Nothing was more convincing than a product you could touch. Pretty PowerPoint slides and high-flown promises were no match in comparison.

"We'll need seed units from Robotics of the new bend-module designs," she said on the phone to Hank. "Preferably the spherical ones, they're the most impressive. Ten would be great, my colleagues will need some too. Do you think that's possible?"

"I'll have to disappoint you there. We only have four spherical seed units at the moment, and they're all needed here for development. I should be able to get hold of a few wave-shaped ones though."

"That would be great."

"I'll mail you an order form straightaway so we can process the request internally. The spherical ones can be borrowed in exceptional circumstances – I'll send you the information you need so you can request them."

"Fantastic. Thank you so much."

Delighted, she went to see Thomas.

"Hey boss, I've just been on the phone about the seed units so we can show the bend-modules at client meetings. I've got the order forms already, they won't cost us a thing."

"Very good, let's discuss it tomorrow at the team meeting."

Hugo's eyes lit up and he said he needed two for Roffarm. Everybody else nodded and requested one for themselves. Except George - although in the general euphoria no-one noticed. Thomas didn't insist on having one for himself.

"I'll only take one if there are enough to go round," he said. "Otherwise I'll borrow yours; I won't be calling on a client alone anyway."

He thought for a little while and then looked at Alex again.

"It's best if you order the units for everyone. It doesn't really make sense for us to ask from different sides and Hank is your contact, after all."

"I'd be happy to."

After she had ordered seed units for everyone, Nobu was next on her to-do list. Alex wanted to hear the latest news, as her colleague in Seoul had been talking directly to Natioba's development lab supervisor. From what Hank said, everything was going well so far. Natioba had named a project manager, with whom he had already been in contact.

It was Chris, who had taken part in the first meeting in Florida. He would be transferred to the New York office for the duration of the project, since that was where Hank and Robotics were both based. This would enable them to work closely together, while also minimising potential delays because of different time zones. Nobu would provide additional support through his contact with the lab supervisor in Seoul.

Hank and Chris were currently working together with a small American design company to optimise the design for the bend-modules. The plan was to present the pilot project to the public in

September. Hank had suggested September because that was when the annual PsoraCom developer conference took place, to which all clients and important partner companies from the ecosystem were invited.

This year it was being held in Asia to showcase the latest developments in the region. The exact location had yet to be decided, but Tokyo, Seoul and Taipei were all being discussed. Of course, Seoul would be huge – and it was home turf for Natioba's development lab. But they had no influence on the venue. Individual departments at PsoraCom presented the latest developments and there were a number of partner booths with solar module and inverter manufacturers, as well as plant surveillance systems and software.

Upper management staff from PsoraCom gave different speeches, with the greatest significance attached to the chief executive's opening presentation. In it, he spoke about the path forward for the next year and the company's future prospects. The event was perfect for the project, as there would be a significant media presence there. And although their own participation wasn't assured yet, Hank had already established initial contact with the relevant event managers.

Since Nobu was an early bird, Alex rang him in the evenings from home. The time difference in both directions (Hank was six hours behind; Nobu nine ahead) would significantly increase her workload in the next few months. Nevertheless, the prospect of a successfully completed project made it a worthwhile price to pay. Her colleague picked up after the second ring.

"Hello Nobu. Are you awake already? I've just spoken to Hank. We might have the chance to unveil the project at the developer conference."

"I'm wide awake now! That would be fantastic. We'd get great publicity for it. Say, Alex, could you do me a favour? I've been trying to get in touch with Natioba's lab supervisor for days. I've left him a few messages but he still hasn't called back."

"I can give him a try, if you like," she offered.

"Yes please. The supervisor is Italian; perhaps your charm can help persuade him to return our calls."

"That certainly won't be the reason he calls back," Alex smiled. "But it wouldn't be a bad idea for me to have his contact details – in case you're on holiday and we urgently need a decision."

"Exactly. One more thing, Alex. There's a renewable energy conference in San Francisco soon. I want to meet different clients there and could do with your support to help present the Vabilmo technology."

"I can't make any promises," she hesitated. "We need international trips to be approved by management. Besides, we're not planning to target the US and Asia until the first phase is complete."

Although every employee booked flights and hotels independently, approval was needed for trips to other continents. Even if expenses were higher for business meetings in Europe that lasted several days. Those were the rules.

"I understand," replied her Korean colleague. "But people are coming to this conference from all over the world, and we need to be represented. Some of your clients also have offices in the US – we could make a few additional appointments. I'll send you the request by mail, along with my last suggestion. That way you can justify it."

"Good, I'll put it to my boss," she assured him.

Prior to the meeting with Premve's head of purchasing, Alex had gone through the slides she'd prepared together with Marco. He hadn't made any real changes except for a few comments here and there of a cosmetic nature. She really liked the fact that he wasn't very bureaucratic. Although he had dealt with Premve for years sales-wise, he allowed her to take the lead. Of course, it might have been because he still didn't know very much about polymer-based solar cells. The slides had been cleared with Brian, and George had given his seal of approval too. He wouldn't take any part in the meeting himself, although Hugo would be there. In George's opinion, four representatives from PsoraCom would be more than enough.

When the day came Alex felt slightly nervous, and decided to conceal her anxiety with one of her best trouser suits. She never wore a skirt at first meetings. She drove to Premve with Marco.

While they were preparing everything in the meeting room before the start of the presentation, Marco spoke to Brian.

"We'll leave the presentation to Alex, she's done a fantastic job there. Only if she gives the sign are we to help her out. But I don't think we'll need to."

Brian bent down over his trolley. "Yeah, we'll hold back. I'm sure Alex will bring home the bacon."

Hugo nodded in agreement, giving the thumbs up as he smiled at her. Since the presentation wouldn't go into great technical detail, his role would be minimal. The reason he was there was to meet those involved from the client's end, as he might have to deal with them directly later on.

Along with the head of purchasing and his assistant, Premve were represented by two additional people from development. After the obligatory round of introductions, Alex began her presentation.

"Good morning and many thanks for taking the time today to get to know our latest technology, codenamed "Vabilmo." To what extent are you already familiar with PsoraCom and our product range? I have a number of introductory slides outlining key company data, which I am perfectly happy to pass over if need be."

The head of purchasing glanced briefly at one of his colleagues before giving her an appreciative nod.

"We are aware of PsoraCom, of course, but I don't know absolutely everything, so please take us through all your slides."

She didn't need any further encouragement and soon all her nerves had evaporated. Now she was in her element. It was always the same at important meetings. She was nervous at first but, as soon as her presentation began, pleasure and self-confidence prevailed: there was nothing in the slides she couldn't relate to. She went through the figures one by one and described the company's matrix structure, only to be interrupted many times by Brian. A few things he said were useful, shedding light on details she hadn't mentioned; others were completely unnecessary, as he was just repeating what had already been said in his own words.

Marco rolled his eyes. Brian didn't seem to notice once he got going. Alex let him be: she would never dream of interrupting a colleague in front of a client, let alone cutting them short. She waited instead for an opportune moment. Brian paused briefly for thought and that was that. Marco took the floor immediately and steered things back to Alex's presentation. It wouldn't be the last time Brian interrupted to give his take on things. As soon as he snatched a breath, Alex thanked him for his comments and continued with her presentation.

At times it seemed as if even the head of purchasing was afraid he wouldn't see the presentation through to its finish. He acted with less restraint than Alex and began to interrupt Brian directly, albeit politely. Towards the end, time really was a bit tight. Alex concluded her presentation and, with a wink, pulled out her trump card.

"It has come to my attention that your company has formed a committee tasked with making a decision on your next photovoltaic power plant," she said, fixing the head of purchasing directly in the eye. "What do we need to do to present the Vabilmo technology in front of such a forum? Would you have any suggestions for me?"

The head of purchasing took the bait immediately.

"That's no problem," he assured her. "You have my support. We can use my boss to get through to the head of logistics' secretary; she coordinates all committee meetings. Revise your presentation so that the main focus is on joint developments, and clear it with my assistant as before. He'll be able to give you an indication of the existing plans for the new power plant. Then the two of us should have another meeting before you take it to the committee. How does that sound?"

"Sounds like an excellent plan!" Alex gave him an impish grin.

After they had said goodbye to their two colleagues, Marco took advantage of the drive home to speak his mind.

"I could've absolutely murdered Brian," he began. "We specifically said you'd do the presentation. But no - he just can't help himself. He always has to put his two cents in. The mad rush at the end could've been avoided if he hadn't gabbed away so much. But you managed to sort it out. Absolutely top class!"

"Some of his ideas weren't so bad," Alex responded. "I've only been here a few months and I'm glad of any support. OK, so some comments were pretty irrelevant, but I don't think they did any harm."

"Maybe not, but his conduct didn't do him any favours. The way he sat in his chair. Behaving like he was the head of purchasing's best friend. The guy's pretty matter-of-fact: you had the right approach. It was your sense of humour that finally got him on side."

"Don't exaggerate now, Marco! Although I have to say hearing that is music to my ears."

Alex felt very flattered and was far too psyched about the outcome to be annoyed about Brian's remarks.

"I'm not exaggerating," he insisted. "I never thought we'd make such quick progress with them. I mean, the committee members are only one level below the board of directors. With a big corporation like Premve, things normally don't happen so easily. I'm pretty sure that Brian wouldn't have been able to manage it."

"Nothing's set in stone," Alex voiced her concerns, "but the head of purchasing seems like the kind of man who keeps his word."

Almost as if to let off more steam, Marco lit a cigarette and opened the sunroof. They both fell silent, abandoning themselves to their thoughts. It was only now that Alex realised Hugo hadn't said a single word during the meeting. He had only spoken to the developers briefly at the end - although that, of course, had been the plan.

The next morning, Alex was caught off guard by a very unusual email. Overnight Brian had written a call report entitled "Significant breakthrough with Premve". The mailing list contained not only the Vabilmo team, but also lots of colleagues from the US and Asia, as well as various executives. Wolfgang was naturally included, as was Bill. Nothing of the sort had been agreed the day before. In principle, there was no reason why he shouldn't write the report and keep management staff up-to-date, as they were expecting this anyway. But the tone of it was far too sensational for Alex's liking.

At midday, Thomas collected her for lunch.

"So tell me," he said on the way to the canteen, "how did it go yesterday?"

"Very well," Alex replied. "Things are looking good – but it wasn't exactly a breakthrough. The meeting still has to take place."

"Well, it sounds like a very promising start," her boss remarked.

"Yeah, but the next obstacle is to convince the committee and get an OK for the project. That would be a great result, but it's meaningless until the project is actually implemented. Even if the project is successfully carried out, there's still no guarantee that Premve will decide to equip their next plant with Vabilmo technology, let alone that a solar module manufacturer will be involved too. So you see, a genuine breakthrough is still a long way off. I need to speak to Brian because he never cleared the email with me. With my clients, I want to be the one who decides when and how something is communicated."

"Don't worry about it," he tried to calm her. "Brian's always writing mails like that. It's common knowledge; no-one takes them too seriously. That's just his way of doing things."

The remark didn't exactly soothe Alex's nerves, quite the opposite. Not to be taken seriously was considerably worse. If expectations were set too high, then at least you could work hard at achieving them. She needed to clear things up with Brian.

In the future she would write the call reports for her clients, or at least together with a colleague. She remembered what her father had drummed into her again and again: "Always stand by what you say! That way you'll think long and hard before you make any promises. Otherwise you'll have to face the consequences."

It was a principle she had kept to ever since; and one she hoped would help her gain appreciation and respect at PsoraCom.

After several attempts, she finally reached her colleague.

"Hello, Brian. Thanks for writing the call report but I think your language was too flowery. We shouldn't be talking about a breakthrough after a first meeting."

"Well, I was only trying to help," he defended his actions straightaway. "The company still sees us as an underground project. It's time we made some waves. Besides, I think the meeting was a real milestone. Premve is one of the biggest PV plant manufacturers, and this committee could decide to build a new plant with our polymer-based solar cells without even commissioning an initial project."

Alex didn't agree with him in the slightest, but chose not to pursue it further. It would only have provoked a lengthy discussion. Besides she had already seen how he took advantage of any opportunity to steer the conversation over to his past achievements. She didn't have time for that now.

"In the future I'll use your template for reports," she ended the conversation, "and send them to each team member. If there's anybody absent from the mailing list, you are more than welcome to forward it. Alright?"

"Fine, no problem."

It didn't take long for George and Hugo to reply to Brian's mail. The former congratulated them on a good result, singling Alex out for special praise. No dissent. No criticism. The latter wrote enthusiastically about how interested the developers had been; they had agreed to remain in contact.

Her netphone rang. It was George.

"A fantastic achievement," he said once more. "Great result for a first meeting."

"Thanks, but it wasn't just me. Brian and Marco were equally important. Besides, we still don't know when the meeting will take place.

"OK, but from what Marco told me, it was mostly down to you."

Alex gave up contradicting him and allowed herself to be persuaded.

As promised, Nobu had arranged a few meetings around the San Francisco conference and officially requested her assistance. Hank and Chris would also be there to meet with the design firm and discuss the form of the solar modules. As a result, she would be supporting colleagues and visiting clients at the same time. Thus armed, Alex went to Thomas to get the green light for the trip.

Her boss put off making the decision; somehow Alex had the feeling he wanted to cover himself first.

Since she still had an overload of emails, she decided to keep working once she got home. Sandro must still have been at the tennis club, even though it was almost eleven. Just as Alex was switching off her computer, her netphone rang suddenly. It was a Korean number.

"Buongiorno Signore," Alex took the call, using her sketchy knowledge of Italian. "Thanks for calling back. How are you?"

She had left a message for the development lab supervisor in Seoul an hour before.

"Buona sera Signora," he replied gallantly in his native tongue. "I am very well, thank you. How are you?"

"Excellent."

Their conversation carried on in Italian for a few minutes more. He seemed to appreciate her efforts, even if what came out was grammatically suspect.

"How is the project progressing?" Alex asked. "Are we on track?"

"Yes. Chris has been keeping me up-to-date on your activities, I'm very satisfied so far."

"That's good to know. However, there's still one very important issue: the question of how we present the project to the public. What are your views on that?"

"I think we need to make a Big Bang, as the Americans would say," the lab supervisor replied without hesitation. "We really have to shake the industry up."

"That's how I see it too," she agreed. "We're discussing our options internally at the moment. We might be able to unveil the project at our annual developer conference in August. Though nothing's been decided yet."

"Your developer conference," he probed, "how big is it and where does it take place?"

"Not as big as the annual photovoltaics conference, but there'll be a few thousand industry players there. Aside from the usual media presence, we're also expecting hundreds of bloggers. It's in Asia this year. Taipei, Seoul and Tokyo are in the running still."

"That sounds exactly like the Big Bang I had in mind. If you can swing it, count me in. Just let me know if you need anything specific. The best way to reach me is by cell phone."

"Good, I'll keep you posted," she promised. "But Nobu is still your point of contact."

"We'll need to clear it with headquarters, of course," he added. "We're not completely independent. We have our own budget for projects that are trend-setting or in line with market requirements but we still rely on assignments from Research and Development in Italy. But leave the Italians to me; I'll persuade them."

"Fine. I didn't think there'd be much of a difference between your lab and the Natioba group as a whole anyway."

"No, there isn't. But high-profile appearances where we showcase our own activities need to be authorised by headquarters."

Tired but exceedingly satisfied, Alex realised it was already past midnight. Sandro still wasn't back. Recently he had been coming home very late from the tennis club. Even if she wasn't exactly worried, she was still pretty annoyed.

Sandro went to Switzerland for Easter as usual with a few members from the club. Alex didn't go anymore. It just wasn't her thing. She would have liked to spend Easter alone with him but she knew how important this trip was. So she let him go just as she did every Good Friday, waving him off as he drove away in his car. Suddenly she was afraid that something might happen and she would lose him. An accident? She quickly abandoned the thought: Sandro was a good driver. Freezing cold, she went back into the flat.

Anna came by on Saturday. She was just back from a stint in South America and they had a lot to talk about.

"Hola, fish face," she said as she stood in the door. "It's good to be back in the Harley café, sweety."

"Hey, pudding chops," Alex was delighted. "I'm glad you made it home in one piece. Do you want a latte, gorgeous?"

"Of course I do. Best coffee in town."

"So, how was Brazil?"

"Fantastic. The project went really well, even if they don't do things the same way as us over there. It's like they have a different concept of time. I had a few little run-ins with colleagues who weren't aware of just how urgent things were. If there was still nothing happening after a bit of friendly cajoling, then I'd take it upstairs. Well, there's no way around it, is there. If we hadn't finished on time, the client would have made a compensation claim and that might have cost the company dear."

The afternoon had gone by quickly and they were both hungry. Alex had no desire to cook.

"Should we order a pizza before you go causing chaos in the kitchen?"

Anna laughed. She knew what Alex was referring to.

"Do you have to bring it up every time? I mean, it's been ten years."

"Until our dying day."

Whenever they met, they had a laugh about Anna's defrosting skills. Alex had once asked her friend to defrost some steaks she wanted to grill later in the garden with Moritz.

"Use the bowl here," she had said to Anna, as she gave her a plastic bag containing the frozen, already-marinated steaks. Then she had disappeared into the bathroom to take a shower. When she came back into the kitchen, each of the steaks was outside the bag swimming in red-brown water. Anna had speculated about what kind of "strange meat" it was. Still, at least the steaks were defrosted and after a bit of seasoning, they even tasted pretty good. Moritz had creased himself with laughter. Since then Alex gave precise instructions whenever Anna helped out in the kitchen.

Anna continued her story over pizza and beer.

"Luckily, I tacked on a little holiday after the project to get to know the country and its people a bit better. The conditions there take some getting used to, but I'm not too fussy. You know me, I don't need luxury; I'd rather save my money for bungee jumping and stuff like that. Here's a photo of me sky-diving."

"Well, you've certainly looked better," Alex laughed, seeing how the wind had contorted Anna's face.

"Hey, how's it going at PsoraCom? I can't just sit here and do all the talking."

"Why not? That's what you always do. If it gets too much, I'll just stop listening."

Anna jabbed her in the ribs.

"The new job's a dream," Alex gushed. "It's really fun and completely international. One of my main clients is based in Italy, I've got a project on the go with South Korea and I might be flying to San Francisco in a few weeks to help a colleague at a client meeting."

"What kind of project is it?"

"I can't say: that's still confidential. But we're planning to unveil it to the public in the autumn. Perhaps even in Asia."

"And what are your colleagues like?"

"Great. Everything's going really well. My team colleagues have helped me a lot these first few months. They let me sit in on client meetings right from the start. It's a really colourful crowd, everyone's very different. One of them, our visionary, does the whole surfer thing; the next is a real-life dandy and a walking encyclopaedia to boot; the third could have sprung straight from a Boss advert: he's even called Hugo; then there's Carl, the devoted father and least remarkable of them all; and finally my boss. He's a study in elegant restraint, although he's begun to thaw out recently – no need for you to put him in a bowl of warm water. All the other people in the office are really open and kind."

"Sounds cool. I'm so happy for you."

"It's so good to see you again. Although I hate to say it, I've missed you."

"I've missed you too, honey. How are things with Sandro? Everything OK there?"

"Yeah, fine. The same as ever. He's spending a lot of time at the tennis club at the moment but he's got a few tournaments coming up."

It was a little after three in the morning when they finally went to bed.

On Easter Sunday she visited her parents. She was greeted by the smell of homemade apple pie, evoking memories of her childhood, an altogether simpler time. Her mother had returned from her health cure only a few weeks earlier and was still weak. Chemo and the operation had left an unmistakeable mark and she had lost weight.

Still, it was clear that her body was fighting and slowly beginning to recover. Her eyes appeared less sunken and there was more colour in her cheeks. At first, Alex had found it difficult to adjust to the changes in her mother and had to fight back the tears. But Ricka had always been a courageous woman, someone who took things in her stride. That was why she had insisted upon baking an apple pie, even if it used up a lot of her energy. The work also provided her with the semblance of normality she needed. Besides, Jenny would be there too and Ricka always went to great lengths for her favourite daughter. Fortunately it had never rubbed off on Alex's sister, who was younger by a few minutes.

Alex still called her "little" sister; for everyone else it was taboo. In contrast to Alex, whom nature had almost certainly intended to be a boy, Jenny had grown up more like a little princess. But she was in no way conceited. Sometimes they had switched roles for fun. Then Alex had cut and styled her hair, while Jenny had cleaned and fixed the bikes. Nevertheless, this kind of role reversal had remained the exception.

Alex laid the coffee table, while answering her father's questions.

"So, anything new on the sales front?" Franz asked, interested as always.

"Everything's going according to plan. The last client meeting was very good, but there's still a lot to get through. Dad, can I ask your advice on something?"

"You know you can always talk to me."

"At the last client meeting, there was a member of the team there who's been dealing with this topic for a year. I asked him to come along because he knows the back-story and I thought he'd be able to assist with questions. But it seems he took it too literally and spent a lot of time interrupting the presentation. By the end he was even being thwarted by the client and afterwards another colleague complained to me about him."

"I suppose you can't always choose your colleagues," her father gave voice to his concerns. "If somebody's experience makes them important for a meeting, then you can't very well do without them. I think you really need to establish some ground rules about who's responsible for what during meetings. But if there's any danger of someone else's conduct jeopardising your own reputation, then I wouldn't take them along. Does this colleague need to be there?"

"He does the same thing as I do. Our boss said only recently that we don't all have to be there at meetings."

"Then I'd listen to what your boss says," her father advised. "If your colleague doesn't absolutely need to be there, then do the meeting on your own."

Suddenly there was a ring at the door and Jenny came whirling in. For the rest of the day conversation revolved around the job offer she had received from a Hong Kong bank allowing her to work for two years while she completed her master's. She had already spent a little time thinking about it.

"Not only the position, but the city itself is interesting in a number of ways. They have a very European mentality there."

Franz wasn't so sure.

"But since the end of British colonial rule, the autonomy of the special administrative region has been steadily eroded by China. The Chinese influence has become even greater. That's right, isn't it?"

"Yes, you're right," Jenny responded, "but after the crash a few years ago a lot of the western financial markets collapsed. The tables have turned in Hong Kong. They have one of the most powerful stock exchanges in the world now. The Chinese prefer to remain in the background so they don't shoot themselves in the foot."

Alex said more as a joke: "Yeah, go to Hong Kong. Then I can come to visit and take a trip to see my client in Seoul at the same time."

Her mother smiled bravely. No-one knew what would happen with her illness. With Jenny so far away, they would seldom see each other. Perhaps only at Christmas. The way things were looking at the moment, Ricka wouldn't be able to visit Jenny in Asia. But she would never ask that her daughter stayed put for her sake. From a professional point of view, Jenny's stay in Asia would win her a lot of brownie points. Her father also nodded in agreement. With that, the committee had made its decision.

Alex found saying goodbye particularly difficult this time. She saw the sadness in her mother's eyes about Jenny. Still, at some point children had to go their own way. No-one could say what the future held or when they would see each other again. Late that evening Sandro came and greeted her with a fleeting kiss.

"I'm so damn tired," he groaned. "We were in a jam for ages. Do you mind if I go to bed straightaway? My eyes are already drooping."

Alex had imagined the evening slightly differently but what could she say? It was normally very important to him that they went to bed together. When they hadn't seen each other for a few days, they usually had a bit of catching up to do. But perhaps not this year.

After Thomas had approved her trip to the US, Alex got straight down to making reservations. Despite two additional nights' accommodation, the cheapest option – flight, hotel and car rental included – was to fly out on the Friday. Spending a weekend was the ideal way to explore the city. She wouldn't claim for expenses: she would have needed food and drink at home as well.

Nobu was delighted at the news. Alex spoke to Hank herself, arranging a meeting with him and Chris for the morning after the conference. That way, she could fly home on the same day.

Alex informed her colleagues about her visit to the US at the next team meeting, where everyone except Carl was taking part personally. There were no objections.

"It's great that you're taking the Vabilmo message to the guys in the States," Brian commented.

George nodded and agreed for once: "Yeah, it's good that you're doing it. Personally, I wouldn't have any desire to fly over there again so soon."

With that, the topic was resolved and Hugo could address a question much closer to his heart. Development with Roffarm was beginning to flag. They were trying to choose an inverter manufacturer. For solar modules with polymer-based cells they needed more efficient inverters than were currently available. Three potential manufacturers were being considered. For weeks Hugo had been trying to assess with Roffarm which company was the most suitable. So far, all companies seemed equally possible.

George had Hugo outline the selection criteria in every last detail, although Alex was sure they must have done so more than once already over the phone. The two of them went through everything together hypothetically, describing what made each of the companies suitable. As usual, George was in his element when illuminating technical details. Despite everything, after an hour they still hadn't come to any conclusions; Thomas, who had just sat there in silence the whole time, ended the meeting after two hours.

"I am certain," he summarised, "that together with Roffarm you'll make the right choice."

Then he stood up and left the room. Alex looked at him in surprise, wondering how long this game of ping-pong would go on for. Hugo had been saying for weeks that he and Roffarm were on the verge of choosing an inverter manufacturer. Only somehow there had still been no progress.

"Is it not better," she broke in, "to make a decision now? If all three are possibilities, then choose any one you like; roll a dice or draw straws. I don't see there being any other way at the moment. I mean, you've looked at each different argument from every possible angle several times already, haven't you?"

"You know, you're right," Hugo agreed. "At the end of the day it doesn't matter. Perhaps we should go over the selection criteria again? But if no company is obviously better than the other, then there are no front-runners."

Alex was getting pretty impatient. "You're not going to make any progress this way. At some point, you'll have to make a decision. Why don't you just start with the second company? It doesn't matter who you work with, you'll learn something whichever one you choose. You can always adapt later. In the worst case scenario you'll lose a few weeks. But that will happen anyway if you don't make a decision now."

Brian didn't seem to be listening anymore. He was two-finger-tapping away on his laptop.

"Alex is right, Hugo," George began to speak once more. "It's the same risk with every company."

Hugo nodded pensively, although he seemed pretty frustrated.

Later George called Alex at home. "Hugo's been complaining to me. He felt like you backed him into a corner. He was critical of me as well – but mainly you."

"That's not how I saw it. That really surprises me. For me it was just a normal discussion. And you welcomed my suggestion anyway." She wasn't going to take this lying down and decided to clear the air with Hugo right away.

"George just called about our discussion earlier," she began. "I didn't mean to put you under any pressure. I'm sorry if that's how you felt."

"It's fine," Hugo accepted her apology. "It wasn't so bad."

"Good. Next time please tell me straightaway to my face. That way we can avoid any misunderstandings."

"OK, I will. But it really wasn't that bad."

That seemed to clear things up.

The seed units! Alex had received an email from stock receipt. Half an hour later she was back in the office, holding one of the wave-shaped units in her hand. She made her way to Thomas, beaming like a child who had just been presented with a new toy. On the way to his cubicle she ran into a few colleagues, who accosted her immediately. Excited, they listened as Alex explained to them about the polymer-based cells and the new design concepts. Not everyone had seen the presentation by Robotics in February.

Thomas wasn't there but Alex saw Wolfgang instead, who wheeled his chair away from the desk.

"What have you got there, Alex?" He stretched out a curious hand.

"These are the new seed units for the bend-modules. I got a few from Robotics so the team has something to show clients at meetings."

"Let's have a look. I've never seen these before. How did you come by them?"

"At the conference in February they showed us the bend-modules with thin-film cells on metal substrates. These are the modules we want to use with Natioba, only fitted with the polymer-based solar cells. The seed units were made up specially for us."

"Good work! We call this sort of thing ‚toys for big boys', don't we? If you have anything else like this, please come straight to me. I'm always very interested."

Although he didn't say so, he was clearly proud that his office possessed such seed units.

Thomas came by, took a quick look at one and returned it silently to Alex.

"Isn't it great that we've got the seed units?" she said enthusiastically.

But he had already gone back to his computer. Sometimes Alex just couldn't work him out. At least Brian and George shared her enthusiasm when she mailed them with the news.

5

May

On average, Alex spent two days a week in the office. She often got to hear the latest news from other departments over a quick coffee in the canteen. It was only she and Thomas who appeared in person regularly for the bi-weekly team meetings. The rest came very sporadically, though this was partly due to various client meetings. More often than not, Hugo participated via the network bridge, arguing that driving to the office would lose him valuable project time. Roffarm was eating up more than half his time and he had to put in a lot of extra work to keep pace with the rest of his commitments.

George almost always had other appointments and his apologies often came at very short notice. Even when participating, he usually went straight home afterwards. With Brian, there was no recognisable pattern. Thomas was sometimes surprised by his absence, especially when he didn't appear to have any other appointments that clashed.

Carl tried to participate regularly but he was frequently on the move and had to dial in while driving, so some of his comments were simply lost in the ether. Whether or not individual team members took part didn't seem to bother Thomas much.

In his place, Alex would have demanded greater discipline. The product they were supposed to be pushing was still very young. Maybe she was just old-fashioned, but to her it was better to speak face to face, rather than over a loudspeaker.

Many things were even decided outside the team meetings, without Thomas' knowledge. Sometimes George would call Alex to tell her he had spoken to Hugo or Brian about the team strategy. Afterwards Brian might inform her that everything George said was nonsense. It was true that he'd spoken to George, but he didn't share his opinion. When things like this happened, she suggested they discuss the matter in the next meeting with Thomas. Although the team strategy had been established, it was hardly set in stone. More information was gained with each client phone call or visit and the impact needed to be considered.

There was no point reacting too quickly; rather, it was a question of examining the situation carefully. How could the information be assessed? Did it represent the opinion of an isolated individual or was the whole department thinking along the same lines? What influence did this individual have on the field in question? When all was said and done, who made the client's decisions and who could be held accountable? Which other people or departments needed to be included in discussions?

These sorts of issues were not clarified in one discussion alone. Every single bit of information was part of the overall puzzle, but they couldn't let their entire strategy be dictated by just one piece. Both George and Brian bandied the word "strategy" around rather lightly, and were always eager to abandon established plans. When she spoke to her father, Alex would compare conversations with her colleagues to the work of a flea tamer.

George was a special case, capable of changing his opinion in the blink of an eye. He spun his view this way and that for so long that he often came upon the counterargument himself. Then he always said: "Mea culpa; I am now saying the exact opposite." A lot of the time, it was very funny; sometimes, however, it was just plain tiresome. The only way to prevent it was to never talk for longer than twenty minutes on the phone with him. That was the amount of time he needed to technically underpin his first opinion. As far as the arguments he composed by mail went, it was best to simply file them away and forget about them. Only in their meetings, which often stretched out over two hours, did this become impossible. Then it needed someone to intervene, which Thomas did only rarely.

Brian saw possibilities everywhere. He sent the team press releases or articles, asking that someone take a look at them immediately. Hugo was always grateful and frequently complied, becoming heavily involved in detailed solutions right away. If it was something about Robotics, then Carl normally took it on without a fuss. As Brian seldom sent Alex client information she didn't already have, she never felt particularly obliged to react.

Hugo would complain to her that he didn't have enough time to respond to Brian's demands. Roffarm and other technical developments were keeping him more than occupied. Nevertheless, Alex often read the next day that he had contacted each individual company. Why was he going to so much trouble if all he did afterwards was complain? They had graded many of the companies "irrelevant" at the off-site meeting. But her colleagues seemed to have forgotten that already.

Brian seemed to send information about his own clients with far less frequency, although perhaps that was just in comparison with everything else.

Alex was working on the gradual implementation of her objectives. There was some leeway as far as solar plants and potential robot applications were concerned. Dealing with both areas equally intensively for each of her three clients couldn't be managed time-wise. Besides, she had agreed to carry out an analysis of the most suitable contractors. There was more than enough to do and she needed to focus as never before.

Her list began with Natioba and the project in Seoul. Next were Premve and the preparations for the meeting with the investigation committee. That would be a decisive factor in establishing the way forward. Closely behind was Luxumi, likewise a company that was active in the high-yield grid-connected-plant industry. She had already made initial contact and was waiting for a meeting with their development head to be confirmed. Analysing contractors and working with the robotics departments of her clients - the next two points on her list - were both of equal importance. Here she was still in the information-gathering phase, but she enjoyed that too.

Working out who the best point of contact was, or who would have the most influence on achieving her set objectives, was almost like detective work. It wasn't always the supervisor or manager. Very often there were key people who weren't immediately obvious: background figures whose competence or inventiveness made them effective consultants to the people officially responsible, dispensing advice and sometimes even making the decisions. A glance at the company organisation chart, rarely available from the firm in question directly, often said very little about hidden decision-making structures.

In Alex's career to date, the most important people had often turned out to be those least expected. You had to see the structure behind the structure. It was crucial to find somebody inside the client's organisation who could sell an idea or objective internally. This somebody didn't necessarily need to be high-up on the company ladder. In the past, Alex had managed to win projects by working closely with developers or employees from a specialist department.

All too often the potential of technically experienced, enthusiastic staff was either undervalued or completely ignored. Still, there was no question that management approval was essential for big projects or investment budgets. Depending on company structure and the general economic climate, a decision might even be taken at board level. C-Level, it was called, since that's where all the "chiefs" sat; somehow, that sounded more impressive than board level.

After establishing her immediate priorities, Alex met with Brian. Thomas had suggested she work together with him on a strategic overview for their European clients. She brought along all her information, including a business itinerary complete with timeline showing when she expected certain actions or outcomes to be achieved. Naturally, the focus was on Natioba and Premve. She had also drafted activities for Luxumi, although these were less pressing.

"The first thing you need to do is arrange a C-Level meeting," Brian began after a brief look at the document. "Like I did for Roffarm. That's the only way to do it. The chief executive needs to make it clear to development managers that they should switch to Vabilmo."

"The CEO is important," Alex said, "but it's only one person, and people make decisions based on information they believe in. No board member is going to authorise the construction of a plant using our polymer-based cells without test results that have been checked and corroborated."

"Oh, they're not interested in details like that," Brian snorted. "What are they supposed to do with test results? Don't be absurd. CEOs are only interested in how much money they can save."

"We all know the influence on capital balance and share prices are the decisive factors. But no responsible, economically minded CEO is going to risk equipping a new plant with new products that are completely untested. I'm absolutely sure of it; I've never heard of anyone in the industry who operates differently."

"As far as the financial side is concerned, it will be enough to give a rough estimate. Then the CEO can tell the people in the lower ranks what needs to be done."

"That's not how I see it. First and foremost, we need a base level of experience, which we can only achieve through joint research and development projects. In order to grab the CEO's attention and get an appointment in his packed diary, we need either a preliminary design or results that can be obviously applied to an entire project. This method has served me well enough up until now."

"The wallies on the lower levels won't get us anywhere. You have to arrange a C-Level meeting. You can talk to the people from Development too, for all I care. But you can forget about Research; it won't help in the slightest."

"I wouldn't say that. For trend-setting developments being pushed by two or more companies simultaneously, where each is providing their own individual area of expertise, going via the board would almost certainly be a quicker way of doing things. But we're talking about landing a completely new project here."

She was no fan of arranging so-called high-level meetings, only to tell those present: "we'll cross that bridge when we come to it". She saw the client's time as too valuable for that. It was different if this kind of meeting could be combined with something else, like, for instance, if a CEO was making a presentation at an event or holding a press conference at a trade show. Then a brief, informal conversation, which could be developed into something more concrete later, was a possibility. The main thing there was that their representative should be equally high up in the hierarchy, or at least carry roughly the same level of responsibility.

They discussed strategy for a long time. Brian kept coming back to C-Level meetings and Alex became increasingly frustrated. Her experience in similar technical industries told her that no company would make such a big investment without having all the facts at their disposal, including quantifiable test results. Not in the capital goods market. A pilot project normally began with the research department. Sometimes Research produced results that convinced Development; sometimes Development was so taken by a new piece of technology that they engaged Research to carry out tests to justify its use in a major project. Although Brian was nodding, Alex had the impression he didn't understand what she meant.

Only after they finished did Alex realise that Brian had kept quiet about his own clients. Apart from arranging high-level meetings, she didn't know what he had in mind. Somehow their discussion hadn't quite gone according to plan. The aim had been to show one another how they intended to proceed and exchange information about current activities; that would enable them to draw up an all-encompassing document. But that hadn't happened. Perhaps time had been too short and they'd catch up at a later date.

In her next jour fixe Thomas assured her that everyone was free to proceed with clients at their own discretion. The important thing was that everyone spread the right "message" and operated within the framework of the established team strategy. At the end of the day, results were what counted, whether you started with the chief executive or just an ordinary member of staff.

Alex loved the atmosphere at airports; even on business trips it somehow made her feel like she was on holiday. As much as she enjoyed living in a small country village, there was nothing like travelling. She arrived early as usual and sat in a discreet corner of the lounge, checking her mails, making calls and quietly reading through different newspapers. Unexpectedly, while she was strolling towards the gate, her Zeus68 rang.

"I've finished the market analysis," Carl got straight to the point. "I'd like to go through it with you before I present the results to the whole team."

"Was George not supposed to be helping you with that?" Alex wondered, but immediately agreed to help him.

"Great! I'm not sure if all my conclusions are right and if I'm linking things to our strategy properly," he explained.

"Let's do it as soon as I'm back from the US," she suggested.

"Perfect, I'll schedule an appointment."

With some surprise, Alex realised Carl either hadn't heard her question or had deliberately chosen to ignore it.

The flight time to the West Coast was ideal. You took off in the afternoon and landed in the early evening of the same day. In San Francisco, Alex was greeted by the last rays of the setting sun, which then disappeared slowly as she made her way from the airport into the city. After checking in to her hotel near the Moscone Center, she took a quick glance at her mails. Whatever she managed to do now would mean less work in the next two days. She tried to avoid work at the weekend, preferring to invest more time during the week. Saturdays and Sundays were sacred; only absolute emergencies where a project might be lost constituted exceptions. Two Samuel Adams at the hotel bar would serve as dinner. The beer would make her tired enough to sleep and help prevent jetlag.

The sun streaming into her room woke her up the next morning at half past seven. After a long shower, she set out cheerfully, treating herself to a breakfast of mocha and fruit salad at a coffee shop along the way. The air was fresh, with not a single cloud in the sky; it promised to get very warm over the course of the day. She called Sandro on Market Street.

"Hey, I just wanted to let you know I've arrived safely. Everything OK with you?"

"Ciao, Alex. Yeah, everything's fine here. So, how's San Francisco?"

"I can hardly remember my last visit eighteen years ago. But I have time for a bit of sightseeing today and tomorrow. I want to walk through Chinatown down to the waterfront and have a look at the Harley and Hard Rock shops. Maybe buy a pair of jeans as well."

"Sounds like a bit of a trek."

"Yeah, but at least I'll get some exercise that way. It was a pretty long flight yesterday."

"OK, but promise you'll look after yourself. I've got to go to the club now."

"Of course I will. Nothing's going to happen to me."

Market Street extended horizontally across the city and she strolled happily through the shopping quarter, located at its east end. A little further north at Union Square, a wannabe haven of tranquillity with its palm trees and park benches, she ignored the expensive designer outlets and made a beeline for the huge jeans store. After stocking up with a few new pairs, she moved on in a zigzag up and over steep hills.

Cable cars passed her, but Alex preferred to walk. She had the whole day and could easily ride these historic, romantic trams on the way home. Towards Chinatown it flattened out again. She stared in fascination at the street stalls, which offered all sorts of curious things, from dried fish to pickled ginseng. With a gentle wind blowing at 80 degrees, the weather was just right for exploring the city. After a quick stop in a little side café on Columbus Avenue, she moved on to the freeway crossing, where she had a great view of the Transamerica Building in the distance. Towards the other direction she could already see the shimmering silver-blue sea; it wasn't far now to the Harley shop and Hard Rock Cafe.

A few T-shirts, accessories and spent dollars later, Alex began to drift along the quayside. Her shopping urge had been sated and the sea lions were the only things still left to see. The penetrating stench of fish wafted towards her in the gentle breeze. But the sight of numerous doe-eyed sea lions, both big and small, lolling on wooden planks before diving into the water and clambering back up, made it more than worthwhile. Despite the smell of the animals, Alex was soon hungry. The hot dog she ate on a bench in the sun was no match for the delightful view of the deep blue sea and faraway Golden Gate Bridge. If only Sandro could be here too, Alex thought to herself, and called him again.

"Hey, I'm sitting in the sun by the waterfront, wishing you were here."

"Ciao. That's great but I really don't have any time. The others are waiting for me. I have to hang up."

"OK, I didn't want to disturb you for long; I just wanted to say that I miss you."

Suddenly Alex was shivering. The temperature had dropped at least thirty degrees from one second to the next. The famous fog rolled in from the sea and cloaked San Francisco's landmarks in a veil of cloud. Fascinated, she walked along the pier and watched the thick mist spread gradually. There was still a touch of blue sky above it. Slowly she began to head back: after all, it wasn't only her feet that were tired. Along the way, she decided she couldn't miss out on Lombard Street, with its brilliant displays of flowers adorning its much vaunted curves, or the view from Coit Tower. Up top, she was rewarded with a magnificent panorama of the city and a much clearer sight of the fog.

After a quick nap in her room, Alex began the search for something to eat and journeyed back to the pier. Some of the restaurants were enormous, exuding all the charm of a railway concourse. She decided on a small diner offering fresh fish and live jazz, and savoured the sounds of the nearby ocean over crab cakes and beer, as she immersed herself in the varied images of the day.

Sunday promised to be just as spectacular. Following her usual breakfast of mocha and fresh fruit, she made the trip to the Golden Gate Bridge. Under a cloudless sky, it offered a princely view of everything from Alcatraz to the waterfront and Treasure Island. By chance, there was another Harley shop close by. Further north, Sausalito and Tiburon enticed with a walk along the sea. Grand houses nestled in the thickly wooded hills, proving that it wasn't called Paradise Drive for nothing. Blinded by the sun's rays and the dazzling silver sea, she paused at Beach Park to take in the view of the Bay Area and the sky scrapers of the financial district. She could easily imagine living and working in San Francisco for a few months. With hunger gently asserting itself she decided to search for a nice seafront restaurant.

And search was the right word. Somehow the Americans hadn't managed to imbue their coastline with the same sort of charm that southern European cities were famous for. Instead of countless restaurants and cafés along the esplanade, jetties lined the shore one after the other. There was only a single restaurant to be found. It was slightly beyond the small ferry terminal and had a balcony overlooking the sea; what's more, it was open. Without a cloud in sight, the view towards neighbouring Tiburon and San Francisco was breath-taking. Just as the day before, however, it soon became marred by the thick wall of afternoon fog.

The cold drove her back to the hotel. Having tried to reach him several times during the day, she left another message for Sandro. No word from Nobu either, even though she knew he must have arrived by now.

The event was held at the nearby conference centre, and not even the strong wind could dissuade Alex from walking. She wondered if it ever rained in San Francisco. Nobu called while she was sipping on her mocha, deep in thought.

"Hey, Alex. Sorry about being in touch so late, but I was completely out of it last night: must have picked up a cold at the airport."

"Sorry to hear that. Do you feel better now at least?"

"Yeah, all the sleep helped. I'm on my way now. Shall we meet at the entrance?"

Nobu greeted her with a beaming smile, drawing hastily on a cigarette. The first thing that struck Alex was how someone who smoked like a chimney could have such white teeth. It must have had something to do with Korean food. He handed her a smart card. Fortunately it seemed like lanyards, which dangled from your neck and ruined sweatshirts and jackets with their annoying clip fasteners, had been phased out a few years ago. Only Brian still seemed to collect them, and she couldn't help but think of the dozen or so that hung from his back trouser pocket.

As this was Nobu's third time at the event, he knew his way round pretty well and gave Alex a quick guided tour before the official opening. In the big hall on the ground floor, different companies had assembled stands and were displaying their latest products. The presentations took place in a large room on the first floor that was cordoned off by thick black curtains. Further back, there were smaller rooms that could be hired for meetings. On the top floor a number of seats reserved for working were set up sideways along the walls, while the middle of the floor was taken up by the buffet, complete with tables and chairs for the breaks.

The focus of the event was not on solar plants specifically, but on renewable energy in general. San Francisco had established itself as the yearly venue. A few years ago California had been the first US state to issue a directive stating that within a decade all state power plants were to generate at least a third of their electricity supply from renewable energy sources. For this reason there were a number of people from different industries taking part, as a quick look at the conference documentation confirmed. A few interesting companies were represented. The presentations ranged from the latest developments in windmills, to biofuels and high-capacity battery technology, and even covered electricity generation using hot springs in the earth's innermost core.

The final presentation before lunch was particularly interesting. Alex introduced herself and ended up having a long chat with the speaker. Besides designing power plants of every kind, his company also developed prototypes of modules and other components such as inverters, which were then licensed for production. Originally founded in Germany, the company now belonged to an American corporate group. Without asking for precise details, he let Alex outline the new solar cell technology and was all ears when it came to the market prospects. He immediately promised to make contact with the relevant people in Germany, who could take a closer look at things and then present their findings to him in the US.

The discussion got Alex thinking. Maybe it made more sense to work together with a single company like this instead of lots of smaller module and inverter manufacturers. Working with an established and successful development service provider, which could then function as a multiplier, would make things considerably less labour intensive.

After the conference, Alex and Nobu made their way to the W Hotel a few blocks away, Nobu lighting a cigarette as soon as he was outside. Their first appointment was with an American off-grid-systems manufacturer, who showed only polite interest in what they had to say. His remarks made it clear that he wasn't the greatest of risk-takers – and that he would prefer to wait and see what other manufacturers did first.

Their second meeting, which took place in a modern, elegant steakhouse on Market Street, was slightly more successful; at least, the client expressed an interest in receiving further information and consented to a non-disclosure agreement. Alex promised to take things from there. Like a true gentleman, Nobu paid the check. After a nightcap in a smoking bar Alex was ready to hit the hay, although Nobu tried to persuade her to stay for another. Perhaps it really was true that Asian people didn't require so much sleep, but she needed every bit she could get.

Her netphone was already on its fifth ring by the time she got out of the shower. She could almost sense it was George. He wanted to quickly – half an hour by his standards – clarify something with her before he met a client. Alex smiled as she hung up: astonishingly, he hadn't changed his mind once after the twentieth minute. For the first time he was treating her not as an inexperienced trainee, but as a dependable consultant.

She tried to call Sandro on her way to the conference centre, but again only wound up with his voicemail. He was probably in the middle of a match or already asleep. Still, it meant she could speak to Hugo before the conference; he hadn't really got involved in the Natioba project yet. Admittedly, he had been on the line for a few of her regular phone conferences with Hank, but he had seldom offered an assisting remark. With Roffarm, of course, he had more than enough on his plate and no-one expected him to undertake such detailed project work with Natioba.

However, in her opinion, he could make more of an effort– especially as they were currently discussing possible solar module designs and Hugo's expertise was potentially decisive. Hank's specialist knowledge of robots meant he could be too rigid at times. Besides, Hugo had stressed again and again that when it came to architectural issues, he wanted to be on board.

"How am I supposed to manage all that around my workload?" Hugo complained. "Everyone's trying to rope me in for some project or another."

"Natioba isn't just some project," Alex countered. "They're one of our priorities, set at the off-site meeting. A lot of companies have fallen off the grid, so why are you still bothering with them?"

"The importance of individual companies is defined by consultants and account managers, not by me," Hugo answered defiantly.

"So why don't you just turn down requests if consultants aren't sticking to their priorities?" she asked, surprised.

"I can't take care of that as well; how am I supposed to cope with all this?"

She simply couldn't work him out. He was complaining about having too much work and yet seemed incapable of saying "no". Did he not have the courage, or was he afraid of missing out on something? Maybe his colleagues really were putting him under so much pressure? As a young post-graduate he was taking his first steps in the professional world, and clearly respected the old hands. Be that as it may, Natioba was right at the top of the list, and Alex didn't have to justify requesting his assistance.

"Fine," Hugo gave in. "Because it's you, I'll do it, but only if you arrange a time for me to talk to the two of them. Take a look in the calendar system to see when I'm free. It's always up-to-date."

"OK, Hugo, I can do that. I'll be seeing both of them tomorrow anyway."

The presentations on the second day were less interesting. What's more, their client cancelled. Things like that happened. She and Nobu decided to take up their dinner reservation at the restaurant on Ghirardelli Square anyway. Although it seemed to be very popular with business people, Nobu managed to get them a table right by the huge glass window, from where they enjoyed a breath-taking view.

Just before sundown, the horizon, now free of the thick fog, shone a vivid orange-yellow. Infused with the scarlet red of the Golden Gate Bridge, the bay stretched out for miles in vibrant blue and lilac tones, interrupted only by the dazzling diamond lights of isolated jetties. During the meal, Alex admitted wistfully to herself that she would rather have shared the view with Sandro, though she was grateful nonetheless. Who else could say they'd eaten such exquisite fish against so magnificent a backdrop, without even having to pay for it?

The meeting with Hank and Chris took place near the airport the next morning. She was delighted to see Chris again after their pleasant first encounter in Tampa. She said hello in Italian and he replied with a smile; she had a good enough grasp for basic small talk, and soon a business-like familiarity set in. Chris was in his late twenties at most and thus belonged to a generation that adopted a more relaxed, friendly style with business partners – although never any less professional.

Hank, who she was meeting for the first time in person, greeted her with a firm handshake, and due to his size was forced to bend down slightly. First, he gave her an update on where things currently stood with the project.

"We're already in talks with two small-scale inverter manufacturers," he began. "As we'll be dealing initially with an off-grid-system prototype, based on the amount of electricity we need to generate, we reckon we can take a standardised high-efficiency appliance and modify it. Deciding on the solar module design is a little trickier, though."

"That's right," Chris broke in. "We've decided to use the off-grid-system prototype as an energy source for greenhouses. Not traditional domestic greenhouses but self-contained ones, in which organically grown vegetables can be cultivated in water baths."

He produced a few slides with diagrams.

"From the outside, it looks just like a normal metal transport container," he explained. "But the inside conceals an ingenious high-tech world. Small receptacles containing the veg are tightly packed together on a number of shelves, themselves ordered into five different sections according to the individual stage of development. The first is where the seeding takes place. A nutrient paste is used instead of soil. Robot arms measure the exact dosage into the receptacle and sow the corn seed. The shelves are moved back and forth automatically so that the receptacles can even be placed into the furthest corner of the water bath. Small plants grow from the seed and paste mixture, receiving all other nutrients they require from fertilised water, added by the robots at regular intervals."

Alex looked at the diagrams in astonishment and noticed that Nobu was doing exactly the same.

"Air conditions are regulated by a computer programme that adjusts the temperature, humidity and light quantity accordingly," Chris continued. "After a certain amount of time, the plants are moved from one section to the next by the robot arms until they are ready for harvesting. The crops and plants are then picked by robots and placed into a basket in the side room via a sluice. If you open the door to the side room to extract the harvest, the sluice locks from the inside. That way you prevent most pests from gaining access to the plants. There is thus absolutely no need to use pesticides."

"This kind of market gardening was first developed a number of years back," Hank added. "But it wasn't until a few months ago that a major investor got involved. We at Natioba feel that a significant expansion is just around the corner. Until now, buyers have probably been deterred by the relatively slow payback period of their investment. Anything that takes longer than a year is seen as a non-starter nowadays. Nevertheless, the global demand for organically grown vegetables has grown exponentially. The system's got a lot going for it. Not only can it run without pesticides or staff; it can also supply fresh vegetables at any time of year. The greenhouses can be built in the most remote areas, completely irrespective of the weather conditions. In an extreme case you could even have one in the desert or on an ice cap."

"Only two things are indispensable if the system is to function properly," Chris took up the thread. "Electricity and water. The latter can be integrated into the container via an isolated reservoir. Since the greenhouse is self-contained, water requirements are lower than normal. Generating electricity is the difficult part. With the existing solar technology, it would be necessary to have a relatively large surface area, which in turn would have a negative impact on the payback period. Your Vabilmo technology could help us develop a more cost-effective way of generating electricity."

Alex and Nobu had been so fascinated that they hadn't once interrupted. This could really be something, Alex thought to herself.

It was clear that Chris didn't see this all as mere technical gimmickry, but as a serious prospect for the future. A thought crossed Alex's mind. Perhaps now was the right time?

A closer look at the relationship between the development lab in Korea and headquarters in Italy would be necessary. She didn't think about it for too long.

"What's the situation with you and Italy?" she asked Chris.

"Development there has a lot faith in us," he responded. "They often give us concrete assignments. That doesn't mean they take on every bit of pre-development work we carry out, of course, but they usually do. For the most part our research colleagues in Italy are working on different projects, although we regularly exchange notes."

"But you also develop your own ideas, right? What proportion of your work as a whole does that cover?"

"About half, I'd say. We often develop ideas based on trends arising in Asia. These are then serialised by headquarters."

Nobu and Hank watched the conversation move to and fro as if it was a game of tennis.

"Do you need approval from Italy?" Alex wanted to know.

"No," said Chris, visibly relieved. "We have our own budget, for this project as well. But we usually keep the heads of both departments informed." He added, smiling: "Out of politeness."

"And will you need the approval of Head Office to implement a commercial project?"

"Yes, we will. It's more of a formality for the domestic market though. There won't be any objections. We're on the ground, we can judge the market requirements better, and we have the relevant production capacity. But if the decision concerns the US or Europe, then our role is more of an advisory one."

His last remark made it clear to Alex that Natioba had to be conquered on two different fronts. Seoul was well on the way to being won over, as Chris had been engaged as an internal vendor. He believed in the project and identified enthusiastically with it. But Italy would be hard work.

Alex had already had initial talks with the research department there, although these had been rather sombre affairs. Getting a meeting had been no trouble, but they had all been isolated appointments, where people had behaved with extreme caution – something of a paradox for a development geared towards the future. Maybe it had something to do with company philosophy; but more likely, it was down to the people themselves.

Originally solar technology was something that had been pushed mainly in countries like Germany and the US, as well as Asia. But places like Spain and Italy had been quick to catch up. Natioba's development office in Seoul was right up there when it came to new technology. This could really work, Alex thought, as she slowly went in for the kill.

"As a market leader, PsoraCom is naturally interested in working with its clients on a global scale. That's the reason I held preliminary talks in Italy – and these weren't altogether uninteresting. However, without wishing to tread on anybody's toes, I got the impression that the research department there is more interested in improving existing, rather than developing new, technology. I'm very excited by your greenhouse idea because it covers two bases. Not only is the demand for organically grown vegetables on the rise; autonomous cultivation is set to become increasingly important in the future. This is a hugely innovative project, the sort that not every company is working on. Is the market aware which of Natioba's developments come from your office?"

It was clear that Chris was playing through the different scenarios in his head.

"Is there some way we could help make these developments more public?" Nobu offered, in support of Alex. She'd let him in on everything at dinner the previous evening.

Hank didn't say a word; it was up to the consultants to negotiate.

"That would be useful," Chris replied. "Lots of developments do come from our lab, although very few end customers know about it. Even most of our colleagues in Italy aren't aware where the ideas come from. We could certainly do with a little help; it might even have a positive effect on our budget."

Alex allowed a little time to pass before making her suggestion.

"There are several possibilities. A written agreement would probably be the best thing, making it clear that the ideas came from your end; at the same time any publicity about our joint venture would reflect positively on the parent company."

"I can't make the decision on my own," Chris hesitated. "I'd need to speak to our boss, who'll probably see the contract as a helpful step towards getting the Italians on board. But we have to be very careful about what kind of contract we choose. Guaranteeing resources that have a monetary value won't be a possibility for us. Of that much I'm certain."

"I think it's too early for that as well," Alex agreed. "First we need to wait for the results of the project and evaluate them thoroughly. An LOI might be a possibility then. It would contain all the defined objectives but still offer individual parties enough protection. At our end, for example, we're still not exactly sure when the polymer-based cells will be officially launched."

There remained the slightest possibility that the Vabilmo technology would be discontinued, though Alex was careful not to say as much out loud.

"However, in my opinion, a Memorandum of Understanding would be the better option for us, as both co-contractors are obliged to sign. Besides, MOUs are very often the first step to a further-reaching contract."

"OK," said Chris. "Prepare a draft and send it to me; I'll see that it gets to our lab supervisor. You'll have to negotiate the final wording directly, but I can prep him for that."

That was exactly what Alex had wanted to hear: Chris would help her sell the contract to his boss in Seoul.

There was enough time for Alex to write her call report at the airport. It wasn't a question of penning a novel, just of briefly recording any developments, insights or decisions. Although she often spoke to her colleagues on the phone, the reports were the easiest means of bringing everyone up to speed. They were also a very good way of finding out what people thought – that is, providing the respondent hadn't forgotten to copy all those on the original mailing list into the discussion.

While she was thinking things over, it struck her that most of her conversations were with George and Hugo. They talked about technical details, how things were progressing with Roffarm or the latest client developments. Carl got in touch when he needed information, or to tell her about his client meetings. As they were the newest members of the team, they enjoyed discussing company quirks.

A number of set expressions were in use at PsoraCom; you almost had to speak another language to work there. For example, a I2I was a meeting where the individual participants met in person – that is, eye-to-eye, since a meeting could be anything from a telephone call or conference to an internal discussion or client appointment.

The language of PsoraCom was best described as a collection of three-letter acronyms. There was even an intranet website detailing most of these TLAs. However, it wasn't always kept up-to-date. At times there were two or three different expressions that corresponded to a single TLA, and the only hope was to guess the meaning from the context. Before revealing their ignorance in front of colleagues, Carl and Alex would check with one another to see if they knew what a specific phrase meant. Carl wasn't in the office as frequently and thus didn't glean as much information from the people at work.

At the beginning, Alex had mostly called Brian. But recently she had been getting his voicemail all too often and he rarely returned her calls. For her it was more a matter of discussing the overall market situation with him, a puzzle best solved by exchanging the latest information about each of their respective clients. However, a lot of general information that had previously been distributed by Brian was now more easily accessible thanks to her own contact network in the office.

Half a page was all she needed to describe the meeting with Hank and Chris. Naturally, she found it pretty difficult to contain her excitement. Potentially, they had just taken an enormous stride forward. Apart from Roffarm, no written agreements had yet been made. And while the MOU with Natioba couldn't be compared to the Roffarm contract, news of it would certainly make waves in the market. Other solar plant manufacturers who were normally hesitant to use new technology might be more willing to get on board. It would also spur Roffarm into pressing ahead with their own development.

But for the time being all that was wishful thinking: the MOU hadn't even been drafted yet, let alone signed and made public. Alex mentioned in her report that one of the next agreed steps would be for Hugo to speak with Hank and Chris, and help finalise the design. Her flight was called. Extremely satisfied, she shut down her computer, realising, as she did so, just how much she loved her job. There were so many things she liked about it: developing new ideas, drawing up strategies, building contact networks and achieving set objectives.

He father had always said: "Reach for the stars and you'll make it at least as far as the moon."

The real attraction was setting your aims so high they were difficult to achieve. That way if you did achieve them, the feeling of happiness was indescribable.

When she arrived home, the initial reactions were already there. George approved of the strategy but questioned the need for publicity. In his opinion, they needed to decide whether it was in keeping with PsoraCom's interests. The objection was justified. Brian was absolutely thrilled. Whether he had been able to resist forwarding the message to executives with headings like "breakthrough" and "sensation" would only show in the next few days – and only then if someone from management responded. Hugo expressed guarded optimism, while Carl declined to comment. She hadn't expected a reply from Thomas, rightly in this case, as he only seldom corresponded by email.

    She had also sent the call report to Emily, who immediately acceded to her request for a draft MOU.

Alex had hoped to treat Sandro to a nice dinner at their local. After all, they hadn't seen each other for a few days. But he came back really late and had only just seen her text on the way home. So they decided to order pizza instead.

    "How was your week?" she asked between bites.

    "A lot of work as usual," he replied, still chewing.

    "And at the club?"

    "Nothing special. I lost a match."

    "Did you get my messages?"

    "Yeah, but I wasn't sure when was a good time to call. Did everything go alright?"

    "Fantastic. The city's amazing, and I might have taken a big step forward with one of my clients. I'll know in the next few weeks."

    "Uh-uh. Listen, I'm tired, let's go to bed."

    Sandro really did seem to be tired, as he reacted only hesitantly to her clear advances under the covers. Something felt strange, and Alex wondered if her feelings had been affected somehow by the jetlag. A little later, she too had fallen asleep.

    "Hey, day-tripper, so how was it over there?" Thomas asked Alex over coffee the next day.

    "Very funny," she nudged him in the arm. "It was good. I made a few contacts who might be able to help us out. One of them seems particularly interesting. He's a level below the CEO of an American conglomerate that arose from Volcrea, a German company that designs plants and develops components, which are then licensed. In the next few days I'm going to look into whether a collaboration would make sense. Perhaps Volcrea could serve as a multiplier; that would save us some work."

    "Good, well, take a look. How were your client meetings?"

"Could have been worse. One of them feigned interest, but I don't think he'll take any risks until three quarters of the market are backing our product. The second was more open to the topic. The next stage is for us to draw up a non-disclosure agreement so that we can offer him more information. Unfortunately, the third cancelled at the last minute."

"OK, that can happen. How did it go with Natioba? I've already seen your mail, but how likely is an MOU?"

"It's not a definite yet, of course, but I think it's on the cards. Chris really believes in the project and he'll give us strong support in Seoul. The MOU would be very helpful for us. We could use it to ensure the greenhouse story gets a slot at the developer conference. After all, it fits in nicely with PsoraCom's sustainability strategy."

"So, autumn's still a possibility?"

"Sure. Hank's confirmed he's on it."

"Great work, keep it up."

"Praise from you? What was in your cornflakes this morning, boss?"

"I know, I'm sorry. Normally, my motto is that saying nothing is praise enough."

He went back to his desk with an unusually wide grin.

Alex headed to the canteen to meet Carl and go through his presentation.

"One can see straightaway that the robot market's your area," Alex said appreciatively. "That's a very impressive overview you have there."

"Thanks, it took me an age to come up with the figures."

"Good. So, how does your strategy look? How do you hope to proceed?"

"I'm not quite sure yet: that's why I wanted to speak to you. My priority is household robots. So, my strategy should be to locate all necessary partners and, together with them, offer a complete solution."

"That's right. You need an ecosystem, of course. But for me that's not a clearly defined enough objective. It needs to be more concrete."

"What would you suggest?"

"I'd need a more in-depth knowledge of the market – which at the moment I don't have. Basically, your strategy has to have a quantifiable objective: for example, achieving a specific percentage of the total market share within x amount of time. Only then can we work out how many companies you need to take on as clients."

In the animated discussion that followed, neither of them noticed how quickly the time flew by. By answering her questions and providing an overview of the market, Carl hit upon various points he hadn't previously taken into consideration. What was a realistic market objective? How high could the percentage market share of the polymer-based cells be, and in how many years? What was the product life cycle and how quickly did new products appear on the market? Which companies were the most innovative and which sold the most products? Which functions were currently being developed for robots and which were the most likely to be successful on the market?

It took years for a new solar plant to be developed, planned and built. Robots, on the other hand – especially for household or private use – were fitted with new functions or developed for different purposes every year, sometimes even every six months. The wheel simply turned much faster here. Design also played a significant role, as this was one of the unique selling points.

To make things more complicated some manufacturers didn't make the robots themselves; instead, they assigned them to ODMs, original design manufacturers. The only thing these companies did was assemble the robots according to the designs they had been given. Until recently, that is. For two of the world's biggest ODMs had just opened design offices and were beginning to develop their own concepts, which they, in turn, passed on to robot manufacturers.

Everyone expected the ODMs to start manufacturing the robots under their own name soon. Carl had heard various rumours lately at client meetings. The question was to what extent he should factor this in to his strategy. In contrast to Alex and Brian, he carried sole responsibility for this sector and so his capacity was limited.

Owing to the fast-paced nature of the industry, he estimated he would only be able to deal intensively with three or four different companies. Should he focus on the robot manufacturers alone? What was the state of play with the ODMs? Would robot manufacturers soon task them not only with production but development as well? Again, it came down the question of whether to adopt a push or a pull strategy.

Alex's opinion was that Carl should take both strategies into account. ODMs manufactured more than half the robots for companies worldwide. Market penetration could only be achieved by looking at the total figures, and in this context it was impossible to ignore the ODMs. They could also ill afford to underestimate their influence on robot manufacturers. If the two biggest ODMs were to further consolidate their position, as well as their market share on all robots produced, then they would have a means of exerting pressure on their clients. In the short term, there were no alternative ODMs to which robot manufacturers could turn.

At the moment, however, it was the robotics companies that had the most market influence and it was on them that they needed to focus. Aside from robots, Carl was also responsible for stationary machines. Once again, this market differed quite significantly from the robot market, as there were very few manufacturers that used solar technology. There were no clear market leaders and, at two years, the development cycle was considerably longer.

"Good, then I'll concentrate on the three biggest robot manufacturers and see how things develop with the ODMs," Carl decided. "I can look after two machine companies on the side. What do you think?"

She thought it over. It still wasn't an overall strategy. There could easily have been five people in Carl's department too, but there was only him. Thus, they had to make sure he focused his attentions on the right thing. But what was the right thing? Since they couldn't see into the future and make specific predictions about possible market changes, they needed to base their decision on what they currently knew. They could always adapt and revise if necessary. Alex used what she had just learned to formulate her view.

"I suggest your aim should be to have fifteen percent of all robots fitted with Vabilmo technology inside of the next three years."

"That would mean more than a million robots with polymer-based solar cells," Carl calculated.

"It's a lot, I know," she agreed, "but I think it's a realistic goal if all of us honour the commitments we made internally."

"It's only possible if we get the three biggest manufacturers on side."

"In order to achieve your objective, I see the second biggest robot manufacturer as the most important client. Yes, if you go by the figures they're a good ten percent behind the market leader but, from what you've told me, they've got the most innovative products. The fact that their ROI is two percent higher despite lower revenues is also interesting. It might mean they have more capital available for new developments."

"There could be something in that," Carl agreed.

"The second most important client is the number three on our list," said Alex. "They're snapping closely on the heels of number two, and their finances look very healthy."

"But what about the market leader? I can't just ignore them."

"No, of course you can't. Nevertheless, I don't see them as the number one priority. You mentioned that the market leader has added a second string to its bow by making cheap products for the BRIC countries, thereby increasing its market share. Although countries like Brazil, Russia, India and China offer enormous growth potential, accommodating them has resulted in prices being slashed by half. The company obviously believes that quantity is more important than quality. However, we still need to bear them in mind and keep track of their plans for expansion, in case anything changes."

"You think I should only concentrate on two clients? That's too few; I'll take an ODM as well."

"Exactly, Carl. For your third client I'd take the biggest ODM, as they've just extended their design and development department."

"They've also built another production line," Carl added, "although they're currently only working to 70% capacity, according to my contact. They deal with all robot manufacturers; they're not dependent on any one specific company."

"Building a new production line must mean they've started manufacturing their own products," Alex inferred, "and their last balance sheet looks pretty reasonable. Still, we'll have to wait a few months to see how these investments will affect revenue and ROI."

Of course, there was always the risk that the venture could go south. Moreover, it was perfectly feasible that the new production line had in fact been built for the market leader. Then all the time they'd invested would be wasted. Nevertheless, in Alex's opinion it was crucial they didn't let the opportunity slide, in case the ODM's products were successful. If they positioned themselves correctly, the Vabilmo technology would give them a unique selling point compared with other robot manufacturers. At best, it could even be used by the ODM as its own USP – depending on how innovative the company wanted to appear on the market.

"That's all clear to me," Carl nodded slowly, "but is the risk not still too high? Wouldn't it be better to start with the market leader and just observe the ODM for the time being?"

"You can do that if you like, Carl. I've only used what you've told me today to make a suggestion. In the end, you know the market better and you're the one responsible for the sector. For the moment, though, I'd just watch the machine manufacturers and not waste too much energy on them."

"Yeah, that's how I see it too. I'll revise my slides so I can present them at the next team meeting."

"I'm pretty sure that won't be the end of the discussion," Alex winked at him.

By the time she got home, Sandro had already started making dinner. She hadn't expected him to be there, as he normally went to the club straight after work. Her good mood only improved further and in honour of the occasion she opened a bottle of Valpolicella Classico Superiore. It was the nicest possible way to start the weekend.

"Let's go to the North Sea for a few days in June," Sandro surprised her, as he took her in his arms. "The time out would do us both good. We haven't seen that much of each other recently."

"Yes, please," she said delighted. "I'm ready for a bit of a break."

"So let's take a look and book something right now."

"Yeah, I should be able to take a holiday. It's only two days, and I haven't had a single one yet."

There must have been less pressure on Sandro because he seemed happier and more even-tempered than normal. They spent the whole weekend together, taking trips into the mountains and going swimming. It was almost like it had been when they first met. The only downer came on Sunday evening.

"I'm just going to the club quickly to change my match dates and take my name off the list for when we're on holiday."

"Can you not call? It would be much nicer to see out the weekend on the balcony with a lovely glass of wine. Don't you think?"

"Well, I haven't been there for a few days. I should put in a quick appearance so they know I'm still alive."

She felt a slight twinge of jealousy, which she immediately tried to suppress.

Alex first learned of the missed appointment from Henry. PsoraCom's development executive was flying into Italy next week from the US because there was a new research lab being opened in Como. A number of prominent figures from both the political and business world had been invited to the official opening, while meetings had been arranged with their most important clients.

When high-ranking members of the board visited regional branches, local management would appoint a person as "regent". The job was an honour and a token of recognition, as the regent was the executive's official point of contact throughout the entire visit. Since these visits needed to go off without a hitch, it was best for everything to be centralised through one person.

If something was badly organised, that would reflect on local management. Thus only people deemed capable of carrying out the task were chosen. However, being regent was also something of a nuisance, as all duties had to be performed in addition to one's regular job. Henry – Wolfgang's right-hand man - was overseeing the development executive's visit to Italy, as well as looking after the press. In matters of discipline, Italy was on a solid line to the German office.

Instead of exuding his usual cheerful energy, Henry poured his heart out to Alex while she grabbed a coffee.

"An important client has called off," he moaned. "And now my replacement has dropped out as well."

"That's real bad luck," she expressed her sympathy. "What are you going to do?"

"No idea. At the moment I've got a 45-minute gap I need to fill somehow."

"Has no-one else got a suitable client?"

"Oh, a few colleagues have tried to get something at short notice. But you know how things are – client executives are all fully booked by this point. And it's not possible a level below. An executive from PsoraCom doesn't speak to just anybody."

"Let me have a think. Maybe something will occur to me."

After briefly thinking things over, Alex had an idea. It couldn't be that far away. It was highly unlikely, of course, as she had no direct contact – but she did have the background information. It was worth a try. She grabbed hold of Henry and took him to see her boss.

"Thomas, what do you think of me inviting Natioba's research chief to the opening in Como and seeing if I can arrange a meeting with our development executive? It's a bit short notice, but who knows?"

"Give it a try," he agreed. "We've got nothing to lose."

"It would be amazing if it worked," Henry sighed. "You'd really save my bacon. I think the Vabilmo technology is originally from his division. Let me know what you need – even if it's a helicopter!"

"Of course," Alex promised. "I'll get to work on it right away and let you know."

Natioba's head office was in Milan, only about thirty miles away from the „Lario", as the locals called the lake. Perhaps the proximity gave them a chance.

Chris was more than happy to make contact with the executive assistant, as a meeting like this brought the work done by the development lab in Seoul to the attention of the Italian office. Alex had recently read an article about Natioba's research chief. She tried to find it. It was an interview that had focused, appropriately enough, on future developments. The chief saw Natioba as an innovative leader and was keen to ensure it remained so in future. Thus armed, she composed her invitation.

Two days later, she had an answer.

"Hey buddy, I've got good news for you," she surprised Henry at his desk. "The research chief's just replied to confirm the appointment. What do you say to that?"

"Fantastic, fantastic, fantastic!" Henry was beside himself. "You are my saviour. The schedule is finalised. You've got me out of a real jam. Tell me what you need. Anything."

"Absolutely nothing! He must be a really decent guy. He's coming in his own car; he said he didn't need a limo."

"That's pretty unusual. I wish our executives could hear that. They want every last thing to be organised for them – and we're smaller than Natioba!"

In his excitement, he grabbed Alex by the waist and swung her round in the air. The people nearby looked pretty nonplussed, but the two of them just laughed.

"You'll be there, won't you?" Henry seemed to take her presence for granted.

"Haven't even thought about it yet."

"I can't bring our executive up to speed at such short notice – I need you to be there! At other client meetings, the consultant responsible is always there."

It sounded plausible, and only made the whole thing more exciting. Her first C-Level meeting. And it would be her first meeting with one of PsoraCom's executives.

Alex began to check possible flight routes right away. The meeting wasn't taking place until late afternoon and she had no real desire to spend the night. A direct flight to Milan would have been the best option time-wise, but because of the short notice, it was also the most expensive. She remembered the little airport at Lugano. She had flown there a few times over the years. The price was pretty reasonable but she'd have to compromise on flight time. It meant leaving the house at five in the morning and not getting back until eleven at night. An eighteen-hour day. The things she did for an important meeting…

On the day of the lab opening itself, Alex awoke before her alarm, tense as the strings of a crossbow. In her enthusiasm, she only just managed to stop herself from waking Sandro. She turned this way and that in front of the mirror, admiring herself in her suit. Even her natural red curls, normally so difficult to tame, felt alive, she thought to herself with satisfaction. On the way to the airport she sang along to Pink at the top of her voice; God is a DJ, life is a dance floor. Nothing could dampen her mood.

In order to keep her growing excitement in check, she read four different newspapers and financial magazines on the plane. Henry had sent a shuttle to collect her from the airport at Lugano.

Just like in the German office, all the window fronts in Como were made up of solar cells. The fir-green leather seats were also there, along with the bistro tables. An Italian colleague led her to a bright office with an outside view and Alex began to work. There were still a few hours to go until the meeting and she wanted to get all her papers in order before her monthly get-together with Thomas. Her concentration was broken suddenly by Henry.

"There you are," he uttered breathlessly, as he stormed into the office. "I haven't got much time. Do you fancy a cigarette? Are we still on course?"

"I haven't heard anything to the contrary," Alex tried to calm him as they walked. "So I assume everything's still set. How's it all going so far?"

"Good! Everything's going well. No complaints yet. That's a good sign. At least, I think it is. The executive's supposed to be a real pedant. But he's in a good mood for now."

Henry took a long draw on his cigarette before continuing.

The company responsible had checked the microphone, loud speaker and lighting three times now. Everything was working. The mayor of Como and the regional minister for economic affairs would be arriving in about an hour. Both were set to make a speech after the executive had officially declared the lab open. Local press and European trade journals were represented; clearly, there would be extensive media coverage of the event. No wonder Henry, who was lighting up his third cigarette in a row, was so nervous.

The technology worked, all speeches passed off without incident and the photographers sparked a flurry of flashbulbs. There was even a little time left over for the journalists before things settled back down. Then everyone headed straight for the food and champagne. Alex abstained.

The man from Natioba was extremely amiable: reserved, polite; not at all arrogant or self-important. Flanked on both sides by Henry and Alex, the executives took their places opposite one another. After the formal introductions, they quickly discovered that their respective departments had combined on a state-aided project a few years before. Immediately, their relationship became one of equals.

Henry or Alex couldn't have engineered it better – even if they had known about the project. Both executives talked shop about the developments that had taken place since. Although time was short, and Alex had hoped to obtain the verbal consent of Natioba's research chief regarding the joint project in Italy, she chose not to interrupt. When two kings were holding court, peasants were obliged to remain silent.

But she had an ace up her sleeve. There were still a good ten minutes left. She took a small case from her bag, lying next to the chair, and placed it open on the table before them. Both executives glanced briefly towards it, before continuing their conversation. Alex was certain it would work.

She just needed to be patient, even if the final grains of sand were now falling through the hourglass. Natioba's executive was the first to pause and glance over at the contents of the case for a second time. When he asked what it was, Alex received a nod of encouragement from her development chief.

It was the spherical seed unit. She quickly outlined the most important information about the Vabilmo technology, before smoothly steering the conversation towards the project with Seoul. Her Italian conversation partner furrowed his brow. He spun the spherical Alex had given him around in his hand and asked for more details. Obviously, he was unaware of the project.

She described the self-sufficient greenhouse and tried not to betray any uncertainty when she saw that his right eyebrow was raised. PsoraCom's development chief interrupted and excused himself: he was expecting his next guest. At the same time, he formally expressed the wish that they meet again in six months. Everyone stood hastily while Alex quickly packed up and said goodbye to her superior.

He nodded appreciatively and said: "Those seed units are extremely rare still. You can only get hold of them in special cases."

Alex felt flattered and smiled. Her response drew a slight laugh: "Reach for the stars and you'll make it at least as far as the moon."

On the way out, her guest asked for more details. In the course of her description, the wrinkles on his forehead slowly began to disappear. He seemed to like what he was hearing; Alex decided the time was right. It was now or never. They were standing by the entrance when a hostess came by to offer them a glass of champagne. The man from Natioba helped himself, as did she. If he had turned it down, she would have done likewise. But now they had a few minutes.

"Here's to a successful pilot project," she said, as she raised her glass.

"To a successful pilot project," he replied.

She was about to ask for his support, but he beat her to it.

"Please keep my people in Italy up-to-date. I want to know how the project is progressing. If everything goes well, we'll need to consider it for other types of off-grid systems."

"I'd be very happy to. Many thanks for taking the time to participate in the meeting. I really appreciate it."

"Not at all, it was worth it."

Hopefully Henry was around somewhere; now she was the one that needed a cigarette. And another glass of champagne. It was over and it had gone fantastically well. Henry thought so too.

"Hey, I'm so happy everything worked out in the end. Without you I would have been up shit creek."

"Don't talk crap," she replied. "Meetings can always be cancelled: nothing you can do about it."

"You're right. But still, it wouldn't have looked good. But now we can chalk it up as a success. Thanks again."

On the flight home, she recalled the man from Natioba's quizzical face. He hadn't been able to overcome his curiosity. It confirmed what she had always thought: that most people liked having something to touch. That was the reason she hadn't stopped pestering Hank and his colleagues about the seed units.

A few days earlier, she had taken advantage of the forthcoming meeting to get what she wanted, and the spherical had arrived just in time. During the last ten minutes of the meeting, the unit had helped whip up enormous interest in the project. What's more, she had been given a concrete assignment. An assignment in the form of a spoken request. A trump card she could use with those tentative researchers in Italy. Perhaps she could even play it with development too.

The next morning, her mobile rang almost non-stop. Her colleagues were dying to know how things had gone. .

"So, how was it?" asked George.

"Good, I think. At least, I achieved what I set out to achieve: that is, their research chief is interested in the project, and the path is clear for me to speak with his people."

"If the board members at Natioba are anything like ours, they'll be a bunch of windbags," he added. "It's possible nothing will come of it."

"Come off it! Ours aren't that bad."

"Well, I suppose it won't hurt," he yielded. "But I've had to learn things the hard way. Still, it's great that the meeting worked out at such short notice. Not everyone could do it."

"To what do I owe this compliment, kind sir?"

"You know me; I'm a real softie at heart. I might have a screw or two loose but mostly I'm alright."

"I can't contradict you there, George."

"I just wanted to see how things had gone, before I head off for a few days. I'm really looking forward to Switzerland. I'll still have my cell though – for emergencies."

She had barely put the phone down when Hugo called.

"You've got to postpone the telephone meeting with Chris," he demanded. "It's just not going to work this week. I really need a few days' holiday."

"That's not ideal," said Alex. "But if you can't change it, then we'll have to put him off. Can't you call Chris yourself, or send him a mail?"

"I don't have time for that anymore. I've got some urgent business to attend to with Roffarm. Then I need to be off."

"I hope it's nothing serious?"

"No, but I've got to hang up, otherwise I won't manage everything. So, you'll get hold of Chris?"

Alex sighed. She'd help him out one last time, but he'd have to make the next appointment himself. She had just hung up when the phone rang again. It was Carl.

"So, I've rejigged my presentation. Can you look at it again quickly?"

"If you send it to me now, Carl, I'll get it done today."

There was clearly something else on his mind, though it seemed like he didn't know how to express it.

"Say, Alex, have you ever had to deal with any strange remarks from colleagues?"

"What do you mean? What kind of strange remarks?"

"Almost everyone I deal with internally thinks I report to Brian. No-one's even heard of Thomas. It's mostly colleagues from the US but some of them work here in the German office."

Alex laughed.

"Yeah, that's happened to me a few times. Particularly at the beginning – everyone seemed to think Brian was in charge. It's just that he was one of the first to start work on Vabilmo, and that's what he tells everyone. Thomas isn't the kind of person to hog the limelight."

"And what did you do? I mean, he can't go round saying things that aren't true."

"Oh, you know how Brian is. I usually just set colleagues right and tell them that Thomas took over the department last year. Then I say that the team has got bigger since, and that Brian and I are jointly responsible for the various solar plant manufacturers."

"If you think that's best, then I'll do the same in the future."

Alex wasn't surprised that the same thing had happened to Carl. It was really typical of Brian. But it was a waste of time getting worked up about it; in the end, what counted were actions and results. But it seemed to have affected Carl quite a bit.

6

////////////////////////////////

June

Alex didn't have any official meetings, only her monthly talk with Thomas and an appointment with Emily. Why the hell not, she asked herself, as she strapped on her back protector and slipped into her leathers. During the journey she breathed in the smell of freshly cut grass, while admiring the mountains that shimmered in the clear sky behind her. A little ride was an enticing prospect; she had been working very hard of late.

Some people balanced out their overtime, although there were no rules about this at PsoraCom. Given that they didn't use time cards, it was difficult to understand when some people did extra work since, for the company, everything was done and dusted with the salary. Results were the important thing, and the organisational skills were crucial. Someone who was unfocused automatically did more work than someone who was organised. At least, that was the theory. It sounded very black and white, Alex thought, as she parked her motorcycle.

She never stopped hearing from office colleagues about how their workload was constantly increasing, about how hard it was to find a work-life balance. Even at the weekend, mails had to be checked and answered – the Americans, in particular, always seemed to be online with their netphones. Alex had used two cells for years. One was reserved for family and friends, meaning she could switch off her work phone in the evenings.

During the week, she was happy to work a few extra hours, as her colleagues in the US and Asia couldn't do anything about the time difference. But Saturday and Sunday were sacred; things could always wait until Monday.

She received more than enough money to compensate for the extra work she did on weekdays: her base salary was certainly not to be sniffed at. What's more, if she achieved her objectives to over 100%, there was a nice extra bonus. But the icing on the cake was the enjoyment factor and the feeling of personal achievement: to be at the vanguard of a new technology, to have a decisive say in the success of such an exciting product - not everyone had that. There was no hobby she would rather indulge.

Wolfgang wheeled past her cubicle and glanced at her motorcycle gear.

"Do you know why men go nuts over women in leathers?" he asked conspiratorially.

"Because we look so damn fine in them?" Alex grinned back.

"No, it's because they smell like new cars."

She had expected something a little more risqué, but at least it was a line she hadn't heard before. It was the first time Wolfgang had initiated conversation himself.

"Why don't we have a coffee so I can hear what's happening with you," he suggested. "Any news about Natioba?"

"Did you read about the planned MOU?" she asked. "I'm just writing a first draft. How does that work by the way? Is it you who signs it?"

"Normally it goes through Legal in Strasbourg," he explained. "But they're not involved with Vabilmo yet."

"I've got an appointment with Emily after this to go over the draft," she replied. "The name of the person in charge needs to be at the bottom."

Wolfgang thought it over. "Perhaps we don't need Strasbourg. Check with Emily!"

"I'll ask her. At the end of the day, we report to you. Surely it would make more sense if it was you who signed."

"You're right," Wolfgang agreed. "After all, we're the worldwide competence centre when it comes to sales of Vabilmo! And Sales makes contracts."

Emily promised to talk to Strasbourg as soon as she could.

"It could be very helpful," said Alex. "There are still no agreements in place about the polymer-based cells, except with Hursoc and Roffarm."

"I don't see any reason why the MOU shouldn't be signed by Wolfgang. I mean, he is the managing director of the German office."

"And an agreement like this could be of great use to him internally."

On seeing Emily's quizzical expression, Alex explained that Wolfgang had told her that the Vabilmo technology had a number of high-level critics. One of the reasons was cost. Polymer-based cells were cheaper than traditional cells – but only if they were mass-produced; and by the million at that.

The Vabilmo team had to find at least two end customers prepared to fit their PV plants with the new cells. Otherwise, the technology could be canned in the next few years. Alex had been astonished by Wolfgang's candour. With Roffarm, they had found their first end customer at the back-end of the previous year. The project was still in the pre-development phase but there were high hopes invested in the contract. They anticipated that Roffarm would make a concrete pledge sometime this year about when they intended to use Vabilmo cells in their plants, and how many.

Natioba could be the second company Wolfgang needed to silence the doubters. Even if it was just an MoU, it would still mean they had something to show upper management – never mind the impact that securing the support of another solar giant would have on the market.

Still, it wasn't as easy as all that. Hursoc, a solar module and inverter market leader that George was looking after, had issued a press release about their work with the Vabilmo technology a few months ago. From a purely technical standpoint, they weren't any further on than Roffarm; indeed, it was possible they had even fallen behind.

The difficulty wasn't in manufacturing the first modules with polymer-based cells; it was in developing new inverters able to cope with the higher levels of consumption. Hursoc didn't want to put up the money on their own, and so were waiting for a plant manufacturer to share the costs. Consequently, there was no actual project yet.

There was no question of bringing Roffarm in, as they had worked together with a different module manufacturer for years – who, in turn, remained unconvinced by the Vabilmo technology. To guarantee market success, therefore, they needed not only two plant manufacturers, but an additional solar module manufacturer to go alongside Hursoc.

Emily's face lit up. "Now I see why you've expanded your work with Natioba to include robots and building integration. It isn't just about the off-grid systems."

"Exactly," Alex continued. "Natioba already has a department that deals with building-integrated photovoltaics. We're looking into service robots at the moment. There are companies in both fields that manufacture special solar modules."

"And you want to approach them together with Natioba."

"Correct. Like Roffarm, Natioba doesn't use the Hursoc modules."

"Good, then I'm in the picture. We just need to make sure we don't make promises that bind us to anyone specific. But I see you've been on the lookout for that already. I'll send you an amended version in the next few days. It's possible that the client will want to change a few things as well."

Thomas raised no objections about her draft during their afternoon meeting. With a degree of concern, she told him about her conversation with Wolfgang as well. There was no danger that US headquarters would can Vabilmo, her boss reassured her. He didn't think it would make any sense after such a lengthy research and development process.

Henry had already informed Thomas about how the meeting in Como had gone. Alex supplied a few extra details, before moving on to how things currently stood with Premve. The appointment with their committee had been agreed and would take place in five weeks. She still needed to speak personally to the head of the power plant division, who reported directly to the development director. The former had written numerous articles about different industry trends, all published by well-respected journals; he also seemed to be a popular speaker at conferences. A key background figure, he was someone who would have a decisive role in establishing Premve's strategy – that much was certain. George shared her opinion, having met the division manager once already. Alex had therefore decided to take him to the meeting with her instead of Marco.

She hadn't overlooked Luxumi either: a non-disclosure agreement had been finalised and an initial meeting with the head of development was in place. For this, Alex had asked both George and Hugo to accompany her. In her opinion, discussions were also set to focus on the operational level, as opposed to mere strategy alone.

"Everything's looking good so far," Thomas summarised. He seemed to be extremely satisfied with her results. Alex got up to leave, but he motioned for her to remain seated.

"What I am about to tell you is strictly confidential. No-one from the team is to hear anything about it until further notice. Wolfgang is the only person who knows."

Curious, Alex pushed her chair closer to the table.

"At PsoraCom, managers are not supposed to remain in any one department for longer than two years," Thomas began, sotto voce. "They are then advised to take something else on, and sometimes even deal with a completely different area. I have another eighteen months to go, and I'd like you to be my successor."

"Why me exactly?" Alex asked, flabbergasted. "I've only been here five months. People like George and Brian have been with the company for significantly longer and have much more experience."

"That's true, but you've already proved your qualities in the short time you've been with us. I like the way you do things. You're far-sighted when it comes to strategy, a quality most of your colleagues seem to lack. They spend too much time chewing over irrelevant details. You, however, always work with the company's aims in mind. It shows in team meetings. As soon as things get out of hand, you intervene and steer everyone back on course."

"You're too kind," Alex whispered, blushing.

"No need to get embarrassed, nothing's happened yet. Still, we'll need to work together closely over the next few months and prepare various things, just like we did for the off-site meeting. That way you'll get an idea of what to expect."

"Sounds good. And Wolfgang knows about this?"

"Yeah, Wolfgang's in on it. He approves."

She certainly hadn't anticipated this, especially after such a short time. But somehow, it felt right.

"So, where's your moped then?" Thomas changed the subject, making a point of stacking his papers.

"It's not a moped! It's a Harley," she cried with mock indignation. "Since when have you been interested in motorcycles?"

"I used to have one myself once," he replied. "Not a great lump of iron like yours, but a stylish little racer. I completely transformed it."

"Mine isn't all original either. If I want to make any modifications, I use a friend's garage. It's really practical. He helps out whenever I get stuck."

"Not bad. I don't know too many women who tinker with their own vehicles."

"It's something I've always enjoyed. I find I need to do something with my hands to compensate for all that brainwork. I have my father to thank for it. When I was a kid he always used to take me down to his tool shed whenever he had to look after me. He gave me a hammer and nails and stood me in front of a block of a wood."

Thomas laughed. "It's never too early to get down to brass tacks."

She couldn't stop thinking about the conversation. When Sandro came home from work, she gave him the good news straightaway.

"You won't believe what happened at my meeting today."

"No idea," he shrugged his shoulders, "but I had an absolutely hellish day."

"My boss told me I'm going to be his successor in a year or two."

"Uh huh, and why you exactly?"

"That's precisely what I asked; his answer was a little funny. He said he couldn't imagine my colleagues taking on the role because they weren't focused enough. He doesn't trust them with strategic matters."

"He said that?"

"Yeah, I was pretty surprised he was so open with me."

"Hey, listen, that's great news but there's something I urgently need to finish."

"I thought we could spend the evening together, just the two of us, and toast my success."

"Not tonight. This is really important." With that, Sandro disappeared off to his computer.

Disappointed, she began to tidy the kitchen. Later, she admitted to herself that she was being a little selfish. At the end of the day, she often worked long hours too, especially where the project with Natioba was concerned. Until now, Sandro had always tolerated that. If he had a lot on his mind, it was surely asking too much of him to share in her excitement.

But she was so thrilled that she decided to call her father.

"You must've really impressed these people," he reacted enthusiastically. "It's a great chance and you could learn a lot from it."

"Being in charge of a department," she thought out loud, "would definitely be a challenge for me. I mean, I don't have any management experience. Still I can't deny that climbing the ladder is an attractive prospect."

"You'll be fine," her father sounded sure. "But you shouldn't forget all the admin that comes with a supervisory post. There are monthly reports, salary negotiations, agreeing objectives and all sorts of other paperwork. There'd be much less contact with clients, of course. Outwardly, though, you'd have a much higher position."

"It's not the position that's important per se – and it's certainly not something I want at all costs. For me, what's important is that my sphere of responsibility grows. I don't necessarily need to have a managerial function for that. Take my current job, for example. In future, the product we're hoping to launch on the market will be seen as one of the company mainstays, a major sales item."

"I think that's the most important thing for you too. But the experience you'll gain from taking on an executive post like this will stand you in good stead for the future. And if you don't like it, you can always go back to what you were doing before."

"That's how I see it as well. It's going to be a real learning curve either way."

When she hung up, she realised that Sandro had already gone to bed. He must have had a really hard day. She crept quietly under the covers and put her arm around him.

At the next team meeting, everyone was there in person for a change. Alex had adapted her wardrobe to the summer temperatures and was wearing a dress.

George beamed at her. "Well, aren't you looking chic today, my dear! Why don't you come and take a seat on my sunny side?"

Hugo grinned. "You old lothario, you. Just make sure your sunny side doesn't overheat next to Alex while she's looking so hot. That would be a real mess."

"You're a right pair of charmers today, aren't you?" Alex looked from one to the other. "Good holiday was it?"

"St. Gallen was fabulous as always," George gushed. "You've got Lake Constance and the mountains nearby, and the city itself is a World Heritage Site. I've been going to the Radisson for years; with them, I know what I'm getting. Just don't go in October: there are far too many cows in the city for my taste."

"Shame they're not cash cows, right George?" Brian said snidely. "Then you could've stayed a few days longer. Or don't they offer Texas hold'em?"

"They certainly wouldn't let you in," George countered sharply. "But if you do want to go sometime, I can recommend a good hairdresser."

"That's enough now," Thomas interrupted. "Let's make a start. Alex has invited Emily to the meeting today so that she can bring us up-to-date on the Roffarm contract."

"Thanks, Thomas," Emily began. "Legally speaking, the Roffarm issue is still up in the air. My colleagues from the US are of the opinion that the exclusivity clause is ambiguous and thus open to interpretation. Though that's not necessarily a bad thing, it could provoke a lot of discussion – and that's something we're keen to avoid. We don't want get caught up in a wrangle with our client, and we certainly don't want to wind up in court. My colleagues' internal recommendation therefore is to keep Roffarm informed of our dealings with other solar plant manufacturers."

"That's bullshit," Brian was already in a state. "You're not serious are you, Emily? That's not what I had in mind when I drew up the contract. Our Yankee friends are well off the mark."

"I don't think it's that bad," George broke in. "I'm pretty sure I could persuade Hursoc."

"But Hursoc has a legitimate interest in winning Roffarm back as a client," Alex responded. "Of course they'll be happy to disclose their strategy if it means achieving their objectives."

"Does this affect me too?" asked Carl. "My clients aren't in direct competition with Roffarm."

"I think it mainly affects plant manufacturers," Thomas replied.

"But I have non-disclosure agreements with all my clients – not just with Natioba," Alex voiced her concern. "And we can't give Roffarm any information without their prior consent. If we did, it would be more than simply paradoxical; it would be completely irrational."

"Alex is right," George agreed. "What sort of company would agree to passing on confidential information about new developments to the competition? Taking advantage of your market opponent's lack of knowledge is the only way to get ahead in this game."

Alex thought the clause put them in a very awkward position. What was she supposed to do? Ask Natioba if it was alright to tell

Roffarm about her project with Hank and Chris? How would that look?

Emily was equally unhappy with the situation.

"Of course we shouldn't give Roffarm any information if it means breaking an existing contract with a different end customer," she made her view clear. "But there has to be some kind of solution."

"It's absolutely ridiculous!" By now Brian had worked himself up into a rage. "It's exactly the opposite of what Roffarm wanted from the contract. They wanted the option to talk to other plant manufacturers from their end so they could work together and establish a standard based on Vabilmo. It's all down to Roffarm's divisional director, that bolshie douchebag."

Alex wondered what had got into him. "I don't like the idea of telling Roffarm what's going on with my clients either. It could lead to a real dilemma. There must be a more morally tenable way of honouring our contractual agreements."

"But the Roffarm contract is our number one priority," Hugo broke in defiantly. "Besides, they started working on Vabilmo first."

"Right, and there are already signs of progress," George agreed. "They're miles ahead of the others; I mean, in that sense, the whole thing's pretty innocuous."

Alex wasn't quite so sure. She was responsible for her clients and wanted to guard their projects. If she had to ask her clients for permission to pass on information to their competition, it would make PsoraCom appear over-deferential – and that was surely undesirable. Nevertheless, they had signed a contract with Roffarm, however open to interpretation it was. It was not impossible that Roffam were in fact lagging behind other companies, and a lawsuit simply wasn't an option.

"What do you think about agreeing to give Roffarm a heads-up?" she suggested. "Before any projects are made public, we tell them to expect new information from their competitors. That way, they have the chance to react first."

"We'd really be going out of our way for them," Brian said. "They'd have no choice but to accept! If they don't, I'll just have to go over there and remind them what we agreed."

"OK by me," Carl let his opinion be known.

"Hursoc would certainly have no issue with it," George agreed.

Thomas nodded. "Then that's sorted. It would mean tipping them off two days before we announce anything about Vabilmo with other manufacturers. No details though."

He turned to Emily and added: "Do you think you could negotiate an additional clause that clearly defines Roffarm's rights?"

"I hope so, Thomas. As things stand, the exclusivity clause is not in our interests."

"They're only shooting themselves in the foot, anyway," Alex shook her head. "There's no way they can achieve mass production with the quantities they're asking for – or reduce costs for that matter. The additional money they invest in developing inverters and such like won't pay off until much, much later. Exclusivity will cost them dear."

"That's a good argument," said Emily, turning towards her. "I'll try and formulate the additional clause along those lines."

With that, the topic was dealt with; the next thing was for Carl to present his strategy.

"I'm not convinced about the ODMs," George expressed his concern right away. "I'd wait to see how things develop. By the time you get a look-in important projects with robot manufacturers might be lost."

"I think things with the ODMs might happen sooner than we expect," Alex countered. "That's why I wouldn't ignore them. But, at the end of the day, it's your decision, Carl. You have the most experience in the field."

"I see it differently," George contradicted. "Carl needs to contact the number one robot manufacturer immediately! I don't understand why they're not on his list."

"They're currently gearing their strategy more and more towards the BRIC countries," justified Carl. "Their focus is on cheap mass-produced goods, not expensive new products."

Brian sat tapping away on his laptop, just staring at the screen. He didn't participate once in the entire discussion.

"This is how I see it," Thomas concluded the meeting. "The risk we're taking in approaching the ODM ahead of the number one robot manufacturer is negligible. Carl has supplied us with the figures. I suggest he proceeds exactly as planned. If it turns out to be a dead-end, then he can revise his strategy in a few months' time."

After the meeting he took Alex to one side.

"Carl told me that he went through the presentation beforehand with you. Was the ODM idea yours?"

"We used the data Carl had to work together towards a solution."

Thomas nodded. "That's what I thought."

Naturally, it had been no problem to get two days off. They had both been working extremely hard lately and, apart from their disastrous skiing weekend, hadn't enjoyed a single holiday together. Sandro loved the sea just as much as Alex, and the long weekend went by in a flash. During the day, they lolled on the beach, slept, read, played volleyball and went swimming; in the evening they had barbecues and chatted long into the night over a few glasses of red wine. The last night was their anniversary: their first date had been exactly four years ago. Sandro had reserved a table in a nice restaurant by the sea. Alex was just about to choose the wine.

"The Amarone is very good," Sandro said, before glancing over at the price, "but why don't we try the Bardolino? It'll do the job just as well."

"I know," Alex agreed, "but let's indulge ourselves this one time. It's our anniversary, after all. Come on, let's celebrate: this one's on me. Agreed?"

"No way," he resisted. "I'm paying! But you know my client hasn't coughed up in full yet."

"Yeah, you said. Let me pay tonight," she suggested, "and you can pick up the bill next time. OK?"

"All right…but please don't choose the most expensive wine. It costs as much as the food put together."

"But I really want the Amarone. Don't worry about it. Let's treat ourselves."

The food was excellent and the wine all too drinkable. They left the restaurant a little tipsy and headed for the beach, hoping to conclude the evening in the manner appropriate. The long weekend had done them the world of good.

After the meeting with Premve, they sat together with Thomas in the canteen and talked him through it.

"That was top-notch, the way Alex talked him round," George began.

"Don't over-exaggerate," she scolded him, laughing. "It was teamwork, a simple question of finding out what made him tick."

"Now, don't sell yourself short, what you did was brilliant." With that, he turned to Thomas.

"Our colleague here has a real talent for working out what's important to her opposite number and subtly using it to her advantage."

"What are you talking about?" Alex waved him aside. "I did a little research beforehand, that's all. The division manager is in a position of authority. Not only does he act as opening speaker at the most important conferences; he's also written a number of articles for specialist magazines. A very decent, affable guy, but not someone who likes small talk. He's too busy for it – precisely because he has the decisive say with his superiors. He's the driving force, the person who actually pulls the strings."

"There you have it! Alex was wonderfully well prepared; I think we can trust her to get things done on her own from now on. She certainly doesn't need me anymore."

"I still need you, George. You know that. You can only do so much planning; there's always a degree of luck involved. We definitely had it today. I mean, I had no idea he would jump at the robot thing the way he did. But that just shows once again how quickly he's able to assess things and come up with ideas."

"You're right. The idea with the service robots is just brilliant."

"Let's stop all this beating around the bush," Thomas was growing slightly impatient. "What idea are you talking about? I want details."

"Premve have been using autonomous robots in their grid-connected plants for some time now," explained Alex. "They examine the state of the solar modules and check the inverter connections. The grounds of the plant are fitted with a wireless connection, with the master station satellite-linked to Premve's maintenance centre.

The individual access points are also powered by solar electricity, by the way. Depending on where they are at any given moment, the robots are able to use the wireless network to create an ad-hoc connection. If need be, they can also be remote-control operated from the maintenance centre. This is where the robots ultimately transfer the results of their repair work.

Until now, the machines have run on highly efficient lithium-ion batteries, which have even been able to withstand the harsh surrounding conditions. But the cost lies in the infrastructure, as charging points are needed across the whole plant."

"What they have there is amazingly progressive," enthused George. "And, if our cells really are as efficient as the product specialists say, then this is an area where Premve could make enormous savings. That's why the divisional manager suggested to Alex that they carry out a test project using one of their maintenance robots."

"He suggested it to us," Alex corrected him. "And more to the point, it was only after you made an initial efficiency estimate. That's what persuaded him. Officially, his boss still needs to agree. However, it's more than likely that he'll rely on the judgement of his fox at the heart of the power base. I guess we'll find out when we meet with the committee; the development director will be there too."

"I have to say I like the idea with the maintenance robots more and more," George beamed. "Above all, because it means we'll get a look-in a lot quicker with the grid-connected plants."

"Exactly," she agreed enthusiastically. "Whether or not they use robots has nothing to do with the development cycle of their plants. Premve are no different to other plant manufacturers in that they build new plants at intervals of three to five years. But there's no reason why the robots can't be used in already-existing plants – as long as no expensive modifications are needed."

"Well, that all sounds very good," her boss summarised. "But I need to go to another meeting now."

He left the two of them alone in the canteen. George immediately began scrutinising the technical feasibility of the project.

"We're going to need a smaller inverter," he reasoned. "The sheer size of the ones they use in grid-connected plants makes them unsuitable. The current-transformers in off-grid systems are not designed to be moved or disturbed, and neither are the traditional inverters used in lighting systems. I'll go through the different technical scenarios and synchronise with colleagues. Also I'll try and get Hugo on board straightaway."

"Fantastic," Alex thanked him. "It was really important to me that you were there today."

"Oh, get away. The result was down to you alone. You were extremely professional and you knew exactly how to behave with the divisional manager. I'm convinced we wouldn't have been so successful if you'd just unleashed a volley of suggestions without giving him the time to develop his own ideas."

"I don't mind admitting that that's music to my ears. But why don't we stop there before we fall out of tune? Was the holiday really that good? You seem to be in an extremely good mood."

"The holiday was superb, but my divorce has also finally come through. I'm not really made for relationships. Now I can realise my dreams and enjoy the single life, with everything it has to offer."

"I didn't even know you were married. So did you paint the town red in St. Gallen?"

"Something like that," George grinned mysteriously.

Despite her high spirits, Alex kept her call report brief and stuck to what she perceived to be the facts. The divisional manager was not averse to a joint project, but approval was still needed from above. How things progressed depended on the meeting with the committee. Nothing was set in stone. She sent the report to team members, Nobu and a few colleagues from the power plant and robotics verticals, deliberately omitting management. Brian replied immediately, gleefully emphasising that he knew adopting a pull strategy had been right all along. Naturally, he didn't just send his response to the original addressees, but to management as well, Bill included. Alex was slowly beginning to get used to it. Nevertheless, she hoped people would be able to distinguish between the information sent by her, and that sent by Brian.

Since their last jour fixe, Thomas had been including her more and more in his work. Whenever Wolfgang needed status updates on the various projects, it was she who put them together. When different departments sent in questions about Vabilmo, Thomas asked her to take care of them. First, she would examine the question and decide how best to proceed. Usually it was enough to give them some general information about the polymer-based cells, which they in turn could pass on to their clients. Most of the time there was no prospect of a concrete project, and, if there was, it wouldn't be worth their while. It was vital that all available team resources were concentrated on strategically important clients and projects.

The exception was a request that had come through Christopher via the London office. It was to do with a company that manufactured batteries and developed different power transfer modes for consumer applications. At the moment they were focusing on the wireless transfer of electricity between robots and prototype charging stations. And the Vabilmo technology was of great interest for these stations, which needed batteries to temporarily store electricity.

The London company was planning to increase their efforts to win off-grid-systems manufacturers as clients for their batteries. They also wanted to manufacture charging stations for service robots off their own bat. Alex's ears pricked up when she read that the company had Premve and Natioba specifically in mind. However, before she spoke directly to the client, she wanted to give her colleague in London some general information about Vabilmo, and then wait for his initial reaction. She went to see Christopher.

"Ah, the Vabilmo-woman," he grinned cheerfully. "How's everything going? How many millions have you made so far?"

"Millions?" she looked at him in mock disbelief. "It'll be billions in three to five years, you'll see. We're not bothered about millions. We'll leave that to your team; we don't want you to be unemployed now, do we? We're not completely heartless, after all."

"Oh, how kind! The next billion, I understand. So, what can I do you for?"

"It's about the enquiry from England. How important is the client?"

"They're the British market leader; we do some business with them. They're doing pretty well regionally in Germany. Why?"

"I'm trying to work out how much time to invest in them, what their potential is. For the moment I've just sent some info to our rep in the UK; I want to wait and see how the client reacts."

"Yeah, that's fine. Still, if the client asks, it would be great if you could fly over."

As expected, Luxumi's head of development had brought several colleagues along with him to the initial meeting. After the Vabilmo technology had been briefly introduced, there was ample opportunity for Hugo to present his detailed slides, together with George.

They were a great duo, and they had soon aroused the developers' interest. For questions about strategy, the development manager had referred to Alex. Luxumi's organic solar cell testing and their work with modified inverters had landed on fertile ground with George.

Over the course of the discussion, he had suggested arranging a joint meeting with Hursoc. The development manager had agreed and a provisional date was set aside; the only thing they needed was confirmation from Hursoc.

After George had dropped them at the office, Alex and Hugo sat eating lunch together in the canteen.

"Good that I had the slides with me," he murmured between mouthfuls.

"I was positive we'd need your technical knowledge," she replied. "That's why I wanted you there."

"I clicked with them right away," he continued. "We were on the same wavelength, you know, we spoke the same language."

"True."

"I put a huge amount of time into those slides and they immediately recognised that."

"Yeah, I thought that too."

"There was a few days' work in there."

"The slides were very good, at least from my amateur point of view," she praised him, before quickly changing the subject. "By the way, how was your time off? It wasn't anything serious, was it?"

"No, no, I just had the chance to take a wellness holiday at short notice. It was so nice, with massages, facials and everything else. Absolutely great: total luxury, including a view from the Jacuzzi of the Swiss mountains. It was great to be able to relax finally; the last few months have been pretty stressful."

"So, the holiday was worth it, then?"

"Oh yeah, financially too: I even won a few hundred euros in the casino."

Interesting, Alex thought to herself. So, Hugo had been in Switzerland too. Still, maybe it was just a coincidence.

Alex and Anna were both massive fans of Pink and had been looking forward to the concert for weeks. After they had taken their seats in the arena, Sandro headed off to get some drinks. He didn't seem to be in a very good mood.

"What's up with you, grumpy guts?" Anna gave him a nudge.

"I'm just completely wiped out from work, that's all," he replied curtly.

"Don't be too harsh on him; he's been coming home very late these last few weeks," Alex defended him.

"Then it's the perfect opportunity to give those overworked joints a good shaking," Anna tried to motivate him.

"Just leave it," he said. "Not everyone has ants in their pants like you. Why don't you two go to the front, I'm happy back here."

"Then make sure you hold on tight to your beer, otherwise you'll fall," Anna laughed.

As soon as Pink announced that so what, she was still a rock star Alex and Anna could no longer keep their feet still; Sandro just stood there, downing beer after beer. Every time Alex took his hand and pulled him closer, he loosened his grip. Either he had to go to the toilet or get another beer. After a few more attempts, she gave up and continued dancing alone with Anna. They knew almost every song by heart and sang along enthusiastically – by the end of the concert, they were completely hyper. Anna bought a round of champagne, then Alex a second. Sandro's mood had improved somewhat, although it could easily have been because of the alcohol.

The three of them went back to the car, and Alex put in Pink's latest album. Anna began to dance around in the parking lot, shaking her hips wildly. She wiggled towards Alex, hooked her by the arm and swept her along in a kind of polka. They span each other frenziedly around the car and a grumpy looking Sandro, until a few songs later they were hoarse and completely out of puff. Splitting their sides with laughter, they decided enough was enough. Back at home, Sandro went to bed immediately, mumbling a brief apology en route. Something was up, but no doubt it would blow over soon enough.

Shortly afterwards, she was on her way to Milan with George. The first item on the agenda was a meeting with one of his clients. Hugo was set to join them afterwards for an appointment with Natioba's research department. They had left a day early, as George wanted to wine and dine his client before their meeting the next morning.

He had arranged for them to stay in a very elegant design hotel located only half a street away from Corso Vittorio Emanuele II. The décor was extremely luxurious, a fact reflected in the price. He had waved aside Alex's reservations with the argument that his contact was a big-shot client. After they had checked in, read their emails and taken care of all calls – Alex had got Hank to give her the latest update – they met in the downstairs lobby.

George looked stylish in his evening dress; he seemed to relish the surrounding luxury. Even his client's last minute cancellation couldn't dampen his mood. Nevertheless, after a quick look at the hotel menu, Alex was able to convince him to eat somewhere else. They soon found a little bar slightly off the beaten track, with a single free table in the warm evening sun.

The osteria seemed to be frequented mainly by locals and offered an extensive wine list to go with the wide variety of dishes. George had no hesitation in ordering a whole bottle of Primitivo, as it would go wonderfully with their fillet steaks. With his starter, however, he ordered a Bellini; which would complement his crab and rucola salad better. Just like the wine, it was only later that George seemed to reveal his true self.

"This is how you travel in style, Alex. Don't you worry about anything! The company has enough money. Our executives spend vast sums on the most ridiculous things when they're away on business. They get waited on hand and foot."

"I'm not worried," she replied. "I'm just not used to staying in such grand hotels. I usually choose a standard one. In smaller cities, you can often find decent, independent places that are good value and haven't lost any of their charm. For me, the main thing in a room is that it's clean, quiet and not too small. Naturally, I don't want it to be out in the Styx either. But I don't need anything more than that for a single night."

"I understand," he said. "But we're here as representatives of a big company. How would it look if a world market leader couldn't afford to put their employees up in decent lodgings? They book out whole suites for our superiors; this is peanuts compared to that. No disrespect, but we have to think about how we appear to others, and if that means higher travel costs, then so be it."

"Well, if you say so."

"Trust me: I'm the old hand here. Only a few years ago they used to fritter away so much money; this is like a kids' birthday party in comparison."

His phone rang just as he was ordering an expensive Grappa to go with his coffee. It was Hugo; he probably had a technical question of some kind, even though it was really late. It didn't seem to bother

George, who stood up and moved a few feet away from the tables. Given the volume at which he normally conducted his conversations, she thought it was an extremely polite thing to do. But this time, she only heard a quiet, indecipherable murmur and saw how his lips moved. There was a vaguely conspiratorial feel to it all, as she watched how he whispered into his netphone, head bowed and face strained. All of a sudden his expression changed completely and he looked like a docile little boy. He was smiling, but as their eyes met, he gave a slight wince. It was the reaction of a child caught doing something forbidden.

"These youngsters," he shook his head jokingly, as he came back. "Always worrying about unimportant details."

Alex bit her tongue and just smiled. Like a true gentleman, George paid the bill. However, his attempts to persuade her to join him for a nightcap at the hotel bar fell on deaf ears.

He appeared the next morning freshly coiffed. His bold waistcoat suit and silk neck tie sat perfectly, although his face looked extremely pale in comparison. Still, nothing a few strong cups of coffee couldn't sort out, as Alex had discovered in Florida. In the end it didn't make the slightest bit of difference, since George's client arrived looking equally bleary-eyed.

It turned out they knew each other very well and had met in the hotel bar for a whisky or two late the previous evening; any unresolved issues surrounding the existing silicon solar cell contracts had thus already been settled. That enabled them to concentrate on Vabilmo and possible future collaborations. George's client was very curious and wanted to know how far along they were with the different power plant manufacturers. Alex couldn't give him precise details because it was confidential. He continued to probe mischievously, but she remained steadfast. Out of the corner of her eye, she saw that George was winking at him – though what that meant, she could only speculate. Basically the client was very open to the idea of working together alongside a plant manufacturer.

For the rest of the day, it was noses to the grindstone in the hotel. The meeting with Natioba was scheduled for the next morning and Hugo wouldn't join them until after dinner. George seemed distracted somehow, and was very quiet during lunch. His lack of sleep must have been catching up with him because he almost forgot to pay for their espressos and panini. It would barely have occurred to Alex. She was so used to him paying – even if the gesture was meaningless in itself. The company didn't care who filled out the expenses claim.

Back at the room, she sat down at her desk and went through her emails. A message from Hank put her in a thoughtful mood and her gaze wandered involuntarily from the window into the middle distance. Roffarm's divisional director had announced he would visit the US to get an idea of the latest designs and discuss possibilities. Up until now, only colleagues from Bill's department had been included in the project with Roffarm; no-one from the second vertical, which dealt with machines and robots, had been involved. At least, not yet. Perhaps Roffarm would adopt a similar strategy to Premve in the interim period. That could be extremely interesting, Alex thought to herself.

What she saw through the window was equally interesting, however. George emerged contentedly from the direction of the Corso, heavily weighed down by a number of large paper bags. His new leather jacket didn't look too bad on him. He had been unable to resist the lure of the city of fashion and had obviously wrought all kinds of havoc with his credit card in Milan's shopping paradise. From what he was carrying, he must have purchased himself a completely new wardrobe. Prada and Dolce and Gabbana labels could be clearly made out on the bags.

Personally, Alex didn't care much for fashion labels; the exceptions being articles from Harley Davidson and the Hard Rock Cafe, but collecting them was more of a hobby. Smiling, she was forced to rethink her position and admit that she was a label-junkie too. But not the sort who oriented herself around the latest trends from Paris, Milan or New York. Maybe there was a Harley shop here too? What she did between finishing work and eating dinner with Hugo wasn't anyone's business, after all.

"Nice outfit, George," she teased him, as they met Hugo in the lobby later. "I see you've remained true to your style."

"As have you," he replied. "Didn´t they have a bike in matching purple?"

"Oh, in-colours are so overrated," Alex shook her head.

"I see you've had a relaxing day while I've been working myself up over Roffarm," Hugo broke in jealously.

"Next time you need to rearrange your appointments," George goaded.

"It's not as easy as you make it sound," he countered, somewhat miffed.

"The hotel would certainly have had a bed for you last night," his colleague argued. "You could even have slept in my room."

"Well, yeah," deadpanned Hugo. "Maybe next time, but then preferably on Alex's sofa. So, where are we going to go through the slides for tomorrow?"

"A place in my room is priceless – but maybe your MasterCard limit is enough to keep George happy," Alex intervened, smiling.

"Let's stay here and look for a quiet table in the restaurant," George decided.

The researchers at Natioba were particularly interested in inverters and the different possible module designs, Alex informed her two colleagues. They wanted to discuss the specifications and limits of the new technology in detail at the meeting. Hugo's slides were slightly chaotic and in answering her questions about this or that, he often strayed from the subject.

He tried to explain everything at once, which in turn simply raised more questions. It was very obvious that he wanted to show just how much he knew. When talking about solar cells, he went into the most minute detail, eventually landing in the depths of the polymer's atomic structure. If discussing the demands made on inverters, his third change of topic would see him alight on bipolar junction transistors, used in chopper circuits. By this point he had lost Alex. She was only aware of choppers in the context of minimalist design motorcycles.

There were experts who were specially trained in the technical precision work, she thought to herself in moments like these. Things could get very tricky tomorrow if the detail-loving developers rounded on Hugo and formed their own little group.

The objectives for the next day were to provide an overview of the possibilities for module designs, to discuss inverter specifications and to consider the prospect of a joint project. That didn't mean Hugo should pitch his tent and start developing module architecture. That would be putting the cart before the horse. First they needed to find out which department in Natioba was in overall charge of implementing new technology. Was it the research lab in South Korea? Or was it the researchers – or even the developers – in Milan? They needed to read between the lines. George and Hugo edited the slides together and agreed who would take responsibility for each part of the presentation.

By way of conclusion, the younger of the two turned to Alex and said mischievously: "Remember, you're the flea tamer; you can rein us in if we go off-topic."

An apt turn of phrase, Alex thought to herself.

As it turned out, the discussion wasn't quite so hectic, although both Hugo and George went into too much detail on several occasions. Each one of Natioba's researchers was very interested; however, they spoke of a timeframe of up to seven years. That was beyond long-term and clearly contradicted what the research executive had told Alex in Como. It looked like there was still a lot of persuading to be done at the ground level.

Hugo promised to remain in contact with his counterparts at Natioba and exchange the latest technical information. Admittedly, Alex had hoped for more from the meeting; still, the outcome had been perfectly acceptable. She had briefly mentioned her meeting with Natioba's research executive at the start but hadn't once come back to it. She didn't want it to seem as though working with PsoraCom was a decree from on high.

Playing that sort of game could get dangerous pretty quickly. If the employees in question got the feeling they were being dictated to, they could rapidly dig their heels in and stall the project. PsoraCom already had a joint scheme in place with the development lab in Seoul, which would almost certainly further influence Italian headquarters.

"What a cryptic bunch of screwballs," George railed as they left the building. "They want to invent the future? They're more old-fashioned than their grandmothers!"

"Yes, they are a little sedate," Alex was forced to agree. "But we should keep in loose contact with them."

"Absolute bullshit!" George threw back at her. "It's a complete waste of time. I'm not going to give up another minute for them – and neither should you, Hugo."

"Believe me, I don't intend to," came the immediate response.

"Hang on a moment," Alex continued the debate. "I just promised to pass on further information in there. We have to deliver on that."

"We don't have to do anything," Hugo became worked up. "There are much more important things, like Roffarm."

"Sure," Alex tried to calm things down. "The project with Roffarm is more important for the moment. But promising to pass on information, and then failing to deliver, is no way to treat prospective clients."

"They will have forgotten about it by tomorrow anyway," George tried to placate her.

"Withdrawing silently is not something I'm prepared to do," she countered, slightly annoyed. "I'm the one responsible for this company after all. I'll make a suggestion to you. I'll put a few bits of information together from today's slides and send them off. We still don't know how much influence the research executive has. He could be important for us later and I have no intention of angering his people. There's also the fact that he asked me personally to keep them up-to-date. But I agree that we should watch how much time we invest."

"For all I care," growled Hugo.

"I wouldn't waste another second," George refused to let it go. "But it's your client, so do what you want."

"Good, then we're agreed," Alex decided.

Although she had also found the researchers sluggish (to put it mildly), she was nevertheless surprised by George's energetic outburst. During the meeting he hadn't been able to tell them enough, and now suddenly everything was different. But maybe she didn't need to understand: it was probably just one of his moods.

The next day she discussed how best to proceed with Thomas at the office; it was more than possible that things at PsoraCom were just different from what she was used to. In the power plant industry, projects were usually longer-term, often extending over several years. If a decision was made within a year, that was pretty quick. At PsoraCom, the wheel seemed to turn faster. The company had barely existed a decade, and developments – including all acquisitions – had been very rapid.

"How do you see it then?" Alex asked her boss. "The researchers in Italy are really thinking long-term, but I don't want to put our contact with them completely on ice."

"A lot of departments at PsoraCom, Robotics in particular, have very short project cycles," he replied. "Sometimes they're as little as two or three months. From that perspective, collaborating with the researchers would be a waste of time."

"That clears things up a bit," Alex nodded. "But we still don't know what role they play when it comes to implementing new technology."

"You said that the research executive was extremely open to innovation, didn't you?" Thomas enquired.

"Yeah, he is. He's just taken over the department. That's why it might be good for him to give them a little kick up the backside."

"At the end of the day, you're responsible for your own clients," her boss summarised. "That includes strategy too. Ultimately, we're paying you to base your decisions on your own independent assessment of things. Basically, though, I'd do as you said: keep in loose contact with them but reduce your time investment to a minimum – and include your colleagues only when absolutely necessary."

"Thanks, that's exactly what I had in mind."

"Why did you ask then?"

"I just wanted to check."

"Fine, but the next time it'll cost you!"

"No problem, I'll buy you a coffee."

During conversations with Marco, Thomas or Wolfgang, Alex had heard again and again that PsoraCom didn't give any of their direct clients preferential treatment when dealing with end customers. Rather, they worked with any company that the end customer chose. This approach didn't put PsoraCom at a disadvantage because their client list already included a number of big solar module manufacturers; indeed, it meant that, with the help of the end customer, more companies could be won as future clients. Hugo characterised the approach as agnostic, but that didn't really get to the heart of it, in Alex's opinion.

To prepare for the next joint meeting with Luxumi, Alex had arranged a phone conference with George and his client. The aim of the conversation was to ensure that Hursoc had no expectations regarding preferential treatment. She had liaised with George beforehand and made her objectives clear. She wanted to undertake a development project with Luxumi. For that, they needed a partner not only to build the solar modules, but to design and construct the inverters.

Hursoc, an established supplier of their end customer for years, covered both bases. If Luxumi decided on George's client, all the better; but she would not insist on Hursoc's involvement. She knew too little about her end customer's objectives for that.

On their way to the client the next day, George spoke on his phone non-stop. It sounded like some financial transaction or another, but it could equally have been about betting or horses. Although the salaries at PsoraCom were very generous, George seemed to need other means of funding his expensive lifestyle. Likewise on the way back, the first thing he did was reach for his phone.

"Tanker ships," George said meaningfully, once he had finally finished his conversation. "I can thoroughly recommend them as an investment – you'll make an absolute packet."

"Aha!" She took note of his explanation. "Tell me, how do you think the meeting went just now?"

"Brilliant! It was fantastic! Exactly how things should be. Why?"

"I'm not so sure," she replied hesitantly. "The guy the head of development brought along is probably important in the decision-making process. He already knew your contact at Hursoc, but he didn't seem too happy with the slides."

"What do you mean? The slides were fine," George replied.

"Well, I found them extremely high-flown," Alex said, "but not particularly comprehensive. The head of development seemed to feel the same way. He asked twice how far Hursoc were with the implementation and seemed particularly interested in inverters. But the answers he got were never anything more than vague."

"What're they supposed to say?" George defended his client. "There haven't been any concrete developments yet; we know that. But puff is part of the trade."

"Of course. But you shouldn't raise such high expectations if it's not clear when they can be achieved. In my opinion, it would be better to keep cool and be more honest."

"Oh, come on, it's fine," he said decisively. "They've known each other for years. Besides, they've agreed to a joint project. What more do you want? Hursoc is the ideal partner. They can develop both the modules and the inverter. You're killing two birds with one stone. It's the best thing for Luxumi, and they know that."

"I'm still not sure," Alex remained hesitant. "The head of development might have agreed, but I don't think he was completely convinced."

"Oh, you're imagining things," George waved her reservations aside.

"Maybe you're right," she conceded. "But I'll get in touch with the developer as promised to discuss how we can take things further. That way, I'll see if anything's still unclear."

"You'll see: we'll have the first plant up and running inside two years."

"That really would be very quick."

Alex was more than doubtful about the last point, but chose to keep her thoughts to herself. Maybe she had missed something or was just being too sceptical. At the end of the day, the guy from Hursoc had known his client for longer than she had.

The partners of PsoraCom employees were invited to the company's annual summer party as well. Sandro had accepted. Alex was sitting together with Thomas, Carl and a few others from the office in the big tent, which had been erected on the lawn next to the building. Festively decorated round tables with upholstered chairs had been laid out on a durable, black carpet. The sides of the tent had been rolled up, though the heat of the day still lingered in the air. There wasn't the faintest hint of a breeze. The sun wouldn't go down for a few hours yet, radiating warmth until the glorious summer day came to an end. Exotic-looking cocktails were served as refreshments and the lavish buffet was enough to make your mouth water.

George had just arrived and, after a quick hello, went straight to the bar at the other end of the tent. He was speaking to the barman and gesticulating excitedly. Seconds later, he turned round abruptly and began to make his way back.

"They're total imbeciles," he was worked up. "No whisky before dinner. Only piss-warm beer and red wine. As if half an hour makes a difference. That's too much for me; I'm going home."

He stormed out of the tent without another word. Thomas shrugged his shoulders and went to the buffet. Alex's gaze followed George in surprise.

"What's up with him?" Carl wondered. "My wife will go mad when I tell her what's on offer here."

"No idea; but they certainly haven't skimped on anything have they?" she agreed.

"She would've really liked to come," he continued, "but it wouldn't have made any sense to bring the little ones. Here, take a look: photos of my little pumpkins at the zoo."

Carl spoke affectionately about his two kids. He was a real family man and very proud too – you could tell just by looking at him. Thomas ate in silence and listened to their conversation without contributing a single word, as usual. Hugo and Brian were nowhere to be seen. There was no sign of Sandro either and Alex was beginning to get annoyed. While Carl was getting ready to go home, Thomas stood up to get himself a glass of wine.

"Shall I get one for you too?" he asked her.

She nodded.

"See if you can find a free space outside," he said. "The noise is getting a bit much in here and the DJ's about to start."

Groups of dark-brown rattan sofas and chairs with off-white fabric covering stood invitingly on the lawn. Lots of people had already made themselves at home, but there were still two free seats at a small table a little further back.

Alex looked at her boss in surprise, as he pulled out a leather case and pipe from his inside jacket pocket.

"This is a Bang pipe," he said. The way he stressed it implied it was extremely valuable. While he was filling it, Alex read the tobacco box: Navy Flake Cut.

"Traditional Danish tobacco, cut and pressed into thin blocks," he explained. "The production method stems from the old days, when sailors' provisions were rationed. In those days, the tobacco was pressed into the smallest volume possible because there was only limited storage space on the ships. That's why most of them have names that allude to the navy in some way."

She could hardly stifle a grin, as she saw him puffing away contentedly in his chair. It suited him somehow.

"So, where's your boat, then?" she winked at him jokingly.

"I've got one yacht on Lake Chiemsee," he replied seriously.

"Of course, and I suppose the other one's in the Bahamas."

"I actually do have two boats. Do you know anything about sailing?"

"No, nothing at all."

"One of them is called Bavaria Vision; it's almost thirteen metres long and riding anchor on the Bavarian Sea. Whenever the weather allows, I go sailing there and spend the whole weekend on board."

"That's a pretty nice hobby."

"There's nothing better on a mild summer's night than to be way out at sea, lying under a clear starry sky without a care in the world. You take breakfast at sunrise in full view of the burning red Kampenwand. You don't need much sleep on the water because of the trance-like state it induces."

"And where's your second boat?"

"In Monte Carlo. I've got a Carver 44 Sojourn motor yacht there. But most of the time I just rent it out to a broker; I only fly out once or twice a year for a long weekend."

"For the Formula One?"

"Absolutely not! It's far too chaotic for me these days, and all those VIPs with their wannabe starlets – they really rub me up the wrong way. In the old days I would watch the race with my parents; when there was still real glamour and elegance outside the palace. I've been renting out our holiday home in the hills above the centre for years as well. Along with the boat, it's not a bad source of income. But it's the only thing I still have in common with the beautiful, rich people down there in the city."

"Not bad! It almost sounds as if you don't need to work at all."

Thomas knocked out his pipe and stuffed it back in its case. He left her question hanging unanswered in the air.

"I'm going to head home," he said instead.

Only now did Alex realise that Sandro hadn't been in touch. He hadn't even sent her a message. She didn't fancy going home yet and so joined a few colleagues huddled around one of the bistro tables. Henry was there too, telling everyone how he had been regent for the development executive.

"Alex really saved my bacon," he said, as he extinguished his cigarette.

"Oh, Henry," Alex tried to put the mockers on him. "You're exaggerating everything."

"No, it's absolutely true. Within no time at all, this woman here set up a high-level meeting with her client. And when she produced the spherical seed unit from her pocket, well, even our executive was impressed."

"What kind of spherical seed unit?" one of her colleagues wanted to know.

"It's a new design, using the standardised bend-modules we hope to employ for our Vabilmo technology," Alex explained. "There are only a few seed units at the moment, which our colleagues from the US were good enough to send over for a meeting."

"And what exactly is Vabilmo technology?" asked another person.

Somehow she felt a bit like a circus attraction. While she was explaining everything, Alex was forced to admit that it wasn't such a bad feeling. Quite the opposite, in fact.

"Hey, Henry, is everything set for that charity event?" she changed the subject after a while; it was a company party after all, not a sales pitch. Her colleague had recently mentioned that he was helping organise a benefit volleyball tournament.

"Almost," his brow furrowed. "The planning's sorted, but we still need team T-shirts. I wanted to do something a bit different there. A little mascot or something. If you have any good ideas, let's hear them."

"Let me think," said Alex. "It's got to be something that reflects charity in some way, and if possible it should have something to do with energy or sport, don't you think?"

"I suppose," he agreed.

"OK," she continued to think aloud, "then I'd create a character based on a comic strip. A hero that fights for good against evil. Something very striking: with extraordinary powers generated by solar energy, perhaps."

"Sounds really good," Henry nodded. "I think you're in a creative mood – I'll get you a glass of wine so you can keep your flow."

Alex nodded absently; her head was positively buzzing with ideas. By the time Henry returned with her drink, she had created a solar hero.

"What do you think about this?" she asked, enjoying a sip of her wine, before letting him in on her idea. "The character is highly developed, technologically speaking. Fine wiring, made of isolated, metallurgic material, extends across its body, and is injected into it in the form of nanoparticles. The wires are highly conductive, meaning the character can use the electric energy as a mobile generator, source of heat, or electric weapon, depending on what's required. The energy needed to generate electricity is obtained through the character's double-layered costume. The outside consists of durable aramid fibres, coated with dye-sensitized solar cells; the inside is a flat type battery used to store energy."

"If you've already thought of all that, you must have come up with a name too," Henry joked.

"That depends," she grinned, "on whether you want a male or female character."

"Female, without doubt!" he replied in mock indignation. "You're the one who created her after all; besides female heroes are so sexy, with their skin-tight outfits."

"That's what I thought," she gave him a nudge. "What do you think of the name "Effusiolara"?

"Effusiolara? That sounds very Italian."

"You're absolutely right; it's a combination of effusione and solar. In Italian, effusione means warmth, radiance, but also warm-heartedness."

"So the character radiates energy generated by sunlight," Henry continued her train of thought, "and in doing good, she displays warmth."

"Exactly so, my dear. By the way, in terms of colours I'd use a very dark purple – an allusion to the solar cell dye – and cream. And if you do print T-shirts of this sexy hero, I want one!"

"Of course," her colleague promised. "But I'll need to take your measurements. Let's have a look."

"Don't you dare!"

"It was only a joke; I'll see if I can rustle something up in Small."

She headed home at midnight and heard Sandro's car just as she was opening the front door.

"How come you weren't there?" she asked, disappointed.

"I didn't have any time. If you had as much work as I do at the moment, you wouldn't even need to ask."

"You could've at least told me."

"What am I supposed to do? You must know if I'm not there, it's because I'm still busy. You've seen how hard I've been working these last few months."

"But you've known about the party for ages. If it was important to you, you would have made time for it."

She was torn. On the one hand, she knew what having a lot of work was like; on the other, she was hurt that the evening hadn't been important enough to him. Moreover, midnight was very late, even by his standards. Perhaps they needed a few days' time out together, just the two of them. Maybe their holiday on the North Sea had been too short. She decided to speak to him about it at the weekend.

In the next team meeting, Thomas sat down to the right of Alex.

"Why don't you sit on my sunny side," she asked George, as he entered.

"Nothing would give me greater pleasure," he replied.

Evidently, Hugo had come from the hairdresser, as his curls seemed more artfully dishevelled than usual. Alex couldn't resist the joke.

"Hey, Hugo, did you stick your hand in a plug socket this morning by mistake?"

He appeared to be in a good mood and joined in the fun. "Yeah, in the one with the heavy current. If you're going do something, you may as well do it properly!"

"You've got to take care though," George was involved now too, "hair's not the only thing that curls up. You know that we men share 90% of the same genes as domestic pigs."

Even Thomas couldn't resist a grin.

"Who's got themselves a pig?" Carl asked, having heard only the last snatches of the conversation. He came through the door with Brian, the latter dragging his trolley behind him as usual.

"No-one, and nothing's curling so far," Hugo said smiling, indicating below his belt.

"OK, boys. Enough talk. Let's make a start." The flea tamer had spoken.

The main focus this time was Brian and Carl's trip to Asia the previous week. Alex had only heard about it in passing. Although they weren't planning to request direct assistance from their Asian colleagues until later, it seemed like Wolfgang had finally given in to Brian's non-stop chivvying.

Since there were some robot manufacturers based in Asia, Carl had gone with him. They were now presenting a summary of their seven client meetings. Brian described each company and meeting in such detail that there was little time left for Carl's overview.

"We have to send Hugo to Asia for a few weeks as soon as possible," Brian concluded his report. "He needs to train our people there so that they're able to take on projects of their own."

"Absolutely not," George countered immediately. "Hugo is needed here. There's no way he's going anywhere! We have to restrict ourselves to Europe for the time being."

"I can't do that as well," Hugo yammered. "Roffarm's taking up most of my time as it is. Then there's Hursoc and the rest. It's not possible. I'm already at my limit."

"Although Asia does have its nose in front when it comes to certain technical aspects," George considered his position. "I have to contradict myself here: maybe it's not such a bad idea at all. But then we need a second Hugo."

"There's only one of me!" the response came like a shot.

"You know what I mean," George calmed him.

"The results sound very promising, and intensive training for our colleagues on the ground would be a possible solution," Thomas intervened before an extensive debate arose. "But our resources are limited. That's why we need to consider each company's potential separately in terms of the team strategy. Only then can we assess how much support our sales colleagues in Asia need and to what extent Hugo, Brian or George should be brought in."

"Most of them over there had never had anything to do with Vabilmo," Brian voiced his concerns. "No-one has any idea."

"How much time do you think it would take to prepare and carry out the technical training?" Alex asked Hugo.

After exchanging a quick glance with George, he surprisingly replied: "Two to three months for sure!"

"We can't invest that much time at the moment," Thomas shook his head and turned to Brian and Carl. "I suggest you collate all the facts about potential and expenditure. Hugo, you draw up a more precise timeframe, including work packages. We'll make a decision then."

Carl nodded conscientiously; Hugo chuntered away; and Brian muttered something into his goatee.

7

July

Sandro's birthday was on a Thursday. They had toasted it at midnight with a glass of Prosecco, and Alex had given him his present: a small SSD camcorder, the best of the latest mid-range models. In their first year, she had given him a conventional HD video camera. She had bought it for a good price from a friend, but unfortunately it had gone on the blink. Repairing it would have been exceedingly expensive. She hoped to assuage her conscience with this new camcorder, thus replacing a present that had proved inadequate. Sandro was speechless at first but soon reacted completely unexpectedly.

"This is way too much!" he complained, standing up abruptly.

"What do you mean? Are you not happy?" Alex wondered.

"It makes me really uncomfortable! Such an expensive gift!"

"But you don't even know how much I paid for it. Besides, the price is irrelevant; what's important is that I want to give it to you."

"Still."

"I just wanted to treat you, since your other one broke last year. Who knows how long I'll be able to do something like this."

He stood stock still. In the same moment, Alex knew it was going to turn into another one of those stupid misunderstandings that neither of them needed. She could already see how he was relating everything back to himself and his income. He had got it into his head that he didn't earn enough in her eyes to support a family. That was absolutely not true, but he had always had a complex about it. She had only acted on her assumptions. If she really was looking after a child at home with no income of her own, there was no way she would just spend his money on a camera or similar gadget: she couldn't imagine spending it on anything other than their family.

All this was due to her being used to having her own money. She had started working at fifteen, and had worked here and there all the way through her studies, sometimes even with an office job in the afternoon and bar work in the evening. Her parents had provided as much financial support as they could, but had been careful at the same time. The sweater she had bought with her first pay check was still hanging in her wardrobe.

Besides, she found it easy to spend money on other people. Giving gifts was something she enjoyed, irrespective of their monetary value. It was their spiritual worth – the joy – that mattered. It was too esoteric an approach for Sandro, and it frustrated her that he didn't understand her way of thinking. If he surprised her by tidying the cellar or cleaning the windows while she was away on business, then her joy was as unconfined as his had been when he received the first camera. But it seemed as if her attempt to make things up to him hadn't worked; it was now a question of damage limitation.

"You can see it as both of us gaining something. The camcorder's yours – but either of us can use it on holiday."

With an exaggerated wink, she added: "That is, if you let me borrow it, of course."

"You know I would," he let himself be persuaded hesitantly.

To seal the reconciliation, she took his hand and led him into the bedroom.

The next evening, she hoped to make him genuinely happy with his favourite meal: a Sicilian fish ragout with king-prawns. Just now, she was preparing the dough for the Focaccia; the Prosecco aperitif and mango mousse dessert were ready to be served; while the Chianti Classico Riserva was standing in its carafe, breathing silently and waiting to be poured.

Sandro's appetite was huge. When he thanked her with a passionate kiss over Café Corretto and Sambuca, it seemed as if everything was going to plan.

"What do you think about going to Prague at the end of the month?" she asked.

Sandro gazed thoughtfully out of the window.

"We could visit your relatives in Palermo instead, of course," Alex added quickly, "if that's what you'd prefer. But I thought it would be nice to spend a few days together, just the two of us."

He waited a long time before giving his answer, and Alex didn't press him.

"That's probably doable," he seemed to be going over the work he'd need to take care of in his head. "My client is on holiday for a fortnight from the last week of July anyway. I've never been to Prague."

Prague was one of her favourite cities and she was looking forward to showing him around. They hadn't done very much as a couple recently. Since their return from the North Sea, there had been a tennis tournament every weekend. During the week, Sandro had mostly worked late or gone to the club. Likewise Alex had been hard at work on the Natioba project, and her calls with Hank, Chris and Nobu had often taken up several hours in the evening. At the weekends, when Sandro was at the club or playing tournaments, she had done something with Anna and Renata or gone to visit her parents.

Carl was the only one from the team who dialled in regularly for the weekly phone conferences with Hank. Actually, that wasn't quite true, as Brian was often on the line as well. But he didn't participate in any of the discussions about developments in Robotics. She wasn't even sure if he was listening – or if he was there at all.

George had taken part on just the first few occasions, and her fourth colleague only managed it when his tight schedule allowed. Hugo often logged out after just half an hour: there was always something more important. He had spoken directly to Hank once about the Natioba project, and had cancelled his phone call with Chris at short notice for the second time. It was Alex's client who had told her that, with palpable surprise. Hugo's lack of involvement in the Natioba project rankled somehow; he didn't seem to have any interest in it.

Carl had inherited a project from George that he was to handle independently. A few years ago Hursoc had created a new department that developed and sold solar modules for smaller applications. Carl's task was to sound out whether there was any business potential there.

In the meetings with Hank, he would give regular progress reports. That's how Alex knew Hugo was assisting him and she wondered why he wasn't doing the same for Natioba. Admittedly, the project was currently underway in the US and Seoul but client HQ was in Italy. Was it because of the time difference in New York and the potentially longer hours he'd have to do in the evening? Was the greenhouse prototype too far removed from the sort of power plants he was working on with Roffarm? Nominally, Natioba's potential was considerable, greater perhaps even than Roffarm's. It was a mystery.

If everything went according to plan with the development lab in Seoul, then there'd be more work in store with the Italians. She'd been certain of that since her meeting with Chris in San Francisco. He would move heaven and earth to ensure that the pilot project became a global market product. But that wouldn't happen without Italy or Hugo. Unless Thomas got the OK to employ another architect sometime soon, that is – but they couldn't count on that.

Perhaps Hugo shared George's opinion, that the Natioba project was nothing more than a gimmick dreamed up by a bunch of amateurs. He had to have some reason because he was only supposed to be spending half his time on Roffarm. She couldn't imagine that the project with Hursoc was taking up the remainder of his working day. If it was, however, they had a problem. She would have to speak with Hugo directly. And sooner rather than later. From her point of view, the project with Natioba was just as likely to be successful – or unsuccessful – as the ones with Roffarm or Hursoc.

For more than an hour, Hugo complained that he couldn't keep up with his mails, that he had countless phone conferences scheduled and that he was already doing too much overtime because of Roffarm and Hursoc. He couldn't look after Natioba as well. After all, he had to keep a few hours free during the week for client meetings, in order to act as a technical consultant. It made perfect sense, but he could have told her all that in fifteen minutes.

Hugo had mentioned at least ten different companies that were right at the bottom of the list agreed at the strategy meeting. They were only supposed to be considered if there was time to spare. Natioba was quite clearly on the priority list, straight after Roffarm and Hursoc, what's more, and followed by Premve.

He waved her argument aside angrily, explaining that some of the other companies were needed for the Roffarm project from a technical standpoint. She simply wasn't privy to all the plans. But that was precisely the reason there was a separate Roffarm team, Alex thought to herself. Hugo was supposed to assist with his architectural knowledge, before passing the baton on to his colleagues and slowly taking leave of the project.

But Hugo wasn't accountable to her. She might be able to express the personal opinion that he had taken on more work than agreed, or failed to get his priorities straight; but openly saying so in front of others wasn't part of her remit. That was up to Thomas, if anybody. He was obliged to have regular meetings with other team members and assess their progress in terms of the set objectives, just as he did with her. One thing was for sure: sooner or later there was going to be a problem.

It looked like a project would shortly be underway with Premve, providing the meeting with the investigation committee went well. Meanwhile, Luxumi had agreed to a joint project with Hursoc, although Alex didn't think that was set in stone yet. As far as technical support was concerned, they needed a solution, and fast. She looked in her diary and pencilled in a meeting with Thomas.

Hank called and asked Alex for her help. It was about the presentation at the developer conference.

"Hey," Hank began. "Taipei has been confirmed as the venue. Now I just need a few more details about Natioba, their capability and how we hope to proceed. It's for our CEO's assistant."

"OK, no problem; I'll send you a few slides from my account plan," Alex said. "When do you need them?"

"The next two days would be good. Any additional information about your strategy in general would also be very helpful. I'm still not sure exactly how it all fits together. But at the moment there's an itsy-bitsy chance that our project could be built in to the CEO's opening speech."

Alex paused; she couldn't believe what she was hearing. "Hang on! What did you say? Tell me again!"

"There's a small chance our project could be unveiled by the CEO himself," Hank repeated.

"That'd be amazing!" she cried enthusiastically. "Tell me what you need and I'll get it for you. For an opportunity like this, I'm quite happy to put in a few extra night shifts."

"It won't be quite as bad as that," he reassured her. "But see what you can put together. The CEO's assistant is quite taken by the project and wants to have a closer look. Ultimately, the opening speech is about revealing significant new developments and collaborations to the public for the first time."

"Then I'll be sure to concentrate on innovations and business potential," she resolved.

"If they go for us," her colleague explained, "we'll need to see what we can incorporate into the speech. When the focus is on products, there are usually seed units on display. Unfortunately the greenhouse has the same dimensions as a standard forty-foot cargo container. It's more than debatable whether there'll be enough room for it on stage."

"You mean we might even be able to put the whole greenhouse on show?" Alex asked. "That'd be fantastic!"

"Yeah, there's a chance."

"OK, I'll get down to the presentation and send if off as soon as possible. It'll be in such a way that you can just pass it straight on to the assistant."

"That's great. Thanks, Alex."

"Maybe the MOU will've been signed by then as well," she finished. "I'll see how things are looking with Seoul."

There were numerous ideas swirling around inside Alex's head. What did they need to consider if their project was to be part of the opening speech? If the greenhouse container didn't fit on the stage, what could they use instead? If it did, what overheads would they have to factor in? How high would transport costs be? Who would cover them? Would there be enough sunlight in the exhibition hall? Where exactly in Taipei was the conference taking place? What did the building look like? Could a container be transported inside? How long would it take to ship to Taipei?

The question of where the greenhouse would be assembled during the project had been under debate for some time. A suitable building had presented itself on the East River in Brooklyn, New York. It was easily accessible from Hank's Manhattan office but nevertheless remotely situated in an uninviting-looking dockyard. There were several old containers lying around the grounds already; an additional one would hardly stand out. But the solar modules and reservoir needed to be camouflaged because of the secrecy agreement. The seed units for the cells came from California and, if necessary, a fresh supply could be delivered overnight. There would be one small problem once everything had been completed, however: namely, that the forty-foot container would have to be shipped to Seoul – which could take weeks. Building separate greenhouses in both places would have been somewhat inopportune at this late stage, and would only have further escalated costs.

It had been agreed that each party would bear the relevant project costs. PsoraCom would pay for the solar cells and had negotiated a deal with the design firm in California. The purchase of the container together with the necessary greenhouse components, as well as the costs of adapting the inverter, would be borne by Natioba; they would cover transport too.

After a great deal of to-ing and fro-ing, it had been decided that Natioba should put the final container together in Seoul. The lab was situated close to the airport and was, by Korean standards at least, generously proportioned. At the same time, however, a set of robot arms had been ordered for New York, so they could carry out real tests there – as opposed to mere computer simulations.

Hank and Chris would send the parts they had used separately by plane and relocate to Seoul for the last few weeks of the project. Besides the modification of the inverter and the design of the solar modules, the most important things were good planning and a clear definition of the individual project interfaces. If the interfaces were well enough thought out, then there was little that could go wrong when it came to the final assembly. Still, Murphy's Law could strike at any time; in which case it was a simple question of staying flexible and finding a workaround.

Even though her ears had already started to burn from the numerous phone calls, Alex tried to reach the development lab supervisor in Seoul. Sandro still wasn't home but tonight she really didn't mind. The chance that the project could be part of the opening speech at the developer conference had infected her with energy.

"You must be calling about the MOU," the lab supervisor greeted her. "I haven't had time to look at it yet."

"Actually I'm calling for a different reason," Alex confessed. "You know how we're planning to unveil the greenhouse at our developer conference in autumn – Taipei's been chosen as the venue by the way – well, there's a possibility we could get a mention in the CEO's opening speech. It's just a chance, mind, nothing's set in stone."

"That sounds right up my street," he replied. "A real Big Bang. What do you need from my end to turn the chance into a sure-fire certainty?"

"At the moment, I'm working on a few slides for the CEO's assistant: he's the one who decides if we have a chance or not in the first instance. If he approves, he'll submit our presentation to the CEO, who then makes the final decision. There are two things that interest our top dog above everything else: revenue and technology. From you, then, we'd need current and planned figures for off-grid systems, with a special focus on your greenhouses' potential, as well as anticipated developments in robotics and building-integrated plants. Second, it would be good to have an overview of which projects were developed in your lab and then placed on the market by Natioba. Product development times are of particular interest here. Like any other American company, we're all about the facts and figures. We have to show the CEO that the project isn't just technical mumbo-jumbo with no market potential, otherwise we won't get a look-in."

"I'll see what I can do for you. Some of the figures are for internal use only of course. But we'll find something."

"It certainly couldn't hurt," she added, "to have the MOU signed already. My colleagues need the slides by tomorrow evening, their time. But please don't let that pressure you."

"At the end of the day, I'm the one who authorises it; it just needs to go through Legal first. I'll see that it's checked immediately and then submitted for signature. I'll have the figures for you by tomorrow."

After she had hung up, Alex got to work on the slides, drawing up a list at the same time. She wanted everything to be perfect; after all, the decision would dictate how they proceeded. If they really were to make it into the opening speech, there were a number of things that needed to be clarified. How could the project be demonstrated on stage? Could they somehow make a prototype from the additional set of robot arms? How could they ensure there was enough sunlight? Would they need to shoot a film about the greenhouse? How could they highlight the size difference between the Vabilmo and the amorphous thin-film cells?

There were even more questions from Natioba's end. Would they need the approval of Italian HQ? Interested readers would instantly associate the name Natioba with the parent company. The lab supervisor and Alex were both more than aware of that. These were questions that Alex's client would have to answer. She had learned from Hank that the order of events was scripted – and it was possible they could influence what happened.

After two hours she stared wearily down at her list, a comprehensive roll-call of points that needed taking care of. The only thing for sure was that it was a massive opportunity. And even if they didn't make it into the opening speech, the exhibition was bound to create waves in the industry.

"You won't believe the call I took yesterday," Alex ambushed her boss in the office the next morning. "Come on, I'll buy you a coffee; you look as if you could use one."

Although he had only just arrived, he put off checking his mails. Normally he wouldn't have let himself get distracted. It couldn't have been because of the coffee joke, since everyone made the same one. Hot drinks still didn't cost anything at PsoraCom.

"What is it that's got you so fit to burst?" Thomas asked curiously.

Henry was standing by one of the tables in the coffee room. He was taking advantage of his morning cigarette break to read his mails. He had got himself a Zeus68 as well, after seeing Alex's.

"Wait for it," she stalled her boss, sweetening his coffee the way he liked it. "Hank called yesterday evening to say there was a chance we might get a mention in the opening speech at the developer conference. He asked me to put together a presentation on our project and overall objectives, which he could then submit to the CEO's assistant. I spoke with Natioba yesterday as well. I wanted to clarify what we should include in the part about our general strategy. I can show you what I've got so far afterwards."

"That doesn't sound too bad," Thomas praised her. "It would mean the CEO publicly declaring his support for Vabilmo, which would make things a great deal easier for us."

"That's exactly what I thought too," she agreed. "The Roffarm contract's been mentioned in the press, but nothing more. It would be good to show the market that there are other companies not only interested in our technology, but ready to implement it. In my opinion, we don't need to give any details about how far along we are. That the technology is purpose-adapted should speak for itself."

She was having trouble concealing her excitement. Although nothing was guaranteed, the chance of a mention like this had been so unexpected.

Admittedly, there had been various press releases about the Roffarm contract; its exact contents, however, had not been revealed. The developer conference in Taipei would be the first public presentation of the Vabilmo team's work. It was set to be a huge success.

Thomas nodded thoughtfully.

"First Roffarm, now Natioba," he nodded approval. "You're right: it could certainly create a few waves."

"I'm pretty sure it will, boss. I've seen it happen before. Some companies want to be the first to implement new technology, while others prefer to wait and see. But when two or more players back the same horse, even the more reluctant ones begin to crawl out of the woodwork."

"Good, then let's go through your slides together when they're finished."

Thomas went to get himself another coffee and Alex seized the opportunity with both hands.

"One more thing," she began. "I'm concerned that sooner or later we're going to reach a fork in the road in terms of technical support. I spoke with Hugo yesterday. He's not only heavily involved in the Roffarm project but also with the relevant partners. The technical specifications for the new inverters as well as the architectural design of the modules both have to come from him. He needs to attend client meetings in person to provide support. Currently he doesn't have the resources for additional projects like Natioba – at least, that's what he said yesterday. It's hardly critical at the moment, but there are potentially two more work packages in the pipeline with Premve and Luxumi, and that's only my clients. We haven't even factored in those of Brian or Carl, let alone the training sessions for our colleagues in Asia. What's your take on it?"

"Exactly the same as yours. What we really need is a second Hugo."

"How can we find a solution? There's no-one else joining the team for the time being, is there? That's what Wolfgang seemed to say last time."

"That's right. We're not planning to take on any new staff this year. Whether we'd be able to get another architect at such short notice is debatable, anyway. I'll talk to Wolfgang. Maybe someone from the Roffarm team can provide a temporary solution."

The telephone conference with the Americans from Bill's division took place every fourth Thursday of the month as usual. It was similar to the meeting with Hank, only this time the emphasis was placed on solar power plants. Anything to do with robots was dealt with in passing, if at all. The focus was on the technical feasibility and implementation of existing projects – and thus primarily on Roffarm and the progress with Hursoc.

Up until now, Alex had participated regularly. With Premve and Luxumi, she could only give sales progress reports. The project with Natioba, on the other hand, was really beginning to take shape, although it was something of a hybrid. Historically speaking, grid-connected-plant and off-grid-systems manufacturers counted as end customers and were handled by specialists from Bill's division.

However, this particular project had ended up in the machine and robotics vertical, as they were the ones responsible for the new bend-modules chosen by Chris. The way things would go from here wouldn't be revealed until after the pilot project. In contrast to Bill's sector, there was no group in Robotics dedicated to the latest applications for polymer-based cells. At the moment, it was just Hank.

The potential project with Premve was likewise neither fish nor fowl. Until it was decided who was responsible internally for such matters, it was left to Alex to give separate progress reports to both divisions. The news about the presentation at the developer conference in Taipei was generally well received. She only made passing mention of the opening speech. There was a brief murmur of approval before they moved on to the next item.

Henry must have got wind of something in the coffee room that morning or during their phone call.

"Come on, I'll buy you a coffee," he surprised her at her desk.

"Here or somewhere else?"

"Well, here of course!"

"Good to know how much I'm worth to you!" she laughed.

"So, tell me, what's the latest on Natioba? Did I hear something about the developer conference?" he asked curiously.

"At the moment, we're working on a project with the development lab in Seoul," she said. "We want to unveil it at the developer conference."

"I didn't even know Natioba was based in Korea. What kind of project is it?"

"It's to do with organic greenhouses," she explained, "where fresh vegetables are cultivated with the help of robots. It all happens completely autonomously. The robots sow and plant the vegetables, and then harvest them at the end. The electricity needed in the container is generated by our new solar cells, of course. We're hoping to put the container on display at the developer conference. We might even get a mention in the opening speech, though that's still not clear."

"That's great; you'll get some real publicity for it," he grinned. "With a tasty dressing, you could even offer the salad to people as a snack – that would be brilliant."

"That's not such a bad idea. I'll have to remember it," Alex said, in all seriousness.

"Every year we invite more than a hundred journalists and bloggers to the conference," Henry mentioned. "What we show is then reported in a number of different media. They'll get hungry at some stage and could really go for something like that, especially if I make it sound appetising."

"Are you going to be there?" Alex probed.

"Absolutely," he left her in no doubt. "The invites are always highly sought after and even traded on the internet. I'll be responsible for more than two dozen reporters from Germany alone. It's just like a flea circus."

"I know exactly what you mean," she assured him with a smile.

Henry had already been to Taipei once before and right now he was in a chatty mood. Although the conference centre was actually part of the World Trade Centre, it was fifteen minutes away by car and had been opened only recently. According to his description, there were two exhibition levels, with the exhibitors' stands typically located on the ground floor. The presentations took place on the first floor; and that would also be where the CEO declared the conference open.

Alex could get a rough picture from the photos on Henry's net-phone, but she'd need to find more detailed information online. Their exhibit couldn't fit into a handbag, nor could it be displayed simply on a table. Still, she had her first impression of the centre – and the salad snack idea wasn't half bad.

Sandro was already home and surprised Alex by taking her to dinner in town. The rustic nature of the restaurant brought her back to the reality of village life; the sort of reality where Taipei could easily be mistaken for a type of martial art. After the second glass of wine, Sandro began complaining about how things stood with his project.

"I can write off all the overtime I've been doing this last week. My client won't give me a single cent for it."

"That's really bad," she offered her support. "What did you negotiate with him beforehand?"

"Not enough! It's always difficult to gauge with a project like this; there are so many unknowns. He's taking advantage as usual. It's a question of the contract extension now, and my basis for negotiation is weak."

"A tricky one," she agreed. "If he renews your contract, you've got a secure income for the next few months. But did one of your friends not mention a company that's looking for people with exactly your background?"

"Yeah, that was Ralf," he replied. "But I don't know much about it yet."

"Have you even spoken to them?"

"Not yet. When would I find the time?"

"If you're serious about finding an alternative to that bloodsucker, then you'll just have to make the time. Ralf might be able to help, but he can't do everything for you."

"I'm well aware of that! I just don't know when I can possibly get it done. I'd have to make them a detailed quote."

"But the job description itself fits, doesn't it?" she wanted to know. "They're looking for someone who knows about medical sensors. You don't find experts like you just anywhere."

"I'd definitely have a good chance," he agreed. "I match their profile pretty clearly."

"Well then, if you can't deal with your current client anymore, you'll just have to bite the bullet and set aside a few hours somehow. You don't get anything for free in the business world, sadly. But all this hassle will finish you in the long run."

"You're right. I'll speak to Ralf again, if I can get hold of him, that is."

That night she lay awake for a while thinking about their conversation. In the end it was his decision, and he was the one who'd have to live with the consequences. Either he accepted another contract from a troublesome client without having to make an effort, or he strained to win a new client, who was at least supposed to be fair. If she had to bet on it, Alex knew which option he would choose.

It was no different in their relationship. When it came to joint activities, it was mostly Alex who took the lead. It didn't matter if it was flat hunting or decisions about where and when they went on holiday. Skiing in March had been her idea; he had neither prepared things the night before nor set the alarm for the next day. It was the same for the North Sea and their planned holiday in Prague.

Unless you placed a gun to his head and forced him to make a decision, then nothing happened. But that was a side of him she'd have to learn to accept, even if it didn't come easy. It just wasn't one of his strengths. In its place, she loved his almost childlike naivety; it had brought something innocent and open into their relationship. Like when he stood proudly in the kitchen after cooking dinner or when he drew a comic character offering her a bouquet of flowers. In contrast to many other people she knew, he hadn't built a wall around himself.

That made him vulnerable, but also authentic. You always knew where you were with him. Even if their relationship didn't always run smoothly, she knew she wanted to spend the rest of her life with him. Maybe she could be too ambitious sometimes and wanted everything all at once. Maybe she set the bar too high. As she turned over and put her arm around him, she was surprised to find him return the gesture in his sleep.

Alex preferred pictorial representations to running text. She went through the charts and diagrams that described the Natioba project together with Thomas.

"Where did you get that photo?" he asked, astonished. "I've never seen anything like it."

"I made it with special image editing software," she said, not without pride. "It contains everything currently outlined in the project plan."

"It looks deceptively real – just as you'd imagine it."

"Well, it can't be blown up any further," she admitted, "or you'd see it was just a photomontage."

"You've even included the robot arms."

"I found them in a film and cut them out using a snapshot program."

"You really enjoy doing stuff like this, don't you?"

"It's like a game; I can play around with it for hours. It's a hobby."

She had taken the slides with all the background information on Natioba almost unchanged from her account plan, with the market share and revenue figures from the latest company report represented in graphs. She had even included information about the development lab. It was now just a question of waiting on Natioba's legal department to check the MOU.

"I've taken the general slides about Vabilmo from the last presentation for Wolfgang. Is that OK?"

"Fine by me; you can leave them as they are," her boss approved the slides.

She would wait until the evening for the MOU, before sending the slides to Hank. Until then, she began to speculate once more. What could be shown during the opening speech? Transporting the whole container up to the first floor of the conference centre seemed unlikely. Or was there a way after all? According to the website, there was a vehicle ramp at the side of the building leading to the first floor. However, it was doubtful whether its radius would offer enough space for a lorry and trailer. Certainly, it didn't look like it from the pictures.

There was also the additional set of robot arms that Hank and Chris were experimenting with in New York. The question was whether these would be needed if the container was assembled in Seoul. Perhaps there was something the arms could demonstrate. During what part of the speech would the project even be mentioned? How long would it take to transport the container to the ground floor? She needed more information to anticipate how things would proceed. But first she needed to wait and see if they even made it into the speech.

The MOU came back signed the next day; Emily checked the changes made by Natioba immediately and found them all acceptable.

Alex went straight to Wolfgang to get his signature.

"Let's go for a coffee," he suggested. "Tell me, how are things with you?"

"So far, so good," Alex replied, while she got the drinks. "Everything's going according to plan with Natloba. We decided to assemble the greenhouse in Seoul and then ship it to Taipei for the conference. It's less time-consuming and considerably more cost-effective. The project might even get a mention in the opening speech, though nothing's certain yet."

"Good work, Alex! That would be an enormous help to us internally!"

"Hank from New York is meeting with the CEO's assistant and has asked me to make him a presentation. Thomas approved it yesterday before I sent it off."

"Let me have a look at it too, so I know what's been circulated."

"I'll do that. The MOU's come back from Natioba and Emily has already accepted the changes. She doesn't think there's anything to stop you initialling it. Your signature is just as valid as the European legal department's. It might even increase the document's value in the eyes of the client. As managing director, you'd be giving our collaboration top priority."

There had been several press reports about projects Wolfgang had officially taken on himself, ranging from major clients to governmental schemes. His signature would ensure the project with Natioba carried the same weight.

"That didn't take long," he remarked. "You might be right about the signature; let's have a look."

Vanity makes for a good negotiating partner, Alex smiled to herself, as Wolfgang read and signed the MOU. She didn't feel at all guilty about taking this approach with Natioba: Wolfgang had really taken up the Vabilmo cause. As Thomas had once mentioned to her, there was no other manager worldwide in Sales and Marketing that had so openly declared his support for Vabilmo.

The way he had assumed direct responsibility for the Roffarm team had made it all the more apparent. He was taking a huge risk if things didn't work out and would have to justify the countless FTE-years he had invested. If he was successful, however, he'd get a big pat on the back, and possibly even a promotion. His vanity regarding the client was thus perfectly understandable.

"I like the contract," Wolfgang praised her work.

"We're making good progress with Premve as well." She began to tell him about her other client. "The meeting with the investigation committee isn't too far away. That should finally clear the path for a joint project – the power plant divisional manager has already guaranteed his support."

"A project with Premve would really push things along with Roffarm. They're dragging a bit at the moment. Keep working on them."

As Wolfgang didn't seem to be in any hurry, she decided to tell him more.

"We've also had confirmation from Luxumi that they've got nothing against a joint project with Hursoc, but I'm not so sure. The development manager's agreement at the last meeting didn't seem binding. Somehow I get the impression that implementing a project like this isn't particularly urgent. It could also be down to a lack of resources, of course. Luxumi are currently busy planning another plant. If it came to a project, we'd need additional resources at our end too. But we won't know anything more until the scope's been defined. That's planned for the next phase."

"We can always make a decision closer to the time," he resolved. "The most important thing is that we can show people internally that we're making progress. There are still a number of doubting voices. I mean, I have to defend the Roffarm project at the start of each new quarter – despite the signed contract. They question everything here! Luckily, our superiors are beginning to appreciate that launching new technology on the market can take years. However, with projects like Natioba for example, I can anticipate future demands and achieve quicker results."

"I'll let you know what's happening as soon as I hear from Hank."

"One more thing," he concluded. "Thomas forwarded me your Premve call report. In future, please copy me in on mails like this. I'd rather have too much information than too little. After all, a provisional decision was made at the meeting. I need to know things like that for my phone conferences – I have to be as up-to-date as possible."

That was useful information, although Alex was generally more careful. As long as no decision had been made, she preferred to play down prospects rather than celebrate victory prematurely. She'd have to consider her wording in call reports even more closely from now on.

"Good work, keep it up," he repeated, as he handed her the MOU and wheeled back to his desk.

Alex saw how efficiently Wolfgang worked and how quickly he made decisions. The outcome of their short discussion had been exactly to her liking, she thought to herself, as she scanned the MOU and forwarded it to Hank.

Christopher had received an email from colleagues in London requesting a member of the Vabilmo team to attend a client meeting there in person. He had forwarded the message to Thomas with the question "who normally does this?" and copied Alex in to the discussion. The email mentioned that the English client had already initiated discussions with Natioba about batteries. The wireless-power technology currently under development could also be used in off-grid systems. As a follow-up, Thomas had asked Alex to take a closer look. After she had agreed to a meeting in London, she went to see Christopher.

"Do we have to help your clients now, so that you at least generate a little revenue?" she grinned cheekily.

"I just wanted to make sure you'd actually got a project – that way, you'd finally have something to show for yourself," he fired back.

"You know, we don't normally bother with such small fry. But for you, I'll make an exception."

"How perfectly charming. When does it all kick off?"

"The day after tomorrow."

"Geez, you don't waste any time do you? Very unusual for your team."

"Rumour has it it's down to the new leadership."

"Touché. Well, have fun over there with the islanders!"

Same-day return flights to London at such short notice were almost as expensive as flights to New York. As a result, Alex had decided to fly out the evening before, which was still the cheaper option despite the overnight stay. PsoraCom had an arrangement with a hotel located in a small square near Hyde Park.

Two six-storey buildings from the previous century were connected to each other by a canopied passage that formed the entrance. Inside, it was almost like stepping back in time. The hotel had been maintained in the Art Deco style, and its homely lounge looked extremely inviting with palms and thick upholstered chairs, all under a glass dome roof. The subdued lighting that glowed from the various lampshades infused the room with a uniquely English charm and elegance.

Providence dictated that there was a Hard Rock Cafe nearby. After checking-in, Alex headed straight over, taking a little detour through the park. The fresh air did her good and only served to increase her appetite for one of their amazing salads. Nobu called briefly just as she was looking at T-shirts for Sandro and Jenny in the adjoining shop. She had brought her netphone so that she could be contacted in case of emergency.

It was no big deal to have her evenings disrupted when she was away on business. Back at the hotel, she looked for a quiet corner in the palm lounge. The dull murmur of guests was accompanied by the discreet tones of a piano emanating from hidden speakers. It was the perfect atmosphere in which to check her mails and deal with Hank's questions about their presentation.

Back at the office, Thomas wanted to know how the meeting had gone.

"The majority of the company's batteries are used for household robots," she told him. "Nevertheless, in future they're going to focus more on the off-grid-systems market, as the margins are greater there. That's why they've already spoken to Natioba. The Italians mentioned in passing that they were collaborating with PsoraCom on a new piece of technology and so they asked to meet with us too."

"What did you discuss?" he probed deeper.

"I didn't tell them about the exact nature of our work with Natioba, of course. But since we have a non-disclosure agreement with London, I gave them a detailed presentation and showed them the wave-shaped seed unit. They both made quite an impression on the managing director. He asked his project leader to arrange a workshop straightaway to discuss any questions arising from the meeting and decide how best to proceed. Their interest lies in robots and off-grid systems in particular. We might be able to approach end customers together."

Thomas nodded thoughtfully.

"But I haven't agreed to anything yet," Alex continued. "First, we need to clarify a few issues relating to potential, and second we have to decide if Carl should take over from me as their official point of contact."

"And how do you view the situation as things stand?" he wanted to know. "Shoot straight from the hip."

"Difficult to say," she hesitated. "Initially, it might make sense to approach robot and off-grid-systems manufacturers together. Still, their timeframe of eighteen months seems pretty tight to me. Whether it's actually possible to implement new charger technology in such a short space of time is impossible to judge. There are so many questions that need to be answered first. What's the company's market share in the battery industry? Britain's their home market, but how are things in the rest of Europe? How big is the market for wireless power technology? What difference does it make to the robot market when it's the charging stations that are powered by solar modules, rather than the robots themselves? What kind of batteries are required for robots that obtain their power supply from solar cells? Is this battery more of a short-term buffer in comparison with the long-term storage offered by externally charged batteries? Might there even be competition in a subsection of the industry? As far as the off-grid systems go, the company constitutes an additional sales channel, but nothing more. Whether an off-grid system's battery is powered wirelessly or not makes no real difference to us."

"Correct," Thomas agreed. "The important thing is that the plant generates its electricity using our solar cells."

"The key question from my point of view," Alex continued, "is what priority level a joint project with them would have – if any. The workshop they've suggested is the perfect chance to make a decision. Based on our initial discussion alone, it's hard to say how we'd benefit from getting involved with this company."

"Don't forget the prestige factor," he added.

"True," she agreed. "Even though wireless powering has been employed for some time in small household batteries and consumer electronics, it's never been used in this capacity before. Until now, the charge current has been the limiting factor in terms of resonance induction, and charging times have always been regarded as inefficient."

"And you think the Brits have found a solution that can be commercialised?"

"It looks like it; although we didn't have the chance to look at the details. It would be a pretty good basis for collaboration, as their product might be the first of its kind on the market."

"Something like that could be decisive, of course," Thomas was forced to admit. "If they use our cells, it would mean two new pieces of technology combining simultaneously on the market. That could give our advertising people a real headache."

Alex knew exactly what he meant. She'd heard any number of examples as part of her in-house training. Who was the first man on the moon? Neil Armstrong. Who was the second? No idea. Who was responsible for the first transatlantic flight? Charles Lindbergh. That wasn't true, of course, since two men from Newfoundland had flown to Ireland several years previously – but the feat was popularly attributed to Lindbergh. The second transatlantic flight? Most people didn't know that either.

Questions like this were supposed to make it clear that the first person to do anything was etched in the public's memory. That's why it was always desirable from a marketing point of view to be the first company to launch a product. As long as it had been properly thought-out and there weren't any teething issues, that is. Negative press was just as likely to stick. The view of some communication experts that there was no such thing as bad press was more than open to debate.

"Go and talk to Christopher again," he instructed her. "But otherwise, you have my approval for the workshop."

"OK, and I'll get Carl involved anyway, since it concerns robots too."

"Yeah, do that."

She went straight to Christopher to outline her opinion.

"The Brits are working on a seminal piece of technology," she said. "And even without this kind of electricity transfer, they represent another sales channel for off-grid systems. The workshop would help us judge once and for all whether collaboration would be worth our while. Factoring in both Carl and myself, the time investment should be around twenty hours. Plus travel costs, of course. Afterwards we should have a good basis for deciding how to proceed further."

"It all sounds pretty low risk to me," he replied. "What does Thomas say?"

"Thomas agrees with me. But we wanted to hear your opinion, as it concerns your area."

"My opinion is that I share your opinion. I like how you work – and how you think about things!"

"Well, my time is limited, so I have to consider how much I invest in each project."

"I wouldn't have thought you were capable of it!"

"You shouldn't judge others by your own shortcomings!"

"Too right; come on, I'll buy you a coffee."

Carl was very excited by the prospect of travelling to London with Alex to see a client. It would be their first joint meeting together. Apart from the Asia trip with Brian, he had only ever been on business in the German-speaking countries.

A date for the London workshop was quickly agreed and set for the beginning of August. Next Alex concentrated on the final preparations for the meeting with Premve.

Four people were expected from the client's end: the head of the power plant division and his boss; the development director; as well as the directors of both logistics and technology. To match them, Alex had factored in Thomas, Marco and Hugo. Her boss had declined – even though his participation as team leader would have given off good signals. As the person in overall charge of the client, Marco was obliged to be there; Hugo had been included in case there were any technical questions but had only accepted under duress. Alex had no idea why Brian had assumed he would be taking part, and neither did Thomas. After declining himself, the latter had said half-heartedly to Alex: "You can take him now as far as I'm concerned."

Brian's presence was hardly a matter of necessity, but she thought he could say something about the back-story if required, or talk about the latest trends from Asia. It was as if he had been waiting for just such a suggestion. Right away he was keen as mustard.

Alex was still working on a final slide that would show all possible solar cell applications. On one photomontage there was a power plant installation with wave-shaped solar modules; another showed a solar powered robot in its case; while the third displayed an off-grid system whose solar modules had been fashioned into spheres. She had instinctively omitted the application the divisional manager had mentioned at their last meeting.

They had been granted a ninety-minute slot for the meeting. She calculated that at least half of that would be taken up by the presentation and subsequent questions. The rest of the time would be set aside for discussion and – hopefully – a green light for the project. The fifteen slides contained a short overview of company data, including an organisational chart, and described the Vabilmo technology, along with its possible applications and targeted ecosystem.

Brian had sent two abridged slides from the summary of his Asia trip. These could have been reduced to: "All companies (visited) in Asia wanted to work with PsoraCom to develop solar plants and robots with polymer-based cells", but that would have been too aggressive. Brian was bound to have had something to say on the subject, Alex thought to herself smiling. And if he were to go rogue at any stage, she could rely on Marco to rein him in. Alex sent the presentation to Marco, Brian and Hugo, copying Thomas in as well. It couldn't hurt – perhaps there was something she had overlooked. But there were no objections forthcoming.

On the journey back after the meeting, Alex was struck by a sense of déjà vu. She was sitting alone with Marco in the car. Brian had driven himself and Hugo had to go straight to the airport.

"Completely impossible!" Marco began straightaway. "That's the last time he sits in with a client of mine! The guy's got absolutely no manners at all! Slouching the whole time in his chair next to Hugo, he's so disrespectful; it's a wonder he stood up to greet them."

"I noticed that too," Alex joined in, almost against her will. "But perhaps they didn't. They were sitting facing us and looking in the opposite direction from Brian and Hugo most of the time."

"Thankfully! It's a good thing your slides were so interesting. The one you pieced together with the different applications clearly made an impression on the development director. You've built up a really good relationship with him."

"If that's what you call it," Alex laughed.

"I'm sure you triggered a few associations when you said silicone instead of silicon. That was a classic, I'm telling you." Marco was grinning broadly.

"But he took you seriously despite that slip of the tongue," he went on. "You could see that; otherwise he wouldn't have kept directing questions at you. I think you probably found exactly the right tone with your presentation and slides."

"Could be," Alex acknowledged. "The most important thing today was to get the go-ahead for our joint project."

"Yeah, and we managed that," he was delighted. "Even though your colleague wasted valuable time by prattling on about his trip to Asia."

"A lot of it was very interesting for them," Alex said in Brian's defence. "At least that was my impression. OK, so he was repeating himself by the end. But that's just the way he is. Obviously he's one of these people you have to keep in check."

"I'll keep him in check next time by not bringing him," Marco replied, incensed. "We don't need him! He should be looking after his own clients. You're doing really well. Ultimately, all he wants is to take the credit. Everything's his idea all of a sudden; and his is the only correct approach."

She noticed the disparaging tone in his voice – just as she had after their initial meeting with Premve – and wondered to herself again what was up between the two of them. Inside, she was forced to agree with Marco partly, as Brian's behaviour had rubbed her up the wrong way on occasion as well.

"We almost certainly wouldn't have got the go-ahead without the support of the head of power plants," Alex concluded. "Did you notice how the majority of questions came from the development director and how his colleagues held back in comparison? Just like the old rule: it's the leader's job to ask the questions. But at the end, when it came to making a decision, he acted on his division managers's suggestion. He's the most important man behind the scenes."

"I think so too," Marco agreed. "Next time your pony-tailed colleague comes along with his old C-Level bullshit, make sure you send him to me. We're the ones who decide what happens with our clients – and we've seen today how well that can work."

"That's true, but things mightn't have gone so smoothly if it wasn't for Hugo," she said. "He dealt with the technical questions extremely well, without getting bogged down in too much detail."

"Sure, Hugo did a good job," Marco concurred. "But the thing that really drew them in was you mentioning Natioba and the joint project. The way you batted off their questions made it clear you could be trusted. The development director was visibly impressed."

"Let's not exaggerate now," Alex replied. "It's a standard answer that never fails to go down well. I use it with everyone. Although everyone asks for details, no-one actually wants their own information to be passed on to others if it's confidential. It's a very quick and easy way to rebut overly inquisitive questions."

"But you're right, Alex; it would have been very difficult without the head of power plants. He pounced on your question about how to proceed as soon as the development director passed it on to him. It was almost perfectly staged."

"There was nothing staged about it; it could just as easily have gone tits up," she said.

"Lucky you had some support then. Still, everything worked out in the end," Marco added, in summary. "Now we can give Roffarm a real kick up the backside and arouse them from their slumber. If

Premve keeps on like this, we can leave those boffins trailing in our wake."

"A little competition couldn't hurt, but let's not count our chickens, Marco. There's still a lot to be done before we achieve our objectives."

Alex liked Marco, and up until now they seemed to work well together with clients. He yielded to her when it came to Vabilmo, taking on the more general client issues himself. She had to admit that she found his praise very flattering. Only sometimes he went a little over the top and seemed unable to take stock of what still needed to be done.

Premve's head of power plants had told her something at the end of the meeting that she didn't want to withhold from colleagues. Not without a degree of pride, she entered "Premve approves pre-development project" as the subject line of her call report. Even if it was seen as too meticulous in some quarters, she always began her reports by listing the participants on both sides; it had been a team effort, after all, and she was not about to take sole credit for the result. A first milestone had been reached with the official project approval from the development director and his colleagues on the investigation committee. However, that was only a start – the real work had yet to begin. Responsibilities had to be allocated to people on both sides, and the exact scope of the project, including overall costs and time expenditure, was still to be defined.

Next, they had to schedule a kick-off meeting and decide whether it would make sense to draw up a legal document. Perhaps an MOU wouldn't be such a bad idea here either, as additional support would be needed from different product groups. Having a binding document could be extremely useful; it was all too easy to renege on oral agreements. At the end she posed the question as to whether anyone had heard of other companies voicing similar concerns to those of Premve's head of power plants. After all, it was vital to know if what he said represented a general trend, or if it was merely an isolated opinion.

Premve's divisional manager had mentioned an Asian manufacturer with which his team was currently engaged in developing the next generation of power plant inverters. It was possible this company could be of interest to PsoraCom. He was convinced that companies like Hursoc were becoming less and less suitable for joint development projects because they had become too big and thus too inflexible. That was why Premve, despite working with Hursoc for many years, had gone to Asia with their current project. They had been wowed by their short response times and willingness to change.

In the divisional manager's opinion, this was becoming a decisive trend, as one of their competitors, Luxumi, had also recently worked on a plant together with a manufacturer from Taiwan. For him, that was a sure sign of significant change in the industry and confirmation that the days of manufacturers like Hursoc were numbered. They needed to take what the head of power plants said very seriously and crosscheck it with Luxumi or Brian's clients. If the market trend pointed towards Asia, they would have to take stock and revise their team strategy.

After reading through the report a final time, she sent it to a standard mailing list that she had devised herself. Along with Thomas, Marco and her team, it also included additional colleagues such as Hank and Nobu from the different product fields in the US and Asia. She made sure to incorporate Wolfgang too, as he had specifically asked to be informed of any significant developments. She thought she had earned a glass of Prosecco and went into the kitchen. Unfortunately Sandro wasn't home to toast her success, so she called her father instead.

"Hey pops, everything OK with you? Any news from Jenny? She's impossible to get hold of."

"All quiet on the western front," her father replied. "Your mother is fighting hard and getting a little better each day. We spoke to Jenny at the weekend. She's very well as always, apart from having to deal with tough decisions like whether to go to a barbecue or play badminton instead. What's going on with you?"

"We've just had a very good meeting with one of my clients," Alex told him. "They've approved a pre-development project. But now it's crunch time; you know, scope, planning, resources."

"That's already the second project you've landed," her father cried, delighted.

"Yeah, it's great," Alex conceded. "No-one takes any risks in the energy industry when it comes to new technology; the only way you can gain a seat at the manufacturers' poker table is to prove yourself first. 99% of the time, that means a development project – and only then once pre-development is complete."

"It's a tremendous success for such a short time," Franz said, clearly proud. "But I'm sure you're putting absolutely everything into it as usual."

"I just enjoy my work enormously, and the subject matter is fascinating. From a technical point of view, the developments in the industry are extremely exciting. There's so much happening at the moment. It's like a game where you've got to continually update your knowledge to get to the next level."

"You've always had a competitive streak. Just listening to you, I can really sense your enthusiasm – it's utterly contagious."

Sometimes Alex couldn't believe she'd got this job. There was nothing she would rather be doing for a living. The energy industry had always interested her and she found technology fascinating. Franz understood this only too well with his technical background; he had been a mechatronics engineer and a devotee of biomimetics.

"What's the good news?" Alex's mother asked, once Franz had put her on loudspeaker.

She was feeling better and better, though it was clear her health would never be completely restored. Her body had been ravaged by cancer and was still dealing with the after-effects. There were certain things she couldn't eat and by and large she consumed very little.

The next routine aftercare examination was due in the autumn. Her blood count, checked regularly by the family doctor, seemed to indicate that everything was OK. Nevertheless, Ricka was convinced that the tumour markers weren't always reliable. There were a number of different opinions on the issue in the literature and online. With some cancer patients, the tumour markers corresponded to the symptoms; with others, however, malignant growths were found despite low or non-existent markers.

There was nothing for it but to await the results of the computed tomography in October and hope for the best. Alex still remembered what the doctors had said after Ricka's operation: the outcome was the equivalent of winning the lottery. As a positive person, she assumed that was still the case. Her mother had always lived healthily and the tumour was an error of nature that could be successfully corrected.

While Alex was speaking to her parents, Sandro sent her a message. He would be home late, as he needed to give a coaching session at the club. She didn't wait up for him. It had been a very stressful day and the Prosecco had contributed to her fatigue. By the time he came home, she was already sound asleep.

The call from Hank the next day was a real bombshell.

"We've done it! We've convinced them," his voice almost cracked at the news.

"Brilliant! That's amazing!" Hank's euphoria was infectious. "That was a lot quicker than I expected."

"They do sometimes make decisions quickly here; the CEO liked our project straightaway."

"I need to let it all sink in," she said. "Is the decision final or subject to change?"

"It's final," Hank responded, "unless the developer conference is cancelled or the world comes to an end. Both seem pretty unlikely at the moment."

"I'm relieved to hear that," Alex was quite sincere.

"But wait, it gets better. The assistant asked if we needed a greater budget. He must have caught me in a lucid moment because I rounded up our estimated budget fairly generously."

"And how did he react?" Alex wanted to know.

"He didn't even bat an eyelid. We're getting our budget. It's peanuts in the grand scheme of things."

"Fantastic. You've done a great job. Somebody give the man a medal!"

"Thank you, thank you, Alex. But we wouldn't have got there without your slides. Now it's time for the real work to begin."

"We'll manage it, partner," she promised. "We're a top team - you can count on me."

It was terrific news; the only thing was that it would mean more overtime in the evenings because of the time difference – but that didn't matter. When would she get another chance like this?

"So, I thought," Hank outlined his idea, "we should try and get the whole greenhouse on stage. That would make the biggest impression."

"It would be great if we could," Alex agreed. "I had a look at the halls online, though. It could be pretty tight. Have you spoken to Chris about it?"

"Yes. He says it's his boss's decision. Can you call him? You're on pretty good terms with him after all. Mention that we can help out with the costs."

"Fine," she promised. "I'll let you know as soon as I've got hold of him. But there are other things we need to think about too. Do we need a high-ranking manager from Natioba to appear on stage with the CEO? How exactly will the project be introduced? What information is set to be revealed? Is there a way to transport the container up to the first floor – and will the stage be able to carry its weight? How quickly will we be able to get the greenhouse back down to the lower hall after the speech?"

"Slow down," he checked her. "Don't worry about it. The CEO's assistant assigns internal event planners to look after the individual details. They work with different agencies on the ground, so the local knowledge is there. All we need to do is deliver the project requirements. The speech itself is scripted – nothing's left to chance."

"That's pure luxury," she was absolutely astonished. "But it makes sense. With so much media coverage, the last thing any company wants is to read a detailed description of a major blunder."

"That's why there's a general rehearsal the day before," Hank told her, "so that everything passes off without a hitch."

"Sounds like a theatre production," Alex mused.

"That's exactly what it is. There are still a good two months to go and we're not under any time pressure in terms of organisation. The project should be complete by then as well. We still need to arrange transport from Seoul to Taipei and check that all parts work, but they're the only things we need to plan tighter time-wise – to have a safety buffer for unforeseen events. Additional costs will be covered by the CEO's budget. It's not exactly a blank cheque but we don't need to worry about it for now."

Shortly after she had hung up, Alex received a surprise call from Jenny. It was as if she had known how excited her twin was.

"Hey, sis, what's new with you?" she asked.

"Hey kid, I'm still pretty psyched," Alex replied. "I've just heard that one of my client projects will be unveiled personally by the CEO at our developer conference. I haven't quite made sense of it yet."

"Hey, that's great," Jenny congratulated her. "What's the deal then? Whose shares should I buy?"

"That's confidential, I'm afraid," Alex stalled her. "But it's something completely new. That much is certain."

"So, where's the conference?"

"In Taipei, in the fall. Maybe I'll even get to go. That would be pretty exciting; I've never been before."

"Asia's amazing. That's the reason I'm going to Hong Kong," Jenny backed her up.

"When are you off?" Alex wanted to know. "I'll have to see what we're doing for holidays this year. Apart from a few days in Prague, we've got nothing planned. Hong Kong doesn't sound too shabby and we could stop off in the Maldives on the way back for a bit of snorkelling."

"Yeah, why don't you! That'd be great," her sister replied. "I'm leaving at the end of the August. October would be a good time to come; I should know the lie of the land by then."

In the meantime, Sandro had come home and heard the lion's share of their conversation. She would have loved to share her success with him but he didn't seem particularly pleased for her. The news that she would probably have to fly to Taipei in September to attend the unveiling of a client project was drearily noted; he mumbled something like "good for you". He didn't ask for details. As he almost always did in situations like this, he simply withdrew to his computer: apparently, he still had work to do.

She didn't know what it was exactly, but her mood had suddenly been dampened. Their relationship had come to a kind of standstill. No new flat, let alone their own house – and no decision about starting a family. No interest in her work. He had been absolutely delighted for her when she received confirmation of her new job at the end of last year. Only a few months had passed since, and from Alex's standpoint, not a great deal had changed. Hopefully their time in Prague would breathe new life into their relationship. Nothing major was set to occur until then. At least, that's what she thought.

Alex called the lab supervisor in Seoul first thing the next morning. However, despite a number of attempts, she was unable to reach him and left a short message. Then she drove to the office; with her current adrenaline levels, she would have felt like a caged animal if she'd stayed at home. The initial frantic excitement had given way to a business-like euphoria.

"We did it!" she ambushed Thomas at his desk. "We've made it into the opening speech! Hank called me late yesterday evening."

"Well, that sounds good," he said. From him, she took that as a compliment and beamed from ear to ear. She was on a high now, and went to see Henry next. He was curious to hear all the details.

"That's huge," he was enthusiastic. "It's very rare for projects from the German office to be presented at the developer conference. Mostly it's new developments from the product line or R&D in the US. This is very important, for Wolfgang especially. While we're on the subject, does he know yet?"

"No, I haven't seen him," Alex replied. "But that's the reason I'm in the office. I didn't just want to send the info by mail; I wanted to tell people personally."

"That's the right way to go about things," he backed her up. "Here at PsoraCom, we have an unwritten rule about visibility. It's just like the old saying: if you do something good, you should let people know about it. It's a kind of self-marketing policy that all hierarchy levels have adopted within the company. There are, of course, some who abuse it – much to the chagrin of those of us who are honest." Henry sighed. "Some things are blown up out of all proportion."

"I don't understand that," she looked at him questioningly. "How can you hype something up when there's nothing behind it? The truth always comes out sooner or later."

Henry shrugged his shoulders.

"Sometimes it's not so easy to spot: you can't always measure success in terms of dollars – just like in your work. I'm sure you don't have any sales targets. Am I right?"

"No, I don't," she admitted. "We have certain milestones, since the technology is still very new and the market is geared towards solar power plants in the long run. But you know, with Natioba for instance, I can't make anything up. There's a joint project and a signed MOU with the development lab in Seoul. Now it's been decided that we'll get a mention in the opening speech. But we still need client approval when it comes to how we're going to present things at the developer conference and how much information we're prepared to divulge. I can't say anything more than the client wants me to. And besides, what good would it do?"

"None at all," he agreed. "Still, there are colleagues who do it. I've seen it many times, believe me. Sometimes management just don't want to see the truth and are taken in by the fantasies people dish up."

Wolfgang was visibly happy to receive the good news a little later.

At the weekend, they invited Moritz and Renata over for a barbecue. They hadn't done anything together for months now; finally, they had taken the bull by the horns. It promised to be a really nice evening. Moritz and Sandro fooled around by the grill, while Renata and Alex prepared the salad. The boys emptied a few beers and the girls enjoyed ice-cold champagne. At last they had some time for a good long chat. There were lots of little things to tell each other, but on the whole it seemed that not a great deal had changed.

"Sandro, when are you going to teach Alex how to play tennis properly?" Renata asked, as they sat happily around the grill together after dinner.

"She doesn't want to learn," he replied snidely. "Alex can come to the club whenever she likes. She just doesn't think it's important."

"That's not exactly true," said Alex.

"Yeah, it is," Sandro insisted. "You look down on my friends. You don't think they're good enough for you."

"No, that's not how it is," Alex defended herself, horrified by the sudden outburst. "The truth is, the majority of members I know just have a different perspective on things. They're nice and I like chatting to them at parties. But most of them choose their friends according to bank balance, the latest trends or the hippest events. It's just not me, and you know that. The limited free time I have, I prefer to spend with you, our friends or my family."

She had enough friends and a wide circle of acquaintances through work alone. She met the people she was close to as often as possible. The only exception was her friend Maria, who had moved to Spain a few years ago and whom Alex saw only once every couple of years. They still spoke a lot on the phone. It was exactly the same with former work colleagues, old acquaintances from her student days and friendships that had resulted from previous relationships.

Almost all of them were scattered across the globe and she was only in touch with most by phone or email. But Alex knew these friends were always there for her and that she could call – or even turn up at their door – anytime. Of course, the same was true for them. Alex wanted to use the rest of her free time for herself.

Sometimes, you had to recharge your own batteries too. She had no desire for her free time to become acutely stressful and so she set priorities. The tennis club simply wasn't one of them. Most of the time, that didn't bother Sandro but tonight it seemed to be an issue. Perhaps it was something to do with work. Luckily, the subject was forgotten for the rest of the weekend.

The message took Alex completely by surprise. Besides the entire Vabilmo team, it had also been sent to a number of different colleagues, including Nobu. The mailing list even contained Wolfgang and Bill. She couldn't believe it and was forced to read the email over and over again.

A meeting with Roffarm had gone wrong and somehow Natioba were affected too. In two days, she and Sandro were flying to Prague and now this. Alex paced up and down her living room cursing. She replied to Hank; and soon after, both Brian and George were involved in the written discussion. She still hadn't finished reading when her inbox displayed a new message from Bill. The subject line read: "Strictly confidential – attorney client privilege!"

Alex gulped. Bill wasn't just asking, but ordering all written communication on the subject to cease with immediate effect. Straightaway, she knew what it meant and began to dial Hank's number.

"What the hell's going on?" she asked, thoroughly vexed.

"Pretty fucked up, isn't it?" came the reply from New York. "A colleague's blabbed."

"Tell me, then! What happened?" she wanted to know.

"This colleague asked me for more detailed information about the Natioba project," he ceded. "So I sent him the presentation we showed the CEO's assistant."

"That's OK so far," she said. "There was a header and footer on each slide saying the information was confidential."

"I'm afraid that's exactly what our colleague seems to have overlooked," Hank told her. "He transferred some of it to his own client presentation; stupidly, however, he forgot to get rid of the company name. Earlier this morning, he showed the slides to the divisional director of Roffarm."

Alex remembered Hank mentioning a few weeks ago that the divisional director was visiting Robotics in the US. She hadn't followed it up because it was the internal sister team that looked after Roffarm.

"Shit," the sound escaped her mouth.

"You can say that again," Hank agreed. "The divisional director went absolutely spare when he heard about the project with Natioba."

"He's not the only one who's pissed off," she said, irritated. "I'm about to go through the roof. Why does it have to happen with my client? It shouldn't happen at all! I just hope it doesn't screw things up for the developer conference."

"I hadn't even thought about that. I don't get it. Perhaps I should have made it absolutely clear that the slides were confidential. But you expect people to have a little common sense. I'm really sorry, Alex."

"No-one's blaming you, Hank. Our colleague should have realised that himself – it was plastered all over the presentation. It's no great secret that we speak to different solar plant manufacturers; but he should have thought to handle it with more discretion, especially since it's being unveiled to the public in a few weeks by the CEO himself. The head of PsoraCom doesn't just get involved with any old hat."

"No, you're right. What a fucking cock-up."

"It's OK, Hank. It's not your fault. Let's see if we can get out of this mess without jeopardising our slot in the opening speech. We need to think of something. Let's speak again tomorrow, OK? I'll keep you posted if there's any news."

Alex was seething with rage as she hung up. What unbelievable stupidity. During the conversation she had been pacing up and down furiously, trying to get rid of some energy. It was clear to her that they had a problem in two respects.

First, she knew that solar plant manufacturers communicated with one another. There were contacts on every level. On certain subjects, there were even official workshops attended by equally ranked representatives from rival companies. What would happen if the guy from Roffarm just picked up the receiver, called Natioba and started talking about the project? The presentation had mentioned that the point of contact was the development lab in Seoul. If Roffarm's divisional director was as much of an idiot as Brian always made out, then anything could happen. In the worst case scenario – and this was probably the lesser evil when compared to the loss of trust – Natioba would sue for violation of the confidentiality agreement and demand compensation. That wouldn't only be financially damaging for PsoraCom; it would seriously tarnish their reputation.

And second there was the Roffarm contract, which would now finally be put to the test. How would their co-contractor react? Since the exclusivity clause was open to interpretation, a legal quagmire could arise here too. The situation was more than tricky. Alex was still unable to think clearly and as she played out the different scenarios, her pulse began to quicken once more. She couldn't find a solution like this; first she needed to get it all out of her system.

It was just lucky that this colleague hadn't got in touch directly – he wouldn't have got off so lightly. You could hardly blame someone who was rarely confronted with such things, but a colleague who had been there for years and regularly dealt with clients, well, it just shouldn't have happened. Especially at PsoraCom, where there were strict guidelines about how to handle information about new products.

Discretion was just part of the trade. She stood still. Working off her stress was currently the most important thing if she wanted to think clearly again. Taking deep breaths in between complaints wouldn't get her anywhere. Somehow she needed to let off some steam. There was only one thing for it: jogging would reduce her tension and help blow away the cobwebs.

She had a good hour to think things through. What was their priority now? What needed to be taken into account? Who needed to be informed internally? How could Roffarm's divisional director be appeased? Would he call Natioba? How would the lab supervisor in Seoul react? How many weeks were left until the developer conference? How could they ensure that this news didn't filter through in the intervening period? She urgently needed to speak to Lucas, her colleague from the internal Roffarm team.

He had known about the project with Natioba and the MOU. Alex had met him occasionally in the office and chatted to him over lunch. He had always exuded a stoical kind of quiet, as if he viewed his own work from a gallery up on high. Since Roffarm were dealing mainly with Bill's division at present, he would have to be kept up-to-date as well.

One of the most important things was that all communication on the subject be conducted orally from now on. In the case of a lawsuit, any written correspondence – including all emails – could be used to establish a body of evidence. That was why Bill had ordered it to cease. Was there a way to tell Natioba that Roffarm had a rough idea of the project without revealing absolutely everything?

Alex wasn't much the wiser when she came back, but she was certainly calmer. Her thought processes were more controlled and the initial adrenaline-soaked wave of indignation had been neutralised by the run. Sandro had arrived home in the meantime.

"Everything's a bit topsy-turvy at the moment," she told him briefly, as she peeled off her wet clothes. "We've got a very awkward situation with a client. I've still got a few things to do before speaking to various people in the US. I'm not sure how late it'll be."

"Then I can go straight to the club and eat there," he resolved. "I'd only get in your way otherwise." He packed a few things into a sports bag and blew her a kiss as he left.

"Can you talk?" she called Lucas, after showering. He had accompanied his client to the meeting in the US. "How's his mood? What's the situation with you?"

"Wait, I'll just go outside quickly," he replied. "So, the divisional director is incensed that a research project was begun with a rival company without his prior knowledge. His view is that we should have got permission from him first. Talk about histrionics! I tried to make it clear to him that from our standpoint he's asking for too much. Maybe he's worried that another company is further along with the polymer-based cells than he is. I haven't found out yet."

"That's perfectly possible," Alex agreed. "According to Hugo's reports at our team meetings, there's a lot of talk and not much action. But there's always a risk another manufacturer could be quicker. Not just Natioba."

"You're absolutely right. In the free-market economy, the winners are the ones who are quickest or best. But try telling that to Roffarm. The way it's looking at the moment, it might be difficult to regulate the exclusivity clause without going to court."

"But Roffarm can't seriously want that," Alex expressed her surprise, "and we certainly don't. That's not how harmonious long-term business relationships are supposed to work."

"Correct," Lucas replied. "We need to try and resolve this as soon as possible, through unofficial channels. At the same time, we should be aware that our solution could serve as a precedent for similar problems in the future."

After the conversation, she called Hank. Admittedly, she didn't have any news for him, but her plan seemed to calm him. Even if it was banal and unspectacular, it represented the beginnings of a strategy. It was better than just sitting in shock. The first thing she wanted to do was speak to Thomas and Emily early the next morning.

In the meantime, she could only hope that nothing happened from the client's end. Alex was pretty confident the time difference would act in their favour. The divisional director was still in the US and wasn't flying back to Germany until the next morning. Lucas was with him and would try to distract him. Seoul was currently under darkness. That would give them some time to think.

Thomas wasn't exactly thrilled when he heard but it hardly knocked him off his chair either. Pragmatic as he was, he had no hesitation in agreeing to a meeting with Emily. Everyone except Brian had paid heed to Bill's instructions. He had either seen the mail too late or chosen not to comply, defiantly expressing his disapproval to everyone on the list.

"I've spoken to Brian about it already," Emily began. "I knew straightaway why Bill had marked all further communication as attorney client privilege. From a legal point of view, avoiding additional damage and maybe even court proceedings should be very easy. Alex, you need to get permission from your client to pass on information about the project to Roffarm. The whole thing has to be in writing as quickly as possible."

"You're joking, aren't you?" Alex gulped. "First I'd need to consider what arguments I can use. Any bright ideas?"

Thomas shook his head.

"I suppose we could just keep quiet," he thought out loud, "and wait until Taipei. It's unlikely that anything will happen in the next few weeks."

"For me, the risk's too great," Alex said immediately. "At the end of the day, this could put our collaboration with Natioba on ice for a long time."

"I would just say to them that it's in the interests of market development for us to be able to speak to other companies about the project," Emily suggested. "I can't think of anything else at the moment. But I'll be in touch straightaway if I do."

"That seems a little thin to me," Alex voiced her concern. "I mean, they could turn our argument on its head and ask for details about the Roffarm contract."

"Sure," her colleague replied. "But Natioba are going public with the project in a few weeks anyway; maybe you'll get them that way."

With that, Alex was on her own for the time being and headed thoughtfully back to her desk. What was the best way to solve things without arousing suspicion or angering her client? What angle could she use? What would her argument be?

Inspiration came in the form of an advertising email. Alex regularly received information about events taking place in the renewable energy sector. She had deleted the invitation to a conference in Hamburg at the beginning of September twice already. First because Thomas didn't have any budget for things like this and second because the organiser seemed to be new on the market. A thought crossed her mind just as she was about to delete the reminder. Why not? It could work. It was worth a try at any rate. Risky, but not impossible. She ran to Thomas. He agreed and Alex booked a flight out of Seoul straightaway.

One phone call later and the wheels had been set in motion. The conference programme had been fixed for weeks already but PsoraCom would be a welcome addition as an industry heavyweight. It was even possible that the agenda could be expanded for a fee. But Alex wanted the prime slot, right on the morning of the first day. She might not have had permission from the development lab supervisor in Seoul, but she was certain she could get it.

Now it was up to her bartering skills. She needed to get the conference chief to make space in the agenda; and she also had to sell the idea to Seoul as an additional highlight en route to the Big Bang. As soon as the organiser heard that it concerned a major innovation and that his conference would be the stage for the official announcement of a strategic alliance, he was hooked. Of course, PsoraCom would have to fork out a significant sum of money for the prime time slot; but Alex would pass that on to Hank's colleague – damages, so to speak, for his faux pas.

She told her project colleagues about the plan.

Nobu called straightaway and asked: "Is there any way I can help?"

"There is something, actually," Alex thanked him for the offer. "Can you look after the financial side of things? I should have an answer by this afternoon. Then we'll have to place the order immediately; we'll need the department code and a responsible buyer, though."

"Can your boss not give you an advance?" he asked.

"No," she replied. "I've spoken to him already. We've got a very tight budget and he doesn't want to make a single cent available, only to go through the arduous process of recovering it internally."

"You're right, Alex. The Americans should face the consequences of their actions. Leave it to me and if all else fails, I'll advance some funds from my own budget. We'll sort it somehow, don't worry."

"Thanks, Nobu. In the meantime, I'll try and get hold of Seoul. Let's hope the plan works."

The lab manager in Seoul was, as so often, unreachable. She left a message. Waiting was making her nervous. She went to get a cappuccino, cell in hand, so as not to miss him if he called back. She got a real fright when it rang. But it was only George. He had just heard that Bill was coming to Germany in August and that he'd been appointed regent for the trip.

"Luckily, Bill isn't overly fussy," he began. "He's got a clear idea of what companies he wants to visit and what he hopes to do with his free time. Still, it's a bit of a hassle, especially when you get the information at such short notice. I've got far too much to do already."

"I'm under a certain amount of pressure too, George. But what do you think of arranging a meeting between Bill and the development manager at Luxumi? Not much has happened since the joint meeting with Hursoc. If we're going to get things off the ground, what we really need is a technical project leader. In the long term, Thomas wants to try and find a second Hugo; I mean, he's already overworked as things are. Roffarm and Hursoc seem to monopolise his time to such an extent that he's got nothing left for clients like Luxumi. Perhaps Bill might be able to help there. Developing a new inverter costs a lot of money and means that everyone's resources are tied. But if a new project leader was appointed from his division, it would help us all. After all, it's in his interests to win Luxumi as a client. That's how the Roffarm team originated."

"I like the way you're thinking," George agreed. "It's a good idea. I'll add it to my agenda. In the meantime, you can start working on Luxumi."

"OK, I'll do that. But I've got to get off the line now."

"Alex, could you…"

"I'm sorry, George, I'm waiting for a call. We can speak longer next time."

"Sure, I understand, I've read the emails from yesterday after all. I'm sure you've got a few things to be getting on with. A real catch-22. And Brian couldn't help himself again. That's absolutely typical of him. You know, I'm not in the least surprised."

"George, another time, OK? Ciao, I'll be in touch."

Alex nipped him in the bud before he could ramble any longer. The call from Seoul really was more important. The issue had to be resolved before she went to Prague, otherwise she wouldn't be able to enjoy her holiday – or worse, she'd have to cancel it completely.

Henry picked her up for lunch. He had already heard what was happening from Wolfgang, who had been told by Lucas and Thomas. It seemed as if bad news spread like wildfire.

"It's an absolute disgrace," he bitched. "You can forget about Taipei if it gets out. Who is this idiot from the US?"

"I don't know him either," she replied. "He's a colleague of Hank's."

"There have to be consequences," he demanded energetically. "And they need to be communicated internally so a cock-up like this never happens again."

"There's no need to be quite so harsh," Alex calmed him. "At the moment we still don't know the full extent of what's happened. There's been a huge mistake, one that shouldn't have occurred. Now it's about damage limitation. Roffarm are angry and Natioba don't know a thing. That's the bottom line."

"But you're the one who has to take the heat for this guy. I mean, it's your client. What are you going to do?"

She let Henry in on her plan.

"When I read about the conference," she told him, "I was reminded of a comment the lab supervisor from Seoul made a few weeks ago. He said that in principle Natioba were interested in officially standardising developments wherever possible. That's only possible if other manufacturers are involved too, of course. A standard is only a standard when the majority of the industry uses it. For that to happen, a mutual exchange of opinions needs to take place. As far as polymer-based cells and technology are concerned, Seoul is basically open to discussion. Besides Natioba, Roffarm, Luxumi and Premve are the only companies we are specifically discussing the use of Vabilmo technology with. All three are based in Germany; it would be extremely difficult to persuade them to go to South Korea for a single meeting. It's not really a subject that can be discussed by phone or video conference either. So South Korea have to come here. With their participation at the conference in Hamburg, we could kill two birds with one stone. We announce that PsoraCom and Natioba are collaborating, without revealing the exact details of the joint project. We'll leave that to the CEO at the developer conference."

Her colleague nodded. "From a marketing point of view, it's not uncommon," he thought out loud, "to bring important information to the public's attention in stages. You want to use the conference in Hamburg as a decoy."

"That's right," Alex confirmed. "The event isn't particularly well-known and in terms of media coverage, it will be no match for the developer conference. That way, we're not stealing the CEO's thunder; instead, we're giving people an extra incentive to visit our show in Taipei – or at least keep an eye open for it in the press."

"How clever," said Henry.

"And listen, there's more," she continued. "In the course of the meeting, representatives from Roffarm, Luxumi and Premve can be invited for a discussion with Natioba. In order to arouse the interest of these companies in such a meeting, however, I need to get permission from Seoul to outline the details of our existing collaboration with Natioba."

"If the lab supervisor agrees to it," he began to understand, "then there won't be any violation of the confidentiality agreement."

"That's about the size of it," Alex replied. "Luckily the US slides didn't contain all the details. We can sell the conference as an exclusive high-level meeting to Roffarm's divisional director. Of course, it's Natioba who'd be interested in meeting him, if his busy schedule allows. That way, we'll be able to massage his bruised ego; meetings with Luxumi and Premve shouldn't take place until after he's already spoken to Natioba. He'll be the first to avail of the information personally."

"You, dear colleague, are one sly fox."

"Well, at least that's the theory, Henry. A lot still hinges on factors I can't control. I'm going to need a healthy dose of luck."

"You could offer to pay for the lab supervisor's costs, flight and hotel included," he suggested. "That's common practice here."

"Good to know!" she thanked him for the tip. "But whether he has any time is the issue. The next unknown is the reaction of Roffarm's divisional director. I hope he'll be as easily appeased as I imagine. He's incredibly egocentric – but that could be used to our advantage. According to Lucas, he's not even aware that we've violated our non-disclosure agreement with Natioba."

"You should handle that with as much discretion as possible internally as well," Henry advised. "The last thing we want is for the CEO's assistant to exercise his veto."

"Of course," she said. "We're hardly going to be shouting it from the rooftops. The conference has to be sold internally too. Still, according to Thomas, it's unlikely anyone will have anything against it. The conference is very much conceived as a niche event for the German market."

"The way I see it, you're going to do just fine."

Just as Henry was about to stand up, her Zeus68 rang. Alex sprang to her feet and darted into the corridor. It was Seoul; she needed to find a quiet corner as quickly as possible. Her colleague gave her the thumbs up. She had to really pull herself together to conceal her nerves, although she had gone through the arguments several times in her head. The Big Bang – that was her angle. They needed to announce that they'd made it into the opening speech to build the tension until the project was officially unveiled.

The other end of the line was silent.

"My diary is pretty full that week," the lab supervisor thought aloud. "But it's mostly internal meetings that I can postpone."

"It would be great if it worked out," Alex replied. "The conference occurred to me because it takes place in the domestic market of your competitors."

"The flight time is considerable, though," he continued. "Two days for the trip alone and then two more for the conference. Perhaps it would be enough for me just to take part on the first day."

His last sentence was more of an observation than a question.

"Naturally, I'm hoping our announcement gets the prime slot on the first day of the conference," she told him. "But I won't know for sure until later today. The first day would be the most interesting for all participants."

She realised he was seriously considering it. He had almost bitten.

"You mentioned recently," she tried to reel him in once and for all, "that you wanted to meet with other manufacturers. In particular to discuss design and the possibility of an industry standard. These meetings could easily be combined with your trip. I could try and arrange things for you from here."

"You're quite right," he remembered. "I'm still just as interested, and the timing's perfect. Industry developments are currently in their infancy; that means there's a lot of leeway in terms of standardisation."

"If you like," she suggested, "I can speak to your colleagues from Roffarm, Premve and Luxumi. It's much easier for me, as there's no time difference. Still, I'd need some background information to provide them with an incentive. I think it'd be enough to tell them a little about our joint project, without going into detail?"

"That sounds very reasonable," he agreed. "Your client service really leaves nothing to be desired. I think it's great how you think about procedure, while taking care of everything yourself at the same time."

"It's my pleasure," she said honestly. Even if circumstances didn't demand it, she would help her client wherever possible. "Could you send Chris an email about what we've just discussed and copy me in? For formality's sake; Chris will almost certainly help me compose the slides."

"OK," he promised. "And if things don't work out with me, perhaps Chris can take my place."

That was exactly what Alex had hoped for. In contrast to Roffarm's divisional director, the lab supervisor was a very affable guy, although he wasn't immune to vanity either, albeit in a considerably more charming way. They had taken a great stride forward. The most important thing was that she had obtained his permission to inform Roffarm about their collaboration. The risk that Natioba would file a lawsuit was all but averted. She sent a message to Lucas straightaway, asking that he call her before the return flight. Only now did she realise just how much she was sweating.

Thomas and Emily were relieved to hear the news. However, since they didn't know exactly what their colleague had said in the US, Emily warned against celebrating prematurely. Even though it appeared that no specific details had been mentioned, they wouldn't be out of the woods until the project had been unveiled. Then and only then was the information officially public knowledge. They needed to announce their collaboration with Natioba as soon as possible, taking care not to spoil the surprise effect of the developer conference. The situation was just as tricky as before.

An additional idea was brewing inside Alex's head. She returned to Henry. He confirmed that it was common practice to provide the media with some initial information before the developer conference. The conference programme was merely an index of contents along with the individual sessions of the different product sectors. The exhibiting partner companies were also listed, though product details were absent. It wasn't clear what the board members' presentations were about, either; understandably, such information wouldn't be leaked until just beforehand. Joint press releases with partner companies or end customers were quite rare, although companies were free to publicise details as they chose. In such instances, approval from PsoraCom's press office regarding content and date of publication was strongly recommended.

Once again, Alex was aware of the market position enjoyed by her employer and the level of expectation it brought. If she could persuade her client to issue a press release before the conference in Hamburg, they would be one step closer to resolving their dilemma. That was the only way of reducing the time period in which nothing was known about the joint project. It was possible that Roffarm's divisional director could speak to other companies about Natioba. Admittedly, it was a bit unlikely: he surely had better things to do than discuss the competition; but, as Emily had mentioned, participation in Hamburg didn't necessarily mean the danger was fully averted.

The organiser took his time to reply. Still, it was worth the wait, as he was able to grant them their desired slot. The price he quoted was a little excessive, Alex thought. In principle, the speakers – two in their case – had free entry. Often the organiser even took on the travel costs as well. Alex was certain that at least half the team would be there and so requested three additional passes. The organiser yielded and she was satisfied. Now she could spark the next phase.

She sent the lab supervisor an email informing him about their time slot and requesting an abridged CV and photo. The agenda would be revised in the next few days and changes posted on the conference website. In a further paragraph, she mentioned that she would call the different companies in the hope of arranging a joint meeting with them. As they had previously discussed, the meeting would focus on a possible industry standard for the polymer-based cells.

In this context, she would also inform Roffarm that Natioba and PsoraCom were working together on a project concerning the use of polymer-based cells in off-grid systems. If there was no veto forthcoming from the lab supervisor, Alex would have his agreement in written form – after a fashion, at least. Among businesspeople, silence meant acceptance, and acceptance equalled consent.

Afterwards she arranged a half-hour telephone conference for the next day. The aim was to give all those involved internally a status update, as well as an indication of what would happen next. As long as the sword of Damocles was still hanging over them, communicating by email wasn't an option. Besides team members, the list of participants included colleagues from the US and Asia, as well as Bill, Wolfgang and Thomas. Alex would inform the last two personally; they were only on the list for the sake of completeness. She assumed that Bill would be updated by one of his employees.

"That sounds really good," said Wolfgang, after she had finished. "The conference is a great idea; the Yanks should be happy we saved their bacon."

"We still need to decide who's giving the presentation," Alex said.

"It's Alex's client," Thomas said. "She should do it. I don't think it's hugely important. What do you think, Wolfgang?"

"I agree entirely. That's the job of the consultant."

That was Alex's take on it too. In her opinion, the event wasn't important enough for someone as high profile as the managing director. Better to keep the head honcho in reserve for more exclusive clientele. She hadn't expected anything different from Thomas, as he preferred to keep a low profile. The sound of her netphone interrupted their conversation.

"Sorry, that's Lucas," she apologised. "I've been waiting for him to call. We've already discussed the most important issues."

"On you go," Wolfgang dismissed her.

Lucas only had a few minutes before boarding and was eager to hear the news. He agreed to her proposal. From his point of view, it represented a fair compromise for both sides. His client could almost certainly be appeased by the prospect of a joint meeting. As an answer from the lab supervisor wasn't expected before tomorrow, they agreed to sit on it until then. Lucas wouldn't divulge any information to the divisional director on the return flight. His client was in a really good mood and hadn't mentioned the incident again. Lucas wanted to ensure it stayed that way for the next ten hours.

She drove home that evening exhausted but satisfied. It was important to her that she left her company phone behind when she went to Prague. That meant she needed to take care of as many outstanding issues as possible tomorrow. While driving, she dictated a to-do list to her Zeus68.

"Official order for Hamburg and US budget – Nobu. Answer emails, get CV and photo – lab supervisor. Make contact with Natioba press office – lab supervisor. Consultation about Roffarm meeting – Lucas. Tickets for Hamburg – team colleagues. Hotel and flight – travel agent."

That was enough for the time being. She could think about the presentation slides and her speech once she was back. The same applied to the press release. Prussians weren't that quick on the trigger.

Her suitcase was quickly packed. The weather in Prague promised hot days and sultry nights. A few T-shirts, shorts and a skirt, as well as a warm sweater and flip-flops were all she needed next to her wash bag. She would swap her suit for jeans and sneakers straight after work. That would be ample. A little space in her suitcase needed to be kept because there was a Harley shop and Hard Rock Cafe. Both were on her list of tourist attractions.

Sandro seemed to be completely undecided. He had packed and repacked his suitcase three times now. In the end it seemed more like he was giving up than actually being satisfied. He was taking his new camcorder with him though. She was primed and ready for some time off. Nevertheless, she wouldn't be able to unwind completely until everything had been taken care of tomorrow. She tossed and turned before finally falling asleep.

8

August

The next day, it seemed things weren't going to go smoothly. The lab supervisor hadn't replied and she couldn't get hold of him on the phone. There were only a few hours to go until his working day was officially over.

At least Nobu's luck had been better: he had reached Hank's colleague in the US. He still didn't seem to be completely aware of the situation, as he was reluctant to give up his budget. Alex couldn't help but shake her head, but it wasn't important anymore. The main thing now was that Nobu could help her place the order and guarantee their slot at the conference.

She tried Seoul again. It was almost like a game of roulette, betting on the precise moment he might have time. Finally he picked up and Alex breathed a sigh of relief. He didn't have a CV to hand so he dictated the most important points for Alex to pass on to the organiser. He had already sent the press office his photo and contact details. Besides that he didn't make any additional remarks. That meant he had accepted her proposal. A great load was lifted from her mind.

Time was getting pretty tight. Alex rattled through her list: flight, hotel room, info for the conference manager. She had reserved a pass for Thomas, who to her surprise didn't want to miss out for once. The others could fight it out for the remaining tickets while she was in Prague. Everything else would just have to wait – because her plane wasn't about to.

With every step towards reception, she felt the tension of the last few days simply melt away. Sandro was already waiting outside in the sun. She greeted him with a passionate kiss, but he didn't seem to particularly enjoy it. On the way to the airport, he didn't say much.

As the tension continued to dissolve, Alex was soon in high spirits. She turned the radio up and sang along with gusto. But that seemed to irritate Sandro as he turned the volume back down. She was probably being a bit over the top, but perhaps it would catch on. After a few more attempts, however, she gave up. He didn't seem to be in the mood for tomfoolery. The best thing was to leave him in peace; that normally worked. He perked up noticeably once he'd taken his place at the window seat she'd reserved for him. It seemed the holiday feeling was slowly taking hold.

In Prague it was already dark and the heat was stifling. Even their proximity to the Vltava didn't provide any respite. They dragged their suitcase wheels across the cobblestones while searching for their hotel below the castle. A pleasant coolness welcomed them into their lavish room. The parquet floor and open beams gave it a homely feel. A dark-wood double bed complemented the soft-yellow walls and moss-green satin sofa. The generous bathroom was fitted with a shower and bathtub so they could bathe at the same time. Luxury soaps and creams stood ready and they made use of them immediately.

After freshening up, they headed out towards the Charles Bridge in search of a restaurant.

"So, what do you want to see while we're here?" Alex asked, as she took a bite of her stuffed pancake.

"No idea," he shrugged his shoulders. "The most important attractions, I suppose. I haven't really thought about it; you know your way round better than me."

"OK, good; let's just see where tomorrow takes us. I suggest we start with a leisurely breakfast. We're on holiday, after all."

"Fine by me."

Having eaten their fill, both were deep in thought when a street trader approached their table laden with roses.

"Should I buy you one?"

It wasn't really the question she had been anticipating. Asking a woman if she wanted flowers wasn't exactly romantic. She hesitated. In the end, he bought a rose and gave it to her. Just like that: no kiss, compliment or anything else. OK, so there was a little smile, but even that was humourless somehow.

She was hardly bowled over.

"Let's go to the Charles Bridge," she suggested. "It's beautifully lit by night and you have a great view of the illuminated castle."

"Whatever you say."

On the way there, they walked beside each other in silence. When she tried to take his hand, he pulled away.

"It's far too hot," he declared.

As romantic as their surroundings were, Alex was suddenly overcome by sadness. She was barely able to hold back the tears. Something was missing. The feeling he used to give her. Affection, romance and loving gazes. She didn't know what was wrong. He seemed so distant and didn't react to her attempts at intimacy.

"Is something the matter?" he looked at her questioningly after a time.

She thought about it and swallowed hard. Were they really going to do this on the first night?

"Somehow I get the impression," she couldn't stop herself, "that there isn't much romance in our lives at the moment."

"Don't talk rubbish! What the fuck?" Sandro was unexpectedly touchy. "What do you expect? Am I supposed to line your path with roses or something?"

His reaction didn't exactly reassure her but she had no desire to get involved in a big debate. Perhaps the events of the last few weeks really had rattled her. As if he could sense this, he took her hand in a gesture of reconciliation. Alex began to feel a little better. They stood still for a minute in the middle of the bridge and admired the castle. It was a gorgeous view but the accompanying magic was lacking.

Back at the hotel, they didn't say much to each other. One thing they were able to agree on was that the air-con was too loud to sleep and they decided to leave their two roof windows open instead. Alex snuggled up to Sandro in bed. He didn't give any signals that he wanted more. That was very unusual on holiday, but she wouldn't have been willing to go any further, anyway; it wouldn't have felt right.

Alex was woken the next morning by the warm rays of the sun; She crawled cheerfully out of bed. Even if things weren't going well, she always began the new day with a smile on her face, just like her father. She came out of the bathroom all clean and fresh. Sandro squinted at her through half open eyes and yawned. Normally his reaction would have been different, but not this time. She registered the change but resolved not too think about it too much. The day was young and they had a city to explore. Prague had so many beautiful squares and buildings to offer, to say nothing of its charming baroque coffee houses, earthy pubs and eccentric bars. There was so much she wanted to show Sandro.

Since Sandro didn't have any concrete wishes, Alex suggested they visit the castle, followed by a tour of Prague's Lesser Quarter, as the district was officially known.

They walked along winding cobblestone alleys past newly renovated façades and up towards Hradčany. Enormous palaces bore witness to the renaissance and baroque styles of bygone years. Occasionally gothic façades peered out from in between, all very typical for Prague. The Malà Strana wasn't seen as the prettiest district in Prague for nothing. You got a real sense of how yesterday's rich had sought out a place close to the centre of governance and settled there. With its mighty St. Vitus cathedral, king's palace and raft of museums, the castle grounds loomed large across the city. A sizeable queue stretched out across the castle courtyard in the summer heat, while visitors sought the cool of Prague's biggest cathedral.

"I'm not queuing outside in these temperatures." Sandro had lost all desire when he saw the line. "I'm too hot as it is, and thirsty. The heat's absolutely suffocating here."

"We had warmer days in Sicily," Alex countered. "Look, I've got some water. The inside of the cathedral's really worth seeing; besides, the queue's moving pretty fast."

Her parents had raised her to accept things she couldn't control without complaint and carry on as planned. She wasn't about to be put off by a bit of warm weather. What's more, positives could be drawn from any situation.

"Hopefully it won't take too long. I'm dying here," Sandro grumbled.

"It'd be a lot worse if it was raining," came the response. "I'd rather be too warm. We can always take a break when we're finished with the cathedral."

Sandro nodded in silence. He was in a strange mood again; Alex blamed the heat. The queue moved quicker than expected into the pleasantly cool nave of the church. Sandro took photos of the tombs of Nepomuk and Wenzel, as well as the high vault. He was less interested by the history of the cathedral. Just before the exit, they lit a candle each and Alex thought of her mother.

They could go without seeing the Golden Lane. The entry price had gone up drastically since her last visit and was no longer worth it in her opinion. A nice postcard was a better investment by far.

For the next stage of their trip, they headed westwards via Hradčany Square up through a cool patch of forest. On top of Petrín hill was a small lookout tower based on the Eiffel Tower. Despite the 299 steps, making their sweat pour in the early afternoon heat, even Sandro was forced to admit the journey had been worthwhile. From there they had a magnificent view of Prague.

Alex pointed out Old Town Square; with the prominent town hall spire and gothic towers of Týn cathedral, its outline could be spied even from a distance. Not far from the cathedral was the biggest synagogue in Prague, replete with the treasures of various Jewish places of worship. They couldn't fail to see the Charles Bridge and its baroque stone figures either, their stoical quiet and dusky veneer providing a marked contrast to the scurrying fleets of tourists. St. Nicholas Church could be made out next to it.

Although they were high up on the viewing platform, there was no breeze whatsoever – and Sandro wasn't the only one who was tired and sweaty. They looked for a secluded spot in the shade so that they could take a rest.

"If it's OK with you," Alex suggested the next leg of their tour, "I'd like to take a little detour to the Harley shop. I don't have anything from Prague yet and it's only a short distance by taxi. Afterwards we can take it easy in the hotel and freshen up for the evening."

"Fine by me," he said indifferently, "as long as you don't spend ages browsing."

"I don't think it'll be that big. Before dinner, we could have an aperitif above the roofs of the old town. There's a hotel with a lovely roof terrace not far away from the town hall. From there you get a fantastic view of the castle and the square in general."

A cold shower was currently a far more enticing prospect for Sandro. Although there was Italian blood in him, he found the stagnant heat and muggy air absolute torture. Alex suggested that they set off again before they sank into a deep sleep, and so they headed towards Lobkowicz Palace via the Hunger Wall and Rosarium. The splendid baroque building, home for many years of the German Embassy, provided a historical link between past and present.

"This is where GDR refugees were given their exit permits shortly before reunification. After tens of thousands had laid siege to the grounds, the former USSR lifted part of the Iron Curtain and opened its gates to the West."

While she was still speaking, Sandro began to look around for a taxi.

There was real live air conditioning in the Harley shop. Sandro spied a folding chair and made himself comfortable. Meanwhile Alex made a circle of the exhibition rooms. Her only purchases were a long-sleeved T-shirt for the autumn and some nice underwear for Jenny. There were no curios to add to her little collection.

The roof window shutters were closed, and apart from the isolated crackle of the wood beam, the half-light was broken only by the low murmur of the room's air conditioning. After the shower he had so desperately craved, Sandro was already resting between the cool sheets. The open windows on the taxi journey back had brought only dust into their lungs. There had been faint signals that Sandro's mood was about to take a serious turn for the worse. He seemed happier now, however. The only thing he was missing was a little sleep – followed by a hearty dinner.

Alex let the water on her skin dry without using a towel. She allowed the cool breeze of the air-con to pass over her. It wasn't only the hair standing on her arms that drew attention to her goose bumps. She set the alarm on her cell. Sandro glanced at her fleetingly, plumped up the pillow and gave her a tired kiss before turning on his side. The heat must have really exhausted him.

Even after the alarm sounded an hour later, he had failed to provide the desired response to her subtle advances. Last night's rose stood next to her suitcase on the chest of drawers, its wilting flowers an all too accurate reflection of Alex's own despair. Maybe they should have gone to the coast. She should have realised it would have been hot in the narrow confines of the city in August. Brusquely, she dispelled the thought. They were here now and would just have to make the best of it. At the end of the day, he had agreed to the trip too. It hadn't been her decision alone. He would like the roof terrace bar, Alex was sure of it; those kinds of places appealed to him just as much as they did to her.

"You're looking really good today," Sandro smiled at her, as he emerged from the bathroom. "The skirt suits you."

She brightened up considerably; his compliments were always sincere.

"Thanks. You look good enough to eat by the way."

The evening could begin. They strolled unhurriedly across the Charles Bridge, entering a hotel just before they reached Old Town Square and taking the stairs up to the sixth floor. As expected, Sandro was captivated by the view and immediately pulled out his camcorder. The nearby towers were illuminated by the sun as if floodlit. Steep, red tiled roofs with countless pointed dormers and gargoyled façade edges lined the horizon, an image punctuated occasionally by the weathered verdigris of their copper counterparts. The castle looked magnificent in the haze of the glistening sunlight.

Alex took a photo with her cell and sent it to Anna as a reminder. It was with her that she had first discovered this place, all those years ago. At over 80 pages long, the cocktail menu was as varied as the view. She decided on the interesting-sounding "Prince Julep", made with traditional Becherovka herbal liqueur, while Sandro played it safe with a mojito. Gradually the heat of the day began to fade as the sun slowly set, bathing everything in a violet-pink light.

Sandro tried various exposure modes on his camera to capture the image that lay before him. The yellow lighting of the castle walls increased the contrast between the shaded nave of the cathedral and the intense tones of the purple sky. Below, the lights of prominent buildings were soon switched on, and the main square became submerged in a festive glow. As good as the view was – even after sunset – their hunger began to assert itself stubbornly. Not far away, they spied an earthy, cosy-looking restaurant with tables decked outside. After the exertions of the day, they had both earned a hearty meal.

Their conversation centred on memories of past holidays. Sandro didn't seem particularly keen to talk about their future travel plans and Alex moved onto a different topic as soon as she realised. Up until now the evening had gone off very peacefully and she was loath for that to change. In the wake of their reminiscence, romance finally appeared to blossom once more; perhaps there would be room for a little tenderness back at the hotel after all.

But Sandro didn't want the evening to end. On the way back through the crowded alleys, he noticed a pub populated almost exclusively by students. There had to be time for a night cap, in his opinion – and Alex allowed her arm to be twisted. They were on holiday after all. Two drinks and a spot of dancing later, she finally persuaded him to go back to the hotel. He fell asleep while Alex was brushing her teeth.

Something wasn't right. She didn't know what it was, but after waking the next morning she was hit once more by a feeling of melancholy. Things were different from before. But she couldn't say exactly how. Sandro was still sleeping. She went into the bathroom and sat down on the edge of the tub. What was the matter? Tears began to flow, streaming uncontrollably down her cheeks, until gradually a quiet sobbing set in. She didn't want Sandro to see her like this. What was wrong with her?

It was probably down to the alcohol the night before. Yesterday had been a good day. Admittedly, the heat had been a problem but you couldn't control the weather. You just had to make the best of it and in her opinion, they had done that. It had been an enjoyable evening, from the romantic sunset on the roof terrace through to their dinner time reminiscing.

They remembered how they had capsized the boat on a rafting tour of the Grand Canyon because they couldn't stop kissing and hadn't noticed the approaching rapids. Memories like this had rekindled old feelings. It had to be down to the alcohol, Alex thought to herself. A long shower would bring her back to life, while a little extra make up would mask the slight swelling under her eyes.

The last two drinks didn't seem to have caused Sandro much trouble. Although he was quieter than usual, he wasn't obviously in a bad mood. Over a substantial breakfast of eggs he agreed to her suggestion that they explore the old town. The sky was overcast. With a little luck, it wouldn't be so hot today. It didn't seem like there were many tourists about either.

Alex took some pictures of Sandro posing next to St. John of Nepomuk and his sacred colleagues on the Charles Bridge. Countless street traders tried to peddle their goods. One of them seemed different. In contrast to his neighbours, he wasn't selling the standard postcards and photos, but rather his own paintings. They were unique somehow and weren't painted on traditional canvas. It was coffee sacks made from coarse jute fabric, he explained. Alex had never seen anything like it. After she had bought one – she always liked to take something special home from her trips – they proceeded to Old Town Square.

There was a huge crowd of people standing outside the town hall, cameras at the ready, waiting for the hourly appearance of the apostles. Their popularity seemed to be similar to that of boy-bands, though the target audience differed somewhat, of course.

Sandro was more taken with the astronomical clock and its depiction of moon phases, solar altitude and the position of the planets. It, like all the Rococo and Renaissance style palaces renovated in various pastel tones, was soon immortalised digitally. Why pink – of all colours – was part of the palette would remain a mystery to Alex. Just like in bygone centuries, goods of all kinds were being sold on the square; today, however, the products seemed only to meet the questionable demands of mass tourism. Behind the square they passed by elegant shop fronts on their way to the House of Representatives. At the end of the lane was a café that had lost none of its olde-worlde charm.

"It's almost compulsory to have a drink here," Alex suggested they go in.

Sandro didn't need much persuasion. He was more than happy for a break, even if a cold drink currently seemed more important than the atmosphere.

From the gallery on the first floor, it was easy to abandon oneself completely to the charm of yesteryear. Chandeliers hung on gilded beams from the bright stucco roof, and the high walls were adorned with golden wood-panelling. Uniformed waiters pushed a refrigerated cake trolley from table to table, while a trio of musicians provided light relief with their gentle singing.

In front of the café, actors in fancy dress were selling tickets for the theatre, which was located opposite in a former baroque church. Sandro shooed them away gruffly with a sweeping hand gesture. He wasn't normally so aggressive.

Despite the overcast sky – or perhaps because of it – it had become noticeably more humid, and the air seemed to hang in the streets. There wasn't the slightest breeze. Next, they proceeded to Wenceslas Square, where the main attraction was the bronze memorial that stood in front of the National Museum. With its numerous modern shops and restaurants, except for a single, old coffee house, the square gave no indication of its former existence as a horse market. Sandro's mood was sinking in inverse proportion to the rising heat. Alex was sweating as well, but unlike him she preferred excess warmth to extreme cold.

"Let's take a little detour along the river up to Josefstadt," she suggested. "It might be less sticky on the Vltava than here between these narrow houses. There's an old Jewish cemetery a bit further on."

"No skin off my nose," he chuntered. "It's worth a try, at least."

On the way there, they walked past another old café with great glass panes; he seemed as uninterested as he had been previously.

Sandro's mood improved briefly as they paused on a bench by the river underneath the trees. It was difficult to say whether it was the Vltava or her imagination, but the air certainly seemed to be less oppressive. Rested, they walked on past the magnificent Rudolfinum concert hall and on to the old Jewish cemetery. A graveyard was not normally the sort of place Alex chose to visit; but like Père Lachaise in Paris, this one was worth seeing – even if there was no comparison in terms of size. This final resting place lay wedged in between houses and was only visible through curved iron gates. Ornate tombs stood untidily next to, or half on top of, rough-hewn stones; apparently there were nine different layers of graves.

"That's it?" Sandro complained. "I was expecting a little bit more. We've been walking in the heat forever for what? To see a few chaotically arranged tombstones?"

Alex suppressed an initial wave of anger and took a deep breath; she didn't want to express her thoughts unchecked. Slowly but surely her patience was being put to the test. She had been making suggestions for two days now, as well as telling him the individual story behind every building or square. He hadn't even deigned to look at the guidebook, let alone read it.

They had decided on Prague and now here they were. They couldn't control the weather; the only thing they could do was make the best of it and adapt their plans spontaneously. By taking a break in a nice café or on a bench in the shade, for example. Spending the day in their air-conditioned hotel room until the temperature became more agreeable in the evening wasn't an option – they were hardly in the desert, after all. What was she supposed to do?

"Then why don't you make a suggestion about where to go or what to do? I guess I'm just no good at receiving the faintest signals today and I don't have my crystal ball with me."

Her answer was snippier than she'd intended. Sandro went quiet and didn't say a single thing more.

Something is really not right here, Alex thought to herself again. She just wanted to go back to the hotel and sleep. Maybe the air conditioning would cool her emotions as well. At any rate, she had no desire to traipse through the city anymore. Sandro walked behind her. It made her furious that he didn't say anything. In situations like this, he just remained silent and she had no way of knowing what he was thinking. The only thing that could help was to give him a little time.

They showered silently one after the other, and then lay down in bed. Each kept strictly to their own side. This time Alex didn't set an alarm. Let fate decide how things went from here.

Barely two hours later, she was awake. Sandro was lying next to her, eyes open. She wasn't wearing anything but that didn't seem to interest him in the slightest. She had tried to arouse his passion more than once in the last two days.

"Don't you find me attractive anymore?" she said, hurt. "You wouldn't have hesitated for a second before. What's up?"

"I'm just knackered," he replied. "Why are you getting yourself so worked up?"

That wasn't a satisfactory answer. Above all because it was devoid of any sort of reconciliatory gesture. He didn't take her in his arms, nor did he stroke her hair or kiss her cheek. There was no attempt at rapprochement. When she tried to get close to him, he just reacted even more tetchily.

"Come on, leave it Alex. It's too hot, that's all. You know how difficult I find the heat."

"You're not making any sense," Alex got dressed angrily. "Sicily wasn't any cooler!"

And he hadn't behaved so objectionably there – though she left that part unspoken. What on earth was wrong with him?

"Let's just go and get something to eat," she added brusquely. "We walked past a steakhouse near the castle yesterday."

At least he seemed more enthusiastic when it came to food.

The restaurant had an inviting-looking terrace and a cocktail bar in the vaulted cellar; an enticing prospect for the midnight hours.

During dinner, Sandro still seemed to be in silent mode and couldn't be drawn into anything other than monosyllabic responses. Alex had no desire to play the lone entertainer and keep a meaningless conversation alive. Her mood was approaching its nadir.

She kept asking herself what was wrong. The frustrating thing was that there were no answers forthcoming, giving her no chance to work on a solution. For that was the way her brain operated. Recognise problem, find and implement solution. Basta.

After dinner, she couldn't take it any longer. She had to stretch her legs. She couldn't keep sitting there without losing her composure. Going back to her hotel room wasn't an option – too constricted. So she went towards the castle. Sandro followed silently. Tears were brimming close to the surface, much the same as this morning, but she couldn't describe the feeling that was causing her so much pain. She couldn't hold back the tears any longer; they just kept coming. What was happening here?

There wasn't a single flicker from Sandro. He just kept walking. No physical contact. No tissue. No questions. Nothing. She began to give free rein to her tears. She didn't care about the people walking past. They could think whatever they liked; Alex had lost all control of her emotions. By the time they made it up to Castle Square, her whole upper body was shaking with sobs. Still nothing from Sandro.

"Don't you talk to me anymore?" she squeezed out.

"There's so much going on in my head I have to think very carefully about what I say," he replied.

He's going to end it, the thought flashed across Alex's mind, striking her with hellish force. It was the last thing she'd reckoned with. She wouldn't have dreamed it could happen. Now there was no stopping her tears. She didn't know how to respond. Keep going. That was the only thing she could do in a situation like this. She couldn't go back to the hotel. Not yet.

The castle gate was still open. She went through. Past the cathedral, towards the eastern exit. Down the old castle stairs. Over the Vltava bridge and across into Josefstadt. Through all sorts of alleyways. Past pubs and restaurants populated by smiling people enjoying the mild summer night.

Sandro beside her. Silently. Idly. Hands in pockets. Towards Old Town Square. A gaze in the direction of the roof terrace caused fresh tears to flow. Away from here. Down Wenceslas Square and back again. She couldn't go back to the hotel. Not yet. Further. How many tears did she still have left? Through the theatre district. Right. Left. Where were they?

It didn't matter. A sign on the left advertised the botanic gardens. Still nothing from Sandro. She went right towards the Vltava. Slowly her legs were beginning to revolt. She had ignored the pain in her feet for over an hour already. To sleep, just to sleep. That was all she wanted now.

Back at the hotel, she didn't set an alarm. What for? Their flight didn't leave until the afternoon and she wouldn't stay in bed that long. She would wake up when it got too hot – at the latest. Without a word, without even the slightest gesture, they got into bed. She was crying so much she could no longer think. Eventually her body gave in to exhaustion.

The warmth made it seem light outside, but it was still dark when Alex awoke. Her eyes were so swollen and gummed up that she struggled to open them. Carefully she rubbed a little spit on them so that she could find the bathroom. The cold water alleviated the pain only temporarily. She hardly dared look in the mirror. A bloated pig stared back at her. Even though her brain had slipped into its usual positive morning gear, she was suddenly overcome by the memory of the previous evening. Perhaps there was still a chance though? Maybe he had no intention of ending it. After all, he hadn't said it was over yet. But she could be mistaken. At the end of the day, how was she supposed to know what he had to think about?

She didn't know anything. Her instincts was all she had and they had proved wrong before. First, take a shower, wash away the events of the previous evening and then see how things went from there. Her brain needed to grasp something positive; it was part of who she was. As soon as she came out of the bathroom, however, she knew there was nothing left to salvage. Sandro had got up and was already packing his suitcase. He glanced briefly towards her, then turned quickly away.

"I'm going for a shower too." His first words in more than twelve hours.

Nothing else. The tears began to stream down her cheeks once more. Slowly she sorted her things into her suitcase. Her gaze fell upon the rose, which was still standing in its tumbler. A wilting picture of misery. She started sobbing uncontrollably. What was going to happen next?

They left their bags at reception for a few hours while killing time before the flight. Although it was quite dark inside, Alex didn't bother removing her sunglasses to settle the bill. Better for people to think she was arrogant than to see how wretched she looked. One last stroll across the Charles Bridge into the old town. She spent the whole time drying her tears and wiping her nose.

In front of a glass-blowing shop she stopped and summoned all her self-control to go inside. Her mother would appreciate a lovely handmade glass bowl. Sandro didn't say a word the whole time. He hadn't spoken since he went for a shower. To her it was inexplicable that someone could walk alongside their sobbing partner without displaying the slightest hint of emotion. It only exacerbated her feeling of isolation and caused salty tears to stream forth once more. Soon she would be out of tissues. The day was a nightmare from which she couldn't escape. The hours went by as if in slow motion. She longed to be back in their flat. Her home. There she could shut herself away. But somehow she had to survive the next five hours.

At some point, she couldn't bear to be in the city any longer. How much time was left? Then they would just have to wait at the airport. Sandro went along with everything in silence, walking alongside her without uttering a word. At last they were in the plane, then the car, then back at home. Alex left her suitcase standing in the hall and went to get a beer from the fridge. The tears were flowing again. She had bought cigarettes at the airport. Outside on the balcony she smoked them one after the other. Sandro started doing the laundry, stuffing everything carelessly into the drum.

Then all of a sudden he stopped and shouted: "In the last few months, you've just become too masculine for me."

Too masculine? What on earth did he mean?

"I'm going to move in with my parents for a few days to see if I can get my head together."

That was it. He didn't say anything more, just went to bed. She sobbed. It was just lucky that Moritz wasn't home to see her crying. The rest of her neighbours couldn't see the balcony through the trees, but she didn't care anyway. The pain was intense. It was the only thing she could still feel. It was over. Even though he hadn't said it explicitly, she knew. She dragged herself off to the fridge to get another beer. All she wanted to do was switch off, stop thinking. But she couldn't. She lit another cigarette.

Her brain was like a computer. As long as she was still awake, it was switched on. This time, it was like a circular reference error in a calculation programme. There was a problem she was trying to solve. Only the solution didn't depend on her. There wouldn't be a solution at all without additional input. But it was precisely this input that was lacking.

Sandro had gone to bed. What did he mean by "too masculine?" She rarely put on skirts or low-cut tops and the fact that she hated housework was no secret. He was just as aware of her penchant for gadgets and all things technical. She hardly ever wore stilettos because she couldn't walk in them for long and her meagre collection of handbags would have brought any normal-thinking woman to tears. But that was how she'd always been; she was no different when Sandro first met her.

Her feminine side was reflected more in the home front. She had always wanted him to feel happy there. Whether it was delicious home-cooked meals, informal gatherings with friends or romantic candle-lit dinners. Sometimes, of course, their opinions differed on the number of candles. Was that not feminine enough? Surely she hadn't changed that much in the past few months? Or had she? Had she given him too little freedom? Tried to help him too much? Or did it have something to do with their talk about his career? Had she been too forthright and backed him into a corner?

But surely that couldn't be the only reason. What exactly was it about her that was "too masculine?" She didn't understand. The tissues were all gone but the tears still flowing. She needed a new packet and might as well get herself another beer. The cigarettes were already starting to make her feel sick but she couldn't stop. At least it gave her something to do, even if it only involved sitting there breathing in burnt air. She lifted her feet onto the chair and wrapped her arms around them. Her knees became wet with tears as she rocked herself gently back and forth. It was already dark by the time she had drunk the fourth beer, smoked the last cigarette and gone off to bed. Not even a flicker from Sandro. Her sobbing had almost turned to hiccups. She stopped crying briefly before the tears started once more.

He stood up and went to the toilet. When he got back, she couldn't help it and said: "What you're doing just now, is like watching someone injured bleed to death."

But he asked simply: "What do you want me to do? I've got to think things over in peace first."

With that he got back into his side of the bed and Alex was seized by a fresh bout of wailing. She had to go to work the next morning. If only someone could stop the pain.

After her morning shower, Alex took a cool mask from the freezer and placed it over her eyes. She looked awful. But she couldn't work from home; she needed to be surrounded by people. Sandro had already left. A change of scenery would help raise her spirits to survival level. A few layers of kohl and eye shadow later, she felt disguised enough to make an appearance. As she drove to the office, the tears kept fighting their way to the surface. She attempted to combat the onslaught with a dose of loud music – but she could only sing along falteringly.

There wasn't much time to brood once she was inside the office. First Marco swung by. The organiser of the conference in Hamburg had issued some preliminary information about their presentation. PsoraCom and Natioba were to unveil a joint project in the off-grid solar power systems industry. It wasn't an official press release, more of an ad-hoc announcement about changes to the conference agenda. Lucas had already been informed. They had to react quickly. His client hadn't seen the announcement. He would not be amused if he received the information from anyone other than PsoraCom. Relations were only just on the mend again after the turmoil of the previous week.

The question was how much they could tell the divisional director. They couldn't tell him anything about the project that he didn't already know. They needed to gently inform him about the joint presentation in Hamburg. The hairs stood up on the back of Alex's neck once more. The whole thing was fraught with difficulty. But it was all about playing the exclusivity contract to their advantage.

When Lucas told his client about it, it had to sound as if they were doing him a big favour. The contract endowed Roffarm with special status, that much was certain. Now the trick was to make it seem like they were getting important market information first – without actually divulging anything important. A kind of heads-up, so to speak. If it worked this time, then according to Emily the problem with the clause would be solved. If Roffarm were to approve the procedure for exchanging information about other projects, a precedent would be created; and for the time being, the whole tiresome issue would be resolved. It remained in no-one's interest to settle the matter in court.

"It worked. Roffarm have swallowed the bait," Lucas informed her later with some relief. "The situation's been just as tricky for me as for you. But I can live with the current solution. Still, in future can you keep me up-to-date on client developments directly?"

"Yeah, no problem," Alex promised.

She didn't ask why he wasn't leaving that to Brian. Perhaps Lucas wanted to hear it from both sides. Or maybe he wasn't getting any information at all.

When no-one picked up the phone in Seoul, Alex sent the lab supervisor a mail with a link to the ad-hoc announcement. For information purposes, so that he couldn't be ambushed from the other side. Shortly afterwards, her phone rang.

"I wanted to thank you personally for your efforts," the lab supervisor said. "It's great that the agenda's been changed so quickly and that everyone's already informed."

"Yes, I think so too," Alex replied, concealing her relief. "The conference organisers seem to be a flexible group. And by the way, we've already been in touch with Roffarm. I'll tell you as soon as I know more."

"I really appreciate everything you're doing for our joint project," he added.

It was unbelievable how some things just seemed to sort themselves out.

In the afternoon, Thomas called her in for a surprise meeting.

"Our chief sales officer has announced a visit for the end of September," Thomas opened the discussion. "He's in Europe for a week visiting clients. It's expected he'll attend staff meetings in the bigger offices like Germany and Strasbourg. As with any visit from the upper hierarchy, we need a regent to plan and take responsibility for everything."

Alex wondered what was coming next.

"Wolfgang wants you to take it on," he said, looking her straight in the eye.

She was speechless. She had already heard from Henry that an internal task like this was a real honour.

"But I haven't been with the company for very long," she replied, trying to suppress her excitement. That a newcomer like her had been chosen to look after someone this high-ranked made the decision even more significant. According to rumours in the sales department, he wielded more influence than the CEO himself. Either way, he was one of the most important figures at PsoraCom.

"Don't get too excited," Thomas checked her. "It's a tough gig. You've got six weeks to plan. And your projects can't be allowed to suffer; everything has to run parallel to your normal job."

"How long will he be here for?" she probed.

"The whole day, as far as I know. He's arriving the evening before. At least that's what his agenda says at the moment, though it's subject to change at any time."

"One day won't be so bad."

"Don't kid yourself."

"I won't. You can count on me."

"That's exactly the reason Wolfgang picked you, so make sure you don't cock it up."

The extra job was just what she needed to distract her from the chaos of her private life.

"One more thing," her boss said. "I'm going on holiday for a week in a fortnight's time; you'll be deputising for me. I don't think there'll be a lot to do. But if there's anything you're really not sure about, just ask Christopher."

"OK, no problem."

Besides her own job and role as regent, she'd be standing in for him now too. Just like that, she smiled cynically to herself.

She drove home high as a kite. The news in the office had helped her forget about the dramas of her home life. But all that changed suddenly when she turned into the driveway to see Sandro emerging from the house, bags already packed.

It seemed like he had hoped not to run into her. Before getting into his car and driving off, he said only that he was going away for a few days. Her sadness set in once more. How had it all gone wrong? Why did he have to leave now? Perhaps Moritz was home. She didn't want to be alone, but no-one answered. There was no way he couldn't have heard the loud ring of the bell. She turned round dejectedly.

Then it was back to her diet of yesterday. Beer and cigarettes. She wasn't hungry anymore.

Suddenly, she thought of Maria. It had been ages since they last spoke. Not that it'd harmed their friendship in any way. It didn't matter how many weeks or months it'd been, as soon as they started talking it seemed just like yesterday. The time they had spent together before Maria emigrated to Spain had made them inseparable. There was nothing they couldn't talk about. Although they were both completely different, there was a special bond between them. Maybe it was simply because they were so dissimilar.

Maria had trained in HR after school and been taken on after successfully completing her final exams. She had combined work with studying to be a solicitor specialising in industrial law. After that she had assumed responsibility for the contracts of all employees and service providers until she met her husband, a Spaniard who had been temporarily transferred to Germany.

After barely a year he had returned to Spain, taking Maria with him. Now she was a contented mother of two, working part time at an animal shelter and trying to find new homes for as many cats as possible. With that, all her wishes had been granted. She had never been much of a careerist; besides, there had come a point when contractual issues and everything that went with them had become too dry and abstract. She made an exception for friends though, acting as a consultant in all matters legal.

Alex had met Maria twenty years ago through a university friend. They had seen eye to eye immediately. When Maria couldn't find anyone to assemble her IKEA furniture, Alex was more than happy to step in. It was the beginning of a lifelong friendship.

Maria picked up the receiver, and Alex could hear the kids charging about outside. They didn't eat until late in Spain and she had caught her friend in the middle of preparing dinner.

"Sure, things haven't been perfect between us for a while," the words poured forth, as Alex told her the latest news. "But when are they in a long-term relationship? You always have to make compromises. He didn't give me any signs that something was drastically wrong. He even gave me a bouquet of flowers just before we went on holiday. Who sees that and thinks their partner's about to end things? The holiday was supposed to make us want to do more things as a couple. I've been working very hard recently and he's been taken up with the club. We've been missing out on a lot of free time together."

"Don't give up hope," Maria assured her. "You're such a good couple. You'll get it together somehow. Men sometimes just need a few days' time out to withdraw to their caves and think. Let him have that at least. When he comes back, listen to him; pay attention to his feelings. It's equally important for you to express your own thoughts too, of course. You almost certainly haven't talked to each other enough recently; so just wait and see where things go from here."

Somewhat reassured, Alex hung up. Maria had done it again. That was exactly what she liked about her best friend: she thought with her heart and listened to her gut instinct. Alex was different; with her, it was the brain that took centre stage. Just like in Prague. First analyse the problem then find and implement a solution.

Alex planned the weekend with renewed vigour. She wanted to spend as little time as possible in the flat. She would only end up trapped in her own spiral of thoughts. She spent the whole day hiking and swimming in the mountains with Anna. Her friend seemed to be in two minds about Sandro's behaviour.

"You know, I really like Sandro," she said. "But who can see into another person's mind? There's nothing for it but to wait and see what happens."

On Sunday Alex visited her parents, but didn't tell them anything about the current situation. What was the point while things were still so unclear? They'd only worry. Her mother told her about the aftercare appointment. For the moment, everything was looking good and no new cancer cells had been uncovered. Alex was greatly relieved; Ricka, on the other hand, was more serious than anticipated – in spite of the good news. But maybe she was just imagining it, Alex thought to herself, as she waved her concerns aside.

Sandro was already waiting for her when she got home.

"I'm going to look for a flat," the news was sudden. "It's too rural for me here. Besides, I'd like to have all my things in the one place."

"So are you breaking up with me or what?" Alex's reacted disbelievingly.

"I just need a little space," he said, "and a place where I can think things over in peace. There's no need for us to break up. I just want to look for a flat in the city. It's the best thing for both of us. If we go out somewhere in the evening, neither of us has to drive and you can stay over at mine. It's a temporary solution, not a permanent one."

"And how long do you want to live in a separate flat?"

"I'm afraid I can't tell you that. Only time will tell."

She was anything but thrilled. Still, he wasn't breaking up with her. The prospect of shuttling back and forth between two different flats was hardly appealing though.

The next week went by in a flash and Alex allowed work to monopolise her time. Besides preparing for the Natioba project, she also needed to fly back to London for the battery company workshop. Carl had pulled out at short notice the previous evening, as another appointment had cropped up, despite initially being so desperate to go. But it was his decision in the end, Alex thought a little upset.

Naturally, she'd be able to cope with the workshop on her own; it's just that things would have been more balanced if they'd gone as a pair. Besides, she had hailed Carl as their robotics expert. Any detailed questions the client had about this area might now have to be left unanswered. Life was full of surprises you just had to deal with. Still, there was no point fixing something that wasn't already broken: Alex had dinner in the Hard Rock Cafe, before checking her mails with a nightcap in the comfortable surroundings of the hotel lounge.

Most of the workshop was taken up by brainstorming. There were three possible sectors in which they could work together. First, they could jointly approach robot manufacturers to ensure their products were fitted directly with polymer-based cells from PsoraCom and batteries from London. Second, they could combine to develop charging stations that generated their electricity from solar cells and use them to recharge the batteries of household robots – preferably with the new wireless technology. The final option was similar to the first, only this time focusing on the off-grid-systems market. Both parties would promote each other's products with the different individual manufacturers.

Technically speaking, all three were valid options. But the second possibility contradicted PsoraCom's own robotics strategy in the medium term. At this stage, it seemed most likely they would combine with off-grid-systems manufacturers. Not just yet, however, as the potential the Brits offered was currently deemed too slight. It was exactly the same with the robot manufacturers. They would meet again when they knew more in a few months' time. London saw the flexibility of the bend-modules as a decisive advantage. They would be able to tailor the generation of electricity to the exact specifications of the batteries.

"By the end of the discussion, it was pretty clear they had hoped for more," Alex said, as she gave Carl a quick call en route to the airport. "But it doesn't help anyone if we kid ourselves about the market prospects. What do you think?"

"I agree with you," he replied. "We've only just started looking at robots ourselves. We need to learn from our own experiences before we decide how best to collaborate with them."

The airport was chaos, as there had been a bomb scare. Security measures had been heightened to the limits of impracticability and a number of flights had been cancelled. Weak-nerved businessmen looked likely to have a heart attack when they were told no hand luggage could be taken on board. The exceptions were passports and a little cash so that drinks, snacks and papers could be purchased in the departure lounges. See-through plastic bags were distributed for these items, though they didn't represent a particularly attractive alternative to the customary handbags. Netphones, laptops and all other electronic equipment were forbidden; everything had to be checked in. Situations like this came up the whole time. They were a little unpleasant, but there was nothing to be done about them.

Back at the office, Christopher greeted her with a broad grin.

"It appears the natives have their pride too; they didn't want to keep you either," he teased.

"It's funny you should mention the natives," Alex winked, "because I don't think you'd really stand out there."

There wasn't a lot of time for chit-chat, as she had to take a call from Nobu. He had read her mail about the latest developments concerning Natioba. He too was relieved that her client in Seoul had reacted so favourably to the conference – and so positively to the ad-hoc announcement.

Nobu had liked the Hamburg idea right from the start. She sent the presentation slides over for his information. Thomas had checked and approved them. After all, there were legal aspects to consider when PsoraCom made a public appearance, and he knew more about that side of things than her.

For the next few days, Alex felt like she was in a time-lapse movie. The meeting with Bill and the divisional director of Luxumi went well, but it was more management banter than anything constructive. Both signalled their willingness to work together without taking any concrete steps forward; a development that confirmed Alex's assessment of the situation.

Although Luxumi were interested in the Vabilmo technology, they saw no urgent need to implement it in a joint project with Hursoc. In the meantime, Alex had tried to verify the opinion of Premve's head of power plants. His Luxumi counterpart certainly hadn't denied the company would be turning its attentions increasingly towards Taiwan when it came to the development of solar modules and inverters in the future. George seemed to have ignored that and grasped the initiative on the way back to Bill's hotel.

"Bill," he began, "the way I see it, we need more assistance with the Luxumi project. It's essential we have experienced technicians to work on developing the inverters with the client."

"I understand that," Bill replied. "Of course we need more staff to initiate and carry out projects with plant manufacturers. Without joint projects, we don't get any contracts."

"I'm happy you see it like that. So when can we reckon with additional support staff?"

"There's no need for panic," Bill checked him. "We have to proceed in a structured manner. Today we need someone for Luxumi, tomorrow someone for Premve and the next day someone for something completely different. I'm planning a restructuring of my department and will assign a few employees and product managers to the Vabilmo team. But that'll take a few weeks. Until then, you'll just have to cope on your own."

It was hardly a satisfactory answer, but offered a ray of hope nonetheless. Bill wasn't prepared to promise anything more. He was far more interested in the current state of affairs with other potential end customers.

"The kick-off meeting with Premve's engineers has been set for the beginning of next month," Alex informed him. "After that we'll have a better idea of the scope and amount of time we need to invest. The manager of the power plant division doesn't see it simply as a test, but rather as a preparatory measure en route to product development."

"If they keep this pace up, they could be on the market quicker than Roffarm," Bill whistled through his teeth. "But a little competition never hurt anyone, least of all us."

"You heard about the slip-up with Natioba," Alex continued. "We're going to announce our collaboration at a conference in Hamburg. In the meantime, we've got their permission to pass on information to Roffarm and other competitors so that joint meetings can be arranged for the event. Natioba are very interested in standardising bend-module interfaces. That'd be a great help to our own internal strategy as well."

"I think the idea with the conference is a very good way of rectifying the faux pas," he praised. "Stuff like this isn't normally supposed to happen! I might even make it to the developer conference myself, though I won't know for sure until relatively short notice. I'll let you know; that way you can show me the greenhouse personally."

By way of goodbye back at the hotel, Bill handed her a business card with his cell number written on it. She was still completely unprepared for his spontaneous embrace, however – to say nothing of the brief kiss he planted on her cheek. Undecided about what to do for a fraction of a second, she decided to smile.

"Don't think anything of it," George laughed out loud. "That's his Latin charm, inherited from Spanish relatives. It's how he makes himself popular with the women here."

Both men smiled. Nevertheless, she got the impression that Bill had meant it in a genuine, innocent way. It was just highly unusual in German business culture.

The phone conferences about the chief sales officer's travel itinerary began shortly afterwards. Each of the five countries he was due to visit were represented by a local regent. One of them had assumed overall responsibility and would report directly to the CSO's assistant. An elaborate interim hierarchy.

The first conference was an opportunity for everyone to get to know each other – as far as that was possible over the phone – and to outline strategy. Among other things, they discussed when certain information was to be made available in raw format and what bookings to make. This included hotel, transport, bodyguards and the agenda for each day.

Bodyguards?

Alex thought she had misheard but didn't want to ask. It was decided by when the list of clients should be published. Regents needed to provide detailed written justification as to why these companies in particular had been chosen and present their statements at the next conference. A short descriptive document had to be written for every approved meeting. The briefing could be no longer than A4 in length and was to contain the following information: all key data including client participants, revenue in the last three years, topics of discussion, tone of conversation, current problems and desired outcomes.

Tone of conversation?

What did they mean by that? Did they have to provide the Americans with details that were self-evident now? They estimated there would be six meetings a day on average. With thirty meetings inside five days, the information would have to be brief and to the point. In addition to the client meetings, appointments were also to be scheduled with the managing director, who would supply the current country figures and present the most important projects. If there was any time remaining, a meeting would be arranged with staff; after a short presentation, the chief sales officer would take questions from the floor. More details would be available in the next phone conference, where regents could also raise queries of their own. Regents were to direct any urgent enquiries to the lead regent himself and copy international colleagues in on the discussion. They could thus avoid any overlap. With that, the first conference was over; Alex's head was spinning. She went straight to Henry, who had more than enough experience.

"What kind of hotel would you book for our CSO then?" she asked. "It doesn't have to be the Four Seasons, does it?"

"So, you're his regent," he said. "Only a whippersnapper but you already have the honour!"

"Honour's all well and good," she replied, "but you know yourself how much work it is."

"I'd go for the Grand Hotel," he recommended. "Make sure you get the suite."

By the time she got back to her desk, her diary was already full with diverse appointments. Alex was beginning to suspect she'd been a little naive about the whole thing.

Over the course of the next few days, Alex felt increasingly like she was trying to juggle five different things at the same time. A positive side effect was that there was little time to think about her private situation. While arranging the kick-off meeting and MOU for Premve, she synchronised with Seoul and Chris on the slides for Hamburg. With Henry she was working simultaneously on the key words for a press release, which was to be issued by Natioba's marketing people in Korea. She couldn't forget about the meeting Lucas was coordinating with Roffarm either.

Then there was Natioba's Milan office, which she provided with regular project status updates. Through an additional contact there, she had come upon a relatively new department that was working on mobile off-grid systems; these could almost be described as robots. She arranged a joint meeting with Carl to present the Vabilmo technology.

Alongside her own commitments, a colleague had approached her and asked for assistance with a company called Cellgot. Lisa worked in Marketing and was responsible for finding new companies that could broaden PsoraCom's ecosystem. Until now, Alex had only read about the firm and their navigational technology in passing. Before she could give an answer, she needed to find out exactly what Cellgot had to offer and whether it was relevant for the Vabilmo strategy.

In addition to all this, she was preparing for the visit of the sales boss; indeed, without Christopher, who seemed to have adopted her as one of his own, she would have been in a real fix. She received suggestions from him about which clients to contact, as well as templates for appointment briefings. In some cases, she already knew the relevant sales colleagues, and arranged a meeting with each one to check the lie of the land. What projects were they currently working on? Were there any stumbling blocks where the CSO might be able to assist? What did the client hope to achieve? What support was needed?

Another important issue was whether the client was prepared to travel to PsoraCom. They were all high-ranking managers whose diaries were chock full. Some of them would lose half a day for an hour-long meeting with PsoraCom. At this level, there were a number of prima donnas who preferred to grant, rather than chase, an audience. Nevertheless, all meetings had to take place near the office; otherwise it would be too much of a stretch. The CSO wasn't coming to Germany to undertake a sightseeing tour interspersed with a few client meetings, after all. The whole thing was anything other than a logistical doddle for Alex and her sales colleagues.

She began with a rough draft of the agenda, allowing for a break of half an hour between each appointment. Even the sales boss would have to go to the toilet; perhaps he'd also want to check his mails, make an important decision or call somebody. Generously she set the lunch break at an hour. Maybe he'd need to freshen up in the interim.

Two client meetings would take place on-site; she was conservative with her timing, setting an hour aside for the transfer there and back. On no account could the CSO be late for an appointment, as that would be disrespectful. In the meantime, his date of arrival had been confirmed and Alex had received the flight times from the lead regent. The chief was leaving the evening before Alex was scheduled to fly to Taipei. If he had come to Germany any later, she would have had to cancel her trip. As he was scheduled to arrive at nine in the evening, they needed to decide whether it was worth arranging a "friendly beer" with a trusted client at the hotel bar.

In contrast to her overstimulation at the work place, very little was happening on the private front. Life with Sandro had been placed on the backburner. Her emotions oscillated daily between hope and despair. He remained silent on where things were going. And he was still looking for a flat in the city. How long he would stay there, he couldn't say. Whether they would find a flat together, build their own house and start a family was likewise in the lap of the gods.

All her dreams were being placed on trial. After four years, she had hoped her private life would take on concrete form alongside her professional success. Although it hadn't happened like that, Alex was loath to write the relationship off. If Sandro needed time to think things over in peace; even if he needed his own flat to do it, that was fine. She didn't want to throw the last few years away. There had been so many good times – and despite their differences, they still had a lot in common. It was impossible to find a partner who was a 100% match. Relationships needed to be worked on, even if there were obstacles that prevented it.

Far too many of her generation simply didn't want to make the effort. They broke off relationships thoughtlessly before entering headlong into new ones. Or they sought variety and consolation in affairs. It had never been like that for Alex, apart from a few slip-ups she would rather have deleted from memory. In her opinion, the thing worth striving for most was a partnership that endured until death. She was just as unwilling to abandon this dream as she was to give up on her goal of a house and family. Even if she found it difficult to grant, what Sandro needed was time.

Something he said gave her renewed hope. He told her he had always appreciated her warm-heartedness. Likewise the fact that she had always been there to support him. Still, for the time being there was no way they could plan for a joint future together.

Waiting for a decision she had no control over had never been one of her strengths. On top of that, she had got a sense after Prague that her biological clock was ticking. She had so much work during the day that she could easily find ways to distract herself. It was only in the evening that her thoughts went round in circles.

One evening, she met Moritz and outlined her dissatisfaction.

"If you ask me, Alex," he began, "he's met someone else. You know how much I like him, but maybe he just doesn't have the guts to tell you!"

"No, it can't be," she shook her head vigorously. "Sandro's not the type for an affair. Just look at him."

"Usually, I'd agree with you," he asserted, "but it's the only explanation for your current situation. What's happening – or, more to the point, not happening – with you guys is not normal. Who else do you know who's looking for a flat of his own after you two have been searching for something together for months?"

"Well, I'm the one who's been doing most of the searching," she conceded. "He's either been too lazy or has had too much on his plate, work-wise."

"Now I get the picture," said Moritz, "but I'd be willing to bet he's been spending his overtime with his new lover."

"I just don't believe it," she repeated. "How do you explain him giving me flowers before we went to Prague? Being unfaithful isn't in his nature. Besides, he's almost always at home in the evenings, when he's not at work or in the club, that is. Where would he find the time for someone else?"

"Maybe you're right," he yielded. "I hope so for your sake, anyway. But I'm not convinced."

At the end of August her optimism was put to the test. Sandro had found a flat and was moving out. Alex slipped away to Jenny's for the weekend as she didn't want to be there to see him pack and load his things. She wouldn't have been able to bear it. As so often in the past, Jenny proved to be a patient listener.

"Somehow it feels as if his moving out is the end of our relationship," Alex told her sister. "Instead of getting closer to each other, we're moving further apart. It's at least half an hour's drive to his new flat. I can hardly just drop in."

"There's not much you can do at the moment apart from simply accept it and make the best of it," said Jenny, as she topped Alex up with wine. "His flat could've been on the other side of town."

"That would've meant he had too far to drive," Alex was pretty sure. "His first choice would've been somewhere within reach of the club. Before we went to Prague, he was always staying with a friend if it got late or he'd had one beer too many. I preferred it that way – otherwise who knows what might have happened."

"That's why you're staying here tonight; in case something happens to you on the drive home," Jenny wouldn't take no for an answer.

"I couldn't have taken it at home, anyway. Now I need to decide what we're going to do about our holiday. Originally we wanted to go away somewhere in the fall. Somewhere warm, on the coast. But now that he's bought all that new furniture, he can only afford a week. The idea that it costs more to live alone than to share hadn't occurred to him before now. Well, who'd have thought it?"

She couldn't hide her cynicism. She'd had a very intensive few months at work and wanted to take longer than a week off. Especially since their time in Prague had hardly been relaxing.

"Why don't you come and visit me in Hong Kong, alone?" Jenny suggested. "I'll have found my feet if you come in the fall and be able to show you around."

She was leaving in two weeks; some of her boxes were already packed and ready in the hall.

"Why not?" thought Alex. "You're only staying a year; who knows when the next opportunity will be?"

"It would be good for both of you," her sister said. "Sandro can work out if he really misses you; and you can do likewise. If the answer's no, then at least you'll know where you stand."

"You're right, that'd be a welcome side-effect."

"And I wouldn't go away with him for a week," Jenny continued. "First, you don't have any real basis for a nice holiday as a couple. Second, I can well imagine that you wouldn't be satisfied because you've been hoping for something longer. Come to Hong Kong and treat yourself to a wellness holiday. Take a look at something new or just relax on the beach."

They started to hatch more concrete plans while out walking on Sunday. If Alex came in October, then Jenny would have a few weeks to explore first. She would wait and see how things were with her new job before letting her sister know. The idea of a few days in Hong Kong appealed to Alex more and more. She had always wanted to go and, with Jenny there, she would never have a better opportunity.

Spending a little time in a new environment would certainly do her good. There were loads of beaches on the way to and from Hong Kong that would be perfect for an October break. She should get hold of Renata straightaway, as she would almost certainly have some contacts; at the very least, she would know the best places for people travelling on their own. Spurred on by the thought, Alex sensed her optimism returning.

But it only lasted until she got back to the flat. As soon as she saw the empty side of the bed and the bare wardrobes, she was overcome by an aching sense of loneliness.

9

September

The internal presentation Wolfgang was due to give the sales chief turned out to be a very particular kind of challenge. Christopher had sent Alex a few slides that had been used the previous year. Unfortunately, they were based on an old template and contained figures that were out-of-date. Management were supposed to have drawn up a new target plan months ago.

PsoraCom had always operated with set objectives in mind. However, in order to achieve even greater success, their global company aim had to be projected in further detail from one hierarchy level down to the next. On the lowest level, individual actions were defined for each employee, no matter the department, and then measured against the overall set criteria.

The point was to integrate all management and employee levels, so that objectives could be adapted and revised through the synchronisation of the vertical and horizontal chains. The "catch-ball" principle, it was called. Translated, it meant that employees helped their bosses achieve set goals, so that they in turn could achieve different objectives on the next hierarchy level. Regular progress checks were supposed to ensure that all objectives were delivered on time. Thus, the focus was quite clearly on solutions, rather than problems.

So much for the theory. In practice, not a single person from Wolfgang's department had provided the relevant information yet. The managing director was on holiday and Christopher was standing in for him. Despite Alex's reservations, he encouraged her to approach the department heads directly.

At PsoraCom, there was an abbreviation that could only be used in exceptional circumstances. ST stood for sine tempore. The term, academic in its origins, required the recipient to react immediately. Messages flagged like this were seen almost as orders. It was nothing personal, however. It merely demonstrated that the sender had been given a high-priority task by someone else. The more commonly used abbreviation PD, which stood for "personal duty", had a different meaning. It was often used by colleagues to denote the allocation of responsibilities within a project.

Her temporary role as regent gave Alex the authority to mark target planning as ST. There were still a few days to go before the visit, but preparing the individual information was bound to take some time. After that, it was down to Alex. Everything had to be incorporated into an overall document. Happily, her concerns proved unfounded – most of the department heads replied straightaway and provided a submission date. She had already drawn up a document for the Vabilmo team, based on their strategy; Thomas had approved it on his return without making any significant changes.

Christopher was next to supply the information, despite being extremely busy filling in for Wolfgang.

"You can't imagine how much bureaucracy there is," he sighed, shaking his head. "Central management is trying to exert more and more control over the regional branches. There are any number of reports to be completed; basically each department is after the same thing, only at a different time. For every request made, there's a new spread sheet to be filled out. The only way any of them differ is in the layout. We can't react to things with nearly as much flexibility as we used to. I understand that we need to maximise revenue but ultimately all we're doing is keeping our sales staff away from their clients."

"Can't you tell them?" Alex asked. She was beginning to see what he meant.

"One of our most senior figures has wasted a lot of time agonising already," he said resignedly. "There's no point me doing it too. It used to be different. Upper management would rely on the judgement of the people on the front line; we had a lot more leeway. Regional quirks are no longer tolerated by headquarters."

Fortunately, that didn't seem to apply to the sales chief's appointments. All clients she had suggested had been approved in the end. There had only been lengthy discussions about one; a debate Alex had nevertheless managed to win by producing concrete objectives for the company in question. She had, it must be said, slightly manipulated the facts to her own advantage.

Before Hamburg, there was the kick-off meeting with Premve's engineers. Besides Hugo, Alex had also invited George and Marco. If everything went according to plan, the project had the potential to trump developments with Roffarm. Admittedly, they were still behind Natioba but the power plant divisional manager had promised that if successful, the project would be implemented as a whole. That would mean all future solar plants would be maintained by robots fitted with polymer-based cells. Even Natioba were yet to make an equivalent announcement about off-grid systems. That was less to do with Seoul, however, and more a question of Milan being unwilling to make the switch.

With projects, it was always about going higher, faster, quicker than the rest. The Vabilmo team had to take advantage of this opportunity; at the end of the day, competition was the basis for the free market economy, and the driving force behind new technologies. The sooner end customers brought the polymer-based cells onto the market and used them in plants, the easier it would be in terms of product distribution. Publicly acknowledged references were a more efficient source of evidence than secret projects.

That's why Alex's colleagues hadn't needed much persuasion to take part in the kick-off meeting. They were all dying to get started and achieve something. Even George thought the idea with the maintenance robots was revolutionary. That way, the polymer-based cells could be brought onto the market considerably quicker than expected.

The meeting lasted the whole day, with the discussion being dominated by Hugo. He was in his element and almost became carried away making suggestions and discussing what additional factors needed to be taken into account. George interrupted again and again with his own arguments and viewpoints. There was a palpable sense of enthusiasm about them, which seemed to have rubbed off on Marco, as well as Alex.

Nevertheless, they both chose to remain in the background, as the discussion was focused primarily on the technical aspects of the project. Only occasionally did Alex break in to mediate. She wasn't an expert in robot or navigation technology; nor did she know anything about inverter circuits. By the end of the discussion, a comprehensive work package had been agreed, still to be augmented by detailed requirements.

It was unanimously decided that resources were the top priority. Hugo, together with the engineers from Premve, made a joint estimate of how much time they would need to invest for development.

George agreed under slight protest. In his opinion, the timeframe was too short. One look from Hugo was enough to make him pipe down.

Alex looked on bemused from the second row. She had just realised how vehemently Hugo had contradicted his mentor; and how the latter had yielded almost meekly, eyes on bootlaces. This kind of behaviour was highly unusual. Did the chemistry between them suggest something more than mere camaraderie? It couldn't, could it? Was that the reason they were sitting neither side by side nor directly opposite one another? Marco had smiled quietly to himself. Did he know what was going on between them? Even if he did, it was none of her concern. As long as it didn't impact upon their work, at least. Maybe her hunch was wrong anyway.

There was no mistaking one thing, however. A quick glance at the items still to be covered revealed that Premve were also yet to decide who their internal project leader would be. That would give her a little breathing space, as she still hadn't heard anything from Bill. Hopefully there'd be a chance to speak to him directly again in Taipei.

Then, as if in fast-forward, it was off to Hamburg. Alex travelled with Thomas the evening before; Brian and Hugo wouldn't arrive until the morning. They met Natioba's lab manager for dinner, as he was in town already. He proved just as charming in person as he had been on the phone. However, a combination of the long flight and jetlag meant he made his excuses early – though not before they had agreed on a schedule for the following day. Although having been been unable to arrange a meeting with Roffarm, Alex got the impression her client wasn't particularly upset. From PsoraCom's point of view, the meeting would no longer be essential once tomorrow was over and the press release had been issued by Seoul.

The night was still young, so Thomas invited her for a drink in a floating bar on the Binnenalster, not far from their hotel. When their cocktails arrived, he took out his pipe and began filling it quietly. Over a few raspberry mojitos, it became increasingly clear to Alex why her boss seemed so distant and uninterested sometimes.

"Actually, I don't really need to work," he began. "I could live pretty easily off my dividends and still indulge all manner of hobbies and extravagances."

Alex listened in silence.

"It's my real estate that makes it all possible," he continued. "And not just in Monte Carlo. But you wouldn't believe how bored you get playing golf all day, always seeing the same people. My wife and I don't have any children; it just never happened. So I began looking for a new job and with the help of a few contacts, I landed a managerial post here at PsoraCom. My technical understanding is fairly limited, but that's what the employees are for. A captain steering the ship's course with the aid of his crew, that's more my scene. Things became a little trickier when I took on responsibility for the Vabilmo team; the power industry is a world away from the trade sector. But I have begun to really enjoy it. It's probably because we're both new to the subject and can help each other learn the ropes. You know a lot about the industry; I've been with PsoraCom that bit longer."

Alex was a little taken aback. Thomas had never spoken so openly before. Since he'd made it known that he was planning for her to succeed him, however, she had noticed that he had been different towards her; more attentive. This personal side was something completely new – but she liked it very much all the same. It was so human. It made him seem less stiff, and she could begin to see through the wall he had built around himself. Where this wall had come from was none of her concern and she didn't ask him to elaborate.

The next morning, Alex awoke with butterflies in her stomach. The anticipation of the day ahead dispelled her fatigue, as well as the last remains of mojito swirling around her veins. The elegantly refined luxury of the five-star hotel underlined her feeling that today would be special.

As soon as her alarm sounded, she jumped straight out of bed and into the shower. Terry cloth bath shoes stood awaiting her, and a towel lay draped pleasantly over the heated mounting. The view from the breakfast room over the roofs and, beyond, the Alster only improved her mood further. Work was a pure joy and she wouldn't swap with anyone. It was exciting and took her all over the world. Today it was "only" Hamburg but the day after tomorrow it would be Taipei.

Upon arrival at the conference hall, she was greeted by the organiser and given a green badge marking her out as a speaker. As usual at technical conventions, there were hardly any women present. She felt like a bullfighter entering the ring as she made her way through the room, taking stock of the interested looks along the way. She had often found that the male participants stared at her, wondering who she was and what she was doing here.

Normally, she was lumped into the media category; only seldom that of the developers. Ever since she started working with technically complex products, Alex had loved being a part of this community. She had always found it especially easy to make new contacts at events like this. As one of the few female participants, people were always interested in talking to her. It would be exactly the same this time too, she was sure. After all, she was representing a high-profile company, and was about to unveil a project that would revolutionise the industry.

After the joint presentation, everybody seemed to want to speak to her for a few minutes. That was the appeal of it all. She felt desired, but not as a woman; rather, as an expert. Who didn't enjoy having their self-confidence boosted like this? It didn't seem to be any different for her client, who for one, was clearly enjoying the attention.

Thomas jumped in to assist whenever Alex referred anyone to him. Brian and Hugo, who had only just made it in time for the presentation, were likewise engaged in discussions with various people. Alex took advantage of a brief lull to introduce Hugo to the lab manager from Seoul, so that any technical issues arising during the project could be clarified directly by the two of them. Hugo promised to arrange a more detailed conversation with him for later in the day.

As luck would have it, Alex ran into the managing director of Cellgot. She vaguely remembered how Lisa from Marketing had asked for assistance in her dealings with them. Cellgot developed hard- and software that enabled robots to be controlled by simple gestures. The robots used integrated sensors to recognise hand and finger position in the air. No kind of touch-sensitive screen or input device was required.

Various finger positions represented a range of different orders. A raised forefinger, for instance, acquired a stop function and could pause a given process. Moving the finger sideways to the right would then set things back in motion. With the help of a small machine, the man from Cellgot was able to demonstrate a few basic orders that stirred Alex's interest. She could well imagine that appliances might soon be regulated by gestures as well as voice sensors. A follow-up appointment with the company certainly couldn't do any harm.

She was mad. Hugo hadn't even managed it at the conference. Alex found it difficult to contain her rage. She paced restlessly up and down her flat, phone in hand. Where was the problem?

"You were standing right next to him at the table," she stressed, "you were five paces away for the whole of the afternoon. After I introduced you, you said you wanted to talk to him. You even promised to answer his technical queries. How come it was so difficult?"

"I didn't have any time," he squirmed. "I was busy talking to other people. You saw how many people there were."

"It's not acceptable," she replied. "We reiterate that Natioba are top priority in every single team meeting. Equally, we know that the lab in Seoul potentially exerts a decisive influence over what happens in Milan. And you had the chance to speak directly to the lab director; no phone, no video conference, no time difference, nothing. Just you and him. And instead of answering questions that are important to the decision-making process, what do you do? You say you're too busy. No-one from Roffarm or Hursoc was there! I just don't believe it. The number of off-grid systems is constantly on the rise and through Natioba we have the chance to really establish the Vabilmo technology on the market. And not in five or seven years, I should add, but maybe even at the end of next year with a small flagship contract. We'd be much quicker than people are currently anticipating with Roffarm. That's why he wanted to speak to you – you're the architect responsible. We have to get to know Natioba's technical requirements, coordinate them and see whether mass production is feasible. That way, the design of the solar modules is determined by our two companies together. We also need to clarify which type of bend-module most lends itself to standardisation."

That was precisely why Hugo was part of the team.

"I've got too much to do already," he moaned, "I can't look after every single client."

She was well aware that he couldn't do everything. But she could at least expect his support with a high-priority client. The team strategy hadn't just been set by her, after all, but by all of them together. Hugo too. From her point of view, it seemed like he spent the whole time dealing with Roffarm and thousands of tiny little things, rather than providing active assistance with other end customers.

Admittedly, he had taken part in the kick-off meeting with Premve, but he hadn't been in any further contact with the engineers there.

It was as if he expected everything to be presented to him on a plate. Using his own initiative seemed to be a foreign concept.

But she wasn't some kind of secretary who arranged his meetings. Neither was she prepared to roll out the red carpet just so he could take care of business with clients. Dealing with clients wasn't a game of tag; it was about being pro-active. PsoraCom wanted to sell products that the client didn't know anything about. Ultimately, it was a buyers' market. Even a cosseted global company like PsoraCom had to approach clients tactfully and try to woo them. A standard wasn't going to materialise just like that; you had to work for it. But Alex seemed to be running into a brick wall.

She noticed just how irate she had become. Hugo's excuses had only made her more angry and frustrated. She took a deep breath; there was no reason to be unfair.

"I understand, Hugo. I'm sorry. Maybe that was a little over the top; I'm just frustrated that you didn't make use of such a good opportunity. I've got a lot on my plate privately. Don't take it personally, OK? We need to mention the support issue as quickly as possible and see if we can get someone to help you out."

If Hugo really didn't have the time for a quick chat with clients – and there were still a few doubts at the back of Alex's mind – then the situation had to be resolved urgently. She quizzed her boss immediately.

Thomas still hadn't heard anything from Wolfgang about additional support staff; but he hadn't exactly asked either. He promised to take care of it and bring up the issue with Hugo at their next jour fixe. Why the latter hadn't spoken to the lab director was a mystery to him too.

Things were still just as unclear with Sandro. Since the move, he'd been in touch every second day to ask how she was doing. They'd been to the cinema once, followed by a few harmless drinks in a pub. When they said goodbye, he had given her a quick peck on the cheek. He could just as easily have been her brother. Still, it was better than not seeing him at all.

Everything was set for the sales chief's visit. Alex had been forced to rearrange a meeting a few days before but that was the only thing. This time it was Henry who had approached her. A reporter for a well-known technology magazine had contacted him to ask if it would be possible to arrange an interview with the chief of sales. Alex had been criticised for being too generous with the breaks between appointments and transfers. The interview would allow her to do Henry a favour and tighten up the agenda at the same time.

With the approval of the interview by the lead regent, the agenda was in place right down to the very last detail. Alex had also scheduled for a debriefing to take place at the end of the day. In reality, however, it was nothing more than a buffer. There would almost certainly be a delay with one of the meetings or transfers. The debriefing ensured that client meetings could begin late without having to be drastically cut short. Barring any unforeseen issues, of course. Amazingly, no-one bothered to ask what the point of the debriefing was. The day began with a briefing, after all; it seemed only natural that it should end with one too. Later, she met with Christopher and Wolfgang to go through the final agenda and slides one more time before the visit.

"Everything looks fine," the managing director said. "And I really like the presentation."

"I would never have managed it without Christopher; he was a great help while you were away."

"She would have been just fine without me," he countered. "I gave her a little help selecting the clients but she did the rest all by herself."

"Come on," she said. "Only with selection? I would've had real problems making up the slides as well – there's no way I would've known who to get the market data from."

She was very grateful for Christopher's help, as there were a number of simple points she had taken for granted. Little things such as the cooling of drinks between transfers would never have occurred to her, let alone the fact that the sales chief might have special dietary requirements.

As it turned out, he preferred fresh fruit to biscuits, and preferably cut into small pieces. The upshot of this was that the fruit couldn't be kept in the meeting room all day. Fresh pieces had to be brought in for each client meeting to ensure that it looked appetising. It didn't matter if the stuff being taken away was still edible or not. From Alex's point of view, it was both an enormous expense and a needless waste, but she wanted everything to be perfect. There was no way she would allow her time as regent to stain the reputation of the German office.

Christopher withdrew from the conversation, while Wolfgang went over the final details with Alex.

"We still haven't found a client who's interested in an after-dinner drink with the sales chief," he said. "Providing he doesn't want to be left in peace, we could make use of the time for ourselves."

"What do you think about giving him a more detailed explanation of the Vabilmo technology?" she suggested. "Natioba are set to issue the press release at EOB Korean time. That's two hours from now. Hot off the press, it could be a very good angle for us. The issue of support for Premve is still unresolved; Natioba too – to say nothing of any additional clients we might get. A little help from upstairs wouldn't go amiss."

"OK," Wolfgang decided, "that's a good idea. Although he won't be able to assign someone directly, his support would be very valuable. There are still plenty of nay-sayers and shit-stirrers who regard the new technology as an extremely expensive dead-end. We have to fight them on all fronts. With concrete examples, it'll be much easier for me to argue that there is more than just one client interested in us. He is aware of the Roffarm contract but doesn't know anything about our work with polymer-based cells. Naturally, I'm counting on your help with any questions about individual projects."

Then it was time for them to make their way.

A chauffeur bodyguard drove them from the airport to the hotel in an armoured van. Marc, as the sales chief politely introduced himself with a firm handshake, was a little tired but not averse to a quick nightcap. Over a glass of wine, Wolfgang laid his net. He explained how important he felt the Vabilmo technology was for the on-going development of company revenue, making reference to existing projects. Now and then he gave Alex a nod and let her outline the details. He mentioned the press release from Natioba only in passing, before casually placing his copy on the table.

Marc took the bait and glanced through the article. Alex saw immediately that his interest was aroused. She took the spherical seed unit out of her pocket as if it were the most natural thing in the world and began to explain how Premve and Natioba planned to make use of it. Marc's curiosity was sparked and he immediately saw opportunities with clients in the US. He talked with them for longer than expected, paying particular attention to the industrial robot industry, the sector targeted by Premve. He promised to provide internal support, as in his opinion, it was an area with real market potential. When he requested that she send him an overview presentation without delay, there was a contented nod from Wolfgang.

Back at home, she went over the conversation in her mind. There was so much more she could have said. Despite the lateness, he had become more and more attentive as the meeting progressed. Especially when she told him about the joint presentation in Taipei. How was she supposed to get to sleep now? Everything was so exciting. She would have liked to start work on the slides straightaway but she needed to be back at the hotel in four hours for the briefing. She had to try and rest if she wanted to be fit for the next day.

Like Alex, Wolfgang was there half an hour beforehand to ensure they began on time.

Marc was content with a bowl of muesli while her managing director presented the German office's key data. Why had such an extravagant breakfast been requested? Just in case? Alex helped herself to fresh fruit and pushed the thought to one side. Don't worry about it; just keep to the agenda. That was the way. It was going to be a ten-hour sprint.

She scurried around with her Zeus68 the whole day, as if it were welded to her hand. The individual meetings were conducted without her but she made sure they kept to the agenda. For people who were awaiting client appointments or had just finished them, she was always available. In addition, she monitored the catering, ensuring that fresh fruit and drinks were available for every meeting. Everything went like clockwork. There was a permanent surge of adrenaline coursing through her body. Constantly she was anticipating that something unexpected would come up. Every time her phone rang, she prepared herself for a last-minute cancellation. At lunch, she couldn't eat anything — she was far too nervous and had no real appetite besides. To make up for it, she cadged a few cigarettes off Henry during breaks.

But everything was perfect. Almost. No clients cancelled, but the meetings went on late. Minute by minute. Every client went a little over time. The sales chief had to make an important call between appointments. Another few minutes' delay. In the end there was no time for a debrief at the airport; still, that was the plan and at least they hadn't had to cut any meetings short. Punctual as an atomic clock, Wolfgang and Alex escorted the CSO to check-in. The managing director got a firm handshake, while Alex received a friendly embrace and a kiss on both cheeks. Wolfgang looked tired but extremely satisfied as he wheeled alongside her to the parking lot. Going home was the only thing on Alex's mind as well. She was going to Taipei tomorrow, after all.

The next morning she could just as easily have worked the two hours from home, but she didn't want to miss out on the post-visit office atmosphere. She composed a brief email thanking everyone involved for their support and declaring that the day couldn't have gone so well without them. Wolfgang, Thomas and Christopher were included in copy. Any sales colleagues she encountered thanked her personally in turn.

The interview they had squeezed in had gone well and Henry was back on top form; he grabbed her by the waist and whirled her around in the air. Shortly afterwards, Wolfgang sent an email to all department heads saying how pleased the sales chief had been with things in the German office. He wanted to pass his praise on, to Alex especially. It was a mutual back-slapping session enjoyed by all parties. And why not? The whole thing had gone swimmingly and everyone was satisfied.

"I could learn a thing or two from you," Christopher conceded with a smile. "Very clever, camouflaging a buffer as a debrief."

From him, the compliment sounded more sincere than from most others.

Scarcely thirty hours of travelling later, she fell exhausted into her hotel bed. Normally a seven-hour difference wouldn't have been so bad, but the flight and stopover had sapped her of energy and she hadn't got much sleep in the plane.

Although her spirits were still high after the previous day's praise, she was already looking forward to the next highlight: the CEO's unveiling of the joint project. Who else flew halfway round the world to spend a few days in a busy metropolis where they could hardly read the street signs? And who could combine their work with a stay in a foreign country where not even the taxi drivers spoke a word of English?

The next morning she awoke refreshed and ready to enjoy a day off. She probably wouldn't see Hank and Chris until Monday. They were both dealing with last-minute preparations that she couldn't help with. That left her a bit of time for some sightseeing.

The Taipei 101 was a must, of course: the world's second biggest skyscraper was her first port of call. She didn't think much of the shopping mall that occupied the lower storeys; the view from the 91st floor, however, was sensational. Set against the backdrop of the surrounding green hills, the collection of offices and high rise buildings beneath her seemed so perfectly arranged. The atmosphere in the evenings, with the sea of light, must be amazing. Perhaps she would get to experience it in the next few days.

The tuned mass damper, a hundred tonne steel pendulum construction in the upper third of the building, was equally impressive. Its function was to absorb and offset movements in the building, as Taiwan was part of one of the most active earthquake regions in the world. Not only that; the Taipei tower also had to withstand several cyclones a year.

Back on the ground, Alex surveyed the building once more in fascination, before travelling on to the Presidential Palace, Longshan Temple and the National Memorial Hall by taxi. She didn't have a lot of time, but it was enough for her to form an initial impression of a city that was more than simply aesthetically pleasing. As she moved from one tourist attraction to the next, the smell of freshly prepared food wafted from every street corner. The scent of ginger, cilantro and chilli lingered in the air and made her mouth water. During the heat of the day, however, she had preferred to keep to fresh mangos and cold drinks.

Late in the afternoon, she took a quick detour to the World Trade Centre where the conference was being held. Hank had informed her when the dress rehearsal was taking place and it would be a good opportunity for her to acquaint herself with the conditions there. Everything was going like clockwork. Hank and Chris had really gone all out. After three test runs, the CEO seemed happy and moved on to the next item, which his assistant read out to him like a stage direction. Alex's two colleagues declined her invitation to dinner. They still had a few things to take care off and were absolutely whacked; a sandwich from room service would do them just fine.

However, Chris recommended that she take a trip to Danshui and walk along the estuary at the harbour. She wasn't disappointed; there was a lot going on around the numerous food stalls and restaurants at sundown. From a distance in the evening light, the new-fangled bridges were reminiscent of an enormous floodlit springboard, their cables stretching on both sides from a pylon soaring high above the harbour. Surrounded by smells that tempted her on all sides, Alex finally gave in to her desires at one of the many hot food stalls. She couldn't have eaten any better in a restaurant – though she might have been more comfortable. Henry called just as she was shoving the last remains of a spicy fish curry into her mouth.

"Hey, I'm at the hotel bar now and I could really use a drink," he said. "I've spent the whole day entertaining the German media delegation. Where are you just now? Are you coming down?"

"I'm still out and about," she replied. "Don't be angry, but I'd like to stay here for a bit and take in the sea air. It was really sticky today in town. Besides, I want to be fresh for the morning, so I'll be going to bed pretty soon after I get back."

"OK, no problem. The journos will be arriving any moment anyway."

"But thanks for thinking of me all the same."

"That's pretty much all I ever do, sweet-cheeks."

Sweet-cheeks yourself, Alex thought as she hung up. Henry was a good guy; a little chaotic but endearing nonetheless. Since he seemed to be in good company, she was able to decline his offer with a clear conscience.

After a quick breakfast, she took a taxi to the World Trade Centre. There were hundreds of visitors and exhibiting colleagues there already, milling around like ants, even though the opening speech was still an hour away. Alex caught hold of Hank, looking just as nervous as she was. He had reserved seats for them.

Chris was backstage, checking all the details for a final time. The whole dress rehearsal had passed off without a hitch and they could only hope that things would go just as well today. The room began to fill up and, as the seats were all now taken, several rows of people were forced to stand at the back.

Without warning, there was complete darkness and glaring headlamps bathed the stage in glistening light. People folded their laptops and switched off their cells. All conversation ceased. Loud music began to play and the tension in the room rose palpably. The techno rhythms of a forgotten Springsteen classic made the loudspeakers shudder. "For you, for you, I came for you."

Everyone stood transfixed by the stage, and watched as the CEO walked smartly across the platform. Behind him the company logo appeared on three room-high screens. The next sixty minutes belonged to him. Each one felt like an hour for Alex. Hank hadn't been told when their project would be unveiled. They could only wait. Twenty minutes had passed already. Key company data alternated with comparisons with the competition and observations about developments in the solar industry. Another ten minutes. The CEO of an important client appeared on stage. Just noise in Alex's ear. It must be nearly time she thought, looking at her watch.

Suddenly the lights on the stage went out. Apart from the emergency exit lights, the room was now shrouded in total darkness. The air-conditioning seemed to be working overtime. It became colder. A chill wind began to cut through the room, accompanied by ever louder meditation music. Alex got goose bumps.

"Imagine you are in the Antarctic," a voice resounded from the darkness.

It wasn't too difficult, with the temperature in the room.

"Nothing but ice all around. No trees, no plants," the voice continued. "But you can still eat freshly grown salad for lunch. Don't believe me? Well, PsoraCom and their clients are making it possible."

The rhythm of the music changed, increasing like the waves of rapids. It became louder.

In the front rows, reporters sprang up with their cameras. Something special was about to happen and they didn't want to miss it. Suddenly, the headlamps turned on the audience, shining so brightly that for a brief moment Alex was blinded. Gradually her eyes became accustomed, and the light seemed to have been dimmed back down to an ordinary level.

Flashlights flared. She still had goose bumps. Only now did Alex realise she had been holding her breath. The CEO moved towards Chris, who was standing in front of the container. The broadside was facing towards the public so they could see the robot arms moving inside the greenhouse. Flashlights illuminated the stage once more.

Chris began to explain how organic lettuce plants were cultivated with the help of seed and nutrient paste. The electricity required was generated via PsoraCom's new solar cells. Why had they gone for these? Because the cells retained their flexibility even in adverse conditions. That meant the design of the solar modules could be tailored to the individual structure of different off-grid systems; in this case, the undulating contours of the container. The bend-modules would help to create a production standard for defined applications. One of the most important reasons, however, was that the high efficiency led to an increased current yield, which in turn had an enormous influence on both profitability and pay-off.

Her client was doing an excellent job, Alex thought. His initial nerves had given way to professional expertise. She was delighted that everything was going so well. Hank and Chris had a gimmick waiting to finish. The robot picked a few salad leaves, poured dressing over them in a bowl and handed everything to the CEO.

"Et voila – organic field lettuce topped with supermarket balsamic dressing," said Chris, producing a pack of croutons out of nowhere to sprinkle on top.

The CEO tasted the freshly grown salad with exaggerated gusto, a cheerful laughter spreading through the rows. All those present were invited to enjoy a portion themselves later on the ground floor. The lights went on again to applause all round, and the conference was officially open.

Alex went backstage with Hank.

"Congratulations!" she greeted Chris. "That was a fantastic performance!"

"Thanks," he replied, delighted, wiping a few drops of sweat from his brow. "Compliments are always well received."

A victory grin spread across his features.

"You deserve every bit of praise you get. The two of you have done a terrific job; it was such an enormous undertaking."

"You mean the three of us," he waved the compliment aside.

"Absolutely," Hank agreed. "You did your bit too, Alex. You ensured we didn't have to deal with the bureaucracy."

"Totally," Chris was with him, "and it meant we could concentrate on the essentials, right Hank?"

Their exhibition stand was extremely busy the whole day. The Asian representatives from Premve and Roffarm that Alex had invited also dropped by for an explanation. All of a sudden, it seemed as if every visitor had become a salad-loving solar technician. Henry came past with the media delegation.

It was with some surprise, however, that Alex greeted a very special visitor. Bill swung by nonchalantly just before the end of the day and was visibly impressed by the detailed description he received. After she had introduced him to Hank and Chris, he decided to join them for dinner. Alex had encountered very few executives in her professional career who had remained so grounded. Hank and Chris didn't tire of explaining the gestation process, complete with all its various stumbling blocks.

The evening went by in flash. Just before they parted ways, Alex grasped the opportunity to ask him in confidence for his personal support with Premve. He put a friendly hand on Alex's shoulder and said only: "We'll manage it; don't you worry."

The day after her return, Alex was on cloud nine. George had been the first to call and congratulate her on the presentation. Brian and Hugo had sent an email praising her to the hilt, outlining the positive effects all this could have on the team; comments endorsed likewise by Carl.

A lot of her German colleagues had followed the opening speech online and the knowledge that it was Alex's client had spread like wildfire. It wasn't only Wolfgang and Thomas who asked about the project; everyone seemed to want to talk about it. In the corridor, during coffee breaks, over lunch. Marco, Lucas and Lisa wanted to hear all the details too. Alex explained everything once more, never tiring of using the seed unit to illustrate the topic.

"The whole speech was filmed," Alex turned excitedly towards Lisa. "I've asked for a copy of the clip containing our project."

"That's great," she replied, her eyes lighting up. "We could use it as marketing material. Since we made the film ourselves, we don't have to ask anyone for permission."

"That's right," Lucas broke in and winked at Alex. "Fortunately, the project's become public knowledge in the meantime."

"You've got to send me the film straightaway," Marco said animatedly. "We need to show it to Premve urgently so they get a move on."

He nudged Lucas in the side and said: "That way they won't only overtake Natioba; they'll leave Roffarm hanging as well."

"That could be a really exciting head-to-head," Alex agreed.

Henry came by and listened for a while, even though he had seen the presentation in person.

"You're beaming like a child who's just got a new toy," he noted with amusement after the other three had gone. "But I guess that's how you keep your audience; your enthusiasm's contagious."

"I still get goose bumps when I think of how the lights suddenly came on and the music started," she admitted. As if to confirm it, she showed him the underside of her arm. "Do you see what I mean? The memory's so fresh – it's like I'm reliving it all over again."

"I can well imagine you found it impressive," he nodded. "They always put on a great show. But it was really important for us to be represented this year by a project initiated here in Germany." Then he whispered: "Wolfgang's chest swells with pride whenever anyone calls about it."

Alex grinned broadly. That was good to hear.

"How did your colleagues react to the speech?" he continued. "Have you seen them? Have any of them been in?"

"No," she replied. "I haven't seen any of them. But their reactions were very positive. They all said how great the publicity would be for the team. Internally as well as externally – and that we need projects like this to move things forward. The success even seems to have rubbed off on Thomas. I just caught him speaking to a marketing manager on the phone."

"And? What did he say?" Henry asked, head bowed conspiratorially.

"Alex is my best horse," she whispered impishly.

"Produces the most manure too," a deep voice resounded.

Christopher had entered unnoticed. Henry roared with laughter. With Christopher joining in, Alex was soon unable to resist.

10

October

Holiday at last! Alex caught up on the previous few weeks' lack of sleep during the flight to Bangkok. In the whole eleven hours, she was awake for thirty minutes maximum. Despite her cramped economy-class seat, she slept like a baby; only her legs were a little stiff. The excitement of the last two months at work, allied to the rollercoaster that was her private life, had really taken their toll.

Upon arrival at her Kao San Road guesthouse, she was greeted by a small gecko that watched in silence as she unpacked. Alex was glad of its presence; at least she wouldn't be alone in the few hours she'd be sleeping there. The old palaces and pulsating life all around enticed her to head straight out and immerse herself in this foreign world.

Her first impressions of the city were indescribable. Frenzied and chaotic; lively and colourful; fascinating and exciting; but also dirty and loud. A seductive Moloch, so completely different from home, apart from the enormous PsoraCom billboard that had greeted her at the airport. It seemed there was no escape, no matter where you were, but she had simply blotted it out, just like her Zeus68. And she had no intention of even switching it on in the next few days. There was far too much to explore here, whether by foot or tuck-tuck, the multi-coloured three-wheeled taxi mopeds that travelled constantly at dizzying speeds.

The old Royal Palace, her first destination, was a world in itself with its numerous small temples. There were gloriously colourful towers everywhere, their golden spires glistening in the sun. The smallest tesserae had been arranged into the most elaborate patterns and vied with the murals for artistic recognition. Turquoise-gold geometric patterns alternated with decorations of dark blue-pink and green-yellow. The roofs of the temples dominated with their orange-blue or red-green tiles. Her camera zoom revealed ornate details to be dragons or fiery tongues of flames.

Imposing statues stood at the entrances and stairs of temples or in the lovingly appointed miniature gardens, combining Asian forefathers and mythical creatures in one. Magnificently gilded and adorned with jewels or hewn from natural stone, they bore testament to the leading lights of bygone centuries. Here, before a passageway, was a nine-foot-high samurai complete with helmet; there, a small, laughing Fu dog on the half landing. Although everything was new and foreign to her, Alex was immediately spellbound by the wonderful blaze of colour.

The luminescent buildings and friendly Thais exuded a joie de vivre that proved irresistible. Not even a heavy downpour that left some of the uneven roads knee-high in water could change that. But the heavens closed just as suddenly as they had opened. Black clouds gave way to a dazzling sun that soon bathed everything around it in a misty haze and sultry humidity. Nature had permitted itself a cleansing shower.

In the niche where she had found shelter, Alex unlaced her shoes and waded barefoot through the palace grounds. She had never seen a rainstorm like it. The blazing midday heat made her sweat as if she was running a half marathon, so she sought shade in the various temples. In one of them there was an enormous, gold-coated Buddha that stretched across the length of the entire building, his toes alone bigger than a human head.

Not far away, in a different temple, was the national shrine. A green jade Buddha stood in the gilded room on a gold terraced platform replete with thousands of embroidered decorations. The magnificence of it alone made Alex sink to her knees in respect and absorb the stillness of the room in peace. Next to her, locals sat silently in worship. Taking photographs was forbidden; rightly so.

The mandatory visit to the Hard Rock Cafe would serve as a welcome alternative. Jenny was sure to appreciate a T-shirt and shot glass, as she had begun collecting too. After a quick, refreshing shower, observed by the small gecko from the ceiling, Alex was on her way again. The backpacking district she was staying in was awaiting exploration as well. Bars and restaurants alternated with shops that sold everything a tourist's heart could desire, from music to rucksacks and clothes. Hot food stalls punctuated the street air with the characteristic scent of fish sauce, coriander and chilli. For a few dollars a day, you could undertake a high-speed feeding cure.

Everything smelled delicious, even if the sight of unchilled food lying in the heat didn't exactly conform to western hygiene standards.

Alex decided she'd rather eat in a restaurant. She wanted to sit in peace, enjoy her food and observe the lively to-and-fro on the street.

It didn't matter what day of the week it was; the bars were always very lively in the evenings. The long-term tourists and backpackers had slept in, had their tattoos and piercings done or were finally finishing work in the laundrette. At any rate, it seemed like the nightly party had begun. Alex watched for a while from a quiet seat in the corner, before it became too much for her and she began to drift away through the side streets, leaving the revelry behind her.

The relaxing lounge of a stylishly fitted bar looked an enticing prospect for a cocktail. Just the thing, Alex thought. She didn't want to do anything other than sit in peace, admire the delightful orchid on the rim of her mojito glass and let her mind wander. To enjoy how far she was from home, switch off and allow her soul to float like the water lily in the lagoon outside. To forget.

During the day, she was able to dispel the memory of Prague and Sandro's move but it was harder in the evenings. The mojitos helped a little. She still wasn't sure where things would go from here. It certainly didn't conform to her idea of what a relationship should be. She hoped the holiday would give her some sort of sign. Either they would miss each other and start making plans together again; or they wouldn't.

The next day she paid a few cents for the ferry to carry her across to the other side of the river. It looked as if the vessel dated from the beginning of the previous century. It had been left soaking by the downpour that seemed to recur daily, and the slimy waves almost crashed over the wooden edges of the tiny barque. There were some who might have felt it was a risky crossing but Alex was reassured by the jaded expression of the boatman, his face devoid of any kind of excitement.

From an architectural point of view, the Temple of the Dawn wasn't any less impressive than the Royal Palace but it seemed gloomier in comparison. The closer she came to the city's phallic symbol, the more apparent the effects of the damp climate. With their many colours, the porcelain and glass tesserae of the tower tried to make themselves seen against the mouldy dark backdrop of the walls.

There were other, smaller temples that had recently been renovated. Their orange roofs with gilded spires and towers vied for pride of place with the gloriously colourful mosaic statues standing before them. Alex could hardly get enough of these historic buildings, so completely different and fascinating as they were. She felt as if she had been transported to a bygone era and allowed herself to be drawn in.

For the final part of her Bangkok visit, Alex treated herself to something special. Dinner at The Dome, one of the world's highest al Fresco restaurants. The view of the city was staggering. The food was Mediterranean style; the elegant ambience complemented by the presence of foliage plants all around. A truly uplifting feeling and a striking contrast to what she had been witnessing on the streets. The atmosphere in the open-air bar took her breath away. With the protruding balcony enclosed only by a chest-high glass wall, it almost felt as though she were floating in mid-air. Somehow the carpet of lights beneath her combined with the winding river to create a soothing effect.

From up here, the view of the pulsating, dirty, chaotic juggernaut with its millions of people could only be described as detached. It made her aware of just how many different worlds there were in Bangkok. Thousand-year old culture dominated by Buddhist thought co-existed with consumer luxury for the upper classes. In between was a vast spectrum, ranging from traditional impoverishment, entertainment for alternative tourists, through to cheap shopping paradises for package holidaymakers.

"Hey, sis," Jenny greeted her with a smile, as Alex arrived at Hong Kong airport. "How was the flight?"

"Hey, kid," Alex replied, embracing her. "The flight was good. How are things with you? Looking pretty trendy."

Laughing, she registered her sister's change in style; she wore cool, bright colours that were slightly futuristic in design. The weather had doubtless played a role in her transformation – here, too, one was struck by the oppressive humidity upon leaving the air-conditioned buildings.

"You'll soon get used to the climate," Jenny promised. "It was much worse in August."

"Come on, let's take a taxi to the hotel," Alex decided. "We can afford to treat ourselves a little."

The thought of the throngs of people in the bus and underground made her feel quite uneasy.

Although the YMCA hotel was located on a very busy crossing, the room offered a perfect view of the harbour bay and a panorama of Hong Kong's skyscrapers. It would serve as their joint base for the next few days. Jenny only lived in a small flat; this way they could spend the majority of their time together.

They set off on foot along the nearby waterfront and Avenue of Stars, a walk based on the Hollywood original, paying tribute to local artists. Round the corner was the north-south connection out of Kowloon, formerly known as the Golden Mile. Rows of shops and restaurants extended for mile upon mile. A little north of the Ladies Market, also visited by men, was a whole block named Sportswear Street – not without good reason. The flower market shops were located a little further on, the unmistakeable smell of roses clearly identifiable against the strong, sweet aroma of exotic plants. At dusk the streets became a mass of flashing neon signs.

That was what the province was famous for, even competing with Las Vegas to a certain extent. Her impressions of Hong Kong were very different from Bangkok. It was very colourful here too, and loud and busy, but somehow it was also both neater and tidier. The skyscrapers that had gleamed in the sunlight before, as well as the equally immaculate smaller buildings, were only part of it. The sidewalks were cleaner and, as far as Alex could see, there were almost no electric cables ranging over the streets or between houses. The bilingual notices on buildings and street signs made for an increased sense of familiarity.

Many of the street names bore testament to the British crown's colonial rule, creating a point of reference to the western world. Elegant car-free zones matched the city's financial status, and the authorities seemed just as eager to take action against the claustrophobia of the packed underground stations by ensuring they were kept clean. Nevertheless, a glance into one of the courtyards or narrow thoroughfares with their crazily stacked cardboard and wooden crates was enough to show that Hong Kong could be equally unruly and chaotic. Like millions before her, the thing that fascinated Alex most was the nightly spectacle, the so-called symphony of lights. Here, different coloured lasers shone from selected skyscrapers and buildings of the city; a unique display leaving both Kowloon and Hong Kong Island aglitter.

"If we can," Jenny suggested, "we'll make a tour of the harbour one of these evenings and watch the whole thing from the water. It makes it even more impressive."

But Alex was impressed enough for one day.

In the next few days, her sister took every opportunity to ensure this fascination remained intact by showing her all the different sides of the city. Instead of the underground, they took an antiquated-looking ferry into the world-renowned financial district of Hong Kong Island. They hopped on a short tour of the city on the historic two-storey tram, from a distance reminiscent of London's double-decker buses, rattling through the centre from North Point in the east, right the way out towards Western Market.

"You've got to be careful with some of the carriages," she warned Alex with a smile. "In between times they veer off into Happy Valley racetrack."

It seemed as if the name symbolised the locals' favourite hobby. In the daytime, when the weather was bad, the skyscrapers seemed far less imposing than at night. Even with the sun beaming down, Alex constantly felt like she was standing in the shadow of giants. The heat in the urban street canyons was stifling. It was almost as if the traffic noise had been compressed into a single crater. Red taxis with silver roofs dominated the street scene just like their yellow cousins in New York. Shopping opportunities abounded en masse.

It was tourist heaven in the attractive boutiques around Causeway Bay and Times Square. The latter wasn't really a square, but one of the city's greatest entertainment centres. Its appeal was based on hundreds of elegant air-conditioned shops, as well as an enormous cinema complex. A one-stop-shop-until-you-drop concept, if ever there was one.

Further to the west, whole streets were geared towards the sale of specific articles. There were antiques in Hollywood Road; herbal medicine in Ko Shing Street. The rattan sofas in Queens Road were anything but regal. There was still a hint of colonial charm in Western Market, with its listed buildings some of the last of their kind in Hong Kong.

Various smells wafted through the air in the more overtly Chinese districts, sometimes appetising, sometimes irritating. The variety on offer at the local markets was similar to that of Bangkok. Dried fish of all shapes and sizes was sold next to preserved ginseng and chilli spices. Alex had never seen some of the vegetables available at the fresh market stalls by the ferry terminal. Luxury goods could of course be found in the Admiralty Quarter.

When the clouds overhead finally released the south lying Victoria Peak from their grasp, they took the tram up to the highest point in the city.

"This is one of my favourite places," Jenny said. "I often come here when I feel cramped."

Despite the many tourists, Alex understood straightaway. In amongst the green hills were viewing platforms, whose railings were adorned by small Chinese stone figures. The view was better than fantastic. However, Jenny used her local knowledge to drag her sister a little further up along a narrow pathway, away from the tourist hustle and bustle, as well as the restaurants and souvenir shops commemorating the city's highest landmark. Barely half an hour later, they were presented with a view that was even more breath-taking, stretching over the skyscraper peaks on both sides of the bay and extending towards the green hills beside the New Territories. Alex was convinced it would be a good environment to get a fresh perspective on things.

"Why don't we get something to eat up here," Jenny suggested. "Then we can enjoy the view by night a bit later."

"I know just the place too," she added. "One of the nicest old-style colonial restaurants in Hong Kong is up here; it's outside the budget of most tourists."

"Sounds perfect," Alex said.

She had begun the holiday with the intention of being really good to herself. During the day she didn't need much: just a few Dim Sum or fried noodles. But in the evenings it should be something more leisurely. That way, they could take stock of the day and plan for the next one in peace. In her sister, after all, she had her own private twenty-four-hour tour guide. Jenny had been able to squeeze a few days' study leave out of her boss, but she would have to make it up over the course of the coming weekends. Alex was eager to repay the favour. She silently thanked her employer for granting her the necessary credit card limit.

Jenny hadn't been exaggerating; it was a feast for the senses. Up until now she had avoided talking about Sandro. But there were moments when it seemed Alex couldn't conceal her sadness.

"I wouldn't throw four years away so lightly," Jenny began, after dinner. "Things don't always run smoothly in a relationship. If there's still a chance, you should fight for it."

"That's my attitude too," Alex replied thoughtfully. "But there's a little voice deep inside telling me it's not worth it anymore. I don't know why."

Since the start of the holiday, the doubts had begun to spread in her mind like ivy. Sandro had sent a number of messages telling her to look after herself. But somehow they didn't seem genuine; didn't seem real. Unprompted, Jenny took her in her arms.

"Listen to your gut, sis. But you know whatever happens, I'll be thinking of you – and thanks to the latest technology, I'm there for you too."

Embarrassed, Alex wiped the tears from her eyes.

"Let's really push the boat out this evening, OK?" she quickly changed the subject. "And no arguments: The bill´s on me."

And that's exactly what they did. After admiring the symphony of lights from the summit, it was back to Kowloon. The chill-out zone of the moment was on the thirtieth floor of a building only two blocks away from their hotel. One look at the view, not to mention the prices on the cocktail menu, was enough to send them into a deep trance. But true to the motto "you only live once", they kept the bar staff busy all night and gave themselves over to the magic of the moment; it was something they'd remember for the rest of their lives.

The time went by in a flash, the days consumed by a mix of shopping and sightseeing. A visit to the world's largest sitting Buddha in the green hills of Lantau proved just as welcome a distraction to the big city as a trip to Lamma Island beach. They didn't bother with the other more typical tourist attractions such as Repulse Bay or Stanley Market. As fascinating as the city was, Alex wouldn't have liked to live there. She needed a balance between the lively hustle and bustle of the busy streets and the restorative quiet of nature. After a visit to a nearby district where amateur and professional musicians were performing scenes from traditional Chinese opera, Alex wanted to ensure she toasted her last evening together with Jenny somewhere special.

The majestically positioned Ritz-Carlton, the newest addition to hotels in the city, was close by to where they were staying. They would treat themselves to an evening in the luxurious surrounds of the highest bar in the world: The OZONE on the 118th floor. As if earmarked for them, they grabbed the best spot in the house in the corner of the table-and sofa section by the great glass window complete with a nocturnal view of the financial district. They enjoyed the view in silence for a while. Signature cocktail in hand, Alex soaked up the bar's cool, modern elegance. She felt both grateful and privileged to be there. Travelling to foreign countries had always been one of her passions, but only since she had got her job at PsoraCom did she have the financial means to combine occasional luxuries like this with her plans to save for a house and family. Not everyone was so fortunate, a fact she was all too aware of right this minute. Jenny seemed to be able to read her mind.

"It's a shame mum can't visit me here," she said sadly. "I'm sure she would have liked it."

Ricka's illness meant there was no chance her parents would come to visit. The trip would have been too long and exhausting. They had to make do with the many images and films that Jenny uploaded onto the family website.

Alex knew just how attached her mother was to the younger of her twin daughters – and how much she missed her. It was exactly the same for Jenny.

"I think I know what you mean," she said. "At some point children grow up and move away from home, and it's not always easy for either side."

"Especially when you're on the other side of the world and can't just nip back quickly for a weekend," Jenny agreed.

"Sure. But you can't let it distract you. Who knows what's going to happen in the future, but studying for your MBA is important."

They had to assume that no news was good news. It was Jenny's future that was at stake. Her parents had known what the decision meant and supported it. Jenny – and Alex - had to concentrate on their own lives and make their own mistakes. At the end of the day, they weren't teenagers anymore.

"What you experience in the next few months here in Hong Kong, no-one can take it away from you," Alex continued, trying to cheer her sister up. "Later, when you have a family, it won't be nearly as simple to live abroad. At least, not as easy as it is now. Besides, you'll be home at Christmas."

In order to put an abrupt end to their growing melancholy, she took the menu and asked Jenny playfully: "Which cocktail should we try now, then? I think I'm becoming hypoglycaemic."

"Right, let's give the waiter here something to do," her sister grinned back.

It was another evening that would live forever in the paradise of memory.

On the flight to Thailand, Alex suddenly felt very lonely. But the vacation still wasn't over and the last week on Koh Samui looked to be another highlight. Renata had described it as a picture-book beach holiday. With the exception of Hong Kong, she had relied entirely on the recommendations of her friend to plan her vacation. The sight of the little airport with its reed-covered roofs in the middle of a green oasis, surrounded by turquoise sea, immediately lifted her mood. The hotel was more idyllic than Renata had led her to imagine.

Two-storey buildings were diagonally arranged around a jungle landscape, next to an artificial pond that merged into a stream. Her first-floor room was more like a spacious apartment, from the balcony of which she could look out to sea. The thick green of the banana plants and palm trees opposite combined with the blue expanses of water produced an effect that was immediately soothing.

Inside the room, the dark wood of the floor and furniture stood in elegant contrast to the bright walls and starched white of the four-poster-bed sheets. Stylishly draped purple orchid plants complemented the austere but warm atmosphere and created a pleasant feeling of security. After a quick tour of the grounds, she was sure she'd be able to enjoy the simple luxury and just relax. It was paradise plain and simple, she thought to herself. Abruptly, she dispelled the notion that it would have been more romantic together with someone else.

The only thing was that there seemed to be only couples staying there. She was soon compensated for that, however. During dinner, two middle-aged guitar players went through the restaurant singing, trying to encourage the guests to visit the hotel bar, and regaling each table with a different song. Having got to Alex, they asked if she was all alone. It was pretty obvious she was the only single person. Alex fought back the sadness that briefly threatened to engulf her, but was barely able to conceal a grin when the first bars of Elvis's "Are you lonesome tonight?" began to play. No song could have been more appropriate. She found the affection with which the pair sang for her truly heart-warming.

After dinner, she went upstairs to the bar, located above the pond and covered by a wooden roof. The handfuls of people sitting comfortably in groups made it feel more like a lounge than a bar; and a gentle breeze wafted in through its exposed sides. There would be no wild parties here tonight, that was certain. She didn't feel any desire to visit the nearby entertainment district yet. Besides, she wanted to repay the guitarists with her visit. Cocktail in hand, she made herself comfortable in one of the thick upholstered rattan sofas and listened to them performing their full range of songs.

Before she left, she debated whether it was appropriate to leave a tip. Unable to decide either way, she compromised and arranged for a drink of their choice to be sent over. Completely unintentional though it might have been, the gesture guaranteed her the nightly attention of her two new friends from that point on; as soon as they saw Alex, they would play "her" song or sit down beside her. She registered with a smile how the other guests would turn round surreptitiously to steal a nosy glance. Even on the evenings when she needed to be among people and went further south of the hotel towards the entertainment district, she always made sure to chat to the pair for a few minutes upon her return. Sometimes it was so easy to make people happy.

With its local, fresh fruit and spicy chilli dishes, the ample breakfast buffet fulfilled more wishes than Alex could possibly have in a week. Even freshly prepared fried eggs were brought to the table by courteous waiting staff. None of the guests used their towels to reserve the sun loungers on the beach early in the morning, as was so often the case in other tourist resorts. There were no drunks at the pool bar and the few steps down to the beach meant the peddlers didn't become too pushy. The service was just the way Alex liked it: discreet but on hand as soon as you needed anything.

The end of the holiday drew nearer and Alex felt her sadness increasing. Since arriving on Koh Samui, she had tried not to think about Sandro; and had managed for the most part too, as her surroundings, a good book, or just sleeping had provided ample distraction. In the few moments she had been unsuccessful, usually in the evenings, she had thrown herself into the hustle and bustle of the bars in the tourist district and put her troubles to bed over a few cocktails.

While she waited for her return flight in Bangkok airport, she began to think things over. The little voice inside her head hadn't changed its tune since Hong Kong. Something between the two of them was broken and couldn't be fixed. There was a pain deep within her that she had only felt once before. Back then no common path had been there either. A feeling of sadness spread inside; her instincts were not often wrong.

Without being able to control it, her thoughts turned to life without Sandro. That stung again; her brain wasn't ready to give up on the relationship. But perhaps it was for the best? Her thoughts moved back and forth like a ping-pong ball. Maybe they just weren't a good match? Then it would make more sense to draw a line under things. Her dreams of a family and her own house lay in ruins. Clearing away the rubble and building something new would take a year or two, assuming she found a suitable partner at all.

It was difficult enough at her age to find someone who wasn't already carrying a lot of baggage. She didn't want to have to accept that her concept of a happy family life might be a utopian dream. Her brain was producing all these thoughts relatively soberly, but inside everything was beginning to cramp up. The feeling from Prague spread through her body like a plague. She could now look back at that traumatic time with a little objectivity. Heartless, that was how Sandro appeared. Truly heartless. In those few moments he no longer seemed to have any feelings for her. Perhaps there was another woman after all? In the end, it probably wouldn't make any difference.

"There she is, our little globetrotter," Moritz greeted her with a mighty embrace. With that, all the dark thoughts that had taken possession of her during the return flight were banished in one fell swoop.

"How was your holiday?" Renata was curious. "We've been shopping. You have to tell us all the details over breakfast. No arguments."

"Exactly," her brother agreed. "And no sweeping the dirty bits under the carpet, either."

"Heaven must have sent you," Alex said gratefully.

"Hong Kong was fantastic," she began. "The night skyline with all the lights is just amazing, and the view towards Kowloon and Hong Kong Island during the day is pretty impressive too. There are at least eight million people living there, but most of the streets are cleaner than here. All the skyscrapers make it much hotter and stickier, though. That's why Jenny and I combined the holiday with trips to the surrounding islands – to see the parks and monuments there. We saw the world's largest sitting Buddha as well, of course, although we spared ourselves Disneyland."

"What? You didn't see Mickey and Goofy?" Moritz asked in mock indignation. "I wouldn't have missed that myself."

"You would've fitted in pretty well, too," Alex replied with a smile.

"How did you like Koh Samui?" Renata asked.

"Superb," Alex responded enthusiastically. "Just brilliant. The hotel's an absolute dream; there's no other way to put it. The people were all so nice and considerate. The only down side was that it was only couples. But the location of the hotel more than compensated for that. If I felt I was going stir-crazy in the evenings, I just took a taxi to Chaweng Beach, sat myself down in a bar and watched everything happening around me. Otherwise, I went to the hotel bar after dinner for my own personal serenade."

When she told them how she had encountered her special friends on the first night, Renata and Moritz couldn't help but laugh.

"I can really picture it, how the pair of them ensnared you," Renata grinned.

"Ensnared is perhaps a little OTT," Alex replied. "They didn't want anything from me. Still, I really enjoyed the attention. It made me feel less alone."

"Ah yes, age is no boundary when it comes to romance," Moritz broke in. "Nevertheless, I'm happy you're back safely."

"Me too," said Alex. "I have to say, this holiday was my best yet. What I really liked about the people was they were so trusting and unassuming. Like when I hired a taxi to do a sightseeing tour. It couldn't have been better. The driver listed all the tourist attractions and suggested different routes but he let me decide; he didn't care about me changing my mind on the spur of the moment or stopping to take pictures. Even when we were in the main city, he waited patiently in a parking lot while I strolled through the little markets to pick up silk pillows or what not. He didn't even want cash upfront. The traders weren't pushy either. OK, so everyone tried to sell me their goods or entice me into their shops; but if I politely declined, they just smiled and said have a nice day. That doesn't happen here. Except with Renata in the hotel, of course."

Moritz and his sister were trying very hard to keep her spirits up. For the most part, it worked – but at some point conversation turned to Sandro. There was no way round it, even though talking about him hurt.

"Somehow I started to feel like it didn't make sense anymore," she told her friends, "that something between us is broken."

Both of them looked at her with sympathy.

"But that doesn't mean you have to bury all your dreams with it," Renata tried to cheer her up. "It's not the end of the world."

"Quite the opposite," Moritz agreed. "You know I've got a lot of time for Sandro. But I always had my doubts as to whether you could really make your dreams work with him. I think your gut instinct's right – you should listen to it and forget about your life together. Perhaps Sandro's found someone new; someone he doesn't have to make decisions with. It's possible all that was too much for him."

"How do you work that out?" Alex asked suspiciously.

"Oh, I don't know," Moritz hesitated.

"Come on," she pressed, "spit it out. What do you know?"

"Just tell her."

"OK, fine," Moritz admitted defeat. "I met up with Sandro a few weeks ago. We've always got on well."

He paused and waited for her reaction.

"It's OK," Alex said. "Just because we've been having problems doesn't mean you can't meet up with him. None of our mutual friends should feel forced to take sides. So shoot."

"There's a woman from the tennis club who split with her husband at the start of the year," Moritz continued hesitantly. "Since then, it seems she's been enjoying her new freedom. She and Sandro have been having a relationship since the trip to Switzerland at Easter. He said it just happened, that the two of them have similar interests: no real commitments to anyone, and tennis. Besides, the woman already has kids of school age and that takes the pressure off Sandro for the time being."

Alex had to swallow deeply when she felt Renata's sympathetic gaze on her.

"I don't believe it," she whispered. "Since Easter?"

It was only with some effort that she fought back the tears. Why hadn't she noticed anything? Sure, he had acted strangely this past year and spent a lot of time in the club. But there had been a number of good moments before Prague. She remembered how Sandro had come into the living room, massaged her shoulders and kissed the nape of her neck. Just like he used to. Then there was their trip to the mountains. How could he have been so deceitful?

Renata took her comfortingly into her arms.

"We'll get through this together," she promised. "You can call anytime day or night, if you need something."

Moritz nodded in agreement. She could see from his face that he would rather have kept it to himself.

"I would've preferred for Sandro to tell you personally as well," he admitted. "But he couldn't do it. Despite everything, he's still very fond of you and wasn't happy with this new woman. As far as I know, that's over now too. He didn't want to hurt you. That's why he didn't say anything – even if it only achieved the opposite effect."

But there was nothing to be done now. It had happened, and she needed to deal with it. Her friends stayed until the evening, distracted her as best as they could and built her back up.

After they had left, she called Sandro straightaway. She couldn't put the conversation off any longer, although she wasn't sure what she hoped to gain from it. At least one thing had come out of today. She had got mad. Mad that he didn't have the balls to talk to her about it. To say it directly to her face. To end things himself after he'd cheated on her. No, he had stretched it out like a piece of chewing gum, for months on end; and yet Alex had still held some hope. Why else had he kept calling after he'd moved out, inviting her to dinner or the cinema?

Admittedly, these dates had mostly limited themselves to a bit of hand-holding. But for Alex they'd been a sign that a fresh start remained a possibility. It was only her sub-conscious she hadn't been able to fool. After venting all her anger on him over the phone, she suddenly felt very tired and just wanted to sleep. He didn't have much to say in his defence and sounded a picture of misery when he discovered she knew everything; that the game was up.

"I'm really sorry," he said at the end once again.

But that was no great help. She'd never had a boyfriend cheat on her with another woman before. Nevertheless, she could have forgiven him if he'd written it off as a one-time indiscretion and confessed everything. If they could have sat down together and worked out why it'd happened. The thing that made it so painful was how long it'd been going on – plus his total inability to be open about it. Deeply hurt, she cried herself to sleep.

11

November

Alex upped her speed on the treadmill that was work. Since returning from holiday, she had often toiled late into the evening, with a daily jogging session providing the only interruption. Through the individual projects, she soon sank into a different and exciting technological world; one that allowed her to leave the wreckage of her private life behind. The project with Natioba had turned into a winner. The short film had arrived from Taipei and covered the whole show, lighting and sound effects included. With it, the entire team now had a tangible reference point, something that could be shown to clients and other companies. It was the kind of proof that was needed to successfully establish a new product on the market.

What sort of client would go for a new product when they didn't understand its benefits? And here more than ever, the old adage applied: a picture is worth a thousand words. Especially where new technology was concerned, clients liked to have something concrete in front of them. Just like the seed units Alex had obtained from Hank and distributed to her colleagues. Until now, validation of the Vabilmo technology had come in the form of press releases from Roffarm and Hursoc, both already a few months old. Unfortunately, there had been no updates concerning the current activities of these two companies. Besides, the press articles were only LOIs; neither party had made specific reference to any projects.

At the time, it had been exactly the right thing to do. However, in order to achieve market success, PsoraCom were obliged to report on new phases and developments. Otherwise the impression could arise that the area was a dead end that the company was constantly trying to revive. In addition to her existing projects, therefore, Alex began to make new contacts. New projects didn't always mean that PsoraCom had to take on new staff. Willing partners from the ecosystem could function as multipliers. Once trained, they could relay the message to the solar industry at large.

Volcrea was one such partner. The name PsoraCom, allied to mention of the fact that they had met a representative of the American parent company at the conference in San Francisco, opened doors with Volcrea's German branch instantly. It turned out they had caught them at just the right time.

Among other things, the company was currently working on a new range of solar-powered machines. Alex got Carl involved straightaway. There were a number of different objectives that could be jointly pursued. Volcrea could function as an additional sales and project arm with power plant manufacturers, designing new plants with polymer-based solar cells and developing the necessary inverters for them. It might also be possible to draw on their experiences with inverters in the machine industry and apply them to the robot sector. The transition would be pretty fluid, as many of the machines were already classified as industrial robots.

Carl's interest was pricked anyway, since things were currently very slow with the companies he had been allocated. Most robot manufacturers were predominantly in the market for cheap mass-produced household robots, and the Vabilmo technology was still far too expensive for them. Alex was astonished to learn that Carl – despite the established strategy – still hadn't contacted the number two manufacturer. His primary focus remained the market leader, who, as a result of the expansion of their distribution network into the BRIC countries, had adopted a low-cost strategy, and therefore had little interest in new methods of generating electricity.

This kind of behaviour was called "hammering away" in certain training courses. If, after several attempts, it became clear that the client wasn't interested, it was best to leave them alone for a while. Either a new opportunity would present itself in time or the client would actively approach the supplier. The more you pestered a client in a situation like this, the more you risked undermining your mutual trust and making the client feel that they were not being taken seriously.

Why the second largest robot manufacturer wasn't on Carl's to-do list was a mystery to her. When she asked if there was a specific reason, he just said no and she didn't probe any further: it was his area, after all. That he had altered the agreed strategy without any reason didn't seem to bother Thomas much, as the issue was never discussed in team meetings.

Understandably Volcrea were very keen on the bend-modules. Their new range of machinery, along with a prototype, was set to be unveiled at a trade show in Valencia at the start of next year. They would still have time in the next three weeks to make adjustments and equip the sample machine with the new solar cells, completing the conceptual phase.

As it was a public trade show, Alex wanted to present the project at the next team meeting and check whose approval she needed internally. Her aim was to minimise PsoraCom's involvement by restricting it to the provision of bend-modules and, if necessary, a small contribution to advertising costs. Carl agreed and promised to get the modules from Apircu. He had obtained the manufacturer's contact details from Hank. Presenting the project in front of colleagues was something he would rather leave to her, however.

"Volcrea is a well-established name in the industry," Alex began. "The company works with almost every power plant manufacturer worldwide, most suppliers and a number of robot firms. At no great cost to us, they can take on a significant portion of our work. If they were to equip their machine sample with our bend-modules, then we, as their partner, would be able to approach clients and end customers from a different angle. In this way, Volcrea would be an additional development and sales arm, at least as far as launching standardised cells on the market is concerned."

"I can well imagine machine manufacturers going for it," Carl added.

Her colleagues did not react as she expected. George – sitting directly across from her - snorted condescendingly, smoothed his glossy violet jacket and propped himself up on the table with his elbows.

"We don't need any more public shows creating waves when there's zip to back them up," he said gruffly. "In my opinion, we should restrict ourselves to developing inverters and working with the power plant manufacturers and robot companies – behind the scenes! Who are Volcrea anyway? A mid-sized company with a few hundred employees. They're still living in the dark ages. To the big players in the industry, they're just flunkies without any influence."

Alex looked at him sceptically. Was it just another one of those days when George was at odds with everyone? With his knowledge of the industry, he was surely aware that Volcrea was the largest and most successful contract developer in its market sector. Every R&D department worked in conjunction with them. Sometimes manufacturers let them design entire plants. What was up with him? Had he lost at poker again?

Thomas initially declined to comment and seemingly wanted to wait and see how things developed. But then his cell rang suddenly and he excused himself. He had been urgently summoned to Wolfgang's office. No-one seemed to take exception to this, and so the discussion continued without him. Astonishingly, even Brian took sides with his long-standing rival.

"If we do this project, then we're total amateurs," he yammered irritably into the room.

He spat the last word out with real venom, angrily twirling his goatee between his fingers. Apparently intimidated by the reaction, Carl decided to keep stumm. Alex couldn't begin to understand. Here was an opportunity to present the company's latest technology together with a not-insignificant partner from the ecosystem, and her colleagues were resisting vehemently. It was completely irrational.

Hugo was whispering away quietly with George and nodding eagerly. Although she hadn't heard a word, it was clear he had sided with the majority view. It was to be expected. Alex's additional attempts to convince them of the project using facts, figures and various other persuasive techniques fell on deaf ears. The meeting ended without a decision being made.

Their boss hadn't returned. If her colleagues' opinion was anything to go by, they shouldn't even begin the project, let alone present it to the public. But Alex wasn't quite ready to yield to this viewpoint. In her mind, collaborating with Volcrea was precisely in line with the team strategy. First she wanted to speak to Thomas and hear his take on the matter. Besides, she was angry about the way her colleagues had conducted themselves.

"It was almost aggressive," she concluded, after Christopher had bumped into her in the corridor and asked why she looked so sullen.

"I've never seen you so glum," he said. "Don't get upset about it! You're usually so stoical about those idiots."

But this time his grin could only go some way towards cheering her up.

"The presentation at the trade show in Valencia isn't the main issue here," she began her conversation with Thomas. "It's the opportunities available in general. Of course, it's in Volcrea's interest to work with us; that much is clear. But a prototype presented by the two of us together could prove to be a real turbocharger; and it might help accelerate things with our existing projects. It would provide another concrete example of our work, which could bring interested companies closer to an understanding of the benefits of the technology."

"Sure," he replied. "But why a trade show? A flyer could be an alternative."

She should have seen that one coming. Thomas found arguments for both sides and refused to commit himself. He wasn't about to come up with a deus ex machina solution. In the end all he did was transfer responsibility over to Henry's department; it was the one in charge of corporate communication in Germany, after all.

"I think it should it be his department that decides. That way, the problem with the budget is solved too."

As a strategic move, it was ingenious; one Alex would have to remember.

Perhaps she was just stubbornly insisting on a pipe dream and, in contrast to her colleagues, was no longer aware of the reality of the situation.

"If Henry's against it, I'll say no to Volcrea," she promised her boss. "One more thing: I don't think the tone of our meeting today was appropriate."

Her boss paused. "You mean Brian, don't you?"

"How do you know it's Brian?" she asked in astonishment.

"I thought as much," he said without providing any further explanation. "Let's go and see Henry."

"Actually, I don't think the trade show's a bad idea at all," the latter said, after Alex outlined the details. "That way, we'd be showing continuity as a company. I'm not saying anything new here, but it's not just important for you guys to win clients; you have to make sure you develop the ecosystem as well. You need an approach that's all-encompassing."

Thomas waited for an additional explanation, his face devoid of any expression. In Volcrea they would gain a partner who, together with their clients and end customers, would serve as another piece in the overall puzzle. By projecting all previous press releases and projects onto a timeline, PsoraCom would be able to provide clear documentation of their progress; starting with Roffarm and Hursoc, followed by Natioba, and now Volcrea.

In Henry's opinion, providing evidence of progress was extremely important. He was certain Wolfgang wouldn't have any issues with his office taking on a pioneering role with the Vabilmo technology (something the trade show could now help to highlight internally). Quite the opposite: in fact, the more he thought about it, the better Henry liked the idea.

"OK, fine, that's what we'll do," Thomas decided, before standing up. "You look after the budget, Alex."

"Sure you don't need more?" Henry asked, after he heard its size. "That's peanuts. Tell me something else. Is Brian still around? I mean, does he still work for us? I haven't seen him for ages and I can't remember the last time I got an email from him. Perhaps there'll be a project with one of his or George's clients at the start of next year; then we can incorporate them too."

"Yeah, of course Brian's still here," Alex affirmed.

The more she thought about it, however, the more the question made sense. Most of the time when she called Brian, she only got his voicemail. If he called back at all, it wasn't until days later. She hadn't seen him in the office for a long time, apart from at the intermittent team meetings. Since the summer months someone from the team had always been away on holiday and discipline had clearly begun to wane. Joint meetings were often cancelled. Apart from her, no-one ever came into the office "just because". Out of sight, out of mind. How true.

Meanwhile, Alex remembered she had to return her colleague from Marketing's call.

"Can you do me a favour?" Lisa implored. "Cellgot are organising an internal conference; it's small but exclusive, involving selected clients and representatives from the energy sector. Since a number of the participants are from the solar industry, we're providing sponsorship. In return, Cellgot are plastering their rooms with our banners, and we have the chance to hold a presentation – which they are naturally keen on. Scatty as I am, I've already agreed. But I can't do it myself. I'll get stage fright, and I just don't know enough about Vabilmo. I think it's an excellent opportunity to give the topic a plug."

Out of her nervousness arose a glimmer of hope, as Alex looked through her calendar system and saw she had nothing planned for the day in question.

"If you're going out on a limb especially for us, then we should be able to give you a hand," she assured Lisa. "I'll just clarify it with Thomas."

Secretly, she was delighted by the offer. Recently she had the feeling that she was being seen more and more as the central contact for Vabilmo. That was hardly surprising, considering she was just about the only person from the team who was ever in the office.

Her boss didn't have any objections; he would even accompany her to Geneva. At some point he had to mix with the masses, that is to say, potential clients and partners. The conference would enable him to meet various people all at once and would thus be an effective use of his time.

"But you're making the presentation," he said, making his feelings immediately clear. "I don't want to. Besides, I'm sure you'll do a good job."

"Sure," she replied. Nothing I'd rather do, she thought to herself.

Only later did it occur to her that at no point had Thomas asked if perhaps someone else should go instead of her.

Henry was sure to think it was "really cool" as well, since the conference would provide them with another partner from the ecosystem.

"I already know," he grinned. "I've got their press release on my desk, waiting to be checked. I'm trying to think of a good headline. They're pretty keen to get everything they can from our participation."

Cellgot was still a very minor player with just over one hundred employees. To make up for it they were innovative and nimble where the market was concerned. Still, they could do with the publicity. For Henry it was a perfect match in terms of PsoraCom's pioneering role.

Although Alex was burying herself in her work, her friends didn't allow her to shut them out. Quite the opposite. They were worried that her job was the only thing Alex was living for. Anna, Moritz and Renata pressed for some time together to take her mind off things. They alternated between inviting her to dinner, the cinema or making pizza and fresh popcorn for long DVD nights. Every week they showed her interesting-looking property notices in the paper; because on one thing they were all agreed: a fundamental change of scenery – that is, a new flat – would be the best way for her to get over what had happened. There were too many memories in her current apartment; she couldn't fool her friends there.

When Alex wasn't working, she began to brood and became deeply depressed. It wasn't just that her relationship had broken down. When things got really bad - and that was happening more and more frequently - she saw all her private dreams in tatters as well. She was pushing forty. It would take a long time to find not only a suitable partner, but someone she could imagine growing old with. But she wasn't nearly ready for anyone new yet.

She had loved Sandro and the disappointment that he had forsaken her for another sat deep. But you couldn't change the past. Chin up; that was the only mantra worth adopting right now. There were people far worse off. She still had an exciting job, one that continued to inspire her. She had a good set of friends and a family that was behind her all the way. Not to mention a sizeable bank balance that allowed her various luxuries, like the trip to Asia. It could be a whole lot worse, her positive alter ego criticised. Still, it wasn't enough to curb her yo-yoing emotions.

Thomas had postponed their next jour fixe by an hour.

"What's the latest with your clients?" he asked, as they were sitting in the empty canteen.

"We're approaching the next phase of the project with Premve," she replied. "They've decided to push things along from Seoul. Premve have an office there, like Natioba. I'm certain one of the reasons for the decision is the relative proximity to Taiwan, as that's where the head of the power plant division thinks the dominant suppliers are. Wolfgang's already approved a meeting with them on-site. I'm still waiting for a response from Hugo, though. He's the only one who hasn't got back to me with a definitive yes or no."

She sighed in frustration, before continuing.

"I've sent him two mails already because I couldn't get him on the phone. That's enough, isn't it? I don't have any desire to remind him a third time. If he doesn't have the time, that's OK – but he has to tell me. If he's not interested or doesn't think it's important, then he won't be involved. What do you think? I mean, I'm not his private secretary; I spoke in detail about how things stood at the last team meeting."

"It's certainly a bit strange," Thomas seemed surprised as well. "Who's confirmed already then? If they can cover everything on their own, it should be enough."

"Nobu and Hank said yes straightaway, Marco's coming too and there's someone from Hank's department on the ground there. Hank will probably be involved in other projects in the future as well. Then there's a guy from Bill's department, Phil, who's also confirmed."

"In that case I think you've got enough," Thomas said. "Hugo doesn't have to fly over as well. We can save on costs and he can concentrate on projects here."

"Good, I'll make sure everything's taken care of. That still leaves Chris from Natioba. Hugo's been promising to call him for months but nothing's happened yet. It's extremely frustrating and I've no wish to spend my life chasing him up."

"I'll speak to Hugo about it next time," Thomas promised.

"Is there any news from Wolfgang about additional resources?" she probed.

"Not yet. I'll have to ask him again."

"If things go as planned," Alex predicted, "then we'll reach an impasse sooner than anticipated. We're basically there already."

That was exactly what Marco thought too. As the person in overall charge of the client, he was interested, more than anything, in carrying the project into the developmental phase. Post kick-off meeting, after all, everyone had agreed it conformed to the established strategy and should be implemented. As he so often did, Brian had spoken about far-reaching achievements, while even George had seemed enthusiastic for more than twenty minutes. Internally, however, it had not yet been decided which department would be responsible for each part of the project. The only certainty was that it wouldn't be the Vabilmo team alone. Just like with Roffarm, they would need a project manager and a proportionate number of developers.

A new sector had been created in Bill's department that was to deal exclusively with Vabilmo projects. That was why Alex had invited Phil to the meeting in Seoul; it was possible he would take on the role of project manager. However, since they first needed to fit the robots with the new cells, Hank's department was likewise a point of contact.

Alex was delighted, as Hank had done a great job with Natioba and could be relied upon. He had mentioned the Premve project parallel to Natioba over and over again in internal team meetings. Even his boss's boss, who was in charge of Robotics as a whole, knew that together with PsoraCom, Premve were laying the foundations for standardised inverters; a component that could be universally implemented in robots, irrespective of their operating conditions.

Such an undertaking couldn't stem from Premve alone; or PsoraCom, as they lacked detailed knowledge about robot requirements.

But together they could do it, and though their client was in reality a solar plant specialist that only used robots for monitoring, they saw such a clear advantage in a universal inverter that they were prepared to pioneer the development. If developed correctly, the inverter could even be modified into an alternating-current converter, or an integral part of it at least. That would enable its use in large plants. A noble aim, from a technical point of view. But Premve probably also thought that if you didn't aim for the stars you'd never even make it to the moon.

The project's potential, at any rate, was enormous, as Premve were not insisting on exclusivity. Quite the opposite, in fact: the more competitors that went for the inverters, the greater the distribution of the new solar cells. The higher quantities would result in lower prices, and thus a quicker payback period. The maintenance robots and their equipment were significant factors in the cost of a plant. If savings could be made here – and with a little reconstruction work, that was possible even in existing plants – the overall benefit for Premve would be all the greater. The head of the power plant division was completely convinced by the Vabilmo technology and he seemed to be well ahead of the market in his outlook. Things couldn't have been better for PsoraCom.

Marco had rubbed his hands in delight when Alex told him of their client's all-encompassing approach. There was an even greater chance they would outdo Roffarm with this project. Competition was always good, even when it was in-house. Perhaps they could also find synergies between Natioba and Roffarm, but that was a long way off. First they had to determine resources and responsibilities internally. They had their plane tickets anyway, and were ready to initiate the next phase in Seoul. As the responsible architect from the Vabilmo team, Hugo should really have been assisting them with his technical knowledge, but somehow they'd manage without him. Completely failing to respond to a number of different enquiries was just impolite.

Alex had been annoyed about it for days; after all, Premve stood at the top of the team's strategy list, just like Natioba and Roffarm. Recently, it seemed as if Hugo was undergoing a change, one that was subtly asserting itself in his choice of clothing, increasingly reminiscent of that of George. But that wasn't the only thing. He now seemed to fully expect Alex to coordinate joint meetings for him. He had his wires crossed there, however. Alex was an equal member of the team, even if she had been a latecomer. She wasn't about to take on the role of PA for any of her colleagues. Everyone had to organise themselves. The company provided enough help tools; it was up to the individual to ensure they were correctly used.

Renata had heard about a free apartment from a colleague at work and called Alex immediately. Winter had already created a few issues in the past years and Alex didn't need a crystal ball to see that her flat would soon have another leak. They went to the viewing together. The flat was quite centrally located in the neighbouring village but away from the main road on a hill-top cul-de-sac. All the important shops could be reached on foot. It was barely two minutes' walk away from both the bakery and local pub. The large living room with wooden parquet flooring led out to the garden via a south-facing terrace. Besides the kitchen-cum-living-room and bedroom, there was another small room that would make an excellent office. She didn't need a lot of space and she could work on the patio in summer. The only thing that prevented the flat from being perfect was its lack of a garage. But, then again, she had a covered parking space in the carport. Better than nothing, Alex thought to herself; you couldn't have it all. After a lengthy phone conversation with the landlord, her tenancy was confirmed.

Thomas and Alex were treated like royalty by Cellgot. A limousine drove them directly from the airport to the lakeside hotel where the conference was taking place. The managing director greeted them at the evening reception, together with the marketing chief, who would be personally responsible for them. To begin with, Thomas kept in the background, filling his pipe several times while Alex was introduced to Cellgot's most important clients.

Apart from the hotel staff, there were no women present and once again she enjoyed the attention accorded to her in the male-dominated surroundings. As she spoke longer and more enthusiastically, Thomas started to participate in the conversation himself. Just as in Hamburg, he was soon passionately outlining the merits of the Vabilmo technology.

Naturally, she was nervous. It was the same before every meeting or presentation, no matter how many people were there. Alex had slept excellently and enjoyed a good breakfast. She hadn't seen her boss there but knew that he only needed a coffee to start the day. Her presentation was after the mid-morning break. An excellent time; the audience would have shaken off their fatigue but wouldn't be hungry again yet.

As she approached the lectern, she squared her shoulders and pulled her collar straight. She knew it would go well because she had written the presentation herself. Henry had approved it. For every slide, she had chosen a key word to link to the next page. She didn't need any notes; she knew it almost by heart. The seed units were in her bag for the moment. They alone would guarantee interest levels, of that much she was certain. She positioned herself freely next to the lectern and stared straight out into the audience. Most of them returned her gaze expectantly, although some seemed almost amused. She had seen such looks before, but they only spurred her on. Nevertheless, she began to sweat slightly.

"How many alternatives are there to thin-film silicon cells?" she began. "How can you permanently lower cost and increase efficiency in order to reach grid parity independent of the state's supportive measures?"

Once more she scanned the eighty-odd participants, before taking a step to the side.

"How can you attain a unique design with standardised modules?"

After the third question, the last remaining whispers ceased and heads lifted towards the front. Thomas gave her a nod of encouragement from his seat. Now Alex was in her element and took another step forward. She realised how many of the audience were thinking the questions over.

As usual her nervousness had dissipated and given way to a state of excitement that was something other than physical. Slowly she laid the bait. General market data appeared on the first page, followed by a prognosis for electricity consumption. Alex stood to the right of the screen, ignoring the lectern on the left-hand side. Owing to the predicted shortage in fossil fuels, the interest in regenerative energy techniques in the solar, biomass, wind and geothermal heat industries was set to increase further. Power plants and off-grid systems would use primarily solar energy from now on.

But the possible scope of application was far more diverse, especially since size and storage capacity were areas where battery technology was being constantly developed in order to balance out discrepancies in sunlight availability. What else would solar cells be used for in the future? Which industries would hold a significant market share in solar energy in the long run? It was clear that it was being used more and more in the field of building integration. Perhaps one day home electricity requirements would be fulfilled entirely by an outer layer of solar cells.

"But what else?" she asked. The three words hung in the air like a far-reaching decision urgently needing to be taken. Her gaze wandered purposefully from one participant to the next. She looked every member of the audience directly in the eye, as if she was speaking to each one of them personally; as if theirs was the only opinion this decision rested on.

"Robots."

Slowly she reached into her bag. Some audience members in the back few rows stood up to get a better view. She had been right. Everyone looked curiously at the seed units in her hand.

"In the future, all kinds of robots and mobile machines will generate their electricity through these standardised bend-modules. The flexible design of our polymer-based cells allows the bend-modules to be customised, as you can see from this example. Moreover, the targeted efficiency of these cells is more than twice that of the thin-film cells currently employed. They allow for a significant reduction in the required surface area, as well as the subsequent weight. The intelligent, gesture-based control of robots pioneered by Cellgot is another decisive building block in the trendsetting field of non-autonomous robot technology. To finish, I would like to show you a film recorded during the opening speech of our annual developer conference. It shows how building integration and robots can work together in tandem. In summary, we can say that large solar plants will continue to be substantially involved in generating electricity. However, in my opinion, there will be a disproportionate rise in the number of small plants, whether stationary or mobile, being decentralised or outsourced."

Alex started the film while thanking everyone for their attention. The film had the desired effect. Most of the participants seemed not to have seen it yet, even though some of the journalists in Taipei had filmed proceedings with their netphones and placed the results online. After the presentation, Thomas came to her assistance. Despite the scheduled lunch break and seductive aromas emanating from the buffet in the next room, the majority of audience members only seemed interested in having their questions about the seed units answered.

Exhausted but satisfied, Alex fell into bed late that evening. Still buzzing from the various conversations of the day, at no point did her thoughts turn to Sandro and the depressing recesses of her memory.

"Come on, let's transfer our ticket to an earlier flight," Thomas surprised her the next morning. "We're finished here."

"No can do," Alex replied, fixing him directly in the eyes. "I think it'd be very impolite; besides, it's only on until midday. We can still make use of the next few hours."

She knew this was one way she got on people's nerves, but it was how she had been brought up.

"Finish what you've started," her mother always said; it was a principle Alex kept to unless it became completely untenable.

She added with a wink: "We wouldn't want our travel costs to go up because of the transfer."

Thomas admitted defeat but didn't seem annoyed. He even bought Alex a glass of champagne later at the airport.

"You did a really good job with the presentation," he praised her. "Everyone I talked to said the same. Even the guy from Cellgot said he could do with having an employee like you. But I told him straightaway that you were out of his price range."

"So much praise at once must be a real effort for you," she teased.

"That's true," he replied smiling. "You're not getting any more out of me."

Nothing seemed to have come of the joint project between Luxumi and Hursoc. No progress had been made since the on-site meeting with Bill during the summer. Her suspicions grew even more. The person from Luxumi's development department who had been put in charge was unavailable. His responses to her emails were not only extremely late, but evasive. Right now, the project appeared to be stalling.

Alex knew that Luxumi were planning a smaller 100 megawatt PV plant in Croatia. However, she had already heard from different people there that developments were too far along to incorporate the Vabilmo technology. The planning and specification phase for the next plant – the earliest the polymer-based cells could enter into the equation – wouldn't begin until the end of next year. Until then R&D were busy with Croatia and not really open to test projects.

So, Alex had explored other avenues and called the maintenance department. Perhaps an opportunity would present itself there, like with Premve. Admittedly, Luxumi didn't use maintenance robots yet and still relied on human staff, although there were some electric vehicles available for service technicians. They were set to switch to maintenance robots eventually.

In an eye-to-eye meeting that the maintenance chief had agreed to, a joint test project emerged. A service vehicle was to be fitted with bend-modules and would thus supply the batteries with electricity. Her conversation partner didn't realise how close he was to the competition at Premve. But Alex would take care not to breathe a word. Converting vehicles to solar-power was nothing spectacular in itself, although their range would be a cool third higher than contemporary solar-powered test vehicles. Still, there was one final detail lacking. Cellgot. They would surely want to be involved as well, Alex thought, before suggesting it to her client. In reality, gesture-based control systems made little sense at the moment, but it was a question of making provisions for the future.

The maintenance chief looked at her sceptically. He was probably imagining a service technician driving all over the plant, gesticulating wildly with his hands, before his vehicle finally spun out of control and crashed into a supporting pillar. But Alex had been thinking of integrated help tools such as a telescopic crane rather than vehicle steering systems. It could help minimise the switch harnesses, which in turn would contribute to a reduction in weight. Less weight would mean the vehicle had a greater range. It was still peanuts compared with the bend-modules, which were thirty percent lighter than conventional silicon cells, but every little helped. Slowly he seemed to be warming to the idea.

By the end, they were agreed that Cellgot's solution should be integrated. The maintenance chief called one of his employees straightaway to give him initial instructions. That made Alex feel considerably better than she had in the summer after the previous meeting. It looked like being a done deal. Her client was already thinking aloud about industry events where the test vehicle might be unveiled. Lisa was sure to be happy her Swiss friends were getting a look-in. Doubtless the initiative also conformed to Henry's ideas for expanding the ecosystem; not to mention that there'd soon be a third client commencing tests on Vabilmo.

12

December

Alex flew to Seoul a day in advance to pay the lab supervisor a courtesy call, as she was in his neck of the woods anyway. Chris had arranged the meeting and given her advice about the journey and hotels. Framed by elegant shopping quarters, the office was located near Rodeo Street, on the south side of the Han River that divided the city and its twenty-five districts.

The concentration of luxury hotels, including the Intercontinental where Alex was staying, suggested that most visitors didn't just return home with a pair of Gucci plimsolls. In the taxi to the hotel, her first impressions were different once more from Hong Kong, though both cities were modern industrial giants. Despite a population of more than ten million in the actual city, Seoul seemed quieter and more serene. The people Alex had met so far had exhibited a level of politeness she had never before encountered. Everyone seemed to smile kindly at her, always ready to answer questions or point her in the right direction.

Chris laughed when she spoke to him and the lab supervisor about it over dinner after the meeting. Both had insisted she sample the local cuisine. After all, they wanted her to get a feeling for the culinary traditions of their homeland.

"You just look different to most people here," he explained the phenomenon. "Compared with all the blond tourists, Koreans very rarely see a red-haired woman with freckles. Let alone one who walks around in a classic suit in this fashion-obsessed city."

"A sort of Irish business alien who, they assume, comes in peace," the lab supervisor added cheekily, as he offered her some kimchi, a sweet and sour fermented cabbage dish.

Many local restaurants specialised in a small number of dishes, Alex learned from her hosts. In this restaurant, for example, it was bulgogi, beef seasoned with hot spices. The sliced meat was grilled on a hot stone, wrapped in salad leaves with additional ingredients such as garlic, peppers or rice, and then eaten by hand. If you wanted stew, soup or noodle dishes, then you had to go somewhere else each time. There were no knives, except perhaps in international restaurant chains or steakhouses. If need be, the meat would be cut with scissors. And to make it all the more difficult for Irish business aliens, the chopsticks were made out of brightly polished metal. Environmentally friendly hygiene South Korean style, Alex thought to herself.

After dinner, her hosts insisted on the obligatory soju, the national spirit made from sweet potatoes. It was ordered in different sizes and flavours and consumed from small shot glasses. A single glance at the quarter-gallon bowl, complete with its own tap, was already enough to make a few stray brain cells say their goodbyes. But Alex would never have made the blunder of declining. Luckily, it turned out the alcohol content wasn't much higher than that of a dessert wine. It was unlikely to cause untold damage.

Chris kept refilling her glass, as was the custom in South Korea. All the while, he gave her useful tips about how to move things along with his colleagues in mobile off-grid systems. The greenhouse presentation in Taipei had jolted a few developers in Italian HQ back to their senses. Initial reaction hinted that there was considerable interest. He thought about which systems were currently being developed and where it would make sense to implement the Vabilmo technology. There was something else that might interest her as well.

A small company that had recently been purchased by Natioba, dealing in maintenance and upkeep. Fifty percent of the time, they still worked for other companies. Alex's head was spinning. The number of departments and contacts affiliated to the Natioba group was becoming increasingly complex.

Back at the hotel Alex sketched out a mind map outlining the structure. First, there was the lab in Seoul, which assisted Italian HQ with research and near-operational developments, sometimes even taking overall charge. Then, besides the development department specialising in traditional off-grid systems - PsoraCom's biggest client in terms of production quantity - there was also a new subdivision for mobile off-grid systems. And, on top of all that, was the maintenance unit. That was four divisions in total, excluding the sluggish research department in Milan. She vaguely remembered Chris telling her something about a design department in New York that could likewise be of interest. Five potential clients in one single company. That was sure to provide plenty of variety. She certainly wouldn't be short of work.

The kick-off meeting with Premve provided variety of a different sort. It was a large group, with Marco, Nobu, and Hank and his colleague, as well as Phil. Overwhelmed by the PsoraCom invasion, as he called it, Premve's South Korea director opened the meeting and circulated the agenda. As behoved a proper agenda, it would conclude with the allocation of tasks and responsibilities. Premve were ready to put their money where their mouth was and had already assigned two people to the project in Seoul. Two additional employees from Germany would provide support if necessary and were on stand-by.

Alex caught Marco's eye, and he raised a questioning eyebrow. She responded with a brief nod. She could only hope that her colleagues from the power plant and robotics divisions were well prepared and ready to make a decision. All participants had received the relevant information in advance by email. In addition, they had gone through the details over the phone.

The thought that it might not have been enough momentarily brought her out in a hot flush. Was there something else she could have done? In order to facilitate a decision, she had drawn up a graphic forecast with a timeline based on production quantity and subsequent revenue, largely corresponding to the calculations of her contact at Premve. The figures didn't look too bad at all. If you looked at the market effect as well - assuming additional solar plant manufacturers got on board later - the potential became considerably greater.

But she hadn't wanted to go as far as that and thus provided only an outlook. It made little sense to gaze too closely into her crystal ball and offer a rose-tinted view of things. There had to be a degree of realism - amongst all the optimism. Over the course of the next two days, the individual PsoraCom employees changed their tune as often as a chameleon changed its colours. Hank's colleague, having declared his full support over breakfast that morning, had affected a volte-face by dinner.

Phil, who had been sceptical to begin with, was now indicating approval. Hank would have very much liked to assist but couldn't give a definitive answer, as his additional responsibilities were yet to be clarified. Alex began to sweat blood and tears about who might change their mind again. It almost felt like a game of roulette. After every break, an additional aspect of the project was discussed. With that, new factors entered into the equation and bets needed to be placed once more. By the afternoon of the second day, however, the action list had to be furnished with names – and all those present were obliged to lay their cards on the table.

Alex and Marco committed themselves to all commercial aspects of the project. That meant compiling status reports to be presented to upper management in both companies. But who else could have taken on the role? It was their job, after all. When it came to distributing the technical work packages including overall project responsibility, an abrupt silence descended. Her colleagues looked expectantly from one person to the next.

After an almost never-ending pause, Phil eventually agreed to take care of any future issues that might arise. As far as he was concerned, however, overall project responsibility was the domain of Robotics, since it was a question of autonomously operated vehicles, rather than power plants. Hank and his colleague were thus forced in action, though neither of them seemed to be jumping at the opportunity. Quite the opposite, in fact; both seemed to have ready-made excuses outlining their lack of suitability. Hank's explanation was the only plausible one. So, on that score Premve would just have to wait. Nobu was ultimately able to persuade Hank's colleague to take charge of appointing a project manager. The meeting minutes recorded that a resource was to be made available by PsoraCom within two weeks.

The result wasn't exactly satisfactory but at least Hank's colleague had made a personal commitment to the client. That was as good as a guarantee. There was no going back on it now.

Thomas and Wolfgang, at least, were satisfied with the state of play. Alex had gratefully accepted Marco's offer to write up the minutes and distribute them by email. She sent him her notes, which also contained an aside about Hugo. How was she to know the trouble it would cause?

George was seething with anger at the next team meeting. Why was a mystery to Alex; she wasn't aware of having done anything wrong. Marco had distributed the meeting minutes as promised and appended a list of tasks that needed taking care of. A rather unfortunately phrased remark had been included from her notes.

"That's not how things work here, Alex!" George hissed. "You can't just distribute tasks as if they're orders."

"I've no intention of doing that," Alex defended herself. "That wasn't how it was meant at all. It was about a question I wanted to ask Hugo. There was no mention of it made to the client. It was in my own personal notes, which I sent to Marco only for the sake of completeness."

"I'm sorry," she apologised to Hugo. "It was an unintentional mistake."

He had followed the exchange stony-faced, as if he had lost the ability to speak. But George didn't really seem to be listening. He kept muttering something incomprehensible and vehemently shaking his head. Brian looked up from his laptop briefly, only to immediately start typing again. He probably had more important things to do. Carl sat there motionless; it seemed he would rather be anywhere else. Finally, Thomas intervened.

"That's sorted then," he said, before going through the meeting agenda.

Alex wondered what had got into George recently. That was the second time he had openly criticised her in front of colleagues. On things that didn't concern her, however, he was back to his objective self. What on earth was the matter with him?

"Let's go and get something to eat together afterwards," she offered during the break, by way of reconciliation.

He accepted with a terse "OK".

At the end of the meeting, Thomas kept her back for a minute.

"Sit back down," he said seriously. "Looking at George tells me there's something not quite right at the moment. Do you have any idea what it could be?"

"No," she replied, shaking her head. "I haven't noticed anything up with the others. I'll try and see what it's about at lunch. The thing with Hugo was a misunderstanding. Marco didn't let me proofread the minutes beforehand. Otherwise I would've changed the wording, as it really wasn't appropriate."

Thomas nodded. "OK, fine. Talk to him again and see that you clarify things."

"It could also be about our resource problems with Hugo," she called out behind him.

Brian and Hugo were sitting with George when she came into the canteen. Like faint signals she caught a few meaningless snatches of conversation on her way to the salad buffet.

"With…about…talk…differently".

It could have referred to absolutely any project, though Alex had the impression it concerned a specific client. At least George and Brian didn't seem to be fighting so much these days. Even on the subject of Roffarm, she felt that the two of them had found some common ground. Alpha males and their turf wars, she smiled to herself, as she took her seat next to them.

It was probably just something eating away at him. Later, when they were alone at the table together, she mentioned the email again. But George had already forgotten about it. Compared with earlier, his mood was as bright as his new blond highlights. Her question about whether there was something else he wanted to discuss drew a negative response. After a frantic look at his watch, he suddenly stood up.

"Daily conference call with Hursoc," he explained briefly. "By the way, we should get them on board with the Premve project as soon as possible."

"What do you mean?" Alex asked irritably. "The head of the power plant division explicitly requested that no suppliers be involved for the time being. He doesn't want to give any companies a head-start on development. Not even his preferred choice from Taiwan. He's been very clear about it, and his team in Seoul have backed him up."

"I'll call you about it later," he shouted as he went, leaving her baffled. It seemed he was always good for a surprise. But surprises weren't necessarily pleasant.

"But George," she countered forcefully, when he called her later. "Premve have clearly stated that they don't want any third-party involvement at this time."

"But that just doesn't make any sense," he contradicted her again. "After all, Hursoc know that there's a development project underway with Premve. They've been supplying the inverters and solar modules to the big plants for years."

"How on earth do they know that?" Alex asked in horror. She couldn't believe what she was hearing.

"Oh, come on," George replied. "Don't pretend you're surprised; word gets around in the industry."

Alex had got up from her cubicle and started pacing up and down restlessly. Her adrenaline levels were threatening to increase and she wanted to neutralise them. She could still just about contain her anger.

"Word doesn't just get around with a project like this. My client certainly hasn't said anything. Neither Marco nor anyone else present in Seoul is in direct contact with Hursoc. Besides, we have a non-disclosure agreement with Premve. None of us can speak to a third party about the project. So tell me, how does your client know?"

She thought about it. Only George and Hugo were in permanent contact with Hursoc. OK, Brian had been there at one meeting but that was months ago. Since then she wasn't sure what he was working on. Thomas could be ruled out straightaway. Apart from the conferences in Hamburg and Geneva, he hadn't spoken directly to a single client.

"That's not important," he waved her aside. "What is important is that we get Hursoc involved. The work can't stem from us alone."

"No, George! Premve explicitly ruled that out at the start to maintain neutrality. We've already been over it thousands of times in team meetings. Only when a project specification has been drawn up can we bring the inverter manufacturers into the equation. Hursoc will receive the information at exactly the same time as all other suppliers."

It was enough to drive you up the wall. George simply wasn't listening to her client's argument. But Alex had no intention of abandoning her point of view. They had been aware of Premve's conditions from the beginning. Exactly that had been the attraction. If every supplier had the same level of knowledge, the competitive element would be neutralised, thus increasing the chance of several companies bringing out Vabilmo-compatible products at the same time. That in turn would enable PsoraCom to achieve a greater market presence.

"But that makes no sense whatsoever," George interrupted her again. "Hursoc need to be involved."

Her patience was beginning to run out. At some point, enough was enough. The conversation was as stale as a piece of chewing gum that had been in your mouth all day. She couldn't just hang up; that wasn't the done thing. But she had to get rid of him somehow – otherwise she would really lose it. Alex resorted to a white lie.

"I've got to go to a meeting, George; I'll be in touch later. Please don't say anything else to your client, otherwise there'll be more trouble. All the commotion with Natioba was enough for me."

But he just kept on talking, as if she had no right to end the conversation.

"Don't worry about it. Hursoc are just right for this job."

After two further attempts, there was nothing else for it.

"Speak later, George. I really have to go," she said before turning off her Zeus68 and taking a deep breath. Just at that moment, Christopher came past.

"What was going on there?" he asked. "It sounded like a real drama."

"Well, you know, sometimes George is a real drama-queen," Alex rolled her eyes.

"Come on," he offered, "let's grab a short black one! An honest glass of wine would beat the pants off it but unfortunately we're still at work."

That was exactly what she liked about him: little plays on words and a reassuring equanimity – even though he, like her, was often in the office for upwards of ten hours.

"He'll calm down," he said, after Alex had let off some steam. "Just bide your time. Or else Thomas will have to give him a serious ear-bashing, especially if the client's position was known from the start."

In contrast to Premve, everything with Natioba was running like clockwork. Representatives from the department for mobile off-grid systems in Milan had agreed to a meeting with Carl in person, much to his delight. Recently he had intensified internal contact with Hank's department, as the standardised parts were being developed primarily for Robotics. He was currently experiencing difficulties with his chosen clients.

Manufacturers of traditional household robots were under such financial pressure that the still-expensive Vabilmo technology wasn't an option for them at the moment. There was a chance with special robots, but that was a niche sector. Perhaps he saw the scheduled meeting as an opportunity to finally get the ball rolling.

They had spoken in advance about who would take on what role during the meeting. Alex was happy for Carl to take the lead. During his presentation, he energetically displayed the bend-module seed units that Alex had procured from Hank. When it came to technical queries about them, however, she noticed that he often threw her a quizzical glance. He wasn't especially strong on the specifics, like whether the autonomy period affected the capacity of the additional batteries needed for bridging, for example. The same went for other factors that needed to be taken into account when designing off-grid systems.

Having worked on the greenhouse project, Alex had done some reading on the subject and was able to satisfactorily answer a number of their initial enquiries. More detailed calculations would have to be made, of course, but right now the priority was to provide approximate guidelines. Natioba seemed to be happy at least; by the end of the meeting, there was nothing else standing in the way of a joint project.

The next stage was to arrange an appointment with the bend-module manufacturer so that development work on the prototype could begin. Carl eagerly promised to take care of it. He had already established direct contact with Apircu through Hank; they had developed the bend-modules in conjunction with PsoraCom and would produce them themselves in the future.

Stacks of cardboard boxes didn't exactly make for a good working atmosphere, so Alex spent almost every day in the office. Christmas wasn't far away. The move to the new flat was drawing closer and brought with it a considerable advantage. As she could do with a thorough clean-out, some clutter went, and that even included most of the furniture. She wanted a completely fresh start; it would help ease the pain of her memories of Sandro.

Alex spent the Christmas break with Jenny at their parents' house. She had always looked forward to this period ever since she was a child, as everything was a bit slower and more relaxed. Especially this time: they all remembered exactly what it had been like the previous year, when her mother had been so ill after the operation. But now the cancer seemed to be in remission.

A peaceful blend of roast duck, old holiday film favourites and long chats by the open fire did her the world of good after weeks of intensive work and packing. Louis spent in the kitchen with Jenny and Ricka went by in a flash. Franz kept them company while they cooked, talking all about the technical innovations he had discovered.

Later, in front of a roaring fire, Jenny showed them pictures and films of Hong Kong. She described her experiences of the city in great detail so that her parents could share in her life there; the MBA, work at the bank, different places she had visited. Upon seeing the pictures, Alex began to immerse herself in her own memories of the place, recalling her final evening with Jenny in the bar high above the harbour with particular fondness.

All too quickly, the holiday was over and she had to make the final preparations for the move. Anna came by to help her pack. Although there were already mountains of packed boxes lying around, the whole kitchen still needed to be cleared, along with any number of odds and ends. Her priceless Harley Davidson and Hard Rock Cafe collection was already wrapped in proverbial cotton wool and driven to the new flat.

On the day of the move itself everything went swimmingly. Her father and Jenny had come early in the morning and hauled boxes with Moritz and Anna, before dismantling and reassembling the furniture in the new flat. Renata hadn't been able to get the morning off but supplied delicious food from the hotel kitchen in the afternoon instead. Ricka couldn't be there either. Still, everyone agreed she had more than played her part by providing two different cakes, both of which were praised to the hilt.

Anna stayed on after everyone else had gone. She didn't want to leave Alex on her own and had purposely taken the next day off. The bed was assembled and the kitchen bench stood waiting, but otherwise it was total chaos. Alex wouldn't have wanted to wake up alone the next morning.

"It's really good of you to stay," Alex thanked her.

"You're always there for me too when I need you," her friend replied, before popping the cork of a Prosecco bottle. "Here's to the new flat!"

"To the new flat!" she toasted back. "I'd like to be completely done with the old flat by tomorrow. Do you think we can manage that?"

"If you can conjure me up a Harley Cafe Latte Special from this chaos tomorrow morning, then definitely!"

On New Year's Eve Moritz and Renata surprised her by turning up unannounced at her door.

"Let's go! Pack some things and don't forget your toothbrush," was all they said.

"What? What're you planning?" she asked, confused. "I wanted to finish up with the kitchen."

But Moritz wasn't taking no for an answer and pressed a rucksack into her hands.

"A few friends and I have rented a great little mountain log cabin for a week," he beamed. "It's even got one of those cool old Wamsler stoves, so we can warm ourselves up from the snow and see to it that the mulled wine doesn't get cold."

"Moritz has already taken up enough food and drink to last us a month," Renata joined in. "Anna's in on the plan and is coming too. Everything's been taken care of. There are enough beds and if you get cold, I'm sure one of Moritz's friends will be only too happy to warm you up."

Her friend could barely stifle a grin and Alex knew straightaway who she was referring to. She had met a few of Moritz's friends at a barbecue some years back and engaged in a brief, exciting fling with Luis shortly after. Laughing, she rolled her eyes. Why not? She didn't have any plans for the evening except for watching DVDs and drinking champagne with Anna. An age-old tradition dictated that they watched each part of Lethal Weapon and admired Mel Gibson's naked behind. Anna liked his blue eyes too. Perhaps there would be something else to admire in the log cabin. After all, she was unattached and could do whatever she liked. The thought of a little harmless flirtation started to appeal.

New Year's Eve couldn't have gone any better. A long walk in the snow in the afternoon, with sunshine and fresh air all around. The romance of a log cabin in the evening, with fondue, red wine punch and steamed-up windows. The boys seemed to be confusing the Wamsler with a sauna, no doubt in the hope of getting the girls to remove a few layers of clothing. They greeted the New Year with skyrockets, fire crackers and a wild snowball fight, by the end of which Alex had found herself laughing in Luis's arms.

The embrace and nearness of his touch felt good. She would have liked for time to stand still, but she also didn't want to arouse any false hopes.

"Don't worry," he whispered, as if he could tell what she was thinking. "Let's just enjoy the moment and forget about tomorrow."

That was all that needed to be said.

13

January

The move and subsequent holiday was therapy in its purest form; lengthy furniture-shopping sessions with Jenny at IKEA, followed by discussions about rattan, partitions and shelving. She didn't give her electric drill a rest until the evening, and the neighbours on the second floor must have hoped that she wasn´t always as fit as the fiddle.

Slowly, however, the rooms began to take shape, as did the muscles on Alex's upper arms. She enjoyed manual work; making things reminded her of her childhood. A bit of Johnny Cash or Shania Twain in the background and the furniture almost fit itself.

During the day it brought distraction into her life; only in the evenings did she continue to be overwhelmed by deep sadness. Apart from a few photo albums, there was very little to remind her of Sandro in her new flat. But no sooner had she sat down on the sofa with a glass of wine after a hard day's work than her thoughts turned to the time they had spent together. Sometimes it happened while she lay tired in bed; often she would read for hours to take her mind off things. That only worked until she laid the book to one side.

Memories of joint holidays, sometimes simply of loving embraces and tender words spoken, came flooding back against her will. The worst was when she thought of Prague. Then she relived the whole drama over and over again, shaken by hysterical fits of crying. In moments like this, she fell prey to a wanton melancholy and became more and more depressed. During her nocturnal despair, Alex often sent messages to Renata, which she herself was barely able to read through a veil of tears. Long discussions ensued, always revolving around the same things. Things that anyone who had ever been hurt in a relationship had experienced before.

The answer to the question "why" never came. You just had to learn to accept things you couldn't change. But that was easier said than done.

After her holiday there was more than enough to do and Alex could concentrate on work. For twelve to fourteen hours a day, all disturbing thoughts were banished to the dark recesses of her mind.

Hank's colleague should have appointed a specialist to oversee the project with Premve ages ago. The agreed two weeks were already up. Upon returning to the office, Alex was bombarded by both Marco and her client, each of whom was awaiting a response. She hated situations like this. Hank's colleague had given the client his word that he would take care of it. But ultimately it all rested on her. Her internal enquiries were met evasively. Even Marco, who, as the person in overall charge of the client, had begun to chase him up, was having no luck. Alex kept having to put off Premve's manager in Seoul.

"You can't treat clients like that," she complained irritably to Thomas.

By chance Wolfgang was wheeling past. His ear pricked up straightaway.

"Draft me a mail that I can send to the divisional director of robotics," he offered. "He has to get his own house in order."

Relieved that she had his backing, Alex got to work immediately. Wolfgang's word would certainly carry more weight. They had to make a decision soon, otherwise it could become embarrassing.

A decision had to be made about Natioba as well, and she suggested to her boss that they discuss the matter at the next team meeting. Carl had taken the reins since their last consultation in Milan. Two appointments had already been arranged with Apircu and an additional bend-module manufacturer in Italy. Just as had been agreed. The only thing was that Carl had failed to keep her informed about the individual stages.

She learned about the meetings from her client: an embarrassing state of affairs. A decision about who was in overall charge of the project needed to be made. It made little sense for them to continue appearing in tandem. That would stretch their already-limited resources and force travel costs up unnecessarily.

It was absolutely no problem for Carl to go there alone but she did need to know. She wouldn't have any issues with him running the project either. Categorically placing the emphasis for the project on either his or her department wasn't possible. Mobile off-grid systems could be seen as a type of robot, depending on your viewpoint.

It was an interdisciplinary project and a precedent, which was why Alex wanted to have individual responsibilities clarified and communicated, internally and externally. Maybe she was being too narrow-minded but she knew from experience that unresolved issues surrounding accountability could quickly lead to problems. With that, they had reached the point Alex had anticipated months before.

Thomas didn't allow time for a discussion to develop, although it didn't seem like one was necessary. Astonishingly, not even George appeared to have an opinion on the matter. In record time her boss determined that individual client consultants would be responsible for projects with plant manufacturers, irrespective of whether they concerned power stations, off-grid systems or movable objects. Carl should, of course, be involved, but only in an assisting role. His focus should remain on traditional robot manufacturers as before; that was his priority sector. It was a clear and unambiguous statement.

That meant she was responsible for all her clients' activities, which made sense in her opinion. Carl seemed disappointed by Thomas's decision and, to a certain extent, she could sympathise. He had been delighted to get involved in the Natioba project. For the time being it didn't seem like there was any prospect of a similar project in the traditional robot market. The current price situation was far too tense for that. There was some potential with robots used for specific technical purposes but the requirements were very stringent.

"I'm withdrawing from Volcrea," Carl informed her after the team meeting. "It's not really benefiting me in any way."

"Shame," Alex replied, "because I think Volcrea could be a multiplier for you – particularly where special robots are concerned. Are you still looking after the seed units for Apircu though?"

Carl had originally wanted to take care of things for the bend-modules. But she wasn't about to beg.

"I'm not going to get round to it," he said.

Then that would be down to her as well.

Two telephone calls later, she not only had the contact details for Apircu but their consent regarding the modules. They were sent directly to Volcrea. Good progress was being made with the prototype there and, apart from the usual teething problems, everything seemed to be going according to plan. The first pictures Alex received by email also looked very promising.

"The futuristic design is way cool," Henry said enthusiastically, as she showed him the pictures over coffee. "I'm directly in touch with their marketing manager by the way. We're working on a press release that's to be issued in advance."

Although Alex hadn't heard anything about it, she more than approved.

"Brilliant, Henry. And all that, despite everything you're doing with Spain."

"Oh, that's just a little project, really" he waved her aside, before pausing abruptly. "Wait. The trade show in Valencia overlaps with our exhibition in Barcelona by a few days. We have to take advantage and do something special."

"What are you thinking exactly? Do you need more pictures or is there someone special you want to interview?"

"EUREKA!" he cried, and stood stock still. "We could set up a live feed from Valencia to our press conference in Barcelona. Brilliant! It might just work. That would be really cool!"

The last word sounded more like the sound made by a freshly milked cow giving voice to its satisfaction. Immediately a few heads turned in passing. When her colleague was enthusiastic about something, he always reacted gushingly. Henry was authentic like that. There were still a few weeks to go until the trade show and they had ample time to think things over in detail.

Lisa had promised to arrange Cellgot an on-site meeting with Luxumi to discuss initial details about the project. Alex had proposed to combine it with a second in-house meeting at PsoraCom. That would enable the Swiss to provide her team with a few demonstrations, like the ones she and Thomas had seen in Hamburg and Geneva.

When Lisa entered the meeting into the internal calendar system, however, the feedback was surprisingly guarded. Carl was the only one to agree conditionally; George and Hugo declined straightaway, as did Brian. She had expected more participants for such a new, exciting piece of technology, especially since the company had been officially incorporated into the ecosystem by Henry.

The annual internal planning conference was being held in San Diego this year. Nobu told Alex before Christmas that he was planning a few meetings with additional American solar companies in California prior to the event. Since he was hoping to acquaint them with the Vabilmo technology, he had requested her assistance once more.

Although Thomas had eventually agreed, he had seemed unwilling. It couldn't have been due to the extra cost; it wouldn't be much greater than the original travel expenses. Almost certainly it was linked to a directive from the executive office which stipulated that no holidays were to be tacked on after the conference. It seemed a few employees had taken things too far the previous year. Allegedly Brian had been among them. In her case, however, she could prove the stopover in San Francisco was business related.

She didn't get to see the venerable halls of PsoraCom HQ in Oakland during the layover, as Nobu had only been allocated meeting rooms in the new Executive Briefing Centre. From the airport, the centre was easily accessible via the Bayfront Expressway towards Fremont. Although the meetings went well, Alex wasn't anticipating any big projects in the near future. The current economic climate in the state was all too evident, despite the promise of extensive grants for the local solar industry. The governor had increased the amount of electricity to be generated using renewable energy sources to one third. Only one of the three companies showed any real interest, requesting an internal discussion with Nobu about the possibility of a test project.

There was even time for a quick detour to the Harley shop in Redwood City en route to the airport, where Alex found a few curios to add to her private museum. The trip thus provided an additional highlight; it helped take her mind off Sandro. Although she was very happy in her new flat and her friends were going to great lengths to see she was looked after, Alex was still having problems sleeping. You couldn't deal with the loss of your dreams inside of a few weeks. She was only just beginning to sift through the wreckage of her feelings; completely freeing herself from it remained out of the question.

The nearby Harley dealer in San Diego wasn't forgotten either. Alex had arrived Saturday morning, earlier than her colleagues from Germany, and was thus able to make use of the time for some serious shopping. Anna would think she was mad when she showed her the champagne glasses with the engraved bar and shield logo, or the heavily reduced Christmas glitter balls. Iced coffee in hand, she took a leisurely stroll along the marina, imagining her friend's expression as she went.

In the meantime, her colleagues must surely have landed. As far as she knew, they weren't staying with her in the Bristol Hotel. Alex had realised too late that you needed to reply to the official invitation within an hour to get a room in one of the hotels surrounding the conference centre. There was a shuttle bus, but she was quite content to be staying further out. Walking the five blocks would give her the chance to get a little exercise.

When she still hadn't heard anything from her colleagues in the evening, she called Carl. He was completely shattered and said everyone else was feeling the same. Besides, they were all spread out across different hotels.

Unsure about what to do, she thought about the alternatives to the less than enticing prospect of room service in front of the TV, before eventually deciding to try her luck at the Marriott Hotel. A few people from the German office were staying there and there was bound to be someone at the lobby bar. Twenty minutes later, the loud, unmistakeable laugh of Henry was already to be heard from a distance.

"Hey, Alex, what do you want to drink?" he called out across the bar, while waiting to get served.

"Samuel Adams, if they have it," she called back.

There were some other people there who Alex recognised. A few leisurely drinks and a bit of light-hearted chatter was just the right thing. Christopher appeared a little later and joined their party. Almost his entire team was staying with him in the hotel.

"So, where have you left your boys?" he asked. "Let me guess: Brian's midnight surfing, George's on his way to Viejas casino and Hugo's just about to peel off his face mask."

"You're probably not far wrong," she replied, laughing. "No, actually they're all staying in different hotels and none of them has the energy to meet up. Perfectly understandable. Unlike them, I've already had a few days to deal with Mr Jetlag, and you lot only have to stagger into the lift."

A few beers later, Alex was gradually beginning to feel their effect. It was time to go. She was still in full possession of her speech and able to express herself coherently.

"Why don't you take a taxi?" Christopher suggested. "It's too dangerous outside. We want you in one piece tomorrow."

He couldn't have known the effect that his last sentence would have on her. She just managed to make it to the hotel door before the tears started coursing down her cheeks and she broke out into uncontrollable sobbing.

She hadn't had the feeling that a man was looking out for her for months. It didn't matter that it was Christopher. It could just as easily have been someone else. There must have been a softening agent in one of the beers that made her more sensitive. With the exception of work, she hadn't met a single man in the last few weeks. Apart from Moritz, who she sometimes saw during dinner at Renata's. To be fair, Moritz and Luis hadn't exactly been sparing with their compliments at New Year, but that was different. Both of them were still so young. They weren't in the same league as real men.

Her whole body was seized by a violent crying fit. Through the haze, she could just about still see the road; there weren't many cars at this time of night. At the start of the Gaslamp Quarter, she went into a bar and bought a pack of cigarettes while downing a beer. It was the frustration that made her smoke – maybe it would help a little. She didn't care what the barman thought. He didn't know her and would probably never see her again in his entire life. From what she could see, there was no-one from PsoraCom there; luckily, it was pretty dim inside.

Shaken by another bout of sobbing, she went outside again and walked along the marina. She didn't want to go back through the pub district in case she ran into a colleague. What on earth had she done wrong? Why had Sandro got involved with another woman? What did she have that Alex lacked? In the last few years he had said over and over again how much he wanted kids and his own house. She didn't notice her pace quickening. Why, all of a sudden, did none of that seem to apply anymore? She knew her current state had been brought on almost entirely by alcohol and that it would be very difficult to bring her thoughts under control. The fresh air and that last beer were just beginning to take effect when her Zeus68 vibrated. It was a message from Christopher; he wanted to know if she had arrived back safely. Even as she was reading it, a fresh wave of tears streamed down her cheeks and trickled onto her netphone.

"No," she wrote back. "I'm walking, but in my state no-one will want anything to do with me anyway." The rebuke came only seconds later.

"You dummy. Well at least take care. See you tomorrow!"

She stared at the message like a tiger in a cage, a prisoner of her own thoughts. The tears refused to stop and her sobbing grew into an asthma-like coughing fit. She had to stand still; she stopped walking and leaned against the fence behind her. Slowly she arched her back and crouched down, her head almost completely submerged between her legs. Three deeply inhaled cigarettes later, she was still in the same position, trying to regain control of herself while her whole body shuddered.

Her head was swirling with disjointed questions, but there wasn't a faintest signal to answer them in sight. Would she have to abandon her dreams of a house and family for good? When would she find a new partner to share these aspirations with? What did Sandro mean when he had described her as too masculine? Would it prevent her from ever finding someone new?

This last question reverberated deep within her very soul, like an echo in a mountain range. Pink seemed to call out to her once more from the very bottom of her heart: she had a bad feeling, it was gonna be a long way to happy. Alex forced herself to stand up. Little by little, the greedily inhaled nicotine began to do its job, making her thoughts hazy until finally a loud buzzing noise inside her head drowned everything else out. All of a sudden, the only thing she wanted was to sleep. To sleep and forget. Slowly she crawled her way back to the hotel. Eventually the tears dried up – she didn't have any left. Everything was empty.

Somehow she had still managed to set her alarm. Luckily the first session didn't begin until the afternoon. Her head was throbbing and she could hardly see straight. A long shower, a little ice and a great deal of kohl and eye shadow; that was the only possible cure. Two hours later, she was almost as good as new. She threw the empty pack of cigarettes into the wastepaper basket; disgusted, even though they had fulfilled their purpose. If only they didn't cause so much harm, taste like death or give her such enormous headaches, they would be a great home remedy for emotional turmoil.

For the time being, sleep had washed away her concerns and improved her mood to a tolerable level. The sunrays and anticipated warmth outside did the rest and drove her out to seek the fresh air. There was a meeting with Bill's team taking place in the Marriott, right on the marina. She decided not to take the shuttle; instead she enjoyed the walk and the feel-good songs The Boss was belting out on her iPod.

It seemed she had misjudged the time. Alex hated being late for meetings. The room was already full and her team colleagues were sitting at the front. As there were no spaces left, Alex sat down in one of the back rows. Bill, who was sitting in the row directly in front, greeted her with a friendly nod. She liked him and appreciated his easy-going nature. Although he was only one level below the PsoraCom bigwigs, he was never condescending, and always good for a joke, though it hadn't escaped Alex's notice that he could occasionally be a bit of a flirt. But why shouldn't he be? It was all completely harmless. Bill was a gentleman and would never exploit his position.

The meeting had already started. The first slides from Bill's department were being discussed. Next, her team would present their insights into current projects, as well as their suggestions for how Vabilmo should be marketed in the future. They hoped the meeting would conclude with an agreement being reached on a common global strategy. George had prepared slides in advance with the different members of the team, with Alex likewise contributing information from projects with her own clients and partners.

She hadn't agreed with the sales trend analysis. Nevertheless, her colleagues had insisted on it and Thomas had approved the slides as they were. Having been outvoted to such an extent, Alex had decided to back down. Her market assessment could have been wrong and she had no desire to provoke another argument. At the end of the day, the sales projections were based on a future of between three to seven years. A lot of water would have flowed under the bridge by then. They were all agreed in terms of actual trends, but the figures themselves were too high for her liking.

Still, exaggerating potential didn't seem to be uncommon at PsoraCom, especially where new application ranges or products were concerned. It was a question of convincing upper management to allow you to continue. Because what kind of management would support a concept that had started life as the hobby-horse of a few people if the figures didn't promise million dollar babies? What was the point of arguing against something like that?

A few of her colleagues had been active in the market for longer and knew the lie of the land. Another reason for her restraint was the fact that discussions with George were becoming steadily more laborious. He had masterminded the sales trend projections together with Hugo, basing his predictions primarily on PsoraCom's direct clients. Whether that corresponded with the outlook for end customers was a moot point.

Alex's opinion was that end customers wouldn't allow suppliers to force solutions upon them. In order to avoid a nervous breakdown, however, it was necessary to limit discussions with George to twenty minutes. That is, before he could say "but, when I think about it again". Otherwise, you would become trapped in his verbal clutches, a hold from which Thomas seemed increasingly incapable of releasing the team. He, likewise, appeared resigned to George's discussion frenzies.

Her colleagues from the US presented their market data, which reflected the view of the product managers. Bill played an animated part in discussions, which were punctuated by critical questions from George, Hugo and Brian. That was to be expected. Apart from Alex's team, there was no-one working on the Vabilmo technology in an interdivisional capacity. Her colleagues wanted to expand their area of competence, already acknowledged in Europe; the rest of the world still remained to be convinced.

To be precise, it was the US they needed to convince; that was where the corridors of power were situated. The best way was through detailed questioning that reflected the knowledge of the team. Knowledge which would prove to be far greater than that of the Americans because they were only affiliated to one department: Bill's.

Still, they were playing a risky game in Alex's eyes. On the one hand, Bill's department was needed to assign people to projects and allocate the budget; on the other, they didn't want Vabilmo to wind up exclusively under his control, since that could result in the influence of technologies from other areas being reduced.

Alex left her colleagues to play their own little games; she didn't approve. They were trying too hard to position themselves as experts. She even found some of their questions presumptuous. If they wanted to make their mark, they were going too far. At times, it seemed like Bill shared her view. He stood up to get himself a can of coke and a few biscuits from the back of the room. When he returned, he sat down in the free seat next to her.

"Nice to see you, Alex," he whispered. "When did you arrive?"

"Early yesterday morning; I had client meetings in San Francisco beforehand."

"Who did you meet? How did it all go?"

He was sitting so close that their shoulders touched. Alex didn't think anything of it. They had to whisper and lean in so as not to disturb anyone else; they wouldn't have understood what was being said otherwise.

Her colleagues were up. She looked at the slides and attempted to follow what Hugo was saying. It must have been George who had appointed him as speaker. The master and his protégé. She had been noticing for some time how her younger colleague seemed to be depending more and more on his guide. Even now he was constantly looking over towards George for approval, the latter giving an imperceptible nod or shake of the head.

Normally Hugo gave the impression of being well aware of the effect produced by his height and model looks. With his appearance, no-one ever expected him to have such detailed technical knowledge. Today he was speaking in riddles once again, using lots of specialist terminology and abbreviations. It all sounded very complex and was bound to impress. However, to anyone who had known him for any length of time, he seemed like a child who had got full marks in a test and was now longing for praise and approval. Often he received it straightaway.

It was not uncommon for George to say something like: "Hugo is the most brilliant genius we could ever have employed."

Such gross exaggeration was enough to induce serious nausea in Alex – or at least make the hairs on the back of her neck stand up.

During the presentation, Alex felt like she was in some kind of play; one that she was seeing through another person's eyes. She couldn't help but think about her colleagues as she observed them one after the other. Some things she saw reinforced for the first time. No doubt George had an ulterior motive for identifying Hugo as the number one expert over the product managers and engineers from Bill's department: simply, the admiration engendered by his protégé's detailed description of the market requirements would reflect well on him as mentor.

Were it not for the technical aspect, it would probably have been Brian who spoke; a first-class alpha male who knew everything about clients and end customers, as well as each individual person of influence. If you started digging for concrete information or names, he would be evasive, mentioning only the CEOs of the companies in question: names that were known to everyone.

He regarded himself as an innovative visionary, the spiritual father-figure, without whom it would have been impossible to launch Vabilmo on the market. He was only too happy to be in the limelight. Technical details and other such particulars didn't concern him.

Things like that were for the staff to deal with; they didn't provide enough of a challenge – his mind had been created for more intricate questions of strategy. Of course, in reality that only heightened the sense that he kept his distance from the more intense discussions because he didn't understand the technicalities. His obvious laxity, which had been amusing to begin with, seemed, along with his unkempt goatee, increasingly inappropriate in Alex's eyes.

It was Carl's first time at the annual conference. In him, Alex recognised herself a little. Curiosity, coupled with the excitement of meeting so many new people; both were clearly etched upon his face. He sat quietly in between his two contrasting colleagues, seemingly content with his role as attentive listener.

She herself hadn't been asked by the team if she wanted to speak. That was more than OK by her, as she hadn't agreed with the sales figures and would have struggled to make them sound believable. In the midst of all these thoughts, she wondered where Thomas had got to. Her boss was nowhere to be seen. Perhaps he was sitting with Wolfgang and other important people from the German office. He was another who preferred to leave the nitty-gritty to the team.

Still, in Alex's opinion, it would have been good for him to be there and nail his colours to the mast. Ultimately, when it came to sales, he was in overall charge of Vabilmo's global strategic development. But that's just the way Thomas was. In his position, it seemed, he could pick and choose whatever parts of the job he wanted.

Hugo moved from the sales figures onto the various architectural designs of the modules. The range of applications included the bend-modules and Alex looked to the front with interest. She hadn't got to see this part of the presentation beforehand. But Bill turned to her once again.

"Hey, I see we're in matching uniforms," he said. "Take a look, faded jeans and a grey sweater."

There it was again, the attempted flirtation. But she didn't take it too seriously. His casual outfit underscored his Latin appearance. It went very well with his mischievous charm, reinforced by his steel-blue eyes. Bill paused briefly to listen to what Hugo was saying, only occasionally contributing something to the discussion. After a while, he turned his attention to Alex again.

"We're having a little drink tonight," he said quietly. "One of my staff has hired a small room in the hotel after the boss's opening speech. Come along for a glass of wine; see if you can bring a few girls too; it will make the evening more fun."

Her face blushed momentarily at the thought that he had invited her, a normal employee, so casually; she already had a colleague in mind who might be keen.

"I'll see if I can interest a few girls in it," she murmured softly, before attempting to focus back on the presentation.

But Bill was clearly enjoying chatting to her more than listening to what was being said on stage.

"How are things going with your clients?" he persisted. "Any news about Natioba or Premve?"

Since he was well above her in the company hierarchy, she had no desire to snub him. Part of her even enjoyed the attention. After all, everyone could see that Bill had chosen to sit next to her. She regarded that as something of an honour because she wasn't the only woman in the room. Bill seemed to know everyone else just as well, so it wasn't gender-related in any way. Moreover, she got the impression that, as someone involved with Vabilmo, Bill viewed her as important.

Contrary to Christopher's remarks the previous evening, she could relate Bill's interest in her purely to her professional career and what she had achieved so far. That was why his conduct didn't trigger a disastrous outbreak of tears; instead it elicited an almost euphoric sense of happiness.

In the meantime, Hugo had concluded his presentation and was summarising the requirements. However, nobody could agree on a proposal regarding global strategy. This was hardly surprising; it was often the case in PsoraCom meetings. There would be additional consultations to build on this one, as well as weekly phone conferences, in which the global strategy would be defined step by step.

After the meeting Bill accompanied Alex to the door of the conference room as if it was the most natural thing in the world. A quick glance across to her colleagues told her that they were still chatting animatedly to other people, profiling and trying to make their opinions known. Her gaze fleetingly met that of George. He gave no reaction whatsoever and seemed to be staring straight through her.

As Bill was clearly waiting she decided to leave together with him. The first keynote speech was in an hour. It was mandatory for all employees, and everyone was intrigued to see what surprises the executive team had in store this time. Bill was staying in one of the hotels diagonally across from the conference centre and Alex walked a stretch with him. She could just as easily get back to her hotel via the Gaslamp Quarter. Since they had left the meeting room, he had been asking for further details about her clients and potential partners. She was more than happy to tell him what she was currently working on. The information, especially the news about the planned project with Premve, just came gushing out of her until they reached his hotel.

"You're coming for a drink this evening, then." It was more of a statement than a question.

"I'll see what I can do, what with all my other engagements," she replied with a wink.

The constant back and forth between furnished, air-conditioned rooms and the warm Californian early-spring sun presented quite a challenge to her well-being, not to mention her deodorant. So she went back to her hotel to freshen up.

Her colleagues hadn't exactly looked delighted to see her in the meeting just before, Alex thought to herself. She knew that George enjoyed making a nuisance of himself. Brian had probably been too involved in his own little strategic world to notice what was going on. Even Hugo and Carl had reacted rather brusquely to her greeting. But then again she had arrived late, and hadn't wanted to make a big fuss. It was almost certainly nothing.

After the sweaty climb up the stairs to her room on the tenth floor, which she regarded as a substitute for exercise, there wasn't much time for anything else apart from a quick, refreshing shower. She didn't need much make-up; all her depressing thoughts had been forgotten, yielding to a pleasant sense of expectation.

If someone had asked her what she was so keenly anticipating, she wouldn't have been able to say. Instead of dinner, which would take place at the conference centre in a purpose-built tent, she decided on a banana and mocha with cream. A little caffeine couldn't hurt – there was no knowing when the evening might end.

For a brief twenty minutes she was overcome by a relaxed holiday feeling. The air outside was pleasantly warm and the sun was gradually beginning to go down. You could almost make out the individual rays. The sky took on what would have been a typical colour for a clear summer evening. The hippie colours – orange and pink through violet and dark purple – provided the perfect accompaniment to rock classics like Aerosmith's Dreamweaver on her iPod. Alex soaked up the atmosphere as she approached the marina and saw the bright boats glowing in the red sunset. It was like yoga for the brain or meditation for the soul.

There were already a few people from the German office standing outside the conference centre, among them Henry and Lisa. They were all enjoying the evening warmth. Nobody seemed keen to spend any longer than absolutely necessary in the chilled climate chamber inside. Alex had brought a turtleneck sweater especially to protect herself from the cold. Depending on where you were sitting, the air-conditioning could provide such a shock to the system that it caused tonsillitis.

Lisa didn't need much persuasion to come along to Bill's drink. Alex's colleagues and boss were nowhere to be seen, so she went inside with the others. It was just as cold as she'd expected; apparently people were raised in fridges in San Diego as well.

There followed the usual remarks about the previous financial year. The verbal carrot was dangled in front of employees from Sales and Marketing. Healthy increase in turnover. New markets opened up. Everyone was great. Huge investments had been made in streamlining production methods and in new products themselves. It was coming.

Yes, there it was. The stick. The efforts of the preceding year hadn't been enough. The average retail price of products needed to be increased. Profit margin was still too small; the differences from the competition not great enough. No wonder investors weren't increasing the company's share price. By uniting forces on all hierarchy levels, this year PsoraCom would manage to catapult their share price through the roof.

The room was full to the brim, and polite handclapping grew into enthusiastic cries of approval and euphoric stamping of the feet. As if someone was standing at the mixing desk steadily increasing the volume and bass. Towards the end of the speech, a number of those in the front rows sprang to their feet and began applauding frenetically. The only thing missing was people jumping for joy – though the Americans were capable of anything. The presentation ended without further incident. Everybody wanted to get out as quickly as possible to enjoy an evening beer or network with colleagues back at the hotel lounge. Alex was swept along by the tide of people, waving here and there to various familiar faces she spied from afar. She pulled aside and waited for Lisa.

"Well, that was the same as always," her colleague said. "Though at least we didn't have to swear an oath this time."

Alex couldn't have agreed more. In a saloon in the Marriott Hotel, a few people were already gathered. She spotted Bill deep in conversation who gestured that they should help themselves to a drink from the bar. A few minutes later when they were both armed with a glass of wine, he came over and greeted them warmly. Alex even got a peck on both cheeks.

"Bill, this is Lisa," she introduced her colleague. "She works in Marketing and has been helping our team look for companies in the ecosystem for some time. Among others, she unearthed Cellgot, who we're currently trying to fix up with Luxumi."

As always, Bill seemed very interested and asked Lisa questions about Cellgot and their gesture navigation. Alex stood alongside and listened.

"I'll be with you again in a minute," Bill excused himself after a while. "I've got to speak to a few other people quickly."

They strolled over to the bar and topped themselves up. The Californian red wine wasn't bad at all.

"So, tell me," Lisa asked unexpectedly, "what's it like working in a team of men?"

"Very interesting, but also extremely demanding," Alex replied. "There are a few characters in my team but it's a good mix and makes for varied work. We don't see each other very often, as the others work almost exclusively from home and everyone looks after their own clients. But when we do, it's often very entertaining. A cockfight is nothing compared with our team meetings. Decisions are usually very difficult. Neither of the alphas wants to concede defeat and I don't have another woman to support me."

Lisa grinned. "I'd love to be a fly on the wall. In my team, it's all very even-tempered; most topics are discussed, and decisions made, democratically."

"In my team, democracy only applies to male opinions. If I don't want to be left high and dry on certain issues, then I need to take their side. That means that they have one opinion and I can share it."

Alex sighed before she went on.

"Seriously, I often do that if it doesn't impact upon my work with clients. Countless arguments have taught me that. I don't put things up for discussion anymore unless it's absolutely necessary. The team strategy is set. From there I derive my own client objectives and see that they're approved by my boss. Any decisions that specifically affect my clients and help me achieve these objectives are taken jointly with colleagues from the different departments assisting in the project. I keep my own team up to speed with internal memos and call reports. Sadly, the favour is rarely repaid. If the need arises, I usually have to ask one of them. Before, when we had regular team meetings, we used to start off with a general update about the most important companies. That seldom happens these days; mostly George dominates discussions with his stories, considerations and opinions. He has the most experience, of course. The others express their opinions when they get the chance – and try to enforce them if they disagree with George."

"That sounds pretty chaotic," Lisa shook her head.

"You can say that again," Alex agreed. "There's a separate team for Roffarm though, since there's a really extensive contract to be fulfilled. The company are handled by Lucas and his team; they report to Wolfgang just as we do. I often see Lucas in the office for an unofficial exchange of information. However, if I hear something that affects us all, then I put the topic on the agenda for the next team meeting."

"And what's Thomas like?" Lisa probed.

"Thomas generally keeps a low profile. But that's precisely how he ensures every one of us has the necessary freedom to act independently. He's no disciplinarian and passes every decision on to the team. Still, sometimes that means Brian and George become embroiled in lengthy debates. In those situations, Thomas could probably stand to intervene a little more."

Lisa said, shaking her head: "I certainly don't envy you."

"I think it might sound worse than it is. It's very varied anyway; so I can't complain about being bored."

The next morning began with breakfast from seven to seven thirty in the catering tent between the conference centre and the marina. Once again, Alex was astounded by how smoothly things went.

She met Wolfgang and Thomas together at the very first session. Just as they were about to go for coffee during the break, she took a brief call from Bill, who invited her to another party following the official "Meet our Managers" session. She should see if she could bring a few other people along.

"Hey, are you up for a party tonight?" she asked her companions right away, before adding, not without a hint of pride: "That was Bill, they're doing something in the Gaslamp Quarter."

"Sure, that sounds good," Wolfgang replied enthusiastically.

"I'll think about it," Thomas said.

He and Wolfgang had almost the same schedule as Alex that morning and so they stayed together. During the lunch break, they met Christopher.

"So, curly, fancy shaking things up this evening?" she asked. "Bill's just invited us to a party. Why don't you come? Bring a few people from your department too. The more the merrier, he said."

"Well aren't you astonishingly well connected?" he countered. "Sounds good, though. I'll inform the troops."

She hadn't seen her colleagues the whole day. It wasn't until the final afternoon break that she saw Brian, Hugo and Carl sitting outside in the sun. She went over for a chat, though there wasn't a great deal forthcoming. For some reason, her colleagues were all in a foul mood. Only Carl reacted to her greeting, and spoke briefly – albeit very politely – to her. The others gazed intensely at their laptops, not even deigning to look at her. What was up with them? Under these circumstances, Alex didn't have any great real to tell them about the party that evening. If they didn't like it, they could lump it. But what was the matter?

The "Meet the Management" session took place after dinner outside the Marriott Hotel. It was a chance for PsoraCom employees to meet their superiors and speak to them in a down-to-earth manner. But Alex had no idea what to say to the members of the board. She didn't want to use her projects to talk herself up and so joined Henry, who was chatting to Marco. Of course they were both up for the party. She looked around for Nobu as well, whom she hadn't seen once since her arrival. When she couldn't get hold of him on the phone either, she left a message where they would be.

A little later she rounded up her party-happy troop of ten. They found a big table with enough room for Wolfgang and watched as the bar slowly began to fill up. Work-related topics were soon banned and things began to loosen up with the first round of cocktails.

"Where are you hiding?" Alex asked her host over the phone. "The party's already started."

"Still in the room, just leaving now," Bill replied.

He was there a few minutes later. Even the CEO came, bringing two blondes in tow and livening up the bar with his rich baritone laugh.

"I'm sticking with Alex in future," Wolfgang indicated towards her. "At least she knows where the parties are."

Flattered, she accepted the compliment before Bill swept her off her feet and onto the dance floor.

They danced uninterrupted until two thirty with a motley crew that had turned half the bar into a dance floor. The atmosphere was amazing, the DJ pushing it to the max by alternating between disco beats and rock anthems. Exhilarated but exhausted, Alex collapsed into bed in the early hours of the morning, after Bill had insisted on walking her home. He had shown once again that he was a true gentleman, taking his leave from her with a friendly embrace. Though it went against her instincts, Alex had feared she might have to dodge an embarrassing moment; fortunately, however, it never came to that. Still elated after such a heady evening's entertainment, she remembered just in time to set her alarm, completely oblivious to the encroaching storm.

It happened five minutes before her meeting with Wolfgang; a discussion with Bill was scheduled to take place immediately afterwards. It hit her like a slap in the face. Almost sensing the pain, tears brimmed in her eyes. It was difficult for her to grasp what her boss had said as they walked the short distance from the convention centre to the Omni Hotel. Thomas had told her what had happened so casually – without any prior warning.

The sun was shining as on the previous days and the seventy-degree outdoor temperature stood in welcome contrast to the freezing rooms of the conference centre. The palm trees, blooming cacti and freshly mown lawns in front of the hotels all smelled of summer and had placed Alex in the best of spirits. At least until a few minutes ago.

She had been looking forward to the impending discussion because it was of vital importance not only for the continued development of the team, but also – and above all – for a special project of her own. At least that's how she saw it. Delighted, and filled with pride at the indirect compliment being paid to her, she had agreed to set up the meeting with Bill at Wolfgang's request a few weeks before.

"Alex, you get on well with him, get something sorted for when we're over at the conference," had been his instructions.

A quick email to his friendly assistant, Shane, with whom Alex had been in contact a few times already, had been all that was required to get an hour-long slot. That was a long time; there were a lot of people hoping to speak to Bill, after all.

On no account could she let on that something was up, but that was easier said than done. Still, now was not the time to think – let alone burst out crying. A visibly relaxed Wolfgang wheeled towards them wearing sunglasses. He stopped in front of the hotel entrance, greeted them both with a handshake and asked: "Is something wrong, Alex?"

Silently she shook her head and proceeded to the reserved table on the palm terrace. What she really wanted to do was make herself invisible, or at least excuse herself with a headache or women's troubles. But that wasn't the done thing. She almost regarded it as an honour to be allowed to take part in the meeting. Neither Thomas nor Wolfgang had invited any of her other colleagues to attend. And so there was nothing for it but to pull herself together. At times like these, her father always had a special remedy handy; it would have to help her over the worst once again.

Taking a deep breath she directed her gaze towards the sky, as if observing a passing flight of seagulls. Then she lowered her head and tried to keep it as upright as possible, without appearing frozen to the spot. She knew from experience that she couldn't let her head drop. That would just make her feel even worse. Why that was, she couldn't say. But she knew it was true.

Over the course of the next half hour they quickly finalised all points, and Wolfgang explained what he hoped to achieve with Bill. Thomas didn't say much, only giving a nod here and there. As usual. He was simply a man of few words – Wolfgang, on the contrary, was only too happy to run the show.

Alex was forced to pull herself together over and over again and fight back the tears that were threatening to stream forth like a sudden attack of nausea. At moments like this, she turned towards the waiter or dug her fingernails so far into her skin under the table that her brain was momentarily distracted by another pain.

"You really want me to be there at the meeting with Bill?" she asked almost timidly, when they were finished. It wasn't often you got to take part in an official meeting with the rung below the executive level.

"Of course," Wolfgang assured her. "You set the meeting up, after all. Besides, it's to do with your Premve project."

With that, everything was clear. Shortly afterwards Bill entered in measured strides, dressed in a manner that was typically American. His beige Dockers and dark-blue jacket made him appear less Latin in comparison with his more informal attire the previous day. He greeted them all with a firm handshake and Alex with a knowing wink: "Sleep well?"

She nodded mechanically and pretended to look for something in her papers. Alex had taken special care to ensure the table she reserved was a little out of the way, as the meeting would be highly confidential. It was about future strategy and how Vabilmo was to be positioned; both internally to upper management and externally with regards to the most important clients and end customers. For the German managing director, of course, the most significant point was the role assigned to his sales and marketing department.

Alex was having trouble concentrating. Her mind wandered repeatedly to what Thomas had said just before. She understood the words alright but couldn't fathom their meaning. How had it come to this? What had she overlooked? Why would someone do such a thing?

George of all people; someone she had had her differences with, but never any real problems. Like when he had lost heavily at poker again and turned up in a bad mood as usual the next day; she had been the one to make the peace following their dispute. Or when he had tried to force his opinion on her and at some point her patience had bottomed out. Typical Libra behaviour but she couldn't change the way she was. At the end of the day, everyone had their own area of responsibility and was able to approach things differently, so long as the net result conformed to the overall team strategy and company objectives.

That was the way Alex was used to working and that was why they had been assigned separate clients and responsibilities the previous year. At least that's what she had thought. Companies always requested that employees work individually within a team. That's what it said in the job description too. The path forward was defined in conjunction with the team; it was up to the individual to make sure they brought their own shoes.

It was exactly the same in other teams at PsoraCom, like Christopher's for example. Everyone had their regular companies, which they looked after. Naturally, there were sometimes disagreements about what products were best for the end customers, or which direct client should be engaged as a supplier. The most important thing was that PsoraCom benefited from the solution and generated revenue. Or had she missed something? Because, in principle – and she had been told this internally by various people – PsoraCom were quasi-neutral in their dealings with end customers and their suppliers so long as it was their products that were being implemented.

Alex abruptly interrupted her thoughts and tried to focus back on the meeting.

"Globally speaking, our sales region encompasses some of the most innovative and successful end customers in the power sector," Wolfgang was explaining. "As market-leader, we have so far failed to do ourselves justice."

He paused for a moment to allow the gravity of what he had said to sink in.

"Establishing an innovation centre in Germany could help to remedy this," he continued. "This is how I see it. We stage regular events and conferences on the latest developments, bringing our ecosystem into the fold as well. That way, we can reach the whole industry and further strengthen our position in relation to the competition."

Bill listened attentively, though his face was devoid of emotion.

"There's an area near our office that would be suitable," Wolfgang went into greater detail. "It could even offer space for an adjoining showroom. A kind of solar museum. It's not hard to imagine a number of our direct clients seeing it as a good marketing opportunity. Together with your product managers, they could make demo objects available, providing vivid proof of the merits of our services."

Wolfgang looked him directly in the eyes, without betraying his excitement.

"What do you think?"

It was like a game of poker. Wolfgang had placed his bets but still hadn't laid all his cards on the table. Bill could only guess what he had up his sleeve.

"Sounds good so far," was the latter's initial reaction. "But we already have a museum in Oakland containing historical products. We make sure it's constantly updated; and we can organise events without an innovation centre."

This move was to be expected. Wolfgang looked briefly down at his hands and then lifted his head once more.

"I've already put a few feelers out with Roffarm. They're very enthusiastic about the idea and would take on a leading role. If we could just win you and your counterpart at Roffarm over as patrons…"

The last sentence hovered over the table, turning the tide like a gust of wind that sweeps the autumn leaves onto the streets.

First, Roffarm were one of the most innovative and established plant manufacturers in the world; second, the project driven by Bill's department had stalled more than he would have liked. There had been no official announcement about the progress of the joint venture for over a year, to the extent that even within the company a few high-ranked employees were giving it little chance of survival.

The innovation centre would serve as an additional milestone and might help to give the combined development some impetus. The fact that Roffarm HQ was near the German office, coupled with the language barrier, made an American-led initiative seem incompatible; Wolfgang's team could be more than just auxiliaries here. Bill's patronage would ensure that, outwardly at least, he retained his influence; while the German office also stood to gain through the internal support of one of PsoraCom's vice presidents.

After a while, Bill nodded.

"That could very well be true," he said. "But I won't be able to make the decision on my own. You have my vote: I'll raise it internally with my boss and the CEO together."

"We could do with your support on another matter as well," Wolfgang moved on immediately. "Alex has the details."

Upon his command, Alex switched her brain into work mode and focused on Premve. She pushed all her despair into the background and kept it there. Brimming with energy she described the project, like a fish thrown back into water. The thoughtfulness of his gaze, together with a few brief nods, revealed that Bill remembered their discussions both the previous evening and in Taipei.

"After initially agreeing to it, Robotics has quasi withdrawn from the project even though there's a very high chance of success," she outlined the current status. "Unfortunately Hank, our project manager with Natioba, has been assigned to a different task and is no longer available. For some obscure reason, his colleague doesn't think it necessary to actively support the project. Premve's management has already approved the project and agreed to provide full support with the joint development. It's a question of prestige as well. Premve are being granted a leading market role for certain technologies, which partly places them in competition with Roffarm."

"I see," Bill replied. "What are your objectives exactly and how great is the market potential?"

Alex had all the figures memorised and explained them in detail.

"You'll get a project manager and one of my employees part-time," the vice president promised.

Everything finally seemed to be falling into place, she thought to herself. The endless stalling of Robotics, which seemed incapable of making a decision without Hank, had been more than embarrassing. Alex only permitted herself a tiny smile even though she was rejoicing inside.

Wolfgang must have been feeling the same way: after Bill had gone, he spontaneously ordered champagne. Little successes tasted sweeter when you could celebrate them immediately. All the same, her festive mood didn't endure for long and Alex soon developed a headache. The strain of the last two hours, together with her attempts to keep control of her thoughts and concentrate on what was being said, had taken their toll.

"Do you need me for anything else?" she asked. "If not, I'll head back to my room to freshen up for the evening."

"No, on you go and thanks again for arranging the meeting," Wolfgang said.

Thomas murmured something incomprehensible that sounded like "see you later".

After the pressure of the meeting and the effects of the champagne had worn off, her thoughts again began to revolve around the same question. On the way back to the hotel her head was buzzing like a beehive and the tears began to roll down her cheeks. She was not only extremely glad of her sunglasses, but also of the fact that she didn't encounter any familiar faces. To maintain her equilibrium, she needed exercise, sunlight and fresh air more than ever. If you could talk about fresh air in the context of a busy four-lane road, that is. What had she done wrong? What did it all mean?

Alex didn't understand it. She tried to recall what Thomas had said to her so casually on the way to the Omni Hotel.

"Have you spoken to any of the guys yet?" he had asked. By "guys", he meant the rest of her team.

"No," she had said, "why?"

"Maybe you should think about doing it. It seems there was a bit of trouble a few weeks back."

"Yeah, the thing with Marco's call report. I spoke to George about it; allegedly I'd been giving Hugo orders. But we sorted it out and there was nothing else the matter. At least, that's what he told me."

"George has been to the works council," Thomas had continued, "to lodge a complaint about you. Why, and whether he was alone or not, I'm not sure yet."

That was all her boss had said. George had made an official complaint! But how come? And why it had been George specifically who had gone to the employee representative? He was a member of the workers' council himself. Something here wasn't right. Perhaps it explained why she hadn't seen or heard much of her colleagues until now; why she had been almost aggressively ignored by Brian and George during the meeting with Bill's team.

Her head was buzzing with questions but that didn't make the situation any better, as she didn't have a single answer. But who did? First she had to try and digest what had been said. Only then could she begin to think clearly and plan her next move. Still, she wasn't ready for that yet. Inside, she realised she had already started to build a wall. With each question that sprouted, another brick was laid, only making her more uncertain. If she had bumped into one of her colleagues now, she wouldn't have known how to react. Why hadn't anyone talked to her? Not a single one of the four. And why hadn't they involved Thomas?

Alex moved faster and faster. It seemed her feet wanted to keep pace with the speed of her thoughts. Why? What for? Gradually, the initial shock turned into frustration. She jerked her iPod from her pocket and selected a rockin' playlist. In an hour from now it would be time for the big party, eagerly awaited by all employees. Alex would have preferred to lock herself away in her room but that wouldn't make her feel any better. Quite the opposite. She would feel like a coward – and that was something she had never been. It takes more than that to get Alex Ruby down, she thought to herself. Spurred on by Run DMC, her strides became longer and longer. It was like power walking, only without the sticks.

Her mood changed again, as her body was slowly beginning to produce endorphins. Perhaps it wasn't as bad as she thought. No-one had told her to her face what the actual problem was yet. There was sure to be a perfectly logical explanation for it and the matter would soon be resolved. Things were never as bad as they seemed. Back at the hotel, Alex jumped into the shower with these thoughts still in mind, before slipping refreshed into her comfy jeans. With the lip gloss to match the new orange leather jacket, her mirror image signalled its intent to meet the challenges of the evening head-on with a smile.

The party took place in a bar in the Gaslamp Quarter that had been hired out specially. All those present had their wishes fulfilled on three different levels. From the tasteful lounge with white leather seats and the well-stocked bar with exotic cocktail creations, through to the classic dance floor that positively gleamed under the silver disco balls; there was something for everyone. Alex bumped into Christopher and his team at the entrance.

"Hey Alex, come over with us," he offered cheerfully. "You've managed to ditch those wallies again, have you?"

She paused. Did he know something? She couldn't decipher his cheeky grin. Was he sending any faint signals? A nagging doubt, which she immediately suppressed, briefly threatened to upset her mood. She couldn't let on. She got herself a gin and tonic, something she could hold on to. In a display of contrived cheer, she drank to the health of Christopher and his team, people that had now fully accepted her as one of their own, providing Alex with some much needed protection. With them, she felt part of a group; she wasn't isolated – as was the case with her own team right now. It gave her validation. After a while, Henry dropped by and found her in the crowd.

"There she is, my dancing queen," he smiled.

Alex allowed herself to be escorted briskly to the dance floor. One classic followed hard on the heels of another, with new gin and tonics quenching her thirst, until she began to feel dizzy. Fresh air was a must but Henry wanted to keep dancing. She went alone towards the exit, running into Christopher again along the way. It seemed like his team had left already. As she stepped outside, a fresh gust of wind blew into her face, sobering her up and dissolving her newfound feeling of belonging into thin air.

It was only with great difficulty that she concealed her sadness. She didn't want to head back to the hotel yet. The only things awaiting her there were isolation and hurtful questions.

"What's up?" Christopher wanted to know.

She still hadn't thought about whether she would let anyone in on her problem. Besides, she wasn't even certain what or how great the problem was.

"Oh, I don't know," she dodged the question. "Things are a little strange in our team right now. It'll be fine I guess."

But as soon as she had uttered those words, she wasn't so sure any more. Doubts began to creep into her mind as silently as a patch of fog. What if there was an even bigger problem or if no solution could be found? What would happen then? Questions rattled through her brain, like a program that had been pre-set and whose cycle could no longer be halted. She urgently needed to speak to someone, to pour her heart out – otherwise her head would explode.

Her parents were sound asleep; she didn't want to wake them. But was Christopher the right person? He was equal to her boss in the company hierarchy and knew the whole team except for Carl. She just wasn't sure. While she was still chewing things over, she spied a colleague from the German office smoking a cigarette a little further back. He was on the works' council, if she wasn't mistaken. She could speak with him; he was obliged to keep it in confidence.

"Well, I'm going to take myself off to the realm of dreams; hope I've earned a sweet one," Christopher smiled. "See you! Keep your chin up!"

She began to think he had a sixth sense and could read her mind. As if he had seen her mentally going over the pros and cons and realised what she was about to do. It was a little spooky somehow. Maybe there was such a thing as a specific wavelength, on which they were able to silently communicate with one another.

Travis was the wiry type and it wasn't just his height that enabled Alex to fix him in the eye.

"Hello," she said, "I'm from the German office too. We've met a few times in the canteen."

"Yeah, I've seen you before," he replied.

"You're Travis aren't you, our employee representative? Do you have a minute? I'm sorry if the timing's not ideal but I really need to speak to someone. I'm Alex, by the way."

The words just came gushing out.

"Of course, what's it about?" he asked, surprised, reciprocating her handshake.

"I don't even know where to begin," she admitted. "A colleague from my team has made a complaint about me. My boss mentioned it to me this afternoon in passing. He doesn't know anything more. Since we've been here, I've had the feeling that my colleagues are avoiding me."

Travis listened attentively, before suggesting: "Why don't we walk a little – no-one needs to hear what we're talking about."

"I don't know what I'm supposed to have done," she suddenly began to sob. "Till now, nobody's said they had a problem with me. What should I do?"

Alex blew her nose loudly.

"Yes, George's been to see me," Travis confirmed. "He said he was speaking for the whole team."

The information came as a real bombshell. Its force robbed Alex of her breath. Tears began to stream forth, even though she was trying desperately to prevent them. After all, she didn't know Travis very well and didn't want to seem like a cry-baby. But her body wouldn't listen and she was overcome by a shivering fit deep within. The whole team was against her? What had happened? What had gotten into them? Why? She sensed the blood pouring ever quicker through her veins, until the feeling reached her ears. It became stronger and stronger; eventually her ears were completely blocked, as if in the midst of a rapid plane descent from 30,000 feet.

"All is not lost yet."

The sentence came through muffled. In between blowing her nose and wiping her tears, Alex kept trying to swallow deeply. It seemed to take an age before she could hear his voice clearly again.

"I would have approached you in the next few days anyway so we could talk in person. It's almost certainly a simple question of communication. Problems like that can be solved. The fact that you wanted to make a break from the old hands and go your own way could also be a part of it. It's perfectly legitimate to plough your own furrow, as long as your teamwork doesn't suffer."

He allowed his words to resound in the air before continuing.

"Thomas seems to be affected by the matter too. Normally your colleagues would be obliged to go to him, which they haven't done. We'll tackle it in good time when we're back in Germany."

"Does anyone else know about it?" Alex asked anxiously.

"Not that I know of, no. Don't worry about it; everything will be sorted."

His attempts to calm her were starting to bear fruit. She had been able to order her tear glands to rest and her sobbing was slowly abating.

She didn't want to go back to the party. Christopher and his team had already gone to bed. Henry was probably still causing havoc on the dance floor. But she didn't feel like dancing; and she didn't want to go back to the hotel. Good company, to cheer her up and take her mind off things, would be just the thing. While she was still deciding what to do, her netphone rang.

"Where have you been hiding then, Alex?"

In the background she heard loud music as Bill was trying to make himself understood.

"It was a bit too crowded and noisy for me inside," she repeated twice, until he heard her correctly.

"OK, I'm coming out. Then we can go for a nightcap somewhere."

They agreed to meet in the bar of the Hyatt. A quick visit to the ladies' fixed her slightly dishevelled make-up; the heavy lip gloss would fulfil its purpose, providing a distraction together with the dim lighting.

"He called me, wanted to have a drink with me, even though there are still hundreds of people there," she whispered to her reflection. She wouldn't waste any time wondering why. He must just think she was good company. When she re-entered the room, Bill, who had taken his place at the bar, pulled out a stool for her, sprightly as ever.

"Gin and tonic?" he asked.

"Yes, please."

A smile flashed across her face. Her frustration of a moment ago had been almost completely washed away. Still, doubt was lurking in the wings, awaiting its next chance to strike.

"Great party," he said. "But in retrospect I'm very grateful to you. It's much nicer here. At least you can understand what people are saying – although with some of that lot, mutual incomprehension is a distinct advantage."

Before Alex could say anything, her netphone vibrated. Who could that be?

"Fancy a nightcap? In the pool bar at the Hyatt."

Astonished, she looked to see who'd sent her the text. It was Wolfgang.

"Just sitting with Bill in the lobby bar. Maybe later," she wrote back.

Management wanted to talk to her, but her colleagues didn't. It was a little strange. There it was again, that lingering doubt.

Should she tell Bill about her problem? He must have been wondering why she was never with any of her colleagues. But then again, maybe not. After all, he was never with any of his colleagues; he probably hadn't even noticed. There had been no-one else present at the meeting with Wolfgang except Thomas.

Bill seemed very supportive of women in the company. That's what his department's organisational chart seemed to indicate anyway – at least half the management positions were occupied by women. It showed how seriously he took the equal opportunities policy preached by the company. But did that mean she could confide in him? It was difficult to know how he would react. Would his position preclude him from dealing with team matters such as this?

She suspected that he'd view it as the team leader's responsibility. Besides, she didn't know exactly what her colleagues were accusing her of; only that the way they had behaved was not just unusual but unfair. They had complained about her behind her back, rather than talking to her directly. Bill had almost certainly interpreted her pensive gaze at the empty glass before as a sign that he should order another round. But before Alex could make a decision, Wolfgang came wheeling towards them from afar.

"The youth of today has no stamina: they've all disappeared off to bed," he moaned in jest. "At least we can rely on Alex."

He winked at Bill, who joined in as well.

"Yeah, you've got a good one there, Wolfgang. Works like a horse but still knows how to really let her hair down."

Quick as a flash, Wolfgang replied: "Alex is my best horse – the one who produces the most manure."

It seemed like that was some sort of company saying. The two men laughed, registering Alex's mock outrage with delight. They didn't seem to notice how much effort she was making to conceal her burgeoning self-doubt with a contrived, coquettish gaze.

Surely, it wasn't only a result of the gin and tonics the previous evening and the brief three hours during which she had tossed and turned restlessly. Even after her morning shower – normally so refreshing – Alex felt knackered. Her brain was like mush. It had replayed numerous images and memories during the night, like a jumpy teenager with an incurable case of channel-hopping. Her subconscious must have waded through every little scene with her colleagues in search of an answer. But it had found none. Alex wondered how she would survive until the plane departed that evening.

There was still no trace of her colleagues. It was a complete mystery to her which workshops or presentations they were attending. Still, she was more than happy not to have to come into direct contact with any of them. Even with other colleagues from the German office, she was gradually consumed by a feeling of paranoia. Perhaps something had filtered through?

She became increasingly aware of how difficult she was finding it to look at people without inhibition. It almost seemed to her as if everyone had X-ray vision and could read her innermost thoughts. Of course, she knew that was nonsense. But the others would surely notice she wasn't her usual self. After all, she wasn't someone who would just shyly withdraw into her shell and play a peripheral role in the festivities.

Still, a little company did her good and helped take her mind off things. All the same, she was having trouble suppressing the questions that probed away at her insides, always seeking to penetrate the surface. She had run into Nobu briefly and he had apologised profusely. After being told to be dealing with a number of additional topics in the future, he had thus needed to arrange lots of internal meetings; that's why he hadn't been able to make it to the party. He had assured her several times how much he had wanted to come – and how happy he had been to receive her message.

It was particularly trying at the airport. There were a lot of people from the German office flying home on the same plane. Christopher, his team, Marco, Lisa and Lucas; they were all there with her at the check-in. Alex had called at short notice to bag herself one of the last remaining upgrades.

"Fuck the air miles," she had thought. The last thing she needed on the long flight home was for a coincidence to place her near – or even right next to – one of her team colleagues. Of course, it wasn't impossible that one of them had upgraded as well, but at least then the seats would be wider and you could stretch out and sleep. Christopher was standing in the row in front and also had an upgrade. This was her chance.

She summoned all her courage and said quietly: "Well, maybe we can sit next to each other, then."

Astonished, he examined her briefly before nodding; he didn't ask any other questions.

"We're going to get a few burritos and enchiladas down us. Fancy coming along?"

He waved her over invitingly towards his team. Somehow, he must have noticed that something wasn't right. Relieved, she joined them; it seemed she was safe from her colleagues for the next two hours.

Shortly before boarding, she met Thomas at the gate. He was completely devoid of emotion and stood taciturn in the background. There was no-one from the rest of the team with him and he didn't know where they were.

She didn't see any of them in the cabin on board either and, with some relief, began to make herself comfortable with her iPod, thick socks and neck pillow. Just after take-off, Christopher ordered two glasses of red wine.

"So let's hear it; what's wrong?" he began. "There's something not right with you lot. The only person I ever see from your team is you. Apart from Thomas."

"I don't know, something fishy's going on," she replied, dodging the question just as she had the night before.

Should she tell him everything? What would the consequences be? She liked Christopher, and his manner had always inspired trust in her. But when it came down to it, he was a department head like Thomas. And birds of a feather flock together. Normally.

"Come on, out with it! I know something's up," he encouraged her. "It will stay between us. Scout's honour!"

"George's lodged a complaint with the works council about me on behalf of the whole team."

The words made Alex feel like someone was holding her underwater and not letting go. Their significance weighed so heavily upon her that she could barely breathe. On no account could she start bawling. She couldn't bear that, not in front of Christopher. She forced herself to take a deep breath and tilt her head against her neck.

"I thought it must be something like that," he replied. "You've been so different since yesterday, withdrawn somehow."

"What have I done wrong?" she asked despairingly. "In your team, everyone's responsible for their own clients aren't they?"

He confirmed with a nod. Slowly tears were beginning to fight their way to the surface. Instinctively, she tried to stop them, rummaging around in her bag for tissues. She didn't want him to see how close she was to losing control.

"I'm sure it'll sort itself out somehow," he tried to be optimistic. "It can't be that bad. That lot are known for causing a stir."

"Thomas didn't hear anything about it until after George had spoken to the works council," she replied hoarsely.

"Really? That's very unusual," he said. "It's a mystery what they could want with the works council. What are they supposed to do about it?"

Alex shrugged her shoulders in silence.

"How do you want to proceed?"

"I'd like to get them all together in one room with Wolfgang and Thomas," she said, through clenched teeth. "Have a really good purge. That way, they'd all have to nail their colours to the mast and say what I'd done."

The thought of her colleagues firing off accusations was all that was needed for her to break down sobbing.

"Easy now. I don't think that's a good idea. I'd speak to each of them individually first and find out what's on their mind. They need to tell you what's wrong. Then it's up to Thomas and, if that doesn't help, Wolfgang."

"There was a little trouble with George a few weeks ago. But I spoke to him about it and we cleared everything up. Otherwise, there's nothing. At least, nothing I'm aware of."

She blew her nose. "They can't expect me to go up to everyone and ask if they've got a problem with me, can they? I mean, that's not normal."

"That's how I see it too. Not least because two of them have been here a long time and know how much the company values honest communication. I suppose that just makes it even more appalling. A pair of old hands seizing upon someone new."

Christopher shook his head in disgust. After a brief pause, he added: "If all else fails, you can join my team. My impression is that you're doing a great job. My people get on well with you and there's more than enough to do."

With that, he finished his wine, reclined his seat and plumped up his pillow. "Don't worry; we'll get it sorted somehow."

"They did WHAT?" Franz could hardly contain himself. "I've never come across anything like it in my whole career. It's outrageous."

Back at the flat, Alex had flung her bag into the corner and called her dad. Although speaking to Christopher had been reassuring, the whole thing was still eating away at her. What she simply couldn't understand was why none of her colleagues had approached her beforehand. What sense did it make getting the works council involved?

"The works council is usually there to assist workers when they have problems with the management, not disputes between colleagues. Your boss needs to take some serious action."

He left her in no doubt as to what he thought should be done. A grown-up was expected to solve problems on his own, not hide behind others. Especially not when it impacted upon several different people.

"If you ask me, it's plain cowardly," he continued furiously. "Wretched – there's no other word for it. And what are you going to do now? What's your next move?"

"I'm going to speak with each of them individually," she said, "and see what they have to say for themselves. Then we'll see. At the moment, I'm just poking around in the dark."

"It won't be easy, that's for sure. If I were you, I'd listen to some Robin Williams beforehand. That way, you'll have something to smile about; it'll put you in a good mood."

Her father loved the comedian.

"That's not a bad idea," she thanked him. "I'll make a special feel-good playlist."

A visit from Anna at the weekend also put her in a good mood. She wanted to say goodbye before disappearing abroad for another few months. A project had come up in Indonesia at short notice, on the island of Java.

"Hey, sweety, I'm really going to miss your coffee," Anna said, as she spooned the last bit of froth from the glass.

"Yeah, sure – because they only drink tea on Java," Alex winked, sending her a file from her netphone.

"These are the important addresses, the ones you really need there. There's a Harley shop in Jakarta and one in Bali, directly en route to the capital from the airport. The Hard Rock Cafe is a few streets further on, towards the sea. There's one in Jakarta as well. You know what to do."

Her collection didn't contain any shot glasses or T-shirts from Indonesia.

"I think you must have a screw loose somewhere," her friend grinned. "It'll be your fault if I have excess baggage."

"Better excess baggage than excess weight, pudding chops."

"Can't argue with that! I'll see what I can do for your obsession," Anna promised with a smile.

Alex would have liked to go with her – then she wouldn't have to worry about the problem with her colleagues. But running away had never been a good solution.

14

February

It was a good thing that the first meeting was with Travis. A kind of warm-up, so to speak. Just as in San Diego, he was certain the root cause lay in the lack of communication and that the problem could be resolved.

"I don't understand it, though," Alex reacted. "No-one provides project updates as often as I do. Just look at the call reports. Carl still writes them occasionally but Brian and George hardly ever bother. Hugo gives a quick heads-up on the status with Roffarm at team meetings but that's it."

"But it's not just about the written aspect; it's about talking to each other too," Travis replied.

"I get Brian's voicemail most of the time. Even when I leave messages, he doesn't call back. And he's very rarely at team meetings these days. I've got no idea what's happening with him and his clients at the moment. A few colleagues in the office have even asked me if he still works here."

His one raised eyebrow said more than words ever could.

"You can't speak to George on the phone for longer than twenty minutes," she continued, "otherwise you can forget about working. He's always changing his mind and expects you to agree with him about everything. That's very trying in the long run; and one of the reasons I've been calling him less and less."

To defend herself, she added: "But he hasn't been in contact with me, either."

It sounded childish, of course, but she didn't want to get pilloried.

"Communication isn't a one way street," Travis agreed. "I think we need to look at the causes on both sides. Your plan to speak to each of them individually is very sensible, in my opinion. I'll be talking to all of them as well in the next few weeks. And with your boss too, of course."

It still wasn't clear to Alex why they had gone over Thomas's head. Travis seemed to have an inkling, but he didn't want to share it.

"Let's arrange another meeting when you've spoken to everyone, Alex. If anything comes up in the meantime, don't hesitate to be in touch."

At the weekend she called Maria. Since Sandro had moved out, they had been speaking nearly every fortnight. Maria was always ready to listen and never tired of hearing the same story. It would have been even better if they could have met in person. The last time had been almost a year and a half ago and both of them were dying to chat at length over coffee and chocolate. As Alex didn't have any real plans for the next few weekends, her friend promised to visit.

The talk with Carl was relatively brief. She had actually called to arrange a meeting with him at the office. But he gave the impression that he wanted to avoid speaking to her face to face. He suggested they clarify things right away on the phone.

"Is there something bothering you about me or our working together?"

She wasn't a fan of beating around the bush but rather coming straight to the point. Still, she didn't find it easy inviting him to criticise her.

"I sometimes get the feeling you think I'm a bit daft," he said without hesitation.

"What makes you think that?" she asked in astonishment.

"With clients, I always have the sense that you're trying to show me up as incompetent. Take our meeting with Natioba recently. You elaborated on something I said. I asked you where you got your information from and you told me it was on one of the slides from your presentation for Cellgot; one that I didn't have yet. You said you'd send it to me. What's the client supposed to think? They're going to take me for a complete imbecile."

Alex could remember it vaguely. The meeting itself had gone very well. Carl had delivered the presentation and the client had expressed an interest in the next stage.

"I'm really sorry, Carl! That wasn't how I meant it at all. I just wanted to say that it was a very new slide. After all, we don't always send them to each other straightaway. I had no idea that's how it seemed to you. The client certainly won't have seen it like that; I don't imagine so, anyway."

She hadn't given the remark the slightest thought, only told it like it was.

"And it was you the client got in touch with after the meeting to arrange the follow-up. They wouldn't have done that if you'd made a bad impression, would they? Did I not also introduce you as our robot specialist and tell them that mobile off-grid systems were essentially your domain?"

"Yes, that's right, you did. But remarks like that can come across as pretty stupid to the client."

Somehow he didn't seem that comfortable in his skin.

"I'm really sorry. In the future I'll be more careful. OK?"

She really hadn't thought anything of it. "Was there something else?"

"No," Carl said, after thinking briefly. "I can't think of anything apart from the odd remark. We're still going to see the project through together, aren't we?"

"Of course. Naturally."

How would she have carried on without him? There was a touch of relief in his voice. Had he harboured reservations? But that wouldn't have made any sense. Despite Thomas's decision a few weeks before, she had continued to work with Carl on Natioba. She hadn't even been there for the initial meetings between her client and the bend-module manufacturers. Carl was perfectly capable of managing on his own, and no agreements about strategy had been made with Natioba yet. She had only asked him to provide her with more information about the current status; something he had either forgotten or neglected to do at first.

"Any news about Volcrea?" Alex wanted to know.

"No. I've got more important things on my plate for the moment. That's why I withdrew from the project."

"So, I'm really sorry you got the impression that I made those remarks intentionally. I'll take special care in future. But please if you find something I say inappropriate, you have to tell me straightaway, OK? We should eliminate these misunderstandings as quickly as possible."

"Apology accepted. The next time, I'll speak to you about it."

It sounded like an honest response. All the same, he seemed relieved she was ending the conversation.

The next day wouldn't be such a cakewalk. She had two meetings: one in the morning and one in the afternoon. After a fitful night, she awoke with a queasy feeling. On the drive to the office, she tried to convert her nervousness into energy.

That was easiest with music. Ever since her childhood, various songs had taken on a specific meaning, depending on the situation in which she had heard them. For her, music was a storage device for her emotions. The first bars of any song aroused a particular sensation in her. Rock music or breakdance hits were just the thing for it; reminding her of evenings when she had danced the night away, releasing countless endorphins in the process. Her speakers crackled, vibrating to the pulsating rhythms of Shannon and then Pink, as she gave all the puffed-up machos the brush-off with „U and Ur Hand".

Alex could barely keep her feet still on the pedals. Soon the rest of her body was no longer able to resist the sway of the beat, and started thrashing back and forth in the seat. Alex knew every single lyric and sang along with gusto – as if she were onstage, microphone in hand. She played the same songs on repeat until she arrived at the office. Now she had the strength to discuss things with George. On no account could she weaken and start to cry; she couldn't let her guard down. No matter what happened.

Armed with a cappuccino in one hand and a notebook in the other, she entered the meeting room she had reserved. She was still alone and chose a seat in the middle of the elongated table. The many foliage plants, usually so relaxing, somehow made the windowless room feel darker and more constricted today. One of the overhead lights wasn't working. On today of all days, when she needed their positive influence more than ever.

Her heart skipped a beat when George came through the half-open door. His face was devoid of expression; the affected appearance of solemnity wouldn't have looked out of place at a funeral. He greeted her almost casually, as he rummaged around busily in his laptop case, before taking his seat opposite her. She met his greeting with her gaze, using all her courage to make it seem reasonably friendly. His body language could be described as impersonal, at best.

"I've arranged this meeting today to hear your side of things and get an idea of whatever it is that's wrong."

As she uttered these words, Alex forced herself to maintain eye contact with her colleague.

George seemed to have been waiting for just such an opening statement.

"As you perhaps noticed," he immediately let fly, "we made a conscious choice to avoid you and Thomas in San Diego. We intentionally stayed out of your way."

Although she had been counting on a certain degree of candour, his direct – almost hurtful – phrasing hit her hard.

"However," he continued in the same breath, "I want to make sure no-one thinks this is a simple case of mobbing. You always plough your own furrow. There's no such thing as team work for you; or maybe you've entirely misunderstood the meaning of the word."

Each remark was fired like a gunshot and noted in silence by Alex, her gaze fixed at eye-level all the while.

"You didn't once bring me on board with Premve. What's more, by excluding even Hugo, you displayed your lack of trust in the team. A project had been agreed between Luxumi and Hursoc, but you wanted to do things differently."

Alex held back with her response. A partnership was based on giving and taking; she suspected Hursoc preferred the latter. Nor did she mention the decision of her client to initially carry out the project under their own steam; to avoid involving a specific supplier so that no one contractor could gain a competitive edge.

"As a woman in the high-tech sphere, you're at a disadvantage, and therefore you feel the need to assert yourself. That's why you often come over a bit strong, a little too aggressive. But in the end, it's your charm that makes the whole thing so completely unfair."

Alex thought she must have misheard. How was it possible to be aggressive and charming at the same time? Nevertheless, she bit her tongue once more. Inside, she urged herself to let him spit it all out. It wasn't easy; almost as if to distract herself, she began to write down his comments in even greater detail.

"Taken individually, these things aren't that bad, so we never mentioned them. On top of that you're a woman – a very attractive one too –, which made it all the more difficult for us to overcome our reservations. But at some point, enough is enough."

George seemed to have a list of things which had left them with a sour taste in their mouths.

Had they had a kind of brainstorming session about everything she had done wrong? Alex took a deep breath and prepared herself for the next bullet. He could hardly fail to notice her tension.

"Your Cellgot presentation wasn't approved by the team. Carl should have been the one to hold it, as gesture navigation is closer to Robotics. And we were too late in hearing about your visits to San Francisco and Taipei. It was almost like they were undercover trips. But what really takes the biscuit is this project with Volcrea. Even though the whole team's against it, you don't have the flexibility to change your opinion. So what did you do? You go and pick someone from management who thinks it's a good idea and they allow you to implement it. What the team thinks doesn't matter to you. You just continue stubbornly on your way."

Maybe George had hoped to penetrate her inner defences with that. Alex closed her eyes for a second, imagining the first bars of Moby's „Lift Me Up". Then with a turn of her head, she loosened her neck muscles, which were slowly but surely beginning to cramp. George didn't seem to notice and simply carried on.

"For the first six months you received a lot of input from us, and now you're passing everything off as your own ideas – both with your clients and internally. Take Henry, for example. Without our knowledge you never would've come up with a suggestion like the live feed, which is totally stupid by the way."

Henry probably wouldn't care if he knew what George thought of his idea. Alex had only sown the seed. Meanwhile, she was finding it increasingly difficult not to defend herself and set the record straight. But her father had always said: "He who apologises, condemns himself." Besides, it was always wise to sleep on these things for at least a night. Knee-jerk reactions were of no use to anyone. Let the boys get everything off their chest first.

"And your behaviour with Bill in San Diego last month. That was completely inappropriate. You were sitting far too close to each other in the meeting. Your shoulders were touching and you spent the whole time whispering. That made everyone feel very ill at ease. You should have seen your body language."

George fiddled with his cufflinks. Maybe he wasn't completely wrong about the last point but what was she supposed to do? Put a high-ranking manager in his place? Prevent him from speaking or be so impolite as to simply ignore his questions? Besides, she was pretty certain they'd been very quiet.

"You're always calling people's competence into question at team meetings. I'm not sure whether it's insecurity, cynicism or aggression – it might even be a misplaced sense of humour."

Alex became aware of her brow beginning to furrow. That was much too sweeping a statement.

"Can you give me any concrete examples?" she asked. "Who have I done that to and what did I say?"

"I've seen it often enough, and how it affects the others. I'll give you an example in a minute. There are lots."

George glanced at his laptop and scrolled down in search of an answer. There must have been about three pages of notes. He looked at her and then turned back to the screen.

"I'm sure I'll think of something soon enough. I'll give you some proof points in two shakes."

Alex waited, her brow clearing in the meantime. She felt as if someone was putting a series of weights on her head, which she was obliged to balance.

"Thomas spends far too much time with you. He hardly concerns himself with the rest of the team. You're far too close for my liking."

Alex shook her head in astonishment. "What do you mean by that? In what way are we too close?"

"He looks after you like a little sister. That's one step too far for me. At the same time, he seems to anticipate your every wish. We've been wondering who manages who for a long time now. And as far as we're concerned, it's you who's doing the managing, not the other way round. It's just not on."

George had talked himself into a real rage by now.

"Two of the three others in our team are currently considering whether they should quit."

"What? Why?"

Alex couldn't imagine why even one of her colleagues would want to quit. The problems weren't that insurmountable, were they? Besides, PsoraCom was a top employer, offering a salary that was well above average; to say nothing of the fact that working with the new solar cells was amazingly exciting.

"That's 95% down to you. You've poisoned the atmosphere in the whole team."

Those last words were like a deathly cloud hanging in the air, gradually seeping into her every pore.

George looked at her steadfastly; his eyes still seemed to be shooting poisoned arrows.

Alex swallowed hard. "Do you even know what you're saying, George? I'm one fifth of the whole team. One fifth! If there are people wanting to leave because of me, that would mean I have more influence on the team than the rest of you put together. That's bullshit."

He didn't seem to have thought about it like that.

"How exactly am I poisoning the atmosphere in the team? Can you give me a few examples? What is it that bothers you personally? You've spoken about how the others feel or what you think as a collective. But I want to hear about you. What is it that bothers YOU?"

"You use your connections with management to push your own projects through. The opinion of the team doesn't interest you. And you're always calling the competence of Hugo and Carl into question."

"I've already spoken to Carl and I'm meeting with Hugo tomorrow. Today it's about how you feel, George. What have I said that's bothered YOU?"

Alex hated blanket statements.

"I don't think the situation's going to improve. Too much has happened already. You should start looking for something else outside of the team."

He looked her in the eye for a long second, without any visible emotion. Then he returned to his screen.

A shiver went down her spine. "He's out to finish me," the thought flashed through her mind. But she wouldn't give up so easily. That was the end. The final straw.

"Already saying there's no chance of a solution is just completely unreasonable. Given that none of you even bothered to approach me, don't you think I should at least have the opportunity to speak to all of you first and give my opinion?"

George looked at her briefly for a moment without saying anything.

"If you can't give me any concrete examples now, then please send me some by tomorrow. I have to go now."

Alex snapped her notebook shut, put the pen in her inside jacket pocket and slowly rose from her chair, clearly signalling that the meeting was over. She moved quietly to the door, before turning round a final time as she took her leave. It wasn't supposed to look like an escape – even though she probably couldn't have taken it for one more second in that room. The constant criticism and subdued lighting had made a considerable dent in her protective shield. But she was proud to have maintained her composure.

In the far cubicle of the ladies', she sat with her head in her hands. The tension her body had been placed under in the last hour dissolved itself and soon she began to tremble from head to toe. She didn't feel the need to cry. That was probably due to the shock induced by George's last remark. She just sat there staring at the floor, while her quaking body attempted to neutralise the devastation she felt within. Her mind was a complete blank, incapable of a single thought.

It took almost twenty minutes for the trembling to abate and Alex to regain control. Clumsily she placed the headphones of her Zeus68 into her ear and selected a playlist. Slowly Steve Tyler's voice began to get through to her, and Alex wondered what was wrong with the world today and why she seemed to see things differently to everyone else. Was she living on the edge with PsoraCom; and could she help herself from falling? As depressing as the lyrics were, the piercing beat of the drums coupled with the opulent chords from the electric guitar hauled her back to reality.

"Pull yourself together!" she spurred herself on. That was only George's opinion. He couldn't get rid of her on his own. The more weakness she showed, the more vulnerable to attack she would become. Nothing had been decided yet. She couldn't allow her everyday work to suffer.

There were still a few things to do before meeting with Brian that afternoon. Bill's assistant, Shane, had been made aware of an interesting conference taking place at the same time as the trade show in Valencia, where Volcrea would be unveiling their bend-module machine prototype. Bill had been invited as the high-profile opening speaker.

However, in order to make his trip to Spain worthwhile, additional meetings were to be arranged for him with PsoraCom's direct clients and end customers. Alex saw an opportunity to move things along a little quicker with her clients. After all, Bill was very well placed in the company hierarchy and would be a suitable conversation partner for more senior client figures, with whom Alex was not yet in direct contact.

Chris helped her find the right secretary at Natioba HQ. This time, Alex didn't want to set up a meeting with the chief of research but rather his counterpart from development. She had invited the development manager at Luxumi as well, and there was a chance that the head of Premve's Asian office would also attend. So far, she had only received confirmation from Cellgot, who would be in Valencia anyway.

Alex was working on a few slides detailing the Vabilmo technology's potential for Natioba and its affiliates. Without them, she knew there was no point even trying the divisional board at Italian HQ. In the meantime there were now five different groups within Natioba that stood to benefit from the new solar cells.

First, there was the research lab in Seoul with Chris and his colleagues, who wanted to develop the greenhouse project for production and actively launch it on the Asian market. Meanwhile in Milan, it wasn't just the main sector for traditional off-grid systems that was a potential partner; there was also the new sister department, specialising in mobile off-grid systems. Then there was Maintenance, where the vehicles could be fitted with the new technology and converted to solar power, just like at Premve. Finally, there was the newly acquired design department, which, thanks to the bend-modules, could gain a long-term advantage in the building-integrated industry.

Alex looked down at her slides contentedly; they had helped take her mind off what had been an unpleasant morning. All of a sudden, she was rudely interrupted by the sound of her calendar system's reminder function. Fifteen minutes remaining to prepare herself for the unavoidable confrontation with Brian. Outside in the fresh air, she immersed herself deep in the rich sounds of Bruce Springsteen's guitar until, like The Boss, she didn't give a damn for just the in-betweens. What counted were heart and soul, making dreams real, finding that one face that didn't look through you. It was no sin to be glad to be alive!

Fortunately, the overhead light was working in the next meeting room, only it was considerably smaller. It seemed there was always some sort of compromise to be made. Brian entered in an exaggeratedly casual manner, his numerous key chains hanging from his back pocket as usual. He nodded silently at her, with neither trolley nor anything else in tow. The first thing he did was move the chair opposite Alex further back, as if he wanted to increase the distance between them; before sitting down with his legs apart and hunching his shoulders on the back rest. Was it invulnerability he hoped to demonstrate with such a pose? If so, he had failed in Alex's eyes.

"Hello, Brian. It seems there is some ill-feeling in the team and I'd like to find out why. I've arranged this meeting today to hear your side of things."

She didn't need to say anything more.

"Ill-feeling? The first cracks appeared in March last year. That's when you started to change. At the beginning, I was so impressed with how quickly you got yourself up to speed. Your professionalism and networking were top-notch. But then came the breach of trust. You just flew off to San Francisco without asking for my opinion. I know all the right people there but suddenly my ideas were no good anymore."

Given his cool entrance, Alex was a little surprised by Brian's verbosity. It almost seemed as if he was trying to get everything out of his system before he forgot it.

"The way you speak to Hugo; that really gets me down. Your constant jokes about his Swiss accent and asking if his hair was curly because he'd put his fingers in a plug socket."

Alex took a deep breath before attempting to make things abundantly clear: "That's not how it was at all!"

It was true she had made the joke about the plug socket, but only after she had got to know Hugo a little better. It had been meant as a compliment; she'd liked his hair. Alex was certain Hugo had understood it like that as well. George and Brian had even adopted the joke, using it to tease Hugo for a long time after Alex had already stopped. But she didn't get any further because Brian simply interrupted her.

"I approached Thomas several times. I didn't want to shoot you down but he never said anything about it. Hugo was really hurt when he came to see me. So we talked about it. To me, what you did there's a pretty clear case of harassment. I just can't deal with it, the way you bully him. It really depresses me."

Alex swallowed. These were pretty severe accusations Brian was making. Harassment was taken very, very seriously in American companies and could have far-reaching consequences. Were her colleagues hoping to bring her resignation about that way?

"I only ever wanted to help you. But you didn't want to know. After five months, you'd already started taking decisions on your own, without even asking for my advice. You stopped working with me altogether. What's more, management went along with your decisions. They agreed to let you undertake all activities with end customers completely by yourself."

He shook his head, as if he had never seen anything like it. Alex had no idea what was going on; Brian was always preaching about individual autonomy. It probably only applied to him, though. She let him continue.

"Since all your secret trips, we've lost trust in Thomas as well. He never wanted to hear my opinion either; the two of you have built a wall around yourselves. I had no idea how to even arrange a meeting with you to discuss the matter without getting the green light from him first; without getting permission to speak to the boss's protégé. It's like banging your head against a brick wall; Wolfgang's just the same."

"What does Wolfgang have to do with it?" Alex couldn't make head or tail of what he was saying.

"I wanted to speak to Wolfgang too but what chance did I have, the way he treats people? We're all about ready to chuck it in. The whole team. It's completely shot to pieces. That's why we went to the works council; because that's what you do in harassment cases."

Again, Alex's whole body shuddered at the mention of the word. She continued to note everything down in silence. Then she raised her head and looked him straight in the eye once more.

"And your behaviour with Bill in San Diego last month. Even Carl was upset about it. You showed absolutely no respect to Hugo or the rest of the team. That destroyed the last remainder of trust. You know Roffarm is our flagship project, the basis for all our other work. I was more than willing to help you with any of your clients. But you always knew better. You even wanted to cast Luxumi aside."

That was anything but true. Eyebrows raised, Alex opened her mouth to say something, only then to reconsider. The discussion probably wouldn't have gone very far, the way Brian was at the moment. Everything he said was accompanied by sweeping gestures, each one culminating in him running his hands through his hair.

"If you think I'm jealous of your achievements, then you are sorely mistaken. I founded this unit! Without me, there wouldn't even be a Vabilmo team! I'm the one with the know-how in this industry, and people are always coming to me for advice. What you've achieved so far is hardly earth-shattering. Any greenhouse installer could've shot that film with Natioba. It's just a marketing gimmick. The whole industry's in stitches about it. It's an absolute laughing stock. Just like the project with Luxumi. First you take them off your priority list; then suddenly you want to fit service vehicles with the bend-modules and integrate some sort of strange navigation technology. We've seen it all before. It's old hat. And now Volcrea, that's going to be another showstopper in Valencia."

He paused quickly for breath, tugging energetically at his goatee.

"There should've been at least four of us at the meeting with Premve in Seoul. In terms of personnel, you've got the best team in the whole company here. But we know absolutely nothing about what you've achieved. Don't forget, we're the ones that judge you; how you're seen within PsoraCom is based on the team's assessment. But you isolate yourself. Even Hugo says he's got no idea about your client accounts. I just can't deal with it anymore, the way you hurt him. You're destroying the whole team with your aggression. I don't think there's anything that can be done. I really don't. I'm sure, in fact."

Brian shook his head vehemently, before standing up abruptly. First George, now Brian. Neither of them saw any chance of the team settling their differences - apparently caused by Alex alone - and finding a solution.

"Brian, let's talk about it again once we've both cooled down," she said. "I don't want to give up so easily; I want to work on the problem after I've heard everyone's point of view."

Although, she found it difficult to stay calm after everything that had been said, she still had a residue of inner strength. There was no chance she was about to break down in front of him, even if the prospect of a harassment case still lingered menacingly in the air. He had mentioned it three or four times. Alex had learned at various training sessions that anything a person repeated three times or more was extremely important to them. Clearly, it wasn't just an idle threat. But he had said so many things, some of which seemed completely contradictory.

"It's pointless," Brian said brusquely, before leaving.

She looked over her notes in peace. It seemed like she and Thomas were being cast as some sort of inaccessible double act. It was true that she spoke to her boss a lot, but they were also the only ones who came into the office with any regularity. The opportunity was there for everyone else as well.

Alex didn't think she had received any preferential treatment. Why had Brian taken aim at Wolfgang again, without even speaking to him? It made no sense and reminded her of his outburst in Barcelona last year. Since then, Wolfgang had begun asking her for the latest news. That had started round about the time the exclusivity issue with Roffarm and Natioba had escalated and Alex was working on a solution. Still, it was the harassment claim that shocked her the most.

Just how had he come up with it? OK, so not everyone had the same sense of humour, but she'd never intended to hurt anyone with her jokes – and as far as she knew, she never had. Otherwise, surely someone would've complained. Or maybe not? Humour was important to her. Sometimes she made little jokes to dissolve a tense atmosphere. Every now and then there were situations where it was impossible to resist.

Indeed, her more humorous comments were often cloaked with a certain degree of respect. They were meant more as compliments, and in her opinion colleagues usually took them as such. There had never been any complaints from other people at PsoraCom. Not even from Henry, and he was one of her favourite victims. In fact, he always seemed very pleased to see her. Just like Christopher, who was only too happy to exchange a little gossip.

It was the latter she ran into, just as she was leaving the meeting room.

"Well, well, Alex. You look as if you've been through the mill."

"Yeah, two 12Is today. The first with George, the second with Brian."

"Yikes. Our two prima-donnas. And?"

"One says I should start looking for a new job right away; the other's accusing me of harassment."

"They're crazy, the pair of them," Christopher blurted out. "How exactly have you been harassing people?"

"Oh, it happened ages ago. This one time I asked Hugo if he'd put his fingers in a plug socket because his hair was all black curls. He laughed uproariously; and everyone else seized on the joke, especially George, who made it into a running gag."

"But no-one's seriously going to view that as harassment. You always counteract any funny or ironic comments with one of your charming smiles. It's immediately obvious when you're joking."

He shook his head, his blond locks bouncing up and down as if in defiance.

"Thomas needs to give them a real piece of his mind. It's just childish, what they're doing."

"Apparently, I've been aggressive towards colleagues in team meetings," she went on, "and called their competence into question. It's true, I often ask about the more technical stuff. But that's because I want to understand. A little extra knowledge never hurt anyone."

"Yeah, well, I'm afraid I can't judge that," Christopher replied. "I haven't been at your team meetings. But Thomas must have noticed. Has he ever said anything about it?"

"Not to me," Alex said. "I mean, I'm no innocent; and there is the odd day when I'm a bit moody and things don't come out quite the way I intend them to. But they can hardly crucify me for that."

She couldn't withhold a deep sigh any longer.

"Don't worry! It'll be fine," Christopher tried to cheer her up.

But she was exhausted. Her head was spinning and her neck was sore. Doing something about it was the priority now. She drove home.

Alex didn't know exactly how many endorphins were released after an hour's jogging, but it certainly felt good. The tension was gone, the circulation in her muscles had returned and she felt a bit more sanguine about things. The situation didn't seem so bad anymore, even if Brian and George had brought out the big guns.

Franz was beside himself when he heard what they had said.

"If George was working in the US, he would've had to clear his desk straight after the meeting," Alex's father railed. "That really is the limit. The Americans have no time for stunts like that."

"But we're not in America. Besides, I don't have any witnesses. It's my word against his."

"That's true," he agreed, "but I'm sure they'd believe you. Why would you make something like this up?"

She had the feeling Franz was almost more worked up than she was. He was really suffering with her. He probably would have swapped places with her if he could have, to give that wussy what for.

"The crux of the matter," he continued, "is that your success has set the bar very high for the whole team; it's become the new standard against which your colleagues are measured. If they don't achieve as much as you, people start to talk."

She hadn't seen it like that before. With the exception of Roffarm, it was her clients that projects were currently underway with. Even so, she had involved George's client from the start. It wasn't her fault that neither Premve nor Luxumi wanted to work with Hursoc for now. Especially since both of those projects were still completely in line with the overall team strategy.

Her clients' decisions not to work with Hursoc had been taken without any input from her. She had initiated the joint meetings and suggested what the companies might be able to do together. But there had been nothing forthcoming from Hursoc; in fact, they had neither supplied additional contacts nor arranged joint meetings with other manufacturers. So what was the problem?

And Carl had been brought on board with both Premve and Natioba. Hugo had been introduced to everyone as the architect, only he seemed to think that Alex was some sort of PA. He was old enough to manage his own diary and workload. He hadn't even got back to Premve in the end. She saw no reason why she should chase him up like a schoolboy who hadn't done his homework.

Brian was responsible for his own clients; she didn't interfere or tell him what to do. If he'd had a project the CEO liked better, she wouldn't have got a look-in with Natioba. The same opportunities were available to everyone. How people used them was their own business – but they had to be able to live with the outcome.

"The best people win the game," Franz said. "And that's the way it's always been. If they're too lazy to put in the hard yards and get something off the ground, then it's their own fault."

Alex had often wondered what Brian had been doing in the last few months. It sometimes seemed as if he had disappeared off the grid. But even when colleagues asked if he even worked for the company anymore, she always remained loyal and covered for him, never letting on that she didn't have a clue what he was doing either.

Hugo behaved like a mad thing during his 12I. First he had sent a text saying he was still stuck with a client and would be half an hour late. Then, after forty minutes, he entered the meeting room, hardly giving her a second glance as he slung his coat over the chair and pulled his laptop from the trolley. He took his place opposite her, sliding down in the chair as if he wanted to take refuge behind the computer screen.

"I don't feel as though you respect me," he spluttered. "The way you always ask in team meetings if I know something or if I'm just assuming it. You're the only one who ever probes further, trying to make me out as incompetent. I should've been at the meeting with Premve in Seoul but you totally shut me out."

"Now, hang on," she countered vehemently. "I invited you along from the start, asked you twice in fact. But you never got back to me. All the other participants confirmed within two days. You were the only one I didn't get an answer from – after two weeks. It's not my job to be permanently on your back about an invitation you haven't replied to."

"You have no idea," he complained, "how many requests and emails I get each day. I hardly get round to reading them all, let alone responding."

Precisely that was his biggest problem. Hugo was incapable of prioritising or turning people down when his workload made extra projects impossible. If he had said no from the start or tried to find a workaround, things might have been very different. But he had never conveyed the impression that Premve were important to him and now it had been made to look as if she hadn't involved him. Well, that was the absolute limit.

"We all get lots of emails," she replied. "But it's down to individuals to organise themselves. If there are certain things you can no longer manage because you've already got too many projects on the go, then you have to be more open about it."

Hugo punched something agitatedly into his touchpad, stubbornly focusing on the screen; he seemed to be reading mails at the same time – as if to prove a point.

"In Geneva, the make-up of the group was all wrong," he changed topic abruptly. "It should've been different members of our team attending the conference with Cellgot. I've already spoken to Thomas about it. It's like the project with Luxumi. You just go and decide which of our partners from the ecosystem they should work with.

And by the way, it's not my job to call Natioba or some other client of yours every second day."

Alex didn't want to comment on the last point right now. It would almost certainly have turned into a fundamental debate about how they defined working with clients. Perhaps at a big market leader like PsoraCom, clients were handled differently from what she was used to. Still, Alex was convinced that success with clients was based first and foremost on listening to them. You had to find out what they needed or wanted. Only then could you look for solutions: solutions which best combined their needs with the products on offer; while also accommodating the technological capacity and business objectives of the employer.

Her belief that this was the right approach could certainly strike some as arrogant, but it had served her well enough until now. For her, what counted was how the client regarded her work, and ultimately that manifested itself in contracts, revenue and joint projects.

All the same, she was pretty sure Hugo wouldn't be particularly interested in the evidence she could provide: how one of her former employers had issued a directive stipulating that the sales team double revenue in five years; she had managed it in three and a half with a team where every member had defined tasks and thus contributed to the overall success. He would have just as little desire to hear about the project she had landed for a start-up, which proved to investors that the company blueprint had been right all along. But now wasn't the time to get philosophical about sales strategies or client proximity.

"Who even approved the press release for Cellgot?" he asked tetchily. "We can't afford another announcement like that. It totally blurs the message we're trying to convey on the market."

"Who said that?" she asked with surprise. After all, she hadn't been the one who'd authorised it.

"A colleague from Henry's team. But it doesn't matter. I've had enough anyway. There's just no fun anymore! Everyone from the team's been asking what's wrong. I've told them all I want to do is pack it in. Every plant manufacturer has me on their top-ten list. They'd be only too happy to offer me a job."

For a fraction of a second, he met her gaze before facing back towards the screen. His fingers tapped nervously on the keys.

"I'm sorry," she said, "if my questions didn't come across the way I intended in team meetings – I was trying to get a better understanding of the topic. Why did you never speak to me about it?"

"I thought I'd discussed it with you several times already," he replied. "Really, I don't have any idea how we can resolve the situation."

Before Alex could manage a response, he started packing his computer clumsily and stood up.

"Time for my next meeting. I have to go."

And with that, he headed for the door, without so much as a glance in her direction.

"He should go to one of the plant manufacturers then, if he can have his pick of them; if everyone's salivating over him."

Her parents had called to get an update on things.

"Such a wussy," her father continued. "Doesn't think you respect him because you're interested in the technical details of his explanation. What kind of nonsense is that?"

Alex had asked herself the very same question. OK, so there had been one or two situations where she had reacted a little impatiently perhaps. Like when he had spent months wrestling with a decision about the inverter manufacturer for Roffarm. At least he had eventually made one there. He had even thanked her a few days later for her suggestion that he switch into Nike mode and "just do it". The client had been very satisfied too, he had told her proudly.

Or like when he had presented the reference design for the solar plant fitted with bend-modules, also for Roffarm. She had been critical of what he had said about inverters.

"Module-integrated inverters aren't suitable for our purposes," he had said. "It'd be far too expensive to equip each solar module with a different inverter. String inverters are the only possibility here."

The latter involved connecting the individual solar modules in series with a cable, which was then linked back to the inverter. That way the number of current transformers was greatly reduced. However, there was also a disadvantage; namely, that high voltages had to be transferred across a great distance.

The real sticking point with this architecture, however, was so-called "overshadowing". If a solar module lay underneath a thick, passing cloud and thus generated no electricity, the whole system could fail. Similar to a chain of lights with a faulty bulb. Alex had been interested in the details of how the two methods compared. She had wanted to know, for instance, how the cost of several inverters measured up to that of the longer, screened cables. Hugo had no data to explain why the reference design was so strictly tied down to the use of string inverters. Even George, who had tried to spring to his aid, had seemed incapable of forming a coherent argument.

Her question: "Do you know that or are you just assuming it?" had probably been a little clumsily phrased.

Maybe she was funny that way, but, in her opinion, if PsoraCom were to approach power plant manufacturers and explain how best to fit their plants with polymer-based cells, they needed some data to back up their arguments. She didn't want to be picked apart by a client and sent back home to redo her homework. But she was probably too meticulous in that respect.

"He just can't deal with the fact that a woman in sales knows anything about technology."

For her father, the case was pretty clear-cut. He hated people who were soft and was loath to tolerate them.

Next, she had arranged a meeting with Thomas, as he had wanted to be kept up-to-date on the outcome of the I2I.

"What George and Brian have come out with is simply not acceptable," Alex opened the discussion. She had no intention of sugarcoating the situation. "George thinks I would be better off looking for a new job immediately."

She waited to see what effect this had on her boss. But apart from a slight furrowing of the brow, it didn't seem to have any.

"He wouldn't get away with something like that in the US," she continued, "and Brian's accusing me of harassment. Because of the joke with Hugo, about whether he'd stuck his fingers in a plug socket. He and George have repeated it countless times themselves."

Still nothing from Thomas.

"Hugo doesn't feel like I take him seriously and is so frustrated he's thinking about handing in his notice. Brian too, by the way."

"That's nonsense," her boss broke in, "nobody will be doing anything of the sort."

"Thomas, I know I'm not exactly an innocent victim here. I've got my own little quirks and some days I'm moody. At the end of last year, I was having a rough time of it personally and maybe some of the things I said were a bit off. I'm aware it's a weakness. However, I'm really trying very hard to ensure it doesn't happen again. It's an area I'm more than happy to discuss, so I can work on the criticisms that come up."

Her boss nodded gently.

"But to be put in the stocks like this, as if I'm some sort of criminal," she said indignantly, "well, it's just not on. And painting the situation as hopeless, as George, Brian and Hugo have all done separately, displays a total unwillingness to cooperate on their part. I've apologised to everyone I might have offended. How do you see things?"

"The way I see it there are three elements here: unwanted jokes; things that are true; and differences of opinion or methodology, which are perfectly common. I'll have a think about each one – but you have my backing. Some of this is straight from Kindergarten."

He added straightaway: "Officially, of course, I never said that. In terms of your conduct last year, there were a few instances, but they were exceptions; certainly not something you could describe as a serious issue. I haven't noticed anything amiss in that respect for quite some time. Your colleagues have all made similar errors: who hasn't? We'll get it sorted. Next week, I'm on holiday. If you need any moral support, then talk to Wolfgang. He knows about everything."

"But I can't just go and speak to Wolfgang. That's exactly what they're accusing me of. They'll complain that I'm using my connections to management again."

"OK," Thomas agreed. "I'll tell him to arrange a meeting with you."

"Carl had a few issues as well, but we were able to clarify them."

"I thought as much. Don't worry: everything'll be fine. I'll speak to each member of the team individually once I'm back from holiday."

Gradually, Alex's confidence began to return. Still, not all her doubts had been quelled, and a timid little voice announced itself from deep within sending faint signals.

"I only hope I don't end up falling victim to internal politics. At the end of the day, it's easier to get rid of one person than three."

"That's not going to happen," her boss said vehemently. "We won't let it!"

"And what's with the annual peer assessment? It's due in a few weeks."

That had just occurred to her. Peer assessment involved every individual employee getting feedback from four different colleagues they had worked with. She had asked Christopher for advice about who she should pick from her team, to go with Henry, Lisa and Hank; eventually taking up his suggestion. It would be interesting to see what Brian had to say about her.

"This issue has absolutely nothing to do with your assessment," Thomas made his position clear, "and won't influence things in the slightest. Wolfgang and I have already agreed on that."

His tone left no room for doubt. Before Alex could get back to her desk, she was intercepted by Henry.

"Alex, we have to have another talk about the live feed from Barcelona to Valencia. I've spoken to a few technicians. They're concerned the line could break down or that there could be other obstacles. A lot of companies are giving press conferences on that day, so there could be a few jitters. Maybe we shouldn't run the risk, although I still think it's a great idea."

He looked a little sad and asked: "You got any other suggestions?"

Alex thought about it. A presentation containing photos of the prototype would be good; but moving images were always better.

"Perhaps we could make a short film in Valencia," she thought aloud, "that you could then show in Barcelona? What would you need and by when?"

"That's not a bad idea at all. A film: that would be one alternative! I'll call the technicians right away and find out what they need, then I'll let you know."

While Alex was making her way back to her desk, another thought crossed her mind. Why not? He could only say no, after all.

When Henry came to see her later, she had some good news.

"Listen," she said. "I've just spoken to Bill. On the day in question, he's going to be in Valencia as well, making the opening speech at a conference. I asked him if he wanted to play the lead role in a film to be screened at our press conference."

"And? Don't keep me in agony here. What did he say?"

"After I told him about the idea, he thought about it for a moment; then he said yes."

"That's brilliant." Henry was beside himself. "The technicians think the film's a great idea as well. They only need the rough cut as an

MPEG-4 on DVD two days beforehand, so they can edit it. Do you think you can manage that?"

"If you cover the cost for next-day delivery," she winked.

Volcrea were likewise very taken by the idea. That was to be expected. They had all the equipment at their stand and the DVD itself could be burned within a few minutes, Alex's contact assured her. He had even found out where the exhibition mail service was based. It seemed like good things still happened occasionally at work.

Then, as if on a roll, she received a phone call from Cellgot's marketing chief. In addition to Valencia, they were organising an event at the trade show in Barcelona, which would be similar to their in-house conference in November. They were keen to engage Alex's services as a speaker again, with PsoraCom as a sponsor. She tentatively promised to make some enquiries, as she herself wasn't in charge of the budget.

After a brief consultation, it transpired that Lisa was unsure what to do with her department's and was grateful for the opportunity. She explained that if she didn't use up her allocated budget for this quarter, she would find it reduced next time and she was keen to avoid that. As far as the presentation itself was concerned, Alex didn't want to risk her reputation any further and asked Thomas how to proceed. For him, the timing seemed very convenient; Wolfgang had just suggested that he show an increased presence at events – and with potential end customers. He decided, therefore, to hold the presentation himself.

An email from Maria provided the icing on the cake. She had booked a flight to Germany for the coming weekend.

"HR really need to step in," Maria expressed her displeasure at the current state of affairs, over a third latte. "That's not the way you do things. First, you can't just complain to the works council – especially if you're on the committee yourself. And second it's extremely underhand to rule out a solution from the outset."

"Maybe they're doing it to protect themselves, so that nothing happens to them? Since they were the first to raise it, I can hardly complain about mobbing now, can I?"

"It's an absolute disgrace," her friend said. "And what's all this about harassment? It's just ridiculous. Such a cowardly thing to say! They're not right in the head."

She scraped the last bit of froth angrily out of the glass.

"Your boss needs to give them a good talking to. If he doesn't do something immediately, they'll start walking all over him. I've never seen anything like it in all my twenty years of working. Of course, people have differences of opinion; that happens the whole time. But what's happening to you is beyond the pale. Three against one, how unfair is that? Not counting your colleague Carl; he seems to want to stay out of it, but has to play along to save his own skin."

Obviously, it shouldn't have been happening. Especially not at a company like PsoraCom, one of whose basic rules was that employees communicated openly with each other. It was precisely in conflict situations that they were expected to approach one another and work out a solution together. The open handling of conflict resolution was a watchword at PsoraCom. There were even short educational films on the intranet; every employee had to watch them each year during annual company training.

Appropriately enough, Alex had just completed her training the previous week, together with the mandatory business ethics programme, which outlined the general behavioural standards expected of company employees. With clients, superiors and fellow staff. If the message it conveyed had been strictly observed, her current situation would never even have come about. But when had theory and practice ever been the same?

The weekend went by far too quickly. They had a lot to tell each other: not only about Alex's current work situation but about projects Maria was undertaking at the animal shelter. Even so, they still managed a long walk in the snow-covered Alps. Even the sea-loving, sun-spoiled Maria appeared comfortable enjoying coffee and cake on the south-facing terrace of the mountain cabin. Being out in the open countryside seemed to put everything into perspective, and soon a guarded optimism had begun to set in.

When she wasn't away on client meetings, Alex went into the office as before. Her team colleagues wouldn't be there except for the weekly meetings. Different people like Henry, Lisa or Emily provided her with a feeling of normality. She needed it if things were to continue as before because there was more than enough to do. There were meetings to arrange for Bill in Valencia and, despite his pledge, a project manager was still to be named for Premve; what with the other projects with Volcrea, Luxumi and Natioba, there was absolutely no room for boredom.

As Thomas had promised, Wolfgang arranged a meeting with her off his own back.

"So, how are you then?" he greeted her. "Thomas thought you could do with a little cheering up."

Wolfgang had never been one for fancy talk, but he managed to give her an encouraging look in amongst all the plain speaking.

"So far so good, even if the meetings haven't done wonders for my mood."

Alex briefly outlined what George, Brian and Hugo had said. She didn't spare him the negative assessment of her colleagues or the suggestion that she start looking for a new job.

"OK, so I'm not an innocent victim in all this, and I've occasionally said things that were a bit off," she told him, "but what they've done is unacceptable. I keep asking myself why none of them spoke to me about it beforehand. I mean, I'm hardly an ogre, am I?"

Wolfgang seemed to see through her attempts to conceal her growing frustration with humour.

"As you're well aware," he replied, "there are one or two prima donnas in the team who think their opinion is the only one that counts. They're hardly innocent victims either, and sometimes we all say things that are a bit off. The accusation that you exploit your relationships with management in order to get your objectives pushed through, well, I don't understand it. I think your interest network management skills are superb. The same opportunities are available to everyone, and your colleagues ought to realise how important it is to make their activities known to others."

Interest network management was an important part of the job at PsoraCom. It involved keeping superiors or influential people in the company hierarchy up-to-date on the latest developments, outlining how each of their respective departments stood to benefit, and ultimately securing their long-term support. Depending on the situation, there could be different people involved, but they would all have a common interest in the positive outcome of a project. Even so, it was Wolfgang and Bill who were affected by most of the Vabilmo projects, and Alex had built up a really good relationship with both.

Wolfgang expressed his opinion almost like a schoolmaster: "Networks need to be cultivated, both internally and with clients.

You're the only one from your team I ever see in the office. None of the others are visible. They shouldn't be so surprised that no-one consults them anymore. Out of sight, out of mind. That's the way it is. But don't worry, Alex. I'll make sure we resolve the matter as quickly as possible."

"That would be great, Wolfgang. I didn't have any intention of looking for a new job anytime soon. I'm very happy with the one I've got."

"Just remember: what you do at PsoraCom is my decision! What George said is just laughable. You don't need to have any fear; we've got your back covered."

After the meeting Alex felt more relieved than anything else. It could have gone quite differently.

"If something comes up, please don't hesitate to come and see me," Wolfgang had emphasised. "We'll sort it out. And if anyone should decide they want to leave the company after long years of service, I won't stand in their way."

The meetings for Bill were slowly but surely beginning to take shape. Three had been confirmed already and coordinated with his assistant. Two more were in the pipeline. That seemed to be more than was expected. Alex wished she could print off the mail that had been sent to her and cc'd to her team colleagues, and save it for later – possibly as evidence.

"You're a star," Shane had written. "It's great how you get stuck in and organise so many high-profile meetings."

The mail would be proof that there were people who could find no fault with her; people for whom in fact quite the opposite was true. But she knew it would be childish. Even so, these few lines did her the power of good. Marco replied as soon as he heard about the meeting between Bill and the head of Premve's Asian office.

"Top work, Alex. Hopefully we'll finally get the project moving. Until now even Wolfgang's attempts haven't borne fruit; and the client, as you know, is slowly becoming impatient."

She couldn't disagree with that. Although Bill had promised to allocate a project manager and part-time developer from his team, she still hadn't received any concrete information about who it would be. Perhaps it was down to the department restructuring he had mentioned. It had been easy to get the meetings she had planned with Cellgot and Volcrea.

But Natioba would be more difficult. She had wanted to bring Bill into contact with the head of development but the latter's diary was already full. Now she was working flat out to try and get him to make some space. He already had the slides describing the current status in each of the five relevant departments. There seemed to be some interest on his part; whether it would be enough to arrange a meeting in Valencia, however, was something that remained to be seen.

Lastly, she had asked Luxumi's development manager if he would be in Valencia. That way, she could bring Bill on board for the test project with Maintenance. One of her contacts at Luxumi had indicated that the project would provide the basis for standardising service vehicles in the future. That meant Development was involved; PsoraCom would thus need someone from Bill's department to assist in the implementation stage.

After the welcome events of the previous days, the news caught Alex completely off guard. Ricka had gone in for a routine aftercare appointment, which had uncovered certain irregularities. Nothing was known for sure yet; but further examinations were set to take place over the course of the next few weeks. At least that's what Ricka had told her. Whether the doctors— typical for doctors the world over – really hadn't given any concrete information or whether her mother just didn't want to worry her was difficult for Alex to judge. One thing was certain, though: she was definitely worried now.

Ricka's liver cancer had been discovered at a relatively early stage. The doctors had been very positive after the op, as no further metastases had been found in the surrounding tissue. What's more, her liver had displayed an excellent regenerative capacity: that is, it could develop new cells in place of the old ones, thus helping to rebuild the organ.

Although great strides had been made in cancer treatment in the past few years, one of the most significant weaknesses lay in the early detection of metastasis. Cancer cells from the original tumour could reproduce in the lymph and blood vessels and spread to different organs. So-called tumour markers were supposed to promptly indicate whether there had been a build-up of cancer cells, but they weren't always reliable. Often they could only provide information about the number of metastases and the speed at which they were growing.

However, by far the worst thing about this disease was the uncertainty. Who would contract it, when, and what was the chance of survival? There were simply no guarantees. Whom it would affect next or how it would develop in a person who was already ill seemed to be something that was decided almost completely by chance, as if someone in the far reaches of the galaxy was playing at dice.

Alex tried to keep control of her thoughts – as long as there were no further test results, it made no sense to lose any sleep over it. Perhaps it was just a false alarm and the small, grey shadows that had appeared on her mother's X-ray were in fact scars from a previous internal wound which had lain undiscovered and long since healed.

15

March

Alex received confirmation of the eagerly awaited meetings with Luxumi and Natioba a week before the event in Valencia. Shane was extremely pleased because the schedule was now complete.

Of her team colleagues, only Hugo had arranged a meeting between Roffarm, Hursoc and Bill. But that had been almost forced upon him, as all the participants wanted something from each other. Roffarm's divisonal director had been engaged as a speaker as well. As far as Alex was aware, that had been organised after Henry had approved the joint appearance with Volcrea. Roffarm would therefore be attending anyway. Hursoc wanted to win Roffarm back as a client, as they had been erased from the approved supplier list some years before. Bill needed an end customer that obtained its solar modules from Hursoc so that PsoraCom could win their first client for the polymer-based cells. Roffarm, on the other hand, were interested first and foremost in seeing to what extent developments had progressed with Hursoc, and discovering what other power plant manufacturers they were currently working with.

When Hugo sent a mail to the team informing them of the three-way meeting, it wasn't only George who described the outcome in such typically gushy terms as "absolutely first-class"; Thomas also allowed himself to get carried away with an appreciative and extremely uncharacteristic "really well done, Hugo". Alex was both amazed and annoyed at their reaction in equal measure.

She had arranged three meetings with high-profile directors, end customers whose diaries had been full for months in advance and who weren't even familiar with the subject of Vabilmo. Although it was part of her job, she had worked long and hard to secure an outcome that, in her opinion, hadn't exactly been guaranteed at such short notice. She didn't really count Cellgot or Volcrea, as the meetings hadn't been that difficult to come by.

Naturally, she had kept the team informed of her progress but after the meetings had been confirmed, no-one had been jumping for joy like with Hugo just now. She wouldn't have expected it from

George. And even less so from Brian, as he had dismissed the event in Valencia as completely overrated during the last team meeting. But Thomas at least should have treated them all equally and applied the same standards. She thought he was being unfair; given her current situation, a little bit of encouragement from her boss wouldn't have gone amiss. Especially since Thomas had promised his support. But ever since he had returned from holiday, she got the impression that he was withdrawing back into himself and returning to his old ways. She had to learn to lower her expectations even further.

Upon arrival in Valencia, she received several surprises. Shortly after landing she got a text from Bill asking when she would be on-site. Once there, she was greeted at the entrance by Shane, strawberry blond and thoroughly likeable. He led her through the lecture theatre into the adjacent meeting room complete with forecourt and leather chairs. Bill approached with a friendly smile and gave her a brief embrace.

"You've done some job organising these meetings," he said appreciatively, "high-profile people – and at such short notice. It can't have been easy."

"Oh, it was nothing," she gave him an exaggerated wink.

"I'm especially excited about Natioba," Bill continued. "After your greenhouse project, we have to make sure we gain a stronger foothold."

"That's exactly why I wanted to arrange the meeting," she agreed. "Our progress is very much dependent on what their development chief says. To be honest, I'm just happy we got an hour with him at all. The meeting with Luxumi is just as important because it's about the possibility of developing standardised service vehicles. In the long term, we might even be able to use them for our projects with Natioba and Premve. That reminds me: Premve are the priority today."

He nodded and his expression became more serious as he was well aware of the problem, but he was caught somewhere between a rock and a hard place. His counterpart from Robotics still hadn't officially rejected the project, though a decision had already been taken at project-management level. According to internal sources, there was little chance of support.

Still, if Bill were now to name someone from his own team as project manager, before the department head at Robotics had formally rejected the proposal, it would be tantamount to stealing – as strange as that sounded. At the end of the day, it was a question of who generated the most revenue. It seemed that's how things were at PsoraCom; and the higher your rank, the more you had to play the game. There was no way Alex could explain things like that to Premve, however, as Bill knew very well. Nevertheless, it was a paradox that needed solving. On that point, they were both agreed.

She put her bag down and hurried over to Volcrea, who had just held their press conference to unveil the machine prototype. It looked really good, slowly turning around on a moving platform up on the podium. There was a prominent, though not overwhelming, Psora-Com company logo directly in her line of vision. Alex took a few pictures from different angles with her Zeus68, before immediately sending them off to Henry.

"Very cool, my dear," he replied straightaway. "Take a few close-ups and send them as quick as possible!"

After she'd taken care of that, she promised Volcrea that she'd come by again in the afternoon with Bill. Then it was back to the conference quick-smart. She saw Shane, who had been watching over her bag like a guard dog, and sat down next to him. A nice guy, very uncomplicated, she thought to herself. Good-looking too. If only he didn't live in America, then maybe… Her mind wandered for a brief moment before she snapped herself back to reality; it was time to concentrate on the business at hand.

The conference started and Bill was invited to take the stand. Shortly after his opening speech had begun, Brian suddenly appeared out of nowhere. He didn't sit with them but moved towards the back instead. Hugo was arriving with Lucas the next day for the meeting with Roffarm and Hursoc, but Brian had never intended to come to Valencia.

As far as she was aware, he hadn't arranged any meetings with Bill either. Was he hoping to muscle in on her meetings or was she just being paranoid? Under the circumstances, it might have been helpful to offer him the chance to participate, to let him jump on the bandwagon, so to speak. But even if she hadn't been extremely reluctant to do so, it would have made very little sense, and so she left it. First, he wasn't responsible for her clients and second, besides her, Bill and Shane, there were already three others sitting in on the meeting. A fourth really would have been overkill.

During the first break, Brian went over to Bill to exchange a little small-talk. The rest of the day, he lounged around in the forecourt or paced up and down restlessly, making what appeared to be extremely important phone calls. He didn't try and talk to her, however – quite the opposite. Indeed, she almost got the impression he was trying to completely ignore her presence. Only once, when their eyes briefly met, did she perceive even the faintest semblance of acknowledgement. But then he turned immediately back to his laptop. She couldn't work out what he was doing here, and her schedule wouldn't allow her to make any real enquiries.

As expected, the head of Premve's Asian office requested firmly at the end of the meeting that the situation with the project manager be resolved. His lab team had been waiting since the start of the year and were raring to finally get started. Bill had little choice but to pledge his support. In secret, Alex hoped everything would soon be clarified internally.

She made use of the short break before the next meeting to get a bit of fresh air; despite the powerful air-conditioning system, the venue was hot and sticky – like all exhibition halls the world over.

Brian wandered off, trolley in tow, leaving an empty coke bottle on the table. No doubt he didn't want to deprive the cleaning staff of work but it seemed he had forgotten what sort of effect the mess would have on Bill's business partners. Even though it pained her to clean up his rubbish, Alex cleared the table and put the chairs straight. Defying her colleague wasn't as important as being able to meet her client in hospitable surroundings.

The meeting with Natioba went extremely well, even better than Alex had hoped. The chief of development was so taken with the polymer-based cells that he immediately cancelled one of his following appointments and stretched the discussion out for almost two hours. He had heard about the greenhouse project. Before receiving Alex's slides, however, he had been unaware that PsoraCom already had links to the four other departments at Natioba. He saw the greatest combined potential in stationary and mobile off-grid systems and, together with Bill, was more than happy to promote the use of the standardised bend-modules to generate the energy supply. Alex was to liaise with his department managers and intensify the collaboration with Seoul.

"Well done," Bill gave her a pat on the back afterwards. "Your slides would have impressed me too; they're clear and well informed.

Send them to Shane: I'm sure he'll be able to use them in some form in the future."

"Sure, Bill. But you know I'm only doing my job."

Alex found the praise a little embarrassing, but given the current situation, it did her the world of good. She just didn't want it to show.

The meeting with Cellgot's managing director was, as expected, a cakewalk, but still represented more than just idle chit-chat. Bill received a demonstration of the gesture-based navigation technology and Shane was tasked with arranging a follow-up with Cellgot's US team. With that, all official meetings were taken care of for the day.

Finally, they made a round of the exhibition hall, stopping off at Volcrea to discuss the filming schedule for the next day. After that, it was time to knock off. On Bill's instructions, Shane had reserved a table for three in a small but excellent gourmet restaurant. There was no sign of Brian. She didn't want to leave herself open to any subsequent reproaches, so she left him a message saying where they'd be. It didn't surprise her one bit, however, that he neither called back nor appeared in the restaurant. He hadn't been in touch with her two companions either.

Over the course of the evening, Alex caught herself dreaming idly about Shane on several occasions. At one point he must have been watching her for quite a while; when their gazes suddenly met, he gave her a mischievous grin. Her cheeks became quite flushed. Did he have an idea what she was thinking about? And how would he react if he did? Should she try to find out?

Bill seemed happy to relieve her of the decision. After dinner, he excused himself, saying that there were important calls to be made to the US.

"But you two stay," he suggested. "Shane's got the credit card. Have a nice evening; you both deserve it. There won't be anything happening before nine tomorrow anyway."

With that, he disappeared into his taxi. They looked at each other curiously. For a few seconds, neither of them said a word, both concentrating on gauging the mood instead. Shane was the first to break the silence.

"One for the road?"

"Why not?"

Her attempt to sound cool and laid-back hadn't been entirely successful.

"Well, let's try and find a nice, romantic bar then."

He seemed to make no bones about taking the lead with the mutual flirting. Suddenly Alex became aware of a tingling sensation in her body and a warm, fuzzy feeling that stretched from head to toe. Her hands became moist.

A few streets on, they struck lucky, entering a small, bizarrely furnished bar with a slightly worn but comfortable-looking sofa and rococo-style seats. The only light came from the numerous candles resting in ornate chandeliers or wall holds. The customers at the bar who had turned round as they came in were probably the locals. Shane strode purposefully towards the sofa, sat down and then patted the free space with his hand. It was a pretty clear signal.

He wasn't one of your typical Americans, who viewed their opinion as the only one that mattered. This was probably due to the extensive European travel he talked about. The only American thing about him seemed to be that he had German ancestors somewhere in his family tree.

After the first vodka martini, he put his arm purposely around her and drew her closer. Just like that. It immediately sent a shiver down her spine; a shiver of pleasure, like she hadn't felt in a long time, not even with Luis at New Year. Neither of them looked at their watches; at some point, they just paid and left. On the way back to the hotel Shane placed his arm around her waist, as if it were the most natural thing in the world.

It felt good. A firm grip that wasn't constrictive. Her head was spinning. What would happen now? He must have known as well as her that this wouldn't be the start of something serious. There were six thousand miles and nine hours between them. Besides, they hardly knew each other. What did he want? He didn't seem like a Romeo permanently on the look-out for a bit of fluff. What did she want? She knew what her body wanted. But did her mind want it too? Or would her desire for affection render her mind null and void?

Why not? It wasn't as if she had to answer to anyone. Still, one-night stands had never been her thing. A little fling like this could put a strain on their work together. She would have to deal with Shane increasingly often from now on. How well could he separate private and professional spheres? If they spent the night together, would he expect her to demand more when dealing with her requests in future? She thought about how nice it would be just once to give free rein to her impulses, without worrying about the consequences. He seemed to have guessed what was going through her mind as she removed herself from his embrace at the hotel entrance.

"Listen, we don't have to do anything you're not comfortable with," he said candidly. "All I want right now is to be with you. I don't care how."

She liked how honest he was. There was something reliable and trustworthy about him. The same was true of his eyes, dark blue-green, and incapable of concealing a glimmer of hope within.

"OK."

She didn't say anything else. She didn't have to. Impatiently, he unlocked his hotel room and pulled her closer. They stood behind the door, just holding each other. He had buried his face in her red locks; she felt the warmth of his breath on her neck. Gently he began stroking her back. Almost timidly, he led her to the large bed, sat down and drew her onto his lap, pressing her tightly against him and holding his arms around her waist. Alex savoured his every touch, each one sending a tremor through her and bringing her out in goose-bumps. He made no attempt to be more forward; he hadn't even tried to kiss her yet.

Lightly he brushed her cheeks with the tip of his nose, moving further down towards the neck. It felt good. Kissing would have been too intimate for her right now. Things could get out of hand pretty quickly and that was something she didn't want. But there was nothing wrong with a few tentative embraces and some TLC. It required a lot of self-discipline of course, but the two of them were evenly matched there.

Strange, Alex thought, how they both seemed to be governed by their heads, rather than their physical desires. Was that a good thing or was it better to just get lost in the moment and ignore the little voice in your head? In the meantime, they lay down on the bed and he held her in his arms, her head resting on his shoulder, their feet intertwined. It was an absolutely classic situation. Without saying a word, they knew they had reached their limit. Shane pulled the cover over her while she set the alarm.

Alex awoke the next morning before it could sound. Gently she kissed him on the cheek, then crept out of the room. Shane responded with a knowing nod. The magic of the previous evening had been overtaken by reality.

Her netphone vibrated as she came out of the shower shortly afterwards.

"Breakfast at eight?" Bill asked.

She couldn't help but smile. It felt good to be in demand – even if it was only for breakfast.

Shane was already going over a presentation with his boss when Alex joined them.

"And? Did you two have a nice evening then?" Bill said mischievously.

"Yes, thanks. We found a nice little bar and had a few more drinks. The only thing missing was you. Isn't that right, Shane?"

"Yeah, by the end, Alex and I had run out of things to say each other; it was so boring."

Before the evening could become subject to more detailed scrutiny, however, Alex changed the subject.

"Today certainly won't be boring, I'll tell you that much. We have a number of meetings to get through."

With that she briefly outlined to Bill why the project agreed between Luxumi and Hursoc had been temporarily put on ice. First, it would be another four years before Luxumi built their next big plant; second, they were currently working on a smaller PV unit in Croatia, where the planning phase was too far advanced for the Vabilmo technology to be integrated.

So, she had used her other contacts to help devise the project with Maintenance, hoping to fit the service vehicles with Cellgot's navigation technology. There was a chance the project could provide the basis for a future standardisation of these vehicles. Luxumi might even bring Volcrea on board to assist them with certain development assignments, as Hursoc were already involved in Croatia. Luxumi never put all their eggs in one basket.

Bill nodded thoughtfully; no doubt there were any number of things racing through his mind. Alex knew how important it was to find an end customer that would work with Hursoc. Nevertheless, they couldn't forget that it was ultimately a question of establishing the Vabilmo technology on the market. That could be achieved with the help of various different companies. She would keep a low profile in the meeting and leave Bill to make his own decision – after all, she needed his support for Luxumi too.

The staff at Volcrea were all waiting expectantly in their starting positions, cameras at the ready. During filming, it was impossible to ignore how much Bill seemed to enjoy playing the role of the experienced technician. He had exchanged his jacket for some clean, blue overalls, and looked very comfortable in them. At each stage of the demonstration, he peered directly into the camera, almost as if he was flirting with it. Yet he maintained his professional aura at all times.

It was a very special mix, and Volcrea were just as taken with it. They only needed two takes before it was in the can. Now it was just a question of assembling the visuals; the sound would be added later as it was far too loud for that here. Henry's technicians would take care of that in Barcelona; they already had the storyboard. Alex would return in two hours to collect the DVD footage.

The subsequent meeting with Luxumi didn't start off quite according to plan. Alex had some trouble concealing her emotions as the development manager updated them on the current status. His words caught her completely off guard. The project with the service vehicles had also been put on hold. It transpired that one of her colleagues had called Luxumi and played down PsoraCom's interest in the proposal. He had said it wouldn't be practical in the long run, mentioning that it only partly conformed to the Vabilmo team strategy as well as that of the company as a whole. A joint focus on solar plants was more important and that was what they should be pushing for instead.

Bill cast Alex a curious glance, which she returned in kind. She had no idea what had happened. It wasn't clear how the situation could be rescued without making PsoraCom seem like a shower of idiots who were completely unaware of each other's activities.

"It's true that one of PsoraCom's chief interests lies in fitting solar plants and off-grid systems with the Vabilmo technology," she began. "No-one's about to deny that."

Nodding agreement, Bill allowed her to continue.

"However, we have also learned that the standardised bend-modules are extremely well suited to the machine and robotics industry, and offer considerable savings on costs. A number of different companies have already expressed their interest in undertaking joint projects with us. Nevertheless, owing to limited resources, we currently feel that we need to focus our attentions more on regular customers, a group that includes Luxumi."

The development manager let what she had said sink in. Alex could only hope that her verbal balancing act had conveyed the right message, namely that they were still interested in collaborating with Luxumi on the project.

Bill's facial expression told her he agreed.

"There's a prototype here that generates its electricity supply through the Vabilmo technology," he added. "Volcrea built it using seed units from PsoraCom. Perhaps that would be of interest to you? It's not a service vehicle, admittedly, but it should be enough for you to get a general picture."

"You're already working with Volcrea?" Luxumi's development manager asked.

Bill nodded.

"We're also collaborating with them on several projects," the former went on, "and we're extremely satisfied with their work so far. Although Hursoc provide a good service, they're no longer innovative enough for us. As a result, we're seriously considering allocating Volcrea more project work when we come to build our next solar plant."

"We've had very positive experiences with them as well," Bill replied, "and would like to intensify our collaboration. What do you think of us reviewing the possibilities offered by the polymer-based cells together with Volcrea? It could pave the way for considerable synergies, both short-term and long-term."

Alex could see just how open to the suggestion her client was. His body language told her everything, as he drew himself closer to Bill.

"I think it's a very good idea," she heard him say. "In the long term, we'd be interested in a solution that makes us less dependent on companies like Hursoc. Although we need them, involving them in the early stages of the development process gives them an unfair advantage over their competitors. Unfortunately we can't afford to bring every supplier in on a project from the outset and then choose the best one. We've been in a cycle of dependence for years, and it's something we'd like to change."

Competition would be tough, Alex thought to herself. Bill was sympathetic, though there must have been a hint of bitterness about Hursoc. Luxumi had just expressed the same opinion as Premve had some time ago, albeit in a slightly different way. In the long term, a turnkey supplier such as Hursoc could encounter serious difficulties on the market or, at the very least, find it increasingly hard to skim profitable contracts. That certainly wouldn't please George.

"So, where do we go from here? Should I ask Alex to set up a joint meeting with your people and Volcrea?"

The development manager nodded in agreement, before going a step further. "We should also arrange some sort of summit meeting with Volcrea's CEO when the first results are available in a few months' time."

Bill concurred.

And so the meeting had gone better than it'd seemed it would at the start. All the same, Alex needed to make some urgent enquiries into who had been responsible for the call to her client and the subsequent mess. Hopefully, there was a suitable explanation; otherwise, it was close to sabotage.

After the meeting Alex said goodbye to Bill; he embraced her warmly, thanking her again for everything she had done. She would have to hurry if she was going to get the footage away to Barcelona on time. There was no sign of Hugo, whose meeting with Roffarm, Hursoc and Bill was scheduled to take place in an hour; not that Alex was particularly upset. Shane accompanied her to the exit, so he could spend a few extra minutes alone with her.

"Keep in touch. I'm sure I'll be back in Europe before the year's out. And you should let me know beforehand if you come to the US."

The way he looked at her told Alex it was more than just an empty platitude.

"I promise."

Her heart began to beat a little faster as he embraced her, gently kissing her on the forehead before she climbed into the taxi. She had to go; the train to Barcelona wouldn't wait.

Things seemed to have run smoothly enough with the DVD. At least, Henry hadn't been back in touch since she'd handed it over that afternoon. Now she could concentrate on more important things and attempt to find out who had made the call to Luxumi. She finally reached her contact on the third time of asking; he was just as surprised as she had been.

She paced nervously up and down her hotel room: it transpired that Hugo had spoken to his "counterpart" at Luxumi. That is, the employee who had been put in charge of the joint project by the development manager after the three-way meeting with Hursoc and Luxumi; the employee who had seldom responded to emails or phone calls because he was busy planning the PV unit in Croatia. Hugo had got round to calling him now, having previously put it off for more than half a year.

Alex's contact had been informed that the discussion was extremely aggressive. Hugo had demanded that the Vabilmo technology be implemented in Croatia, meeting protests that the project was already too far along with accusations of intransigence on the part of Luxumi. His argument was that Hursoc had committed to the polymer-based cells at short notice, so why couldn't they? He had gone on to describe the proposed project with the service vehicles as an impractical gimmick, at odds with PsoraCom's overall strategy.

It was an abomination! She could hardly believe her ears. What did Hugo think he was doing? Luxumi had ruled out the use of the Vabilmo cells for Croatia from the start, and despite repeated demands to the contrary, they hadn't once moved from this standpoint. Alex had just accepted it.

You couldn't force yourself on clients; being too forthright was likely to do more harm than good. That was picked up by most right-minded consultants during their initial training. It was another example of hammering away. Just like Carl and the biggest robot manufacturer, who, it seemed, he was still trying to win as a client. What had Hugo hoped to achieve? Not once had a colleague ever gone behind her back like this.

After the phone call, she needed to calm down somehow. She was so angry she threw a towel against the wall. In this mood, she could neither write up her call report from Valencia, nor make any other calls. She couldn't risk someone else having to serve as her punch bag. She just couldn't. One way or another, she needed to let off some steam. There was a choice between unhealthy and healthy. Either a few drinks and a pack of cigarettes in one of the little tapas bars nearby or some serious exercise.

She thought about it briefly, before deciding on a jog up to the mountain-top stadium. Writing call reports while under the influence wasn't really a practical solution. Her hotel was right next to the exhibition centre at the foot of Montjuic. Running would help ease her bitterness over Hugo's call and enable her to think clearly again. An hour later, exhausted and sweating all over, she was back. The more she had thought about what had happened, the faster she had run.

After a refreshing shower, still absolutely outraged, but with regained composure to a certain extent, she felt relatively capable of speaking objectively about Hugo's actions. At some point that evening she was bound to run into Thomas, as he was speaking at tomorrow's conference. A few hours later she glanced over her reports contentedly, satisfied that she had outlined the facts and agreed course of action in an objective manner.

The information that Luxumi were hoping to intensify their collaboration with Volcrea in order to become less dependent on Hursoc wouldn't be to George's taste. It was equally probable that it wouldn't do anything to improve relations as they stood. But she couldn't just sweep important information about the future development of the Vabilmo team under the carpet for the sake of keeping the peace. Especially since Bill had agreed with the development manager to increase their joint collaboration with Volcrea. All was not yet lost for Hursoc; but George's client would have to exert themselves more in the future.

Premve and Luxumi were two industry heavyweights, and they were sure to wield significant influence on future developments in the solar market, as well as making a lasting impression on the supplier structure. In addition, neither Roffarm nor Natioba were currently working with Hursoc, and there was no sign that this was set to change anytime soon. Taken together, these were the four most innovative companies in the European solar industry; there was only a Spanish company that was in anywhere near the same league. The rest of the business was spread out among lots of minor players, but they didn't have enough clout for Hursoc.

There were a few American and Asian companies as well, though the competition in China was considerably closer to success. Innovation, low-cost quality and efficiency; these were all factors which could help Hursoc reassert themselves on the market. For that to happen, however, a fundamental restructuring would need to take place within the company and Hursoc would have to trade in their illustrious status as market leader for a little more flexibility.

Alex had deliberately left Hugo's phone call out of her call report, saying only that new questions had arisen about the project with Luxumi. She wanted to speak to Thomas first and get his opinion on what she should do next.

The opportunity came after dinner, during which Alex had run into Christopher, as well as a few other colleagues from different departments. Her group was just moving into the hotel's atrium garden when she saw Thomas sitting at a table smoking his pipe. He signalled that she should join him.

"What happened with Luxumi, then?" he asked. "I've just had a quick look at your report. What questions have arisen?"

Alex came straight to the point.

"I learned from my contact that Hugo called his equivalent at Luxumi and told him we were only interested in large solar plants and off-grid systems. Supposedly, he described the project with the service vehicles as a gimmick."

"Aha." Thomas waited for her to continue.

"What's more, he's said to have become very aggressive about the PV unit in Croatia, which has Luxumi working flat out at the moment. Apparently, he described the fact that they couldn't use our cells because of time constraints as intransigence on their part. At least, that's what my contact there says."

While she was speaking, Thomas had furrowed his brow.

"Can you give me any reason why he would do something like that with my client?" she asked without hesitating. "Did he tell you about it or speak to you in advance? Did he mention anything about service vehicles in particular?"

"I can't make any sense of it at all," her boss shook his head. "I've got no idea why Hugo would claim mobile solutions aren't part of our strategy; or what's caused him to make these remarks."

"The service vehicle project is still in line with our current team strategy, then?" Alex probed.

"Yes, I mean I haven't heard anything to the contrary," he replied. "It'll all be clarified, Alex. I'll put it on the agenda for the next team meeting."

Relieved by what he had said, as good as a declaration of support in her eyes, she ordered a gin and tonic. Shortly afterwards, Thomas disappeared off to his room. Christopher had been looking over constantly.

"So, how are things with you," he joined her. "What are your divas up to?"

As usual, he couldn't resist pulling a face as he tilted his head and waited for a response.

"Ah yes, my divas. Things are a bit tricky with them actually. Mildly put, I think they're going to enormous lengths to take no notice of me or my work."

"What do you mean? What have they done now? Have things not sorted themselves out yet?"

"No, unfortunately not." She explained briefly what had happened.

"It's not about Hugo calling my client. I've been waiting for him to do that for more than half a year. No, what's annoying is that he wants to change course all of a sudden. There's been a plan in place for months, all approved by Thomas. Hugo should've spoken to me first. Or what do you think?"

"Of course he should," he agreed. "Assuming that you kept the team up-to-date on the project. Did you discuss your client strategy openly with the team? Including the role played by each individual client employee?"

"Not in detail," Alex replied. "But no-one does that. I met Brian one time last year so that we could compare client strategies. The conversation was very one-sided; we only talked about my clients. I never had another go after that. Brian began returning my calls less and less, and then at some point he just seemed to almost completely disappear. It's a good idea, though. Maybe I should do it for all my clients at one of our team meetings."

That was exactly what she liked about Christopher. Talking to him always gave her a fresh perspective or new ideas.

Before breakfast the next morning, Alex was dismayed to see how many mails had been sent overnight about Luxumi. Reading them over, she felt a real knot in her stomach.

George commented spitefully that the project was nothing more than a useless widget; Brian bemoaned the lack of a client strategy; while Hugo went one step further. He said he wasn't surprised that further questions had arisen: there was no account plan and the right people weren't at hand. None of them mentioned her explicitly by name, but everyone receiving the mails knew she was the consultant responsible for Luxumi.

In her view, her colleagues' reaction was tantamount to a declaration of war. The more she thought about it, the more it seemed like merely the continuation of what her colleagues had said during the I2Is: namely, that they didn't think the problem could be solved, and that she had better start looking for a new job.

She looked for Thomas in the breakfast room. He couldn't allow her colleagues to behave like this; something had to be done. But she couldn't find him. Frustrated, she realised she would have to wait until the Cellgot event was over.

The convention took place in the exhibition centre and began at exactly the same time as PsoraCom's press conference. Thomas's presentation was before the first coffee break – she'd be back by then. But there was no way she was going to miss the press conference. She had never experienced anything like it before, and at the end of the day, she wasn't just curious to learn how Volcrea's footage had turned out; she wanted to see how it was received as well.

Cellgot's head of marketing sympathised with her schedule and promised to save Alex a space next to him. She had been flattered by his attention in Geneva too; it seemed he was that rarest of beasts: a true gentleman. Realistically, however, she knew it was mostly down to the pre-eminence of the name on her company business card.

The press conference was held in front of the exhibition hall, in a vaulted antechamber. As always, the length, including time for questions, had been specified in advance. The sequence of press conferences, all of which were followed by a fifteen-minute break, had to be observed to the letter.

There were already two hundred people in the room, each person obliged to show ID on entry. Security paid special care to ensure that only media representatives or company employees were granted access, along with anyone else whose attendance had been authorised. Henry spotted her straightaway and whispered that there were more journalists present than he'd been expecting.

"The DVD's turned out brilliantly," he whispered enthusiastically. "Volcrea had some additional material we were able to put to good use. It's pretty cool; Wolfgang really liked it too."

He was clearly excited, though that was nothing new.

As the lights were dimmed, the room went quiet. Only a dull murmuring could still be heard.

A whole third of the half-hour press conference was devoted to Vabilmo. Just as Henry had said, the individual projects were introduced in chronological order, thus reflecting the company's progress. First Roffarm and Hursoc, followed by Natioba and Cellgot. Volcrea occupied more than half the time. Accompanied by the characteristic tones of "Eye of the Tiger", the movie was pretty lively, containing a graphic animation of the different possibilities offered by the bend-modules to go with its striking narration. Alex thought it was absolutely superb.

"See what I mean?" Henry hissed quietly, not without a certain amount of pride.

"Volcrea must have spent a good deal of money on 3-D software programs to get that much detail," she whispered in his ear. "You can even see Apircu's name clearly."

"It certainly won't have come cheap," her colleague said.

"I have to show this to Apircu," she replied enthusiastically. "They're the manufacturers, after all, the ones who Hank got the seed units from. They didn't even want anything for it."

Henry nodded and said: "When I think about what it cost us, and what we're getting in return, it almost brings a tear to my eye. Here's to our next project!"

On the way back to Cellgot, she called Apircu. As chance would have it, her contact was at the company stand in Barcelona and was naturally very interested in seeing the film. Henry had given her a copy, including a press kit, straight after the conference. Alex promised to come by when the convention was over.

She slipped into the seat that had been reserved for her just in time for Thomas's presentation. His slide set, which they had coordinated together a few weeks previously and supplemented with some of Alex's information, was good. But he didn't have the bend-modules; they would have aroused even greater interest.

During the coffee break, Alex noticed Brian, Carl and Hugo at the back of the room, seemingly about to leave. None of them gave her or Thomas so much as a second glance. They didn't bother to speak to anyone else either, even though there were a few prospective clients among the participants. Why had they been there at all? To appear on the list of participants? So that everyone who read the list – and Alex was sure that most people, like her, would – would find their names there? Inwardly shaking her head, she joined the small group that had formed around Thomas. She, at any rate, wasn't going to pass up the opportunity to make some new contacts. You never knew when they might come in handy.

"That's sensational," the man from Apircu cried, completely beside himself. "I've got to get a copy for our management. Can I keep the DVD for the time being?"

"Unfortunately not," Alex replied. "It's my original, but you're more than welcome to copy it onto your netbook – or I can send you a DVD tomorrow."

"Then I'll copy it now quickly. Our product manager from China is coming tomorrow. He has to see this. If you need any more seed units in the future, just let us know. We'd be glad to help out again."

Apircu had got a lot more out of the film than they had invested in the seed units. But the real credit had to go to Volcrea, who had done most of the work. PsoraCom had only made a small financial contribution, besides the hours Alex and Henry's technicians had put in. But in return, they were getting a fantastic marketing tool which could be used worldwide without restriction. How had Henry described it again? A sure thing.

She met Thomas in the airport lounge as agreed. They were both taking the same flight back. At last, Alex could speak to him about her colleagues' email responses, a topic that had been preying on her mind all day.

"It just isn't funny anymore," she began straightaway, all het up. "Behaviour like that is unacceptable. Even more so when you consider the mailing list the replies were distributed to. Since when has the project with Luxumi no longer been in line with the team strategy? What's your view on all this?"

"Take it easy," her boss replied. "The project is still part of the overall strategy; nothing's changed since yesterday evening. As far as I'm aware, at least. But I see now there's another issue that needs to be resolved."

"That's my view too! If you like," she suggested, "I'll go into more detail about the service vehicle project at the next team meeting, mention what the situation is with the solar plants and when we can expect new projects to emerge in that area. What do you think?"

"OK, that makes sense," he agreed. "It would be a good idea to prepare a few slides."

"They're done already; I have everything in my account plan. But I'd like Brian and George to provide an update on the state of play with their clients too. There have been absolutely no call reports about their last few meetings, nor any information via email. Do you know what's going on with their clients at the moment?"

"More or less. I'll let you know; an update certainly wouldn't hurt though."

Alex was very interested to learn what Brian had achieved these past six months. Like many in the office, she had noticed that very little had been seen or heard of him recently. She just hadn't said it out loud yet.

Back at home, the first thing Alex did was call her mother, whose PET scan was taking place the next day. The so-called Positron Emission Tomography exam was used to locate tumours.

"Hi, Mum. How are you?"

"Oh, you know, could be better. My stomach's really bad and I've been feeling awful all day."

"I don't blame you. It's a huge stress. The scan tomorrow won't be easy either."

Alex once had only had a computed tomography; she still had terrible memories of all the contrast agents she'd needed to drink.

"It's not so bad," her mother replied. "They inject you with a radioactive tracer these days, so you don't have to drink anything. It lasts a while, that's all. After the injection you have to rest for nearly an hour while the tracer spreads throughout your body. The scan itself lasts about another thirty minutes, though that depends. You have to go in on an empty stomach."

"Hopefully you won't have to wait as long as last time," Alex said. "I'll be thinking of you tomorrow afternoon, anyway; I'll make sure all my fingers and toes are crossed."

Ricka could really do with catching a break. Still, as long as they weren't sure what was wrong, there was no point agonising over it.

"Hope dies last", that's what her grandmother always used to say.

After the call, Alex just about had time to unpack her case and slip into something more comfortable. In her absence, Renata had decided they would cook together more often, beginning tonight. She thought it would be one way of ensuring they both ate healthily. Otherwise they would just grab a hotdog or something. The idea appealed to Alex, as she really enjoyed cooking – just not for herself. An hour later, she was sitting at her friend's house, stomach full, recounting the sights and sounds of the previous few days.

"Valencia was amazing and the client meetings went very well overall. There was a bit of a storm kicked up about one, which still needs to be dealt with internally. The shoot with Volcrea was fun, though."

"Could there be another reason for the glint in your eyes, I wonder? Is there something I should know?"

"Well, OK," Alex gave in, "I had a little thing with a very attractive colleague from the US."

"And? God, do I have to drag it out of you?"

Renata topped their glasses with red wine, a conspiratorial look in her eye. It wasn't until she had heard all the gory details that she gave a contented smile.

"In your shoes, I wouldn't have wasted any time faffing around in the hotel," she said frankly. "That's an opportunity missed. He's not married, is he?"

"Not that I'm aware. He didn't exactly seem like a notorious womaniser either."

"Well, then I understand you even less. I'd have made sure I really indulged myself."

Alex could well imagine it. Renata was a bit less inhibited about things like that; she enjoyed life to the full, without wasting any time worrying about the consequences. Sometimes Alex wished she could be like that too, but there was something in the deepest recesses of her mind that prevented it – and maybe that was a good thing.

"What are the chances you'll see him again?" her friend asked.

"Not bad actually," Alex reckoned. "His boss is here pretty regularly, so I'm sure he'll accompany him every now and then. Maybe I'll take a trip across the pond sometime too. I still don't have any idea where I'm going on vacation this year, or when."

"I've been thinking about taking a trip to Barcelona this summer," Renata told her. "That reminds me, how was it there?"

"Impressive. The film presentation went down really well. I have to show it to you - it turned out great. But things are getting a bit hairy with my colleagues. There were three of them there at the conference, but none of them so much as glanced at me. What's more, they're undermining my efforts with a particular client, as well as making use of our enormous mailing list to torpedo the project internally."

Her friend shook her head in disbelief.

"And what does your boss say about all this? Or is he still maintaining an elegant distance?"

"No, I've spoken to him and he wants to make it an issue. He agreed to my suggestion that I go through all my slides in detail at our next meeting. But I've also requested that my colleagues talk about their clients too. I've got no idea what they're working on. They don't ever write call reports or send status updates, let alone tell me what they're up to in meetings."

"Things are pretty weird with your guys at the moment," Renata voiced her surprise. "A little more leadership from your boss would be no bad thing. If he keeps on like this, your colleagues will do exactly as they please with him."

"I don't think things will get that far. The last time we spoke, he assured me that he'd resolve the problem. It'll all be fine."

But as soon as she uttered those words, Alex found herself wondering if she really believed them. What if she was just burying her head in the sand, in the hope that the storm would soon blow over?

16

April

A week after the trade show in Barcelona, Marco came to Alex and informed her that from now on he would be in charge not only of Premve, but of Natioba and Luxumi as well – an encompassing responsibility no-one had previously held.

That was fine by her, as she got on very well with him. She couldn't blame him for wanting to take on two additional clients. After all, they had some promising projects on the cards and she could do with the extra support. She was still happy to work twelve hours a day, though she knew it couldn't be sustained. In her last job, she had come within an inch of losing her hearing thanks to the stress, and she wasn't about to risk that a second time. After their conversation, Marco notified her colleagues of the change; there was no response forthcoming.

Alex entered the meeting room with a slightly queasy feeling. It was the first team meeting since Barcelona. She was the first there, and took her place on the long side of the horseshoe table. The meeting had already been cancelled twice, as everyone apart from her and Thomas had been away on client calls. According to the agenda, Emily would also be there to provide an update on the legal position with Roffarm.

Her colleagues arrived in dribs and drabs, each choosing a seat on the opposite side of the table; Emily was the only one to sit next to her. Thomas arrived last and looked around indecisively, before finally going over to the male side. No-one sat in the middle section. It was five against two, as if some unwritten rule from the Middle Ages dictated that men and women mixing together was a punishable offence.

Alex was glad that Emily at least had sat down on her side. Her colleague was an ally, even if she knew nothing about Alex's current situation. Whether it was down to said situation or just her outrageously short skirt, Alex wasn't sure. All she could say with any certainty was that her male colleagues were taking just as little notice of Emily as of her. Hugo was the sole exception, stealing a glance at Emily every now and then out of the corner of his eye. From a purely aesthetic point of view, she could have been his type – if he even knew himself what that was.

There had been further developments with Roffarm concerning the interpretation of the exclusivity clause, though neither party was quite ready to make an amendment to the existing contract in writing. The reason for this was the client's request that the contract be supplemented by a penalty clause, in case of a proven violation of the non-disclosure agreement.

A request like that was not uncommon in the industry. Besides a drop in revenue, there could also be a considerable loss of face if a competitor was the first to launch a new market product, despite another company having previously worked on it. It seemed strange, however, that this particular request hadn't been made until after the trouble with Natioba and, moreover, that Roffarm had directed it exclusively at PsoraCom.

Her superiors in Legal had tasked Emily with reviewing the situation internally. She had to clarify who from the team was involved and then assess the risk of information being passed unintentionally from one client to another. None of the lawyers had been so naive as to assume this could never happen. In such cases, however, it was necessary to build in a protective clause so that any careless or intentional contract violations on the part of PsoraCom would need to be proven.

From a sales point of view, there was only an extremely small risk of this happening, as the devil lay in the detail and depended entirely on the realisation of a project. For Emily, someone in Hugo's position posed a far greater danger. He was more than happy to deal with her questions, providing an extensive description of his activities with the client as well as the technical implementation of the team strategy, and peppering his discourse with all manner of complex specialist terminology. It seemed like he had learned a thing or two from George, who sat alongside signalling his agreement. The longer Hugo spoke, the fewer notes Emily took. Her facial expression, initially friendly, had become increasingly stony as the meeting progressed.

"So, Hugo," she summarised, eyebrows raised, "you say you're working internally with colleagues from the US on a kind of solar-module standard, based on the existing fluorescence collector architecture together with the Vabilmo technology. To be used especially in solar plants."

"Yes, that's correct," he confirmed. "We're about 90% ready; we're just missing a few details. Then we can publish the architecture as a reference and make it available to all solar plant, solar module and inverter manufacturers."

The pride in his voice was unmistakeable.

"Is that not very similar to the development at Roffarm?" Emily wanted to know.

"There is some overlap," he conceded. "But we've only been carrying out developments internally with this architecture."

"And who's responsible for it? Is it you?"

Alex had an inkling where her colleague was going with this.

"Yes, that's right."

"I'm certain it'll be clear from your detailed project notes," Emily continued, "that the structure itself, as well as the individual technical components, are the fruits of internal labour alone. How have you ensured that an idea developed in your joint meetings with Roffarm hasn't been used for the standard?"

"All the ideas are my own."

"No-one's doubting that. The point is, can you prove they were all developed internally, and independently of client meetings, if Roffarm were to ask?"

His previous self-confidence had given way to irritated silence. He glanced over to George for help, but he seemed to have recognised the problem as well and chose to keep quiet.

"We should set up a separate meeting and look over the whole thing carefully," Emily said, turning to Thomas. "I want to make sure we have watertight proof that we developed the standard on our own, without client input."

It was clear that Emily wasn't about to make an overt judgement. Nevertheless, Alex suspected that Hugo – and Thomas too, therefore – were both skating on very thin ice, as far as their working methods were concerned. Unless they had explicit proof that there had been no wrongdoing, PsoraCom would never agree to a penalty clause being added; given the current situation, it would only open the door to large compensation settlements. Without such an agreement, however, there was every prospect that negotiations would become increasingly protracted.

After an hour, Emily had to rush off to another meeting, and all of a sudden Alex felt completely lost. The meeting was scheduled to last four hours whereof she would have to survive the remaining three with a seemingly insurmountable distance separating her from the team. Even Thomas made no attempt to adopt a more neutral seating position after the break and bridge the gap between Alex and her colleagues.

She didn't receive a lot of attention from her colleagues as she went through her slides on Luxumi and provided a status update on the situation with their solar plants. It seemed Brian had important mails to answer. Hugo and George, meanwhile, spent the whole time whispering to each other; Alex only picked up snatches of their conversation: words such as "untenable" and "irrelevant".

Her boss asked her to clarify a few things but when that didn't generate any discussion either, he simply stopped. It wasn't until the final slide that George eventually weighed in. The slide displayed the possible revenue and numbers of solar cells required for the large grid-connected plant Luxumi were planning to build.

"That can't be right, not in a million years," he said. "You obviously haven't checked your figures with Hursoc. The unit in Croatia could generate half that revenue alone – and it's only about a third of the size."

She immediately stopped herself from asking where George's information had come from, as this could easily be misinterpreted as another attack on his competence. Her own figures had been calculated according to Luxumi's estimated performance, while also allowing for the internal price structure of the polymer-based cells.

Naturally, there was a degree of uncertainty in her projection, as there was no way of knowing how much the products would fetch on the market. The time scale was simply too great. However, it was anticipated that increased market presence would result in lower prices. Alex had therefore deducted a sum from the grand total: better to be conservative than speculative.

"There are, of course, certain unknowns," she conceded. "Let's compare the figures together with your client, George. We could also take the opportunity to assess the overall potential for grid-connected-plant manufacturers. Perhaps we could check where Hursoc have been hawking the Vabilmo technology, how high the potential success rate is and which companies we could target together with them."

"Yeah, we could do that," he replied. "I'll set up an appointment with you, but first I need to check my calendar. I'm up to my eyeballs at the moment."

He didn't seem to think much of her suggestion, and Alex wondered if the meeting would ever take place.

The next point on the agenda was the team strategy. Hugo was supposed to inform everyone of the latest technical developments and outline the consequences for the overall strategy.

First of all, he went into great detail about the individual developments relating to the planned standard. Many of the points mentioned were very technical. Alex only had a very limited understanding of what was being said, though once again she refrained from probing any deeper.

Hugo would never have believed she was doing it just out of interest. Brian's expression as he looked at the slides was completely blank. Either he was somewhere else entirely, or understood even less than she did. If his questions were anything to go by, it was probably the latter. Even so, in answering them, Hugo chose his words with a care that had been previously lacking.

George willingly supplemented some of his colleague's remarks without, however, interrupting in the usual manner. Miraculously, he seemed all of a sudden to have donned the kid gloves; and there was no sign of the traditional cockfighting between the two. Even Brian had slipped into his role without batting an eyelid: that of the good student, hanging on his favourite teacher's every word. Carl brought up the rear, completing the picture of harmony by nodding avidly in agreement.

Had her team been taken over by aliens? Alex could hardly believe it. In comparison with the previous year, the behaviour of her colleagues was so contrived. Unfortunately, it wasn't one of those awful cliché-soaked TV series where you could just change the channel; this was one she'd have to see through.

After she had resigned to her fate, the meeting took an unexpected turn. Hugo was presenting his findings and their impact upon the team strategy. He was unveiling the NEW team strategy. There had been no emails, no discussion about it in advance. The different points had been neither debated nor agreed upon. Alex hadn't received any information, and neither, by the look of him, had Thomas.

The crux of the new strategy was that mobile solutions which couldn't be categorically seen as robots were impractical and thus excluded. Alex looked at Thomas, shocked. His gaze was devoid of any emotion. If this new direction was approved, it would render all of her current projects invalid in one fell swoop.

Hugo concluded his remarks.

"We have to increase our focus," George offered his support straightaway. "We can't allow ourselves to get distracted by trivialities. Our goal is for the Vabilmo technology to be built into every large solar plant in the future. At the same time, we need to win over the leading robot manufacturers."

"That's my view too," Brian joined in.

"Mine too," even Jen's voice could be heard now.

Thomas remained silent, impassive as before.

For Alex, it was all very reminiscent of how things were done in Japan, where every decision was made beforehand and the meeting itself was a mere formality. Her head was spinning. There was still a very small chance that the Premve project could be taken on by Robotics. Strictly speaking, of course, they weren't dealing with assisting devices there but machines that performed robot-like duties. There was also the fact that an internal project manager had yet to be named. If, despite Bill's approval, there was no support forthcoming from his department, her argument would be scuppered immediately.

Things were different with Luxumi. According to the new definition, the project was clearly no longer in line with the team strategy. Alex would have to inform her clients that PsoraCom's involvement was at an end. That would be more than embarrassing, as she had laid the groundwork at the end of last year and already informed the partner companies. That Bill had recently persuaded the development manager to enter into a joint collaboration with Volcrea would only exacerbate things further. She couldn't help thinking of the commotion caused by Hugo's questionable behaviour over the phone. If they were to suddenly can the project of their own accord, it might seem like PsoraCom had no idea what they wanted.

Naturally, internal circumstances were always shifting and targets constantly being adjusted. But Alex couldn't think of a single good reason for her colleagues' change of heart. In her opinion, the potential of projects with companies like Luxumi or Premve couldn't be ignored. Admittedly, the amount of cells used by the individual service vehicles was pretty small; if the whole fleet was taken into account, however, the revenue generated could be considerable. The question of a standardised design, which would significantly reduce development costs, was one that deserved serious reflection.

In fact, the more she thought about it, the less sense this strategic about-turn made. With some frustration, she realised it was only her clients that stood to be affected. Brian either didn't have any or wasn't particularly concerned about losing them. He had blithely declared himself in favour of the change at any rate – as had Carl. George was only interested in Hursoc and, as so often, Hugo seemed to take his lead from him. With the renewed focus, there was even a question mark hanging over their work with Volcrea, a pledge made by Bill in Valencia, independently of end customers such as Luxumi. Things weren't looking good at all.

They weren't looking great for Ricka either. Alex called her straight after work.

"How are you? How did the scan go today?"

"Not too well," her mother replied. "I feel awful; I haven't been able to eat the whole day. First I had to wait two hours before they injected the tracer. After that, I had to lie down for an hour and wait for it to take effect. That stretched out for considerably longer; then there was the scan itself."

"Oh, you poor thing. I'd be feeling awful too. Were the doctors able to give you an initial prognosis after the scan?"

"Yes, I got a report from them."

"And what does it say?"

The more she had to extract the information from her mother, the greater her fear that the news wasn't good.

"We can talk about it when you're next here, Alex. That way, you can read the report too."

"No, Mum! Let's talk about it now. Tell me what's wrong, I want to know. I'll read through the report later."

There was a deep sigh at the other end of the line. It was obviously difficult for Ricka to talk about. She probably hadn't processed it herself yet.

"They found two new tumours, as feared. In the lung."

Alex swallowed hard.

"What do the doctors say? What treatment have they suggested?"

"They've ruled out surgery for the moment," her mother told her, "as the tumours are too big. Before they can perform any sort of operation, there'll be a course of chemotherapy to shrink them. Radiotherapy's a possibility as well, but that only kills the tumour's growth; it doesn't remove them. That could lead to some pretty serious long-term consequences, and the chances of recovery aren't great. For now, the best solution looks like chemo followed by an operation."

That was another thing with this disease. Even when it was discovered at a treatable stage, there was no guarantee of a cure. It all depended on how the patient responded to the therapy; if the drugs took effect; then whether the growth of the cancerous cells was blocked or even reversed altogether. But nothing was certain.

"How long does the chemo last, then?"

"That depends. One treatment unit lasts six weeks. After that, a CT scan determines if the chemo's had any effect. There can be as many as six individual treatment units. At the moment, they can't say how many I'll need. After each unit, the results are presented to the presiding doctors, who decide if and when to operate."

There it was again, Mother Nature's unpredictable game of chance, leaving everyone helpless in its wake.

That was exactly the feeling that overcame Alex after she had been so hopeful of Ricka's chances. What if the treatment didn't work? If they couldn't operate? How much time would they have left? Alex was choked with sadness. First she lost her partner, then the time bomb at work and now this. Everything weighed so heavily on her that she was powerless to halt the depressive spiral of her thoughts.

Was there any hope for her mother? Would she ever see her daughter get married? If not, who would be responsible for the flowers? No-one else would be able to arrange them so lovingly. Would she meet her grandchildren, if Alex managed to find someone who shared her dreams for the future? Would Ricka be there to provide moral support at the birth? Whose advice could she seek when the little one was sick? Who would know which natural remedies worked best against common complaints? Who, if not her mother?

The longer Alex thought about these things, the deeper she plunged into the abyss. The tears streamed down her face, but she didn't make the slightest effort to stem the tide. She couldn't take it in the flat anymore. She had to get out, and began walking aimlessly through the village. It was dark already. There was no-one else about – hardly surprising given the weather. It was cold and drizzly.

After the first op, the doctors had been so positive; it was like winning the lottery, they had said. How could everything have changed so quickly? And why Ricka? She was still so young. She had eaten well her whole life, didn't smoke, and drank only the odd glass of wine. How could someone like that get cancer? And how much longer would this deadly disease give her? Years? Months? She kept coming back to the same thought; a vision of a wedding reception, the bride weeping uncontrollably.

And all of a sudden, she felt shabby. Hoping her mother would be at her wedding, in some remote future. How could she be so selfish? She wasn't the one who had to deal with chemo and its side effects, or go under the knife for a risky procedure; to say nothing of the drawn-out recovery process. Since when had she become so self-absorbed?

Carl called the next day.

"Can I get the Volcrea DVD off you?" he asked. "I want to show it to Apircu so they get an idea of what their modules can do."

Alex could hardly believe her ears. Originally, he was supposed to have been involved; it had been his job to get the seed units from Apircu. However, he had baled once he had discovered that Brian and George were vehemently opposed to the project. In the end, he hadn't even helped her with the seed units. Hank had got them and passed her directly on to his Apircu contact. Now, after the work had been done, the support of a high-profile manager secured and the whole thing unveiled to the public, Carl wanted back in so that he could raise his profile with the client. Just like that, without any qualms. But he was too late; he should've been quicker off the mark.

"Sorry, Carl, you should have told me sooner. I already showed it to Apircu in Barcelona, just after I got the copy. The opportunity was there."

"You might have realised that I would want to show it to them myself. They're my client, after all," he replied angrily.

"I had no idea you were still interested in the project. You never replied to any of my emails about the project status."

Alex didn't feel any particular need to justify herself. He really should have got in touch earlier. She thought he was being distinctly opportunistic. Even so, it was sure to provide her colleagues fresh ammunition. Yet again, she had taken things into her own hands, directly approaching a partner company that Carl was responsible for in

Europe. She could just imagine George and Brian railing about it. But thoughts like that wouldn't get her anywhere and would only spread negative energy. There were other things she needed to concentrate on.

There was still no project manager for Premve. Bill had been stalling them ever since Valencia. Since the project appeared to be neither one thing nor the other, it wasn't clear whether the revenue generated would be credited to Bill's department or Robotics, so he had decided to take it to the highest level. A decision also needed to be made on who carried overall responsibility for the Vabilmo technology on product-related issues.

A CDC had thus been called. At a Chief Decision Council, all vertical and horizontal department chiefs convened to establish the basic conditions for dedicated procedures. The decision would naturally impact upon the relevant section of Robotics, perhaps resulting in its dissolution and integration into Bill's department. Equally, the CDC could freeze an internal project, or bury it completely.

At PsoraCom, anything was possible. The latter option was extremely unlikely, however. More information was needed for such a radical step, particularly when the data available pointed to significant growth potential. It was more likely that the timeframe would be the sticking point, as they didn't anticipate breaking even for another three years.

Bill called Alex and told her he had received some unexpected support from the sales chief during the CDC.

"The meetings he had in Germany last year were still fresh in his mind. It almost seems like he has just as much influence on the company's future development as the CEO himself. Despite the naysayers, who still see Vabilmo as a dead-end and associate it primarily with the Roffarm contract, the technology was given the company's overall backing."

Alex listened with relief, as he continued.

"There's no question that one of the decisive factors was the projected revenue from Hursoc and the companies specialising in household robots. They must have waved a few million dollar signs in front of the CEO. I conference-called Wolfgang in so he could explain the figures."

Not the first time Alex was astonished by how free and easy PsoraCom were with their revenue forecasts. The only thing that compared was politics; during economic crises, billions of taxpayers' money was used just as unashamedly to award credit, even when there was little chance of a return. Sometimes it really did seem like there was a whole class of people who had simply lost touch with financial reality. Alex had tried over and over again in team meetings to make the forecasts more realistic and include risk calculations. Her suggestions had always fallen on deaf ears. She discovered from Bill that Wolfgang had taken her colleagues' figures and rounded them up! He didn't seem to realise how much he was putting his own neck on the line.

As with any high-tech company on the stock exchange, PsoraCom's CEO found himself under enormous pressure from shareholders. If the projected figures were to be believed, within a few years Vabilmo alone would increase company turnover by over 30%, thus giving the CEO the chance to significantly increase PsoraCom's stock price value. Of course, he had wanted to believe Wolfgang; and so had approved the Vabilmo technology until further notice. In addition, it was decided that Bill's department would be in overall charge of product-related issues, meaning that any revenue generated would be credited to his account. The only exception was traditional household robots, though their limited prospects ensured they were of little interest to Bill anyway.

Despite being highly critical of the revenue forecast, Alex took care not to share her views with him. The decision meant that the project with Premve had been clearly assigned to his department.

Still, that didn't mean Alex's problem was solved. It wasn't only behind the scenes that George and Hugo were drumming up opposition to the service vehicles; their written correspondence established Hursoc, Roffarm and Brian's clients alone as the most likely revenue generators. Bill knew nothing of the internal squabbles and was understandably taken aback by the mixed signals he was receiving from Alex's team regarding Premve. He requested that Wolfgang and Thomas clarify the matter.

Alex was more than frustrated. Were her colleagues concerned that she would exploit her relationship with management again? A few months ago, they had been enthusiastic about the project. Everyone had been happy about Bill's involvement. But now everything was different and the project was seen as a threat to business with Hursoc.

Thomas really ought to have given George a good hiding; he was insisting more than ever that his client be involved in all projects with end customers. If a project was being undertaken with Premve, then Hursoc had to be there, too.

"George's argument is that his client should do most of the work," Alex explained to Thomas in their monthly jour fixe. "But that's precisely what Premve don't want. We've talked about it so many times. First, they're no longer convinced by Hursoc's performance and second, they don't want them obtaining information that gives them a decisive edge over competitors. Premve are interested in a standard which encompasses all end customers. That's why they're looking for a neutral partner to implement it. In their eyes, we're neutral; Hursoc aren't."

Thomas had avoided Alex's gaze the whole meeting. "I think that's for your client to decide," he said vaguely.

"But they did that long ago," she replied in frustration. That was what she'd just been saying.

"Hursoc are a direct client," her boss made his position clear. "It's important for the team that a plant manufacturer gets into bed with them. I don't mind which manufacturer that is. But with our current team situation, we can't afford to be too picky."

Reading between the lines, his message was pretty categorical.

"What about Brian's clients?" she probed. "It could just as easily be one of them. There are sure to be companies he can approach together with Hursoc."

So far, George hadn't been able to find an end customer for Hursoc. Roffarm seemed just as reluctant to take the bait.

"That doesn't apply here," her boss dodged the question.

Apparently not. Apparently, her client represented the only option. Even when Premve had a very different view of things; one, moreover, that didn't conflict with PsoraCom's interests. But that seemed to have been overshadowed by political concerns.

"You just have to persuade Premve to bring Hursoc on board," Thomas said.

It was hard for her not to get angry. There was no point; her boss was about to add insult to injury.

"As you can see, not a lot's changed since February. Your colleagues are still keeping their distance and things don't seem to have calmed down yet. That's why I suggest you admit defeat with Luxumi."

Alex swallowed hard. "I don't think I'm quite sure what you mean," she said hesitantly.

"In the next team meeting, I'd like you to discuss how things currently stand with Luxumi and ask your colleagues for advice on how best to proceed."

To her that sounded like an absolute cop-out. It would be a tacit admission that she didn't know what to do next with her client and had had no real plan to start with. That was asking too much, damn it.

"Do you not think that's going a bit above and beyond?"

Thomas shrugged his shoulders casually.

"I don't see any other option. I've already had meetings about your clients with the rest of the team. It's the only way to bring everyone back together."

It just got better and better. Her colleagues were inviting her boss to meetings in order to specifically discuss her clients? She hadn't known anything about it, hadn't received a single piece of information.

She thought about it briefly and took a deep breath.

"If you think it'll help get things back on track, then I'll do it. But I expect the rest of them to discuss all options in a constructive manner. PsoraCom doesn't gain anything by safeguarding the interests of one or two employees. Things can't just be about Hursoc – especially since Bill wants to keep working with Volcrea."

"Fine," Thomas seemed satisfied.

"But if it doesn't work," she added, "then the big guns need to be brought out. What they're doing is nothing short of mobbing. And it shouldn't be tolerated!"

It was the first time Alex had said the word out loud. But the knowledge that people were discussing her clients behind her back had infuriated her.

Thomas gave an almost imperceptible wince but didn't say anything more about it. Alex let what she had said hang in the air briefly, before changing topic.

"Henry's asked for my help on something," she said. "There's a field test for autonomous vehicles taking place in Greece in June. The university responsible wrote to Henry asking if PsoraCom would fit the cells. Wolfgang's already approved it."

"OK, and what exactly would we be doing there?" Thomas asked, without any particular interest.

"Since the field test is of no great importance and isn't even on most of our clients' radars, I would keep our involvement down to a minimum. We could bring Volcrea on board, as they've got a large office in Greece. They could do most of the fitting. Henry's got a small budget. The only thing they'd need from us would be the seed units and some help with questions on Vabilmo in general."

"The team won't be very happy about it," he said. "I can tell you that much now. But if Wolfgang wants it and the only thing it costs is time, then we'll support it. You'll act as the main interface between Henry, the university and Volcrea. Get Carl to help you with the seed units."

She would have done that anyway, assuming Carl was willing. But that was sure to depend on what the others thought and how much influence they had on him.

Alex stood up to leave. She didn't have anything else to discuss.

"I've got the results of your peer feedback here," he mentioned, almost in passing. As if he wanted to get it over with as soon as possible, without any real questions coming up. He tossed a few sheets across the table.

"The first one's your assessment; take it home and read it over in peace. The second sheet contains details of your salary raise, which has been calculated based on the peer feedback. The other two are copies, which you need to sign as confirmation of receipt."

She wasn't about to sign something she hadn't read. The assessment wasn't too bad at all, she thought to herself, as she glanced over it briefly. Her responsibilities at PsoraCom were outlined. This was followed by a list of achievements, which didn't take only her work with Natioba, Luxumi, Premve and Volcrea into account. Her regency, as well as the assistance she had provided in London and her presentation at Cellgot's in-house conference were all mentioned in glowing terms. Descriptions like "always professional" and "receives outstanding feedback" were accompanied in the attached summary of her strengths by the phrases "settled in very quickly", "independent and focused work" and "extraordinarily adept at building solid internal and external contact networks".

To finish, her character was described as "well organised, very motivated and reliable". The fact that she was always "ready to take on responsibility" and "meeting her commitments" hadn't gone unnoticed either, nor had her ability to "quickly adapt to changes". Overall, it read very well. Up until the point where her weaknesses were listed and the overall assessment provided.

It was urgently recommended that she "work on her communication skills"; her ability to operate as part of a team was specifically called into question.

So the whole fiasco had found its way in after all. Alex could hardly imagine that Henry, Lisa or Hank had given such an assessment. If so, they were extremely two-faced. That seemed more than unlikely. The comment could only have come from Brian.

Still, she wondered how a single comment could possibly be more important than the rest of the evaluation put together: her overall rating lay somewhere in the middle. Admittedly, she had been described as "successful" but based on PsoraCom's in-house system, that was only equivalent to a "C". Since Alex had achieved her quarterly set objectives to more than 125% in each instance, she assumed she would have at least "surpassed expectations", which corresponded to a "B".

"I don't quite understand," she said, irritated by the obvious contradiction.

Thomas had assured her two months ago that the situation with her colleagues wouldn't impact upon the peer feedback. It seemed he had hoped to conclude the matter without further questions; but Alex wasn't about to do him that favour. Ultimately, it was about the bare financials too, as the percentage increase in her salary was determined by the overall assessment. And in her eyes, the raise had been negligible.

"I never said that we wouldn't take your colleagues' complaints into account. There's no way round it: one of the criteria is the working environment – and that's something every employee contributes to."

This remark was in direct contrast to his earlier statement, with which even Wolfgang himself had agreed.

"Who disputed my ability to work as part of team?" Alex wanted to know.

Unfortunately, she wouldn't get to see the individual reports written by Henry, Lisa, Hank and Brian.

"I'm sure you can work that one out yourself," Thomas replied.

"How is it that one negative assessment so comprehensively trumps three that are positive?"

"Because the working environment is an important criterion."

"But I still don't quite get it. I've surpassed all my set objectives; and on one occasion I even helped you and Wolfgang out. We reduced my percentage from 150% to 125% so that Wolfgang wouldn't have to bat off any tricky questions."

No comment was forthcoming from her boss.

"And where does what I think come into it? After all, my working environment has been affected too. I'd even go as far as to describe my colleagues' conduct as hostile. Has that been taken into account?"

Somewhere along the line, fairness had fallen by the wayside – and that was before her salary raise was even taken into account.

But Thomas seemed to just want to bring the matter to a close.

"It is what it is," he said. "We can't change it now. Not unless you want to speak to someone from European Management?"

Alex gave in and signed the papers, even if she hardly felt good doing it. Wolfgang had obviously also approved the assessment. The cards had been reshuffled commencing a new game, where the support that Wolfgang and Thomas had promised her only weeks ago no longer seemed so assured. Perhaps her fear that she'd draw the short straw for political reasons would prove well-founded. She hoped not. But how realistic a hope was it?

Dejected, she reluctantly went to see Marco to tell him about the change of plan with Premve. Instead of unveiling the new project leader to their client after months of stalling, they were now performing a total U-turn. Marco wasn't impressed either.

"George always has to get his own way, doesn't he? It seems like your boss doesn't have the guts to tell him what for. The project make-up's been known for months. Why the change all of a sudden?"

Alex couldn't give an honest answer without telling him what was going on with her colleagues – and she didn't want that.

"Well, I suppose Hursoc represent the most likely chance of generating revenue with the Vabilmo technology," she replied. "There are probably senior figures within the company who have certain expectations about what we achieve as a team."

It took a great deal of effort for her to be so diplomatic.

As expected, Premve weren't exactly thrilled by the faint signals they could read in-between the lines. The argument that involving Hursoc would ensure the project was implemented considerably sooner, thus increasing the benefit for both sides, didn't go down too well.

Alex thought it was pretty lame too. But she hadn't been able to think of anything better. She could only hope that neither she nor the company would come across as completely incompetent after all the to-ing and fro-ing with the project leader. Premve asked for time to consider their options. The ball was in their court now; but somehow Alex no longer felt so good about the project when she hung up.

"Hey, if it isn't the Vabilmo team's token female. How's the state of the union?"

With his cheery manner, Christopher always managed to at least raise a smile from her.

"Yeah, well, it could be better."

"Come on, let's go for a coffee," he suggested. "I've got a few minutes before my next phone conference and could do with a little break. The Yanks want every last bit of data on thousands of different Excel sheets."

Alex told him briefly about the assessment and her grading.

"That surprises me," he said. "At the start of the year they asked me if I had any suggestions for the internal employee achievement award. It's given every six months to someone from the German sales and consultancy team. I put your name forward for your work on the Natioba project, as it caused quite a stir internationally."

"And? It's the first I've heard about it."

"Wolfgang thought it was a great idea to begin with, but then he changed his mind and removed your name from the list. Thomas was completely indifferent to the whole thing and would've gone with whatever Wolfgang decided. From what I gather, George and a few others are going to get it now for their work with Hursoc. But you didn't hear that from me."

"Hear what?"

Alex wondered if it was sometimes better not to know certain things; that way, you'd never be disappointed.

"This beats everything!" Franz gave full rein to his displeasure. "I can clearly remember you telling me that both your boss and this reprobate of a managing director were going to keep it out of the assessment. Now all of a sudden, it's not possible and they never said so in the first place."

He was sitting with Ricka next to the phone loudspeaker as Alex read her assessment aloud and told them about the meeting.

"The salary raise is a joke; after all you've done for the company." Even her mother, who normally didn't get involved in matters of business, was outraged.

"When I asked him how many other people had managed to get a flagship project like Natioba off the ground within such a short space of time, my boss just said "oh a few". Then when I probed a little further, he couldn't give me any concrete examples. I mean, that's pretty strange."

"Very strange," her father agreed.

"And the stuff about the award," Alex continued. "That's more than odd as well. I suppose they could still change their minds, or maybe my boss's colleague isn't up to speed. But it'd surprise me if George got it, since there's no concrete project I'm aware of."

"You might have lost a battle with the assessment," Franz ruminated. "But that doesn't mean you can't win the war. Don't let things get you down; you need to grab the managing director and this boss of yours by the scruff of the neck."

That was precisely what Alex intended to do. She certainly wasn't about to lie down without a fight. The question was how to go about it.

17

May

Even admitting defeat with Luxumi didn't seem to achieve a great deal. Her colleagues just sat there whining, before eventually coming to the decision that a joint workshop needed to be arranged with Luxumi's marketing and development department. Brian, George and Hugo were to take part.

The plan was to make Marketing so hot for the new products that they urged their own developers to switch to the Vabilmo technology for the PV unit in Croatia. Any objections on the part of the developers would be rendered null and void by the modules Hursoc supposedly had up their sleeve. It was a method Alex would never have condoned under normal circumstances. She had been completely unaware that the sleeves of George's client were hiding anything other than sketches and prototypes.

In her opinion, her colleagues were being extremely presumptuous. Her carefully phrased objection that Luxumi would have invested considerable brainpower in drawing up their schedule was met only with stiff resistance, while her boss offered no support whatsoever. It looked like there was nothing left for it but to arrange the workshop. Maybe her colleagues would finally believe her when they heard it from the horse's mouth.

Alex was sitting at Renata's enjoying a glass of wine after dinner when her Zeus68 rang.

"Hey, Alex, is this a bad time? It must be nine o'clock in Germany." It was Chris; he was calling from Natioba's New York office.

"No problem, Chris. You can call me anytime. As long as you know I'm normally sitting on the sofa with a glass of wine by now."

Chris laughed.

"You're the best. So, enjoy the wine. Listen, I'm calling because we've just had an internal meeting and a project's been approved. It involves us building 1000 greenhouses in Mongolia. I'd like to work with you again, if you're interested. Our aim is to collect and analyse data spread out across the whole year, then use it as the basis for the global series launch."

Her hands had already begun to sweat. Fitting 1000 greenhouses with Vabilmo technology was no mini-project; this was something bigger altogether.

"Of course I'm interested," she replied, as calmly as possible.

"I thought you would be," he said. "We're going to produce the solar modules together with our design department. The quantity means their short run capability will be stretched a bit. So, we'd need solar cells from you, as well as your assistance with any technical questions. Once the project's underway, I'm sure we can discuss the appropriate marketing strategy to inform the outside world of our joint efforts."

It was getting better and better. With their appearance in Taipei, it seemed like Natioba had found some enthusiastic support.

"Can you mail me the information so I can distribute it in-house?" she asked. "The decision isn't mine alone; we need the approval of the product division. They'll supply the seed units and technical support."

"I'll send you all the key data by tomorrow," he promised. "Is it still Hank and his team in charge?"

"We've had a bit of an internal reshuffle. It's Bill's department now – you met him briefly in Taipei. Hank and his team will be focusing more on household robots."

"OK, Alex. I'll send you everything. Have a glass of wine for me too! And thanks for getting stuck in."

"No problem: with offers like that, you can call me anytime."

She'd have an extra glass of wine for him, he could be sure of that. The news had to be celebrated. If the project really turned out the way Chris had just described, it could put Roffarm's work in the shade. Despite a year's head start, the latter were still fiddling around with prototypes and keeping quiet on further developments; not providing any details about whether and how soon they might be able to implement the technology.

Natioba could give them a real kick up the backside and steal their thunder if they were to unveil another project in public. Roffarm might have to be forced to go with PsoraCom. Any competition for the role of most innovative company was good and benefited all parties.

"So, what are we celebrating?" Renata asked. "Have they finally carpeted those mobbing colleagues of yours?" Her friend laid the dishtowel to one side and topped their glasses up.

"That'd be nice. No, that was my favourite client. They want to do another project with us; it sounds very promising and could be extremely lucrative in the long run."

Against the backdrop of her dissenting colleagues, a little success like this could be just what Alex needed. It not only helped safeguard her position; it validated her work. A soothing tonic for her shattered peace of mind.

The next morning, there was an email from Chris as promised. It contained a detailed outline of how many solar modules were to be built, based on the different container sizes, and an initial estimate of the number of polymer-based cells required. There was also a detailed timeline, marking when the greenhouses would be built and the different vegetables that would be grown. In addition, certain organisational aspects were mentioned, such as when the project would be unveiled to the public and at what point they expected the first data analysis to take place. That would denote the earliest possible time a decision could be made on whether to go ahead with a series launch.

As usual, she admired the élan and passion that Chris had for his job. It was something they both shared – and no doubt one of the reasons they got on so well. The email contained all the important information Alex needed for an internal decision to be made. As a result, she was able to rapidly compose a circular, which she then distributed to all her colleagues, including Thomas, Wolfgang and Bill, as well as Nobu, Hank and Henry. To supplement the client data, she also attached the relevant company figures and a conservative revenue forecast.

Christopher had drummed into her time and time again that it was all about the facts and figures at PsoraCom, irrespective of the decision that needed to be made. Given the possible revenue and relatively brief timeframe, Alex was certain there would be nothing standing in the way of a green light. The likelihood of a reasonably prompt payback would surely appease even her colleagues, as it would benefit the entire team if proof could be provided internally with customer contracts. That's what Alex hoped, at least, even if her optimism bordered on the naive given their last meeting.

Alex's hope for a drastic change in the team dynamics was dealt another blow. Her colleagues' reactions were anything but positive. As usual, George was the first to express an opinion, shooting the new project down completely. It was ridiculous, he said, that a plant manufacturer – and one specialising in off-grid systems at that – should even attempt such a project without the aid of a recognised solar module and inverter company. In his opinion, the project was doomed to failure from the outset, as they were bound to "cock it up" somehow. Hursoc would be a much better choice but since Natioba didn't want to work with them, the project would be a total waste of PsoraCom's time. Brian was next to chime in, describing the idea as pie in the sky; a project for the kids from R&D to invest their toy money in. Then, equally predictably: Hugo agreed with George, and Thomas refrained from making a comment.

Her frustration reached new heights. She had a creeping sensation she was missing something. Developments taking place in the background; invisible threads that someone was spinning, waiting for her to trip over; encrypted signals being sent that she had no code book for to decipher. Her old projects had been upended and new suggestions were being torpedoed immediately. She could no longer rely on the support of her boss. He had intervened only once, when her colleagues tried to veto the field test in Greece. At least then he had explained that the idea was Henry's – and that Wolfgang had approved the request for assistance. Only under a great deal of protest had her colleagues let the issue slide.

Still, all in all, she got the impression that she was gradually being taken out of the loop. The few mails she received from her colleagues were very general: newspaper articles or the like. She hadn't obtained a status update about Brian's clients for months, let alone any information about scheduled projects. Since she had started at PsoraCom, there hadn't been one single project undertaken with his clients. Even Wolfgang seemed to be discreetly distancing himself from the whole thing.

That evening, utterly dejected, she called her parents.

"If I was in your shoes," her father said angrily, "I'd send the managing director a very forthright email. Things can't go on like this."

"It's my boss who needs to put his foot down," she replied.

"Yes, but he seems to have a backbone made of jelly," her mother countered.

Although she had liked him at first, in the last few months Ricka's opinion of Thomas had undergone a fundamental change. It was strange. Despite having far more serious things to contend with, she seemed much more interested in Alex's situation at work. The whole thing seemed to provide a distraction from her miserable diagnosis and the debilitating effects of chemo. It was just the same for Alex: in comparison with her mother's illness, her own problems were almost completely insignificant. That was something she tried to keep in mind at all times.

"I'd go straight to this Wolfgang," Franz suggested. "In his position, he can't simply be willing to accept what's happening. It makes an absolute fool of him. At the end of the day, mobbing reflects badly on him. He's the guy running the show after all."

He was right, of course, but Alex didn't want to just go over her boss's head. Before she approached Wolfgang, she needed to talk things over with Thomas. But maybe she was too peace-loving.

"I'll have a little think about how you could write a mail like that," her father continued. "Then I'll send you my ideas. Things can't go on like this, anyway. It sounds like an absolute circus there at the moment and there's no way that can be good for business."

Hearing the indignation in his voice had done her the world of good, as had Ricka's reinforcement; It was something she'd been in dire need of.

As expected, Premve had absolutely no intention of bringing Hursoc on board for the service vehicle project. The development manager from Seoul had requested that Alex give a clear indication of whether PsoraCom would support the project or not.

Nothing had changed from his end. They wanted to develop the specification for a generic inverter that could also function as an alternating-current converter, thus paving the way for an industry-wide standard that would offer them greater independence from manufacturers such as Hursoc. Alex knew this strategy was also in the interests of Natioba and Luxumi, though she couldn't tell Premve that at this precise moment.

The only thing certain was that a decision needed to be made. She was tired of all this and didn't want to stall her client for months on end again, so she arranged a meeting with Thomas right away. It was up to him to say what was what. If her colleagues still weren't prepared to offer their support for the project after such a clear statement from the client, Bill wouldn't assign them a department employee; of that much she was sure. With that, the project would be upended once and for all. There was no point reproaching Bill for it. How was he supposed to know about the internal squabbling that was responsible for all these mixed signals?

At the weekend, Alex spoke to her sister for a long time on the phone; Jenny was extremely concerned about Ricka. The chemo had produced some severe side-effects and was eating away at their mother's strength.

"There's no way you could have known last year," Alex tried to calm her. "None of us could have known that this awful illness would strike again. Going to Hong Kong was the right decision."

She could understand the guilty conscience but it wasn't helping anyone.

"If something were to happen," her sister said, "it's not like I could just fly over for the weekend."

"We shouldn't be assuming the worst, Jenny. Everything'll be OK. If all else fails, we'll find a solution. Don't make yourself crazy over there. You've got to live your own life, and both your studies and your job are extremely important right now. Mum is so proud of you! Precisely because you had the guts to go there alone and do your MBA."

Jenny didn't want to just chuck everything in; that wasn't in her nature. But she also couldn't exactly hop in a car and drive home from Hong Kong. At least she had applied for some leave in the summer and would be back in July for a few weeks. For now, though, she needed to concentrate on her exams.

"There wouldn't be much you could do if were here, you know, except talking to her and being by her side. OK, so you could do the washing or vacuuming but that's hardly going to help you get your MBA."

"You're right, Alex. But sometimes I just feel so crummy. Especially after we've just spoken or chatted online. She really loves hearing about it all. At least I can look after her when I'm home in the summer, I suppose."

"Exactly! In the meantime, you just concentrate on your exams and exploring the city. You never know when you might get another chance."

In her next jour fixe with Thomas, she came straight to the point.

"Things can't go on like this. You must have seen the responses to the email about Natioba."

"Yes, I've read them," he confirmed.

"The way they're conducting themselves can't be in the interests of the company; it's time something was done about it. I did as you asked and admitted defeat with Luxumi but that didn't help. My colleagues aren't prepared to make even the slightest compromise where I'm concerned, and I don't see why I should be forced to bow to their demands. You have to take some serious action."

She looked at Thomas insistently and was amazed to discover that he was shaking like a leaf. His hands shook so violently he had to press them on the table to quell the trembling.

"Alex, listen," he said, pausing briefly to swallow. "I have to take you off the team."

"Excuse me?"

"It's the only way," he continued, gaze lowered. "You can see yourself it's not working. The team's still avoiding you. You can see it in the meetings when everyone sits as far away from you as possible. I thought we could resolve the situation, but there's no other way. I have to take you off the team."

He looked at her momentarily before diverting his eyes back towards the table. His voice sounded dry and husky.

Alex was shocked. She hadn't been expecting this. Neither of them said a word, while she tried to process what he had just told her.

"And how did you come to this decision?" she asked in disbelief.

Without looking up, her boss explained.

"There was a meeting between Wolfgang, Brian and myself. Brian arranged it. He went on about your treatment of clients and said that some of the team were prepared to quit because of you. But after a while, the discussion became more constructive. Ultimately, it was decided that you had to leave the team."

She swallowed hard. All of a sudden her throat seemed to be swollen. Her brain tried to decipher the exact meaning of what had just been said. Her eyelids felt heavy, oppressed from within. But she wasn't about to lay herself open and show weakness. She couldn't have coped with the ignominy.

"You and Wolfgang, it was your decision?"

After looking at her for a second he nodded, then continued to avoid her gaze. He kept his hands folded in his lap; his quivering bottom lip, however, couldn't conceal his unease.

"So you're backing my bullying colleagues! Are you even aware that mobbing is a punishable offence here in Germany? You, as the boss, will be held responsible. If you know it's going on but don't do anything about it, you make yourself an accessory. The constant attacks on my character, saying I have no idea what to do with my clients, the torpedoing of my projects; these are all clear examples of mobbing."

No response, merely shaking.

Alex sat there bewildered. She simply couldn't understand why no-one was listening to her side of things. Why her boss couldn't see things from her point of view.

"And what are you expecting me to do now? Should I quit?"

"That would be one possibility," came the swift response.

That was one favour she wasn't about to grant. Although she had been close to tears just now, she suddenly felt a deep surge rising from within. Her colleagues were making her life a misery, her boss had retracted his initial support and now, on top of all that, she was expected to quit? Had the whole world gone mad? Alex became absolutely furious.

"No, I won't quit!" she hurled back defiantly.

"You have three days to consider your position." His response sounded like an ultimatum.

"Are you offering me any alternatives? What am I supposed to think about for three days."

"There are no alternatives at the moment."

She swallowed. If they really wanted to get rid of her, she wouldn't go without a fight. Nobody backed Alex Ruby into a corner.

"I won't quit. There are client meetings taking place tomorrow and the next day that I intend to honour. They can't just be cancelled."

"Then go to the meetings. You can tell your clients yourself."

The hell she would. Nothing had been decided yet, no use to unsettle the clients.

"If you have to fill my position, just make sure you don't hire a woman! Actually, better still, hire two! At least then the ratio would be a bit more even."

She knew she sounded stubborn. But she wasn't prepared to conceal her displeasure about what she perceived to be an injustice any longer.

For the first time in the whole conversation, Thomas looked her directly in the eye.

"In future, I won't be hiring any women at all. I'd have exactly the same problems, and the team would split into two factions again."

How Alex wished she had recorded what he had just said. It beggared belief. Her boss was as good as admitting that the real problem wasn't based on fact, but on mobbing combined with discrimination. That was pretty full-on.

She couldn't help but feel sorry for Thomas.

"You must know," she said seriously, "that none of them would have quit. Brian and George are more than aware they won't find such a well-paid job anywhere else in the industry. Neither of them could go without the money – they enjoy surfing and gambling far too much. Hugo would never leave without George, and Carl has a family. It's blackmail pure and simple, what they're doing to you. If you give in now, then you've lost. In future it'll be you they shoot down, just like in my I2Is. They'll do exactly as they please."

"I don't care, I can live with that."

That was easy enough for Thomas to say, of course, since his private wealth meant he didn't need the job. What Alex didn't understand was how he could still look himself in the mirror in the mornings.

"Is there anything else?" she asked. "Otherwise I'm going straight home. I'm sure you'll appreciate that I'm not feeling too good right now."

She stood up abruptly, even though the meeting was due to last an hour. Everything had been said, and she had absolutely no desire to engage in phony small talk.

Within a flash, she'd taken her bag from the desk and was heading towards the exit. Most people would be going for lunch in a quarter of an hour; she wanted to make sure she was gone by then.

She met Christopher outside in the parking lot.

"Clocking off already?" he teased.

But he must have seen straightaway that something was seriously wrong.

"Can I reach you on your phone?" he asked. "I'll call you later and you can tell me what's up."

She could still just about hold it together, fighting back tears of despair. Oh, to have a boss like Christopher. Considerate and understanding. At least he was concerned for her welfare.

"Tomorrow and the day after I'm with clients," she told him. "But you can call me in the evening. I've got to go home now, I really don't feel good."

Alex climbed into her car and drove away. She had barely got past the barriers before the tears began to stream down her cheeks. She couldn't hold them back any longer. All of a sudden she felt awful. Truly awful.

Back at home, she couldn't eat anything, despite having had no breakfast. Instead she went straight to bed and tried to sleep. That was usually the best therapy. For a long time she was kept awake by penetrating voices inside her head, before finally being overcome by exhaustion. How much more did she have to put up with? How could they condone injustice like this? Where would things go from here? Could she transfer to another department? Just what had she done wrong?

Sleep brought only temporary relief. As soon as she awoke, her head was in a swirl. She needed to speak to someone, otherwise she'd go mad.

Furious about the latest developments that Alex described on the phone, her father promised to draft a mail immediately. Half an hour later, he called Alex to get her opinion on it.

"If I were in your shoes," he said, "I'd send the mail as it is straight to the managing director."

"It's pretty harsh, what you've written," Alex said, after she had read the email. "I'm not sure if I can put it like that, given my situation."

She read the mail through again.

"I like the start. Naturally, my motivation was high to begin with, and it helped me achieve my aims; I had that confirmed on many occasions. It might sound harsh to describe my colleagues' behaviour as mobbing, but given that they complained to the works council and tried to force me out of a job, I think it pretty much hits the nail on the head. After all, it's been going on for months – we're not talking about an isolated incident here."

"And that's exactly what you have to make clear to Wolfgang," Franz insisted. "It seems he's not aware of what's going on in his own company. I don't know anything about your clients or your projects. But accusing you of having no strategy, without reference to the facts; torpedoing projects from the outset: for me that's character assassination."

"You're right," she agreed. "But I still can't say 'I was hired neither as a water-carrier nor as a servant – or to be objectified by macho colleagues; or that it's demeaning and completely unacceptable.'"

Although what he had written conveyed her own feelings exactly, there was no way Alex could express herself like this, other than in a private conversation.

"When I consider your career at PsoraCom, it all becomes extremely clear to me," her father summarised. "Your colleagues simply can't deal with your success or the speed at which you work. That's why they want to get rid of you. Take your project with Natioba, which was unveiled in public. None of them wanted to help at first. Then, when it was a success, they wanted to bask in the limelight – as if they had been responsible for it. Exactly the same happened with the Volcrea project in Valencia. All of them railed against it. But when it was mentioned in the press conference, your colleague suddenly wanted to raise his own profile with it."

"I hadn't seen it like that before," Alex replied. "But I don't understand. They have exactly the same opportunities as me – more even, since they've been with the company longer and know more people. Any one of them could have made it on stage with a project like Taipei or Valencia."

"Maybe it was too much effort for them. You've almost certainly raised the bar internally. Now they have to pull their fingers out and get their hands dirty. You represent a danger to their cushy existences."

Perhaps it wasn't quite so extreme; nevertheless it made sense, what Franz said.

"Personally, I think the wording is more than appropriate," he said firmly. "I would phrase it even more harshly, but it's only supposed to be a springboard for your own ideas. Your problem needs resolving, and fast. If this stretches out for months, it'll finish you."

Alex couldn't argue with that. In the last few months, she had noticed how it was becoming increasingly difficult to come into the office. She felt oppressed there, even though other people like Henry, Lisa or Marco behaved as they always had done towards her. After today's meeting, it would only be more tricky. Thomas had assured her than no-one else apart from Wolfgang knew about the meeting. But her colleagues must have suspected something and were no doubt waiting for precisely this moment. She couldn't imagine Brian not telling them anything about his meeting with Thomas and Wolfgang. It would be just like him to gloat about the outcome, after all.

The next day, just as she was checking in for her flight, her netphone rang.

It seemed Travis, the employee representative, had been informed of the current situation by Thomas.

"Alex, as I see it, you need to get an objective opinion on the matter. It's your decision, of course, but I would urgently recommend you arrange an initial meeting."

"Thanks, Travis. I also think it'd make sense to get a legal perspective on the whole situation. Things aren't looking too good."

"All is not yet lost," he tried to encourage her. "You still have a little leeway. But if you leave it up to management to find a new position for you – and remember that could be either outside Germany or simply unappealing – in the worst case they might serve you with a notice of dismissal pending change of contract."

Now that was a rosy prospect. Alex made an immediate mental note to speak with Maria; she was bound to have some good advice.

The client visits went as planned. Only Alex found it very difficult to hide her true feelings. She was constantly thinking about her current situation. During the meetings she had to push these thoughts right to the back of her mind. That cost a great deal of energy, sapping her of her usual light-heartedness and enthusiasm. She couldn't let her clients get wind of what was happening.

But the paranoia was gradually beginning to set in. Did her clients know something already? Was that why the greeting was a little stiffer than usual? Had they noticed that she was more hesitant than normal in assenting to their requests, since she didn't know whether they could be granted? Or was all this a mere figment of her imagination?

That evening in the hotel, she composed a mail to Wolfgang. Her father was absolutely right: the situation needed to be resolved quickly.

She had worked on it for over three hours, gone over what she had written countless times word for word until she was satisfied. One last time, she looked at the mail. Then she clicked on send. Now she needed something strong to soothe her nerves, perhaps even numb them. She was dying to see the reaction. Thomas and Travis had both been copied in, for form's sake, although she wasn't expecting an official response from either of them. The ball was now in the managing director's court. After sipping deeply on her gin and tonic, she read through the email once more:

Wolfgang,

Barely eighteen months ago, I started work at PsoraCom with high expectations and not inconsiderable enthusiasm, bringing several years' valuable experience of the power plant industry with me. After a brief settling-in period, my passion for the role assigned to me as Vabilmo team consultant continued to grow steadily.

My ability to make new contacts and establish a client network that also incorporated the higher echelons of management enabled me to meet my own expectations, as well as those set by my manager. This was confirmed to me on many occasions during individual meetings.

After scarcely a year, for example, I had initiated projects with my clients Luxumi and Premve, as well as playing a decisive role in promoting a successful reference project with Natioba, which was unveiled to the public by our CEO during the company developer conference in Taipei.

The projects mentioned above were all in line with the established team strategy, a point on which I sought clarification from my manager.

Then, however, a fundamental shift in the team took place, with opinion turning drastically against me; a development I do not see as justified and one that was only communicated to me by my manager. None of my colleagues – I was given no concrete information about how many were involved – approached me in order to discuss the matter constructively, as is the custom here at PsoraCom.

When a formal complaint was lodged with the works council, I actively sought out all my colleagues to arrange 121 meetings with them.

What I experienced can only be described as mobbing. George and Brian declared during initial meetings that the situation was hopeless from the outset. George immediately urged me to start looking for another job, while Brian has repeatedly denigrated my work both behind my back and, together with George, in internal email communications. This conduct is unacceptable.

I myself have never at any point ruled out a solution and to this end have approached colleagues in team meetings and separately arranged discussions on several occasions during the last few months.

Overall, the progress I have made with clients either corresponds to or surpasses the targets I was set:

In the coming months, there is a follow-up project planned with Natioba involving the use of polymer-based cells in 1000 greenhouses in Mongolia. This is a large-scale trial in preparation for the series launch of solar-powered greenhouses. In addition, Carl and I are working together with their central office in Milan on further uses for the Vabilmo technology, focusing specifically on mobile off-grid systems such as tents. Joint projects with Natioba's maintenance department are also developing promisingly.

Despite our rejection of the "service vehicle" project (a move enforced by changes made by colleagues to the team strategy), Luxumi are still very interested in working with PsoraCom. They have agreed to arrange a workshop in order to discuss the planned PV unit in Croatia. In addition, after an initial discussion with Bill in Valencia, Volcrea have agreed to a joint meeting, which has since been fixed internally.

In spite of the unsatisfactory state of affairs regarding the project that began last year (standardised inverters for autonomous service robots and power station modules), Premve remain interested in collaborating with us. Here, however, there is an urgent need for a clear decision concerning whether PsoraCom will provide support for the above-mentioned project. The planned collaboration was originally regarded in an extremely positive light by my colleagues; a fact which makes their subsequent claim that the project no longer conforms to team strategy impossible for me to comprehend.

If, despite the recent official assessment and excellent feedback received from both many colleagues outside the team and US management, my superiors in the German office no longer see a role for me in my current department, then I am more than willing to discuss potential alternatives within the organisation.

My ability to familiarise myself with new topics and make successful use of acquired knowledge would, I believe, stand me in good stead in Marketing.

With this in mind, I will endeavour to consider my options in greater detail and remain open to your suggestions.

My goal is to continue being a valuable member of PsoraCom's team and make a decisive contribution to the company's on-going success.

I place trust in your fairness and ability to resolve the situation described above, thus ridding the German office of a stain that has no place in PsoraCom's company culture.

Best wishes,

Alex

The sound of her netphone startled her from her thoughts. It was Christopher.

"So, what was wrong yesterday?" he asked. "I've never seen you looking so distressed. Can you talk?"

"Yeah, I'm in my hotel room. What happened yesterday, I've never come across anything like it! Neither personally – nor among friends or acquaintances."

"So, what happened then?"

"Thomas said he had to take me off the team. Some time ago Brian arranged a meeting with Wolfgang, who then got Thomas involved. Brian must've had a really good bitch about me: said that I didn't know what was going on with my clients etc. Afterwards, they apparently got a little creative and decided that I had to be taken off the team."

"That's really not good news," he admitted with some concern.

"Wait, it gets better," she went on. "When I asked Thomas if they were expecting me to quit, he just said that it was an option."

"OK, don't panic. There's no way you're quitting. We'll find a solution somehow."

He thought for a moment, before continuing.

"Why don't you join my team? I can always use good, hardworking employees and my people enjoy working with you. Someone mentioned to me only yesterday how great he thought you were, how quickly you'd given him the information he asked for."

Alex drew hope.

"That wouldn't be such bad idea."

Working in his team was something she'd really enjoy. She knew a lot of them already, since Vabilmo was a topic that was forever coming up in consumer retail.

"Don't you worry about it," Christopher reassured her. "I'll speak to Wolfgang and Thomas. We'll get this sorted."

Relieved, Alex hung up. The situation looked distinctly more promising, she thought to herself. A quick resolution was in everybody's interest. There was no way Wolfgang could be anything other than glad of Christopher's suggestion. What Alex didn't know, however, was that she was missing an important piece of the puzzle – a piece that not even Christopher seemed to have.

The response to her email came a day later.

"That sounds like a bit of a rush job to me," Franz said, after Alex had read it to him.

"I just don't think they're taking the matter as seriously as they're making out," she said. "My colleagues have been railing about my conduct with clients for weeks. Since then, I'm not at all sure I'm getting wind of everything, or if there isn't something completely different happening simultaneously."

She added in frustration: "I don't get the impression there's someone telling them they should meet me halfway."

The managing director had defended the decision in his email. Her hope that he would have reacted differently now only seemed naive.

"That's one thing," her father agreed. "The second is that his justification sounds so phony. They're not taking issue with your professional capabilities or performance because the problem lies in the field of interpersonal relationships. How did he put it again?"

"He wrote," Alex replied, "that ‚even without a detailed analysis of the root causes' – and they had ‚conducted such an analysis both conscientiously and in all seriousness' – they would have come to the same conclusion sooner or later. Namely, that changes had to be made in order to do justice to all members of the team. Team spirit needed to be salvaged if they were to re-establish motivation and happiness within the group."

"If they really had conducted such a serious analysis," Franz snorted with contempt, "then he wouldn't have to underline it specially. It all seems far too artificial to me. If he attaches so much importance to interpersonal relationships, then why hasn't he commented on the behaviour of your colleagues? What they've done is so insidious. They've ganged up against you behind your back and lodged a complaint without even bothering to speak to you about it. That's not the way to defuse a situation."

"Yeah," she replied. "What team spirit? That's been missing for ages, if there ever was one in the first place. Right from the start, Brian and George were fighting like a pair of roosters on a dung heap. That was extremely obvious in every team meeting. Hugo's forever clinging to George's coat-tails and never makes a decision without him. Admittedly, Carl is a nice guy and I thought we got on well, but he's another one who won't express an opinion. Since they're in the majority and he's the newest member of the team, he probably reckoned it'd be a bad move to take my side."

"You urgently need to arrange a meeting with this Wolfgang," her father advised. "Even if he doesn't seem to think so, I'm certain the problem is one of professional competence. All that stuff about interpersonal relations is just bluster."

"What do you mean?"

"Brian hasn't had anything to show for himself for a long time," he explained. "You said yourself there's been nothing forthcoming from him in the last half year, and other people have asked if he's even working for the company anymore. So his aim, in my opinion, is to take over your clients. That's his only chance of survival. George is only interested in his own clients. He'll do everything in his power to promote them, and to achieve that, he's allied himself with his arch rival. Carl and Hugo are too weak to take their own stance. They're just blindly going along with it, happy they're not the ones doing the dirty work. Your boss has no backbone and is only interested in doing his own job, which, remember, he doesn't even need. He chooses the easiest path with as little resistance as possible."

"I'm really disappointed in Thomas," she replied. "I wouldn't have thought he'd just cave in and allow himself to be blackmailed. If Brian and George really did plan it like this, well, it'd be staggering."

"Did you not also mention once that the revenue forecasts were far too high in your opinion?" Franz asked. "That you were getting different figures from your client but that your colleagues wouldn't listen to your objections? Your managing director needs to be told that his current plan, which is based in all probability on details provided by Brian and George, is unrealistic; and that there's no way it'll allow him to achieve his own aims."

"You're right," she agreed. "I'll prepare an overview and arrange a meeting with Wolfgang."

But the overview was no use to her either. The managing director didn't seem to have the slightest interest in it; indeed, he appeared to have a different agenda entirely. His remarks caught Alex completely off guard and her hopes of a fair and constructive solution dried up like water in the desert. She felt like it was a completely different person in front of her compared with the man who had pledged his personal support only a few months before.

"There have been concerns about your personality for some time now," he explained. "Thomas came to me with them at the end of last year."

That was news to her, but she didn't interrupt.

"The key question is whether your conduct is fitting of the image PsoraCom seeks to project; or if we'll simply be deferring the problem by transferring you to another team. We've already given it a lot of thought. In this regard, however, I am something of a prisoner of the system and am not free to make the decision for myself."

What did he mean by that? If he wasn't going to decide, then who would? It sounded almost as if he was about to fire her.

"But I've no interest in a dismissal pending change of contract," he continued. "Scaling the department down or giving someone the boot is the last thing I need. Especially someone capable. Ultimately, we shouldn't have been dealing with this issue for half a year. But if we transfer you to another team, we need to think very carefully about how to communicate our decision to top brass. After all, the question of why you left a department in which you were so successful is bound to come up. And the answer has to ensure you can perform just as well in your new role."

Absolutely right, Alex thought to herself. Bill was sure to ask for the reason behind it. But what was all this about dismissal pending change of contract? Had he made a prior arrangement with Thomas?

"The decision is yours entirely Alex; it's your behaviour that's the issue here. Are you prepared to make a fundamental change to the way you behave?" He pierced her with his gaze. Alex felt like a criminal.

"But I've already met my colleagues halfway," she defended herself. "I've made a series of compromises and done exactly as Thomas asked. What about the behaviour of my colleagues? What do you think of them dissing me behind my back and lodging a complaint without even talking to me first? No-one's meeting me halfway!"

Defiance blossomed within her. She wasn't prepared to be viewed as the sole culprit.

"Your colleagues feel frustrated by your behaviour," Wolfgang replied, "and I can well understand why. Thomas and I have spoken about it a lot. They've been very open with their feedback to you. You've attacked them on a personal level, right where they're vulnerable."

It just got better and better. Now suddenly she had attacked her colleagues on a personal level.

"That's not the way I see things," she countered. "What about all the other people from different departments who get on well with me? Did you speak to them too? Surely what they say has to be taken into account as well."

But it seemed like arguing on an objective level was no longer possible.

"We place much greater emphasis on the work carried out in your own team than on loose networks formed with colleagues over coffee. They don't count for anything."

Things were just getting absurd now. Her relationships with people like Henry or Lisa were hardly a loose network. Indeed, Wolfgang had benefited from their working together on more than one occasion.

"I worked very closely with both of them for the presentations in Geneva and Valencia. That wasn't only coffee. Why is it that these people aren't involved in the mobbing?"

"There is no mobbing," Wolfgang replied brusquely. "Your team colleagues are frustrated by your behaviour, understandably so. They spoke to one another about it and a certain team dynamic developed. That's all."

Team dynamic. Alex was left dumbfounded at how the situation was being spun, with her cast as the sole culprit. She was tilting at windmills here.

"What alternatives do you suggest?" she changed the subject. "Which team could I work in?"

"I can't tell you that," Wolfgang evaded the question. "I still haven't spoken to any team leaders, as Thomas and I wanted to keep this under wraps – that's in your interests too. As I said, it all depends on whether you're prepared to fundamentally change the way you behave. At the moment, I don't see any particular willingness on your part to do so."

Alex couldn't believe what was happening here.

"But Wolfgang, you know me," she spluttered, almost in despair. "I'm the same person as I was a few months ago. Until now you've always said that you like how I go about things."

"And I still do. I always need capable people. The best thing would be for you to think about where you'd like to be transferred. In the meantime, I can speak to a few of my managers and let Thomas know."

She couldn't really make anything of what Wolfgang had said. After the meeting, she felt absolutely wretched. It couldn't all be true, surely. She had only tried to do her job to the best of her ability. Who had she ever done any harm? Even Wolfgang and her boss had ultimately hung her out to dry. That made it six against one.

Given the circumstances, she really didn't have any other choice but to perhaps join a different team – maybe with Christopher or Henry. And to think, she had started at PsoraCom with such enthusiasm, such élan. Just last year they had all been so excited about her projects and Wolfgang had been constantly enquiring about the latest developments. What had happened to make everything change? Tired and hurt that Wolfgang had merely increased the pressure, all she wanted to do was head home and go straight to bed. The dull throbbing in her ear had returned like an uninvited guest and she seemed to be drained of all her energy. Even her legs felt heavy as she walked; as if there was lead in her shoes.

On the way out she ran into Lisa, who was just coming from one of the meetings rooms.

"Hey Alex, are you not feeling well? You don't look too hot," she asked, concerned.

"Oh, could be better," Alex replied evasively.

"Come on, let's go in here," Lisa suggested. "There's no meeting scheduled. We can talk privately here. I'll just go and get us some coffee."

While she waited, the merry-go-round of her thoughts began once more. Should she tell Lisa what was going on? Would that be of any use now? Could it do any harm? She was sure, at any rate, that Lisa would treat what she told her with the greatest discretion.

But her colleague already seemed to have a hunch, as she reappeared with two lattes.

"Say," she began, "something's not quite right with your team, is it? I've just seen Brian and George. When I asked about you, they launched into a tirade; it was pretty close to a declaration of war. Even a fool could see that."

"You've hit the nail on the head there." Alex began. "Please don't tell anyone what I'm about to say to you. I don't really know what to think anymore. Apart from you and another colleague, no-one knows anything about this. At least, I don't think they do."

"Of course," Lisa promised firmly.

Alex took a deep breath. Whenever she thought about her situation, she felt an oppressive weight on her shoulders. Her head was throbbing, like after a heavy night on cheap wine. It was becoming increasingly difficult to speak about, as repeating the facts only etched her predicament deeper into her consciousness; the hopelessness of her situation clear.

"My colleagues lodged a complaint about me with the works council at the start of the year. In the I2Is I arranged subsequently, they described the situation as irreconcilable and urged me to start looking for another job. To begin with, management assured me it was all nonsense and that they were behind me; that we would find a common path, if necessary in a different department. But their support began to wane a week ago and has since vanished completely into the ether. Last week, Thomas told me he was taking me off the team. Then he suggested indirectly that I quit. As a result, I drafted a mail to Wolfgang, in which I outlined the situation from my point of view and requested a meeting so we could find a solution. I've just come out of there now; it did not go well."

Lisa looked at her for a few seconds, speechless, as if she first needed to process what had been said.

"That's unbelievable," she said indignantly. "I had a hunch something was up with your colleagues but the fact it's so bad really makes me think. What did Wolfgang say exactly? That's very important for me too: it'll show whether the equal opportunities policy they pretend to take so seriously here actually means anything in practice."

"Interesting that you should mention that," Alex replied. "In our last meeting I advised Thomas not to hire a woman as my replacement, unless he hired two at the same time. And do you know what he said? He said he wouldn't be hiring any more women in future at all because it would only lead to the same situation!"

"He said that?" Lisa could barely conceal her astonishment.

"Almost verbatim," Alex confirmed. "I even noted it down."

"And what did Wolfgang say to you just now? Any similarly choice phrases?"

"Not in so many words. Wolfgang said my behaviour didn't conform to company culture and it wouldn't make any sense to transfer me to a different department unless I was prepared to change it fundamentally. He waved aside my description of the situation as mobbing, labelling it simply a team dynamic that was entirely understandable in light of my recent conduct. In his opinion my colleagues have good reason to be frustrated."

"Incredible," her colleague said. "I just don't buy it! How can your colleagues be frustrated? You don't only push the Vabilmo technology with clients, but internally as well. That benefits the whole team. Almost no-one is as open as you about how things are progressing with their clients. And by the way, I'm still really impressed with how you resolved the secrecy issue with Roffarm and Natioba. It was a masterstroke in my opinion, as things could've become very tricky marketing-wise too. Your colleagues could take a leaf out of your book. Hugo, in particular, if I understand things correctly. We've just had a meeting with Emily about how to market his standard design. Emily reckons it could land us in serious hot water, in terms of the exclusivity clause and Roffarm's compensation claim. None of your colleagues, she said, not even your boss, would have paid such stringent attention to the letter of each individual clause as you; that was confirmed again at the last team meeting. I think you're a great person to work with. And from what I've heard, it's not only Emily who shares my opinion, but people like Henry as well."

Lisa shook her head emphatically once more.

"I could well imagine that Brian's frustrated," she continued. "Henry let the cat out of the bag a little there. Apparently Brian was offered the chance to head the Roffarm team last year. But he turned it down. Now he sees that he could've had four or five people under him. It's too late for that now, though, and he needs to set something up on his own, which naturally requires a lot of work. On top of all this, his relationship with Wolfgang isn't great anymore. He learned that a few deals Brian had allegedly landed with Roffarm were nothing more than hot air. It came up after Lucas made a detailed comparison with the client. But I don't have any sympathy; Brian should really have known better."

"But then I understand even less why Wolfgang is taking their side and pillorying me," Alex said. "There must be another reason for it."

"You're right there. I think it probably has something to do with the CDC. Wolfgang made very high revenue forecasts for the next three to five years there. I had a closer look at them and in my opinion he's stuck his neck way too far out."

"Correct," Alex continued the thought, "and if three of my colleagues were to quit then the team would be disbanded in one fell swoop. That would not only jeopardise his forecasts but damage his reputation with upper management."

"Which could have serious consequences for him," Lisa concluded. "But that's surely a fallacy. None of your colleagues would ever seriously consider quitting and leaving the company. They live the life of Riley here. It would be stupid of them to give it up. I'm absolutely baffled as to why Wolfgang and your boss are allowing themselves to be blackmailed. Ordinarily, he'd be above this sort of thing."

"That's what I don't understand either. As well as all that, one of Thomas's colleagues has offered me a place in his team. He said he'd be glad to have an employee like me – he even had enough work to justify creating the position. I've had a lot of contact with his people and they've all told him they get on well with me. At the moment, that's the only chance I have, unless there's something in Marketing."

"I don't know of anything at the moment, unfortunately," Lisa was forced to disappoint her.

Alex let out a sigh that came from the depths of her soul. What was it her grandmother used to say?

Hope dies last.

Alex's mother wasn't faring much better, though the causes lay elsewhere. The first round of chemo had taken effect and the tumours had shrunk. That was seen as a good sign, so a second round was prescribed.

The worst thing was the side effects, which caused her a lot of suffering. Extreme nausea and stomach trouble alternated with headaches, and were sometimes even eclipsed by them. During their nightly phone calls, both mother and daughter tried to surpass each other in playing down their respective physical and psychological conditions. Neither Ricka nor Alex wanted to overly worry the other.

"Now tell me what's happened, take your time."

Maria was waiting to hear the latest developments; she had taken on the mandate from Alex pro forma.

"That's pretty intense," she said afterwards. "But let's try and approach the matter objectively. Your managing director wrote in his mail that he was prepared to discuss alternatives. But in the meeting itself he qualified his statement by making it conditional on you modifying your behaviour."

"Although exactly which bit of my behaviour I need to modify, he didn't say. He dismissed my working relationship to the people I get on well with as coffee-room chit-chat. I think that's pretty unfair."

Alex really couldn't make anything of Wolfgang's behaviour.

"As I see it, what's happening to you at the moment is a clear case of mobbing. The disparaging attacks on your person and work are not isolated incidents, but recurring episodes taking place over a number of different weeks. Additionally, in your last meeting, your boss suggested that your situation contained a discriminatory aspect, as he expected to be confronted with the same issues if he hired a woman again. The managing director hears of all this only in passing and is challenged by you to put an end to what's happening. When he hears the word mobbing, his initial reaction is self-defence, as he can hardly admit it's taking place in his office. If he did, that would reflect badly on him, and he'd have to reckon with legal action, as well as a possible compensation package."

She had to admit that Maria's hunch was probably very close to the truth.

"But I have absolutely no intention of suing. It's just not for me. First, I'd be tilting at windmills. At the moment, it's six against one, and the company surely wouldn't think twice about getting the best legal representation. Second, I don't have the most important statements – that I'd be better off looking for a new job, for instance – in writing, nor do I have any witnesses apart from my own notes. Third, even if I were to win a case like this, it would probably reflect badly on me anyway. I mean, who would sue such a famous company?"

Maria agreed.

"That's the worst thing about mobbing. It's so insidious and very hard to prove. Basically you've got two possibilities now. The first is to go on the offensive and remind your managing director that he has a duty of care, which he is obviously not fulfilling as matters stand. Officially involving a lawyer would ratchet up the pressure a notch. That way, you can slip into the background and negotiate with the company via your legal representative. However, once battle lines are drawn, you could easily end up in court. The second possibility – and this is what I'd advise you to do – is to try and reach an amicable settlement by transferring to a different team. This guy Christopher wanted to help you. Why don't you wait and see what he can do."

Maria was absolutely right. As long as both sides were still willing to talk, they should try to make use of it.

18

June

Although Renata couldn't offer any legal advice, she tried to provide her friend with some emotional support.

"What you really need is a change of scene, a little distance. Jogging every day isn't enough anymore."

"A holiday would be pretty nice!" Alex sighed. "But there's no way I can go now! When I still don't even know which department I'm going to end up in. I just hope they've taken Christopher up on his suggestion and the switch to his team's soon done and dusted."

"I hope so too," Renata replied, "but if I were you I'd schedule a vacation in pretty soon. This whole thing's been going on for months. And they're still keeping you in suspense about their decision. It's almost two weeks ago now that your boss's colleague said he'd take care of the situation. If things keep on like this, you'll end up punching your own ticket; and we'll be the ones who have to drive you to the hospital. That's not really something I want to do."

Alex knew exactly what Renata was getting at.

Ever since she'd spoken to Wolfgang, it wasn't only the dull throbbing in her ear that was plaguing her; she was also finding it increasingly difficult to sleep. Every evening she lay in bed, tossing and turning between the sheets, before her brain finally granted her entry into the world of dreams. Even that wasn't always a great alternative.

In the mornings she was exhausted and had no desire to get up. The fact that she was in an indefinite state of limbo also meant her sphere of activities was constantly diminishing. Officially, she was still a member of the Vabilmo team; unofficially, of course, she was now unattached. She hadn't heard anything more from Christopher. As he was currently away on holiday, the decision was bound to stretch out for at least another week.

After consulting with Thomas, she had been forced to reject Premve. Her explanation was that owing to internal company directives, priorities in the Vabilmo team had changed. The joint project had by no means been shelved, merely temporarily put on ice. Naturally, it had been impossible to say exactly for how long that would be the case. And so it was that the project, which had aimed to standardise inverters for solar-powered service robots and had initially been so lauded by George and Brian, ultimately fell prey to internal politics.

The time for the workshop with Luxumi had been arranged and the agenda co-ordinated with the rest of the team. However, in defiance of their original promise, Alex's colleagues had only replied tentatively to the calender invite; then, two days before, they cancelled completely. Apparently there had been a meeting scheduled with Hursoc at short notice, which, regrettably, could only take place on that particular day. Since Hursoc had top priority, they would no longer be able to assist with Luxumi.

Thomas's reaction to the incident was devoid of emotion as usual. He didn't let her call things off entirely; just postpone the meeting indefinitely, so that a slight loophole remained. Regarding Natioba, there was still such stiff resistance to the follow-up project in Mongolia that Alex was leaning towards handing it to Nobu. First, he was their man on the ground and second, his position was bound to ensure he could provide clients with the relevant products.

The field test in Greece was drawing closer and closer. It was the last project she was taking care of under her own steam. Carl had only participated half-heartedly, and ended up leaving her hanging. He was supposed to have obtained the seed units Volcrea needed from Apircu, but in the end she had had to chase them up for weeks on the phone. There weren't any other projects she could actively push forward, as making binding pledges to her clients was currently an impossibility.

In passing Alex also learned from Marco that Carl had flown to Milan with him to discuss the promotion of mobile off-grid systems with Natioba HQ. Just like that. He hadn't breathed a word of it to her. As she knew neither the date nor the outcome of the meeting, calling Natioba now would make her look like a fool. After all, responsible consultants should at least know what was going on with their clients if they found themselves unable to attend meetings.

By this stage, she was only going into the office for appointments or team meetings. There had been just one recently, but that had proved more than enough. Even on the way there, she had felt queasy and her hands had started sweating. Together with Pink, she had tried to persuade herself that she wasn't dead yet, just floating. But her whole body, specifically the area around the neck, had tensed up, thus exacerbating the dull thud in her ear. Just like an anaesthetic, the effect of the feel-good playlist only lasted for a limited period of time.

During the team meeting itself, her heart had been beating so fast she had barely been able to concentrate on what was being said. None of her colleagues had even deigned to look at her as she entered the room; nor had they commented on her arrival. Alex had forced herself to keep looking straight ahead, even though she would have preferred to scan the floor for crumbs.

It had taken an enormous amount of effort during the meeting just to show her colleagues she still existed. Despite her remarks eliciting no response, she was not going to allow herself to be dissuaded from expressing an opinion – on topics that concerned her clients, that is. Otherwise she had maintained a low profile. Nobody had treated her with open hostility but they hadn't exactly paid her any attention either.

While walking around the building she got the distinct impression that people were glancing sideways at her. As if they knew what was going on. Gradually, a feeling of complete paranoia started to creep over her. She was in a real catch-22.

Staying at home and lounging in a deck chair with a good book wasn't an option, even if they were slowly phasing her out. Simply pulling the covers over her head wouldn't do much good either. If someone were to discover she was unavailable during working hours, the company would immediately have grounds for dismissal. She had no intention of providing them such an easy target.

Nor did she want to take sick leave. What was wrong with her? A loud throbbing in her ear, a tense neck and a few dodgy nights' sleep. That wasn't an illness. Somehow taking sick leave would seem weak and shabby, as if she couldn't deal with the situation. Still, she couldn't exactly spend the whole day working; there wasn't enough to do and besides, what little she did get done proved enormously taxing. Ultimately she had decided on a compromise that was bearable but increasingly frayed her nerves.

In the mornings, she would stay in bed for an extra hour or two with her netphone beside her, checking her mails every thirty minutes and responding immediately if one came. Afterwards, she would get up and spend the rest of the morning updating her client account plans with the latest info on each company. After lunch she had to lie down for at least an hour when the rumbling in her ears got out of control and she developed a headache. Often she felt that she had only narrowly avoided a migraine attack.

In the afternoons, she would surf the internet to keep herself up-to-date, ploughing through RSS feeds and microblogs in search of industry news and trends, her phone and mailbox always within eyeview. But there wasn't much doing. Although she sent a few emails during the day herself, a sign of her increasing desperation, she received as good as nothing from her team colleagues in return.

If there was something, it was usually trivial information she already knew about. Her incoming mail contained ever-fewer client requests, and now consisted almost entirely of newsletters and internal communications detailing product training sessions. There were fewer calls too. Maybe her colleagues had already plundered her clients, just as pirates raided trade ships laden with booty. Only her colleagues had none of the charm of a Jack Sparrow.

Renata's idea to take a vacation probably wasn't such a bad one after all. At least then she would be justified in doing nothing for a week or two. Perhaps when she returned, a decision would finally have been made on whether she could join Christopher's team.

Alex pulled herself together and arranged a meeting with Thomas.

"What's the latest?" her boss asked her straight out.

"I was about to ask you the same," Alex replied, confused. "Wolfgang was going to discuss alternatives with you and the other managers."

"I don't know anything about that. Perhaps you've changed your opinion in the meantime and see a future for yourself outside of PsoraCom?"

What on earth made him think that?

"No," she said vehemently. "My opinion hasn't changed. I still regard PsoraCom as a very good company and I remain committed to them. When do you think this situation will be resolved? Things can't go on like this. My colleagues are excluding me more and more and have already begun to organise meetings with clients behind my back."

"I have no idea," was his evasive reply, arms folded in defence. "That's not something I can say for sure."

The whole conversation was obviously so embarrassing for him that he seemed almost delighted by her vacation request. Without giving it much thought, he granted her two weeks. How could he possibly have objected? It wasn't as if she had urgent project work to carry out.

Although part of her was relieved at the prospect of some time off, there was another part of her that wasn't. In a week's time she would get a fortnight's breather, and she wouldn't have to pretend she was going about her work with the same old enthusiasm. Before that, however, she had to finish off one of the last projects she was still officially responsible for.

After all, Henry was relying on her support. Through gritted teeth, Thomas had agreed she should fly to the field test in Greece and spend a day on-site there to answer any questions. Only reluctantly had he conceded that the university students equipping the service vehicles today could be the development engineers of tomorrow.

On the flight home, she had enough time to consider potential holiday destinations. Actually, thinking about them wasn't the problem: the real issue was taking a concrete decision. Did she want a beach holiday? Asia would be very cheap right now. Still, was the flight not too long for just a week? In her professional life, she had covered similar distances for even shorter periods – but there were nice beaches in Europe too.

Would she prefer Italy or Spain? In Italy she could brush up on her language skills. Apart from Lisbon, she had never been on the Portuguese coast either; while the beaches in Eastern Europe were also supposed to be wonderful. Or would it be better to take a cultural holiday and explore a new city? Perhaps one on the coast? That way she could combine it with the beach. Rome maybe? But being alone for a week in a foreign city could also become depressing.

If she booked an all-inclusive holiday in a resort, she might get to meet some nice people. All the same, there could be a certain amount of peer pressure to undertake activities, and she didn't want to feel restricted on her holiday. Another option would be just to stay at home and go on day trips. As long as the weather played ball, she could go hiking in the mountains or on motorcycle tours. Then she'd also be able to react quickly to any changes at work. But perhaps it would be better to go further afield so she could truly switch off.

Since when had she become so hesitant? What had happened to her decisiveness? Was she still capable of being spontaneous? It seemed as if the events of the previous few months were beginning to have more of an effect on her than she was willing to admit. Frustrated by her indecision, she closed her eyes and tried to gather her thoughts using autogenic training. Luckily, the decision was soon to be taken away from her.

At least everything in Greece had gone smoothly, she thought to herself. Only one situation had caused her an almost-sleepless night.

Henry had collected her from the airport, since he had arrived the previous day. After dinner in a cosy restaurant, they had strolled back to the hotel via the marketplace, passing a warden along the way. As if he had somehow received a cue, Henry suddenly began speaking about the relationships within her team.

Caught off guard, Alex had briefly considered revealing everything to him. All sorts of questions were racing through her mind. How had he got on to this exact topic? Perhaps someone had already filled him in? Or had Lisa let something slip by mistake? Maybe he was even supposed to be checking up on her? He normally got on pretty well with Wolfgang. Had he been instructed to question her? Looking at his face, he didn't appear to have an ulterior motive. He had probably just asked out of interest.

Still undecided, she had thought about telling him everything and asking for his help. But why should he help her? Because he liked her and respected her work? Because they had gelled during joint projects? Because he despised injustice? Would that be reason enough? After all, in order to support her, Henry would have to take a clear stance and position himself against her colleagues. Would he risk the situation backfiring, in case things escalated further? Maybe he would react completely differently and spurn her? That was a possibility as well, as Wolfgang and Thomas's behaviour had proved. Perhaps she had only imagined that she and Henry got on well, and everything had just been a political game?

Eventually, she had decided against speaking to him. It seemed unlikely that an equal-ranking colleague would stick his neck out for her. Nevertheless, responding diplomatically, with a contrived wink and raised eyebrow, hadn't been easy. He knew how crazy her colleagues were, she had said, before quickly changing the subject. Henry hadn't probed any further. She had lain awake a long time that night, with the same questions going through her mind over and over again. But she had reached the same conclusion each time.

Back on the plane, her thoughts revolved around those same questions once more: was there anyone in the company she could – or should – turn to? Who would be willing to oppose the top boss and deal with the potential fallout? She would need at least ten people to offset what her team colleagues were saying. Or someone more senior than Wolfgang. Surely Bill was too far out of it, though. Would he talk to Wolfgang and intervene in a sphere that was removed from his own? It seemed highly unlikely. Birds of a feather flock together – usually, anyway.

Perhaps HR would afford her the necessary help? Alex had heard of mediators who negotiated when there was a problem between employees. But in the end, HR was also answerable to Management. How could they dispute a decision taken by the department director? It had also been the individual department that made the final decision during the hiring process. HR had only looked after the contract.

The works council had already assumed a mediating function. Another option would be to go to Marketing in person and ask if a switch was possible. That was an area which would greatly interest her. However, Lisa had said there were no vacancies at the moment and besides, what grounds did she have to make such an approach?

As Wolfgang had noted, she was very successful in her current job, and not only as far as the German office was concerned. Who, in her position, would want to transfer just like that? It was bound to lead to speculation that something was amiss, and that would do her more harm than good. After turning it over and over in her mind, Alex again came to the conclusion that Christopher was her only realistic chance as matters stood. If he could argue that his team required additional personnel, and justify the investment with the appropriate sales forecasts, then Alex would be saved.

Back at home, her private routine provided her with a short-lived distraction. Before heading to Renata's for dinner, she called her mother. Ricka was still struggling with the side effects of the chemo, but putting a brave face on it.

She advised Alex to go away somewhere for her vacation.

"Go explore. Take a city break with a cultural programme, or book a holiday in a resort geared more towards young people. That way, you won't be alone and you might meet some nice people. It will take your mind off things. You'll just mope around if you stay at home."

Her mother was right, of course. But Alex was still nowhere near making a decision. The decisive factor proved to be a message she received while at Renata's.

"In Paris next week. Could tack on a weekend. Up for it?"

Since Valencia, she and Shane had exchanged a few messages. It seemed like he couldn't talk right now but he wanted her to know that he'd soon be on her side of the Atlantic. His message came at just the right time. She had always wanted to go to Paris. The opportunity had never arisen until now.

"What are you waiting for?" Renata gave her a little grin. For her, there was nothing to think about.

"What if somebody in the company gets wind of it?" Alex replied hesitantly. "It'll be just another thing they can use against me."

"What are they going to do about it? First, you're on holiday and second, your private life doesn't concern them in the slightest."

Alex still wasn't completely convinced. "I don't know what he's expecting from me. There's no way I'm ready for a serious relationship yet."

Her friend merely shook her head. "If you don't go, you'll never find out. Be good to yourself for a few days! What've you got to lose?" She was right there.

"Go on," Renata urged her. "He's probably wondering what's taking you so long."

Alex replied that she'd love to meet him in Paris.

He promised to send her his itinerary so she could book her flights accordingly.

19

July

The first week of her holiday stretched out like chewing gum. Temperatures in the mid-fifties and constant rain didn't exactly fill her with desire to leave the comfort of her four walls. Between reading, sleeping and internet research into the current job market, her only distractions were the long phone calls with her mother and the various dishes she prepared with Renata in the evening.

On one occasion Moritz made his first appearance for a long time, having made the seamless transition from skiing to mountain biking. He was proudly telling them of his latest acquisition.

"No, it's not a girlfriend," he began. "You two would like that, wouldn't you? I've bought myself a new bike. It's made completely from carbon, apart from the tyres of course. Shimano pinion gears, Racelite handlebars, equalizer bars for single-track biking and freeriding and, naturally, hydraulic brakes. The absolute number one currently on the market. The finest there is."

Moritz was almost bursting with pride and didn't skimp on the specialist terminology.

"All this stuff about the finest is slowly beginning to grate," Alex grinned, "it's everywhere. The finest buffet, the finest beer or wine and now the finest mountain bikes."

"What my dear brother won't tell you," Renata said with mock indignation, "is that the money he spent could feed a family of four for months."

"A new girlfriend would cost just as much in the long run," Moritz replied cheekily. "And I'll get more from the bike."

"At least one of us has got his priorities straight," Alex laughed. "Or maybe there's still no blueprint for the finest girlfriend."

"While we're on the subject," Moritz began hesitantly. "I met up with Sandro last week. Hope that doesn't bother you."

"Not at all," Alex shook her head. "I've already told you. Your friendship is nothing to do with me. Sandro likes you and it'd be a shame if you guys didn't see each other on my account. What happened between us is my concern only. Yes, it affected me deeply and threw me off track; I'm sure that'll prey on my mind for some time yet. But I played my part too. The cause never lies with one person alone."

"You could well be right," Moritz nodded. "You probably just put him under too much pressure with your hopes of raising a family and finding a house."

"What?" Renata became reluctantly involved. "He can't hold a candle to you. He didn't have enough backbone for you. You deserve something better."

"No, Renata," Alex countered softly. "You're not being fair on him. What he did was absolutely not right; I'm not going to spin it any other way. But he's not a monster, not someone we should avoid like a criminal. At the end of the day, I was with him for a number of years and know how loving he could be. Maybe we just didn't have enough in common."

With a deep sigh, she added: "What's the use in it now, anyway."

"I don't agree with you on the first point," Renata refused to let go, "but you're absolutely right on the second: onwards and upwards! Paris awaits; it's time to enjoy life!"

As promised, Moritz drove her to the airport on Thursday at the crack of dawn. The nearer to take-off she was, the more nervous Alex became. She had no idea if she'd see Shane before the weekend. During the day he'd be in meetings with Bill, before dining with various clients in the evening.

Since she had never been to Paris, however, she had decided to fly out a little earlier and explore some of the major tourist attractions. The weather was just right for a cultural visit. A light, cloudy sky and temperatures around seventy degrees. The small guesthouse room she had booked wouldn't be much more than a place to sleep for the next two nights; she had a lot to get through, after all.

From the Place de la République - with its monument vaguely resembling a miniature Statue of Liberty - it was on to the Bastille; somehow Alex had been expecting more than simply a tall column in the middle of a busy roundabout. Further along the banks of the Seine, she came to the Hôtel de Ville. The town hall was built in the neo-renaissance style.

But it was the numerous sculptures lining the sandy-brown walls of the building that first caught her eye; they were integrated into the façade and looked to have been extremely delicately handcrafted.

Many of the figures were either armed or, like Roman statues, depicted half-naked in loin-cloth. On the pillars in front of the fenced entrance gates there were statues of nude children with chains around their necks, not even a fig-leaf to conceal their modesty. With some amusement, Alex wondered whether statues like these might not have been belatedly altered in countries such as America and forced into more appropriate dress.

After a quick rest by the garden fountain, she continued upriver towards the Louvre, where the sun and clouds were reflected in the glass pyramid. There was an enormous queue outside the museum. With the exception of architecture, art had never really been a passion of hers. As a result, she was happy to forgo the air-conditioned vaults, as well as the opportunity to steal a glance at the Mona Lisa's smile.

Moving further northwest, her route took her through the Jardin des Tuileries and past the naked female sculptures, parts of which were just as shiny as the bronze statue of Juliet in Verona. She stopped in front of the 3000-year-old obelisk, its gilded decorations glistening in the sun. With the Louvre at her back, the Place de la Concorde lay before her and an admirable view of the mighty Arc de Triomphe in the distance, with the Eiffel Tower soaring high above over to the southwest. It was one of the most impressive squares in the whole city. There was a real feeling of antiquity about the place, immortalised in the ancient hieroglyphs adorning the monolith, dating back many centuries before Christ. Originally created to mark the entrance to a temple in Luxor, the obelisk had been installed in Paris barely two hundred years ago.

Inspired by the charm of her surroundings, she took a leisurely stroll up the tree-lined Champs Élysées and treated herself to an overpriced glass of champagne in one of the exclusive cafés; a decision almost justified by the view of the city's lavish shopping mile. Then it was back via the golden cupola of Les Invalides, until, having walked ten miles, she finally gave in to her exhausted feet and took the metro back to the guesthouse.

After an hour's sleep and a refreshing shower, her destination was a cosy-looking restaurant chosen from the wealth of bars and eateries by the Place de la République. There, she sat with an aperitif, reflecting on her impressions of the day. At last, Shane texted.

"Not a moment's peace until now. Sorry. Hoping to make a move after dinner. Fancy meeting later? Will give you a call. Near Eiffel Tower."

"Sure, why not," she replied, her pulse racing as she did so. "Let me know where. Can take metro."

Though time seemed to be crawling by, the view of the busy square with all the different people provided ample distraction, and the wine accompanying her dinner helped make her feel pleasantly relaxed. She alternated between reading her guidebook and looking at the photos she had taken that day, until her wait was finally over.

"Meet in thirty minutes? Take metro to Invalides."

All of a sudden, she needed to get a move on if she was to be on time. After a quick trip to the bathroom to check how she looked, she set off for the little bar that he had described.

How would he react when he saw her? Had he perhaps remembered her differently? Did she look too casual? How should she behave? Was he just as nervous as her? Should she go back to his hotel, if the opportunity arose? What if he wanted more than she was prepared to give? Alex felt like a teenager on a first date.

The next morning, her concerns of the previous evening seemed utterly superfluous. Shane's carefree manner had made it easy for the pair of them. After sharing a bottle of wine, they had gone back to his hotel room. His obvious advances had flattered her and his careful touch sent shivers of pleasure through her whole body. The alcohol had doubtless made her more responsive, but she had told him in no uncertain terms that she was reluctant to arouse any expectations she would ultimately be unable to fulfil.

Although she wanted to enjoy his affection, she still wasn't ready for a relationship, and certainly not a long-distance one. Stimulated by his inviting gaze, she had suggested they enjoy the weekend without worrying about what followed. Neither of them needed to make any promises or commitments about the future. Whether it would develop into something more serious or not in due course, no-one could say. Shane had agreed. Relieved by the simplicity of their arrangement, she had given free rein to her passion and awoken beside him the next morning with a clear conscience.

While Shane went off to work, Alex – after a breakfast of café au lait and pain au chocolat in a nostalgia-evoking old café – continued exploring the city.

First on her list was the Centre Pompidou. The little streets on the way there, however, were considerably more to her taste than this modern, abstract building with its multi-coloured exposed pipes and red-roofed diagonal escalator. This kind of architecture just wasn't her cup of tea.

In contrast, that of the famous gothic cathedral on l'Île de la Cité, her next port of call, seemed all the more impressive. With her zoom lens, she could even make out the fierce gargoyle sculptures high up on the façade, as seen in films like The Hunchback of Notre Dame. From there, she wound her way through the narrow streets of the Latin Quarter, past the famous Sorbonne University, and up to the Jardin du Luxembourg, the appetising smell of fondue and grilled fish accompanying her every step. With its shaded garden cafés, the sprawling castle grounds were an inviting place to stop and rest.

After a Pastis, she strolled back along the tree-lined St. Michel Boulevard, stopping at a few shops along the way and, after enjoying a sweet crêpe, finding a new favourite T-shirt. Shane texted later that afternoon, once he had a better idea when he could officially begin the weekend.

"Bill flying tonight. Extended hotel till Sunday. Come to Hard Rock Cafe at seven with your things."

After all that fine French cuisine, Shane had a hankering for a real burger and had also remembered Alex's passion. As well as the obligatory shot glass, she bought a new hoodie. It had been a great day but the night was about to get even better.

Although neither of them had got much sleep, the rays of sun filtering through the open window drove them out of bed early the next morning. They took breakfast in a small bakery round the corner, thrashing out a plan together as they consumed their fresh baguettes. The Eiffel Tower was first on the list, its upper platform laying the city below at their feet. Not a single cloud blurred their view not only of the Louvre and Notre Dame, but also the Sacré Coeur Basilica. The wedding-cake style church in the hills of Montmartre was their next destination, followed by a substantial dinner in the Brasserie Lipp.

It was unbelievable how quickly the time was passing, Alex thought to herself later, as they took a boat trip along the Seine through the illuminated night city. She hadn't spent a single minute thinking about work, or what awaited her upon return. Distracted by the sights and sounds of the city, she had allowed herself to be swept away by Shane's unbridled joie de vivre, as if there really was no tomorrow. As he embraced her from behind on the ship's deck, pressing her close, it seemed like he too, despite their agreement, was abandoning himself to romance.

If things had been different, there was no knowing what could have become of them. For a brief moment, Alex thought about telling him about the situation at work. But why destroy the magic? Why exchange exhilaration for melancholy? There was surely nothing he could do except show sympathy, or worse still, pity. He was on the other side of the world, and would have little reason to interfere with matters in Germany that were so far-removed from his own work. She decided it was better to block everything out for as long as possible and simply enjoy the liberating change of scene. The mundanity of daily life would catch up with her all too soon.

During their third night together, their passion for each other remained all-consuming. Neither of them gave much thought to sleep. Although Alex couldn't say exactly what was driving him, it was a different story for her. It had been so long; his constant desire made her feel appreciated, and she was loath for it to end. They had no need of words; only for each other's touch.

After a few dreamless hours' sleep, they slowly began to come back down to earth. By the evening it would all be over. Both would go their own way and return to their separate lives. Even so, they still weren't quite ready to let go of the magic. They spent the remaining hours exploring as much of the city as possible, as if that, in some way, could bring time to a halt.

At Père Lachaise, they visited the graves of Chopin, Oscar Wilde and Edith Piaf, as well as the resting place of Jim Morrison, upon which fans of The Doors had placed half-smoked joints to go with the flowers. After grabbing lunch at a snack hut, they checked out Le Marais, the perfect symmetry of the Place des Vosges, and Rue de Rivoli with its countless shoe stores. Then they walked along the banks of the Seine towards the Louvre, rummaging through the stalls of the bouquinistes for books and postcards, as people had done in their thousands for centuries.

Neither of them said much, just a few things about the city or its architecture. Both were adhering strictly to the agreement and outwardly suppressing their feelings; even if Alex wasn't the only one who seemed to be finding it difficult. They granted their feet one last pause in Café de Flore, before the weekend came to a close. The nearer the hour of departure, the more impatient Alex became. She would have liked to bring time to a standstill, to have remained cradled in the security of her newfound sense of belonging; but she knew this was unrealistic and so longed for the fateful moment of farewell to bring a swift end to the torturous waiting, this eternal clockwatching.

On the way to the airport, they looked at each other mostly in silence. Even when Shane took her hand, neither of them said a word. She would have liked to know what he was thinking. But being unable to say exactly what she herself felt, she decided not to ask.

They embraced each other for a long time as they said their goodbyes. The passion of the previous few nights had now, finally, been consigned to the past. It seemed as if Shane was waiting for a sign from her. But she couldn't give him one, even if she'd been absolutely sure of what it was he wanted. Still, perhaps she was wrong after all. After he had removed himself from her embrace, he kissed on the cheek and said simply: "Look after yourself." Nothing more. Then he took his bag, headed towards the long moving walkway that would lead him to the satellite and waved at her a final time.

As she stood there for a minute watching him go, she sensed the emptiness slowly beginning to take hold once more. Her feeling of security was forced to give way to that of isolation.

Nothing had changed. Absolutely nothing. At least regarding her future position. Alex glanced through her inbox, searching for emails containing news about her situation. Thomas had taken the beginning of the week off at short notice. Christopher was back from holiday, but there had been nothing forthcoming from him either. When she tried calling, she only got his voicemail.

It was enough to drive you mad, she thought to herself furiously. At some point they had to make a decision. They couldn't just leave her hanging like this! Wolfgang had told her in their last meeting that he always needed capable people and that he had no complaints about her performance. But had he really meant it like that? Why were he and Thomas taking so long? They must have known they were wasting manpower, as, in her current situation, she was working with the handbrake firmly on. There was no way that was in company interests. She needed to speak to Christopher urgently.

Finally she got through to him that evening. Unfortunately, he didn't have the news she had been hoping for.

"So, how was it in France?" he asked. "Good enough to take a french leave, was it?"

"You know that envy's a sin, right?" she pretended to be outraged. "And the Maldives – how were they? Did you find Nemo?"

Christopher laughed, before immediately becoming serious again.

"Listen, Alex, I'm afraid there's not a lot I can do for your situation."

"How come?" she asked, dismayed, hoping to at least partly conceal her despair. It didn't really seem to have worked, as Christopher squirmed audibly before letting the cat out of the bag.

"I've spoken to Wolfgang, but my hands are tied. I'm out of it."

"What do you mean, you're out of it?"

"I'm to concentrate on my own affairs," he replied, "keep out of the whole thing. Truly, I'm sorry, but there's nothing I can do."

Now she really didn't understand. Here was a manager who wanted her to join his team because he was convinced about her abilities and could use some reinforcement. At the same time, it would solve a problem currently facing the managing director.

"What sort of game are they playing here?" she asked in disbelief. "There must be something else going on!"

"No idea, Alex," he said and it sounded like he meant it. "I'm really sorry. I would have very much liked to have you on board, to say nothing of the fact that there's more than enough work. But Wolfgang's been very clear. What lies behind it is a mystery to me too."

Before Christopher hung up, he gave her some more information.

"Did you hear? Your colleagues were with Luxumi last week."

That beat everything. Her colleagues had boycotted the workshop she arranged for the beginning of the month, even though they were the ones who had originally requested it. And now they had agreed a meeting behind her back and gone to her client?

Things couldn't go on like this. She called Travis. Perhaps her employee rep knew what was going on behind the scenes.

She could barely conceal her lack of composure when he immediately picked up.

"Do you know what's happening here?" she asked him straight out.

"Maybe," he said cautiously. "Nothing's been confirmed, though. I have my suspicions all the same, and they've hardened in the last few weeks."

She could hardly believe what he told her. If it was true, then it was a farce fit for the stage.

"I heard from American colleagues several weeks ago," Travis began, "that there are global job cuts imminent, which also stand to affect the German office. Not a great deal, mind. One branch has already been sold to an outside company, under the proviso that the employees keep their jobs. Now, there's only a few people they need to lay off. That's why they didn't make a big deal out of it; negotiations have been taking place behind closed doors. A few people close to retirement were persuaded to indulge their hobbies a little sooner than planned by the prospect of a golden handshake. If they were to get rid of you now as well, then Wolfgang will have fulfilled his given quota: problem solved, just like that. It looks like they've spent the last few weeks trying to break you down."

"Well, they've done a pretty good job there," Alex was forced to concede dejectedly.

After hearing that, she needed to sit down for a minute.

"But you can't let them get you down now," he implored her. "They've got nothing on you! They can't terminate your contract as easily as all that."

"What do you think I should do?" Alex wanted to know. "Hire an external lawyer to remind Wolfgang and Thomas of their duty of care? That way, I could force them to find me another job within PsoraCom, though there's a good chance that could backfire. But, the way my colleagues are continuing to undermine me with my own clients is both shameless and provocative. I can't call my customers anymore because I'm no longer aware who's spoken to whom, and when. My clients would think I was a total idiot and my credibility would be absolutely fuc-... well, you know what."

"You're absolutely right," Travis agreed. "The company are giving you no help whatsoever, as far as your continuing success is concerned. Your standing with clients is beginning to corrode; and your reputation could end up being seriously damaged. The only thing you can do is stand firm and keep pressing for a solution."

"That's what I'm doing," Alex sighed, "but at some point my reserves will be exhausted. I'm already having huge problems sleeping, not to mention the constant ringing in my ears."

"We'll find a solution that's acceptable for you," Travis promised. "I'm going to fight your corner for you and approach Wolfgang myself."

It wasn't just bad news on the work front, however. There were fateful times ahead for Alex's mother too. Since the second round of chemo had only had a minimal effect on the tumours, the doctors, after seriously evaluating the risks, had decided to go ahead with the operation.

Such a grave procedure would last for several hours and would be fraught with danger, given Ricka's weakened condition. Her energy reserves were exceedingly low and there was a very real chance they wouldn't be sufficient for her to make a recovery. In a moment of outrageous bad taste, one of the doctors had joked that there were no guarantees Ricka wouldn't be chauffeur driven out of the hospital in a black hearse! The operation had been set for the end of September, so that Ricka could regain her strength and at least partially recover from the chemo – if you could talk about recovery in a case like this, that is.

The news depressed Alex more than her situation at work. It seemed like there was nothing positive in her life at the moment, as she trudged from day to day. She found it increasingly difficult to get out of bed in the mornings. During the day, she sat despondently at her desk looking for something worthwhile with which to fill her official eight-hour quota. As she was using the company network to log in, she didn't want to search for alternative jobs outside of PsoraCom or simply surf the net. She was certain that every website she visited would be recorded somewhere. The last thing she needed was to give Wolfgang or Thomas legal grounds to fire her. At lunchtime, she found herself having to extend her break in order to prevent her tinnitus from developing into a genuine loss of hearing. Sometimes she no longer even heard the chirruping of the birds in her garden, so loud had the ringing become.

At the end of the week, she arranged a meeting with her boss so that they could agree on her MBOs for the forthcoming three months. Normally, she would have made some suggestions, which Thomas would have discussed with her, before officially agreeing on her objectives.

That had been what happened on the previous six occasions. But what suggestions could she possibly make? And how was she supposed to define any MBOs? She was no longer a practising member of the Vabilmo team and in two months she had still not been assigned a new role, this despite having repeatedly reaffirmed her desire to continue working for the company and enquiring about her position on several different occasions. Under these circumstances, she saw absolutely no reason why she should also face a loss of earnings.

Thomas didn't appear to have any great interest in the meeting and very quickly agreed to award her a blanket 100% variable pay for the coming quarter. Alex had argued that there were various factors preventing clear objectives from being set. First, she was to be taken off the team and second, her colleagues were boycotting client meetings, even when they had been arranged together in advance.

The best example of this was the workshop with Luxumi. The fact that Alex's colleagues were stealing her clients and setting up meetings without either informing her or allowing her to participate, was something Thomas completely neglected to comment on. He simply changed topic, impassive as ever, before allowing himself, after some discussion, to be persuaded that Alex had achieved her objectives to 100% for the previous quarter as well.

"So, what happens now?" Alex forced herself to ask the question. It took a lot of effort to phrase it neutrally, without a hint of reproach in her voice.

"That I don't know," Thomas replied, as usual. "I need to speak to Wolfgang again."

"What alternatives have you discussed?" she wanted to know.

It was evident just how uncomfortable he felt. But she had no intention of being fobbed off with a vague response. She felt her ear begin to throb again under the surface.

"As I said, I need to speak to Wolfgang. I don't know the latest."

Her frustration rose. "But what's the latest from your end? When will you have a solution by?"

The throbbing became stronger.

"I'm afraid I can't give you an exact date. I'll be in touch as soon as I've heard from Wolfgang."

It seemed pointless. She wasn't going to get anything out of him.

Maria called at the weekend.

"So, when are you starting in Christopher's team, then?"

"Probably not at all," Alex gave a pained sigh. "The managing director told him not to get involved."

Maria whistled quietly through her teeth.

"He's got to be pursuing a different agenda if he's gagging people trying to solve the problem."

"You're absolutely right," Alex agreed. "The way it looks, it seems like they actually want to get rid of me. The US has announced job cuts; with me gone, that's the quota filled."

Her friend must have noticed the resignation in her voice.

"What a bunch of pigs," she said indignantly. "But you can't let it get you down, Alex."

"That's much easier said than done."

"There's no way you're just quitting now!" Maria resolved. "I understand you're frustrated but let's try and make the best of it. Stick it out a little longer, even if it's tough. I'll help you."

"That's sweet of you," Alex said gratefully. "I wouldn't just resign flat out; that'd be making it far too easy for them. Besides, I'm the one who decides when I can't go on, not them!"

Her reserves weren't completely exhausted; she still had something left.

"Exactly. That's the right attitude! You need to give your superiors a good kick up the ass and demand that they find you an alternative position – even if you do want to quit. You can't make them feel as if you've already decided. We can raise the pressure on them this way, and it'll ensure you have more clout when it comes to the settlement."

Where would she be without friends and family to stick by her and provide encouragement? Alex quickly dispelled the thought; it was too close to incredulity and self-pity.

20

August

Another week went by without the slightest bit of action being taken by management. Alex had just about got through the team meeting, standing up to the cold - almost contemptuous - gaze of her colleagues. Afterwards, she had gone to her doctor for two neural injections. The tension in her neck had become even more severe and was pinching the blood supply to her ears – indeed, almost cutting it off all together.

Not long after, Travis had a little more success from his end. He had finally set up a meeting for her with Wolfgang and Thomas that he would also attend. As employee representative, he could take on the role of neutral witness and thus lend her his support.

Not that there was much to support: Wolfgang refused to become involved in any discussions about her colleagues' conduct and simply waved aside every argument.

"The team seems to have rediscovered its drive in recent weeks," he said.

"My colleagues are stealing my clients," Alex retorted. "Initiating activities without my knowledge, so that I can no longer call clients for fear of losing my credibility, you call that rediscovering their drive?"

His choice of words had caused Alex's blood to boil, but he refused to provide an answer.

"I've thought long and hard," the managing director stressed, "about where best to deploy you. But I'm afraid my hands are tied."

"By whom," Alex probed. "Who, if not you, decides what happens in the German office?"

But he ignored this question too.

"I see no prospect of finding you a new position either in Marketing or with Christopher's team," he made his position clear. "One possibility, however, would be a role in which you analysed biomass resource requirements with a view to processing the solar energy contained within. Biomass will be enormously important to us in the future, representing the second highest revenue generator after Vabilmo."

Even Travis immediately raised an eyebrow at this. Processing biomass in order to generate energy was not one of PsoraCom's core competencies.

"Are there plans to make biomass technologies a core competence within the company?" Alex asked disbelievingly.

"That would be news to me too," Travis backed her up.

"The position still hasn't been officially approved and at the moment there's no guarantee that it will be anytime soon. However, Alex is a permanent employee and we have an influence on where her focus will lie. I think it's an area with enormous potential. Electricity is needed to process biomass and it could be generated using our Vabilmo cells, for example. You'd be directly answerable to me in your new position. Your colleagues - Brian above all - would bite their hands off for a chance like this."

Alex wasn't so sure of that. From the first moment, it had seemed like another dead-end.

"I can't give you a decision today," she said, as a result. "I need to know more about the technology and how its future prospects are viewed. Therefore, I'm going to use the next two weeks to read up on the topic. After that, I'll let you know. I think that's only fair given I've been waiting months for you to come up with alternative suggestions."

"I don't have any issue with that," Wolfgang concurred, and so the meeting was over.

Alex spent much of the next few days deep in thought. What could she have done differently? Could she have made more demands or increased the pressure on them to find her a new job? If she was honest, she no longer trusted either Wolfgang or Thomas. First, they had pledged their support and then they had reneged on it; ultimately, she had been left hanging out to dry for months. Under these circumstances, there was no way she could seriously believe they still valued her as an employee. Was biomass really considered such a promising area for the future or was he just being crazy? Perhaps it was only a placebo: something they could use to sideline her, in the hope that she'd quit in frustration after a few weeks.

After a week, her decision was made. Her father wasn't immediately convinced.

"Who knows, perhaps it could be an interesting position after all?" he ventured carefully.

But Alex didn't share his opinion.

"I've spent a whole week doing research," she explained. "Not just online, but on the internal company forum as well. It's pretty clear from a lot of board members' blogs that biomass isn't seen as a serious issue at PsoraCom. If I accepted the offer, it'd surely only be a matter of time before I found myself in a similar situation and had to look for another job. Since the position hasn't been approved internally, I'd be completely dependent on Wolfgang. He might come along at any time and tell me his department could no longer justify keeping a project like mine afloat. Then my cards would be considerably worse than they are now. The risk lies entirely with me. I don't want to jump out of the frying pan and into the fire. It's time to be more active. I'm not going to let myself become sidelined. Even if quitting does play into the hands of Wolfgang and Thomas, at least I'd be doing it my way and on my terms. They don't want me anymore; otherwise they'd have proposed an alternative a lot sooner."

"You're probably right," her father conceded. "They've had months to think about it, only to come up with such a dubious suggestion."

"If I take it," Alex said, "I'll no longer be able to look myself in the mirror when I get up in the morning; I'll have sold out. How am I supposed to retain any sort of enthusiasm for a job where I've been made to feel so unwelcome by my superiors?"

"It would be very difficult," Franz admitted. "You've got to be realistic about things too: as long as you still work for the company, you'll be seen as a latent threat by the managing director. After all, he's allowed mobbing to take place in his office without doing anything about it. If his superiors got wind of that, he could be in some serious trouble. Especially if he's under pressure from other quarters."

The longer they talked about it, the more they came to the conclusion that there was only one solution Alex could really live with. With that, the decision was taken once and for all.

Now it was a simple question of arranging the details, a job for which Maria was ideally qualified.

"You'll have to put on your best poker face; it's not going to be easy. But I hope your father's idea works. It's extremely unusual. But we need to at least negotiate a decent settlement for you, which you can then chalk up as damages."

"Yes, hopefully this works," Alex agreed. "I've never heard of anything like it. But it's worth a try. Things can hardly get any worse."

"You'll manage," her friend was certain. "Justice is on your side, even if, legally speaking, we don't have a leg to stand on. Still, negotiating was always one of your strengths. You can do it!"

After some initial doubts, Travis pledged his full support – as far as his role permitted – and accompanied her to the decisive meeting with Wolfgang and Thomas.

Alex felt awful and was so nervous that her carotid began throbbing wildly. After everyone had taken their seats and Wolfgang had wheeled over to the table, an expectant silence descended.

She summoned all her courage, looked round the table, fixed her boss and managing director straight in the eye, and said: "I hereby tender my resignation for the end of April next year."

Wolfgang and Thomas looked at her in disbelief, saying nothing.

As proof, she passed her written resignation letter across the table, effective from that point. However, the date was much later than the three-month notice period stipulated by her contract. It was her father's ruse; Maria had dealt with the legal side. The goal was to negotiate a few extra months' salary for Alex as compensation.

The legal position was that an ordinary resignation had to observe at least the statutory regulations, or the period of notice laid down in the contract. "At least", in this instance, meant the contract couldn't be terminated before three months had elapsed – unless there were exceptional circumstances, which justified an extraordinary cancellation. What happened after this three-month period, however, was not defined by law.

Moreover, unlike the employment contract, resigning was a unilateral act; if proper procedure was observed, therefore, it immediately attained legally validity, irrespective of whether the employer agreed to it or not.

Wolfgang and Thomas read the letter of resignation one after the other; it did not, however, confirm their suspicions that they had misheard what Alex had said. It was clear that neither of them had expected such a reaction on her part. Resignation, yes, but not with such a long period of notice, which contractually guaranteed both her job and, of course, her salary.

Travis seized the opportunity and added fuel to the flames.

"In my position as employee representative, I see no reason to object to Alex's resignation," he said. "Nevertheless, I propose that she be released from her contract immediately. Given the current circumstances, it would be entirely unreasonable for her to continue working here. First, she has been repeatedly subjected to mobbing actions from team colleagues and second, I do not anticipate that her new post analysing the biomass market will be approved anytime soon. As a result, I view the request that she stand idly by and await your decision as immoral."

Completely taken aback by Travis's open use of the m-word, Alex tried, nonetheless, not to let her astonishment show. Gratefully, she cast him a brief look.

After a time, Wolfgang seemed to have regained the power of speech.

"I can't say anything about the conditions under which you are leaving. Nevertheless, I am astounded by your resignation, especially after you so categorically turned down the possibility in May."

Alex looked at him steadfastly, silently. Her eyes reproached him for having waited until August to propose an alternative: an irresponsibly long period. It was the start of a power struggle that she could ill afford to lose. The managing director pierced her with his gaze, as if trying to bring Alex to her knees. But she didn't say a word.

"But for me, this is a completely normal situation," he continued. "If people in a team don't get along, one of them leaves. That's normal."

She held his gaze, as she answered.

"I think it'd be a real shame for PsoraCom if a situation like mine was normal, don't you?"

Thomas didn't even seem to be breathing, let alone about to say anything. He twisted his fingers nervously, his eyes fixed upon an imaginary point on the floor. Seconds passed. Alex held Wolfgang's gaze and counted along silently.

Ten.

Travis had cast his net and saw no reason to express himself further.

Twenty.

Everything was between Alex and the managing director.

Thirty.

The magic number during negotiations.

Finally, Wolfgang turned to Thomas and became the first to break the silence.

"I will speak to HR tomorrow and see how they view the situation. Only then can we make an offer concerning the next eight months. From Monday, I'm away on holiday for three weeks and won't be able to do anything."

Thomas cleared his throat and said quietly: "I'm off as well, until mid-September."

That sounded like another delaying tactic, but it was nothing less than had been expected.

Travis immediately became involved.

"It would be in company interests to resolve this as soon as possible," he challenged. "Alex has borne the costs on her own for over half a year now."

She hadn't expected so much support from him.

"We'll do our best to find a solution before my holiday," Wolfgang concluded the meeting, before wheeling out of the door. Somehow his statement seemed less than binding.

"How are you feeling," Renata asked, "now that the cat's out of the bag and you've told them about your decision?"

They were standing in her friend's kitchen again, cooking dinner together.

"I do feel better," Alex conceded. "Everything's still very much in limbo of course, as far as the next eight months are concerned. But at least I've taken a decisive step forward."

Renata nodded.

"That you have – and it can't have been easy. Other people would've just buried their heads in the sand, taken their pseudo-job and done the required minimum."

"I wouldn't have been happy doing that," Alex knew. "Working as a consultant for the Vabilmo team was so much fun. That's the worst thing about all this. It was my dream job and I was really good at it. I still don't understand why they took it away from me."

She shook her head sadly and wiped an embarrassed tear from her eye.

It took seven weeks before Wolfgang and HR finally confirmed that Alex's demands had been accepted.

Seven interminable weeks, during which she tossed and turned every night until five am, before her tortured thoughts eventually gave way to fitful sleep.

Where did things go from here? How on earth had it even come to this? What had she done wrong? The first few days she had lain in bed until lunch in a kind of exhausted waking nightmare. After that, she had asked Maria to call her every day at ten at the latest, and speak to her for a few minutes until she was awake and ready to get up. She didn't want to throw her body's natural rhythms into confusion just because she couldn't sleep at night. Valerian tablets were no use; increased wine consumption wasn't a long-term alternative; and she didn't want to go anywhere near sleeping pills.

The same old questions continued to eat away at her. Why had she been abandoned, left hanging out to dry for months? Was she a different person professionally from privately or had she undergone a drastic change? Was she, in actual fact, just like her colleagues had described her? Selfish and only concerned with her own personal gain?

Her sleeping problems didn't get any better. Some days, she was seized by convulsive fits of crying that came on without rhyme or reason, shaking her whole body, only to pass a few minutes later. On bad days, they extended over the course of the whole day, until her body finally gave way to exhaustion. On better days, she regained control after two or three attacks with Bach flower rescue drops.

After her demands had been accepted, she hoped the tide would soon turn and that she would be able to contemplate her future more calmly.

What would she do now?

Should she call Chris or Premve's lab manager in Seoul and ask if they knew of any other jobs available in the industry? Perhaps her contacts at Luxumi, Volcrea or Cellgot might also have an idea?

But what could she say to them about why she wanted to leave PsoraCom for a different company?

She couldn't tell them the truth because she had no evidence. Besides, who would believe her, if there was anyone prepared to listen to her at all? What was the truth then? It was always subjective, linked inexorably to the eye of the beholder. If she were to tell someone her story, which truth would they see within it?

From Christopher she heard that Carl had already applied for her company car; as soon as she gave it back, he would trade his smaller vehicle in for it. Brian had successful managed to take over the consultancy work for Natioba and Luxumi; he had given up his other clients, who would no longer be represented. George and Hugo had harangued Marco until he eventually set up a joint meeting between Premve and Hursoc.

So, what was the real truth?

Epilogue

Over the course of the next few months, Alex granted herself no respite and continued searching for a new job in the same industry. She rejected friends' suggestions to take a few weeks off. Although the prospect of spending a month or more abroad was extremely enticing, it was a decision she felt unable to make.

Not for financial reasons. She just didn't want to run the risk of something happening to her mother while she was away. Admittedly, the operation on her lungs had passed off without any great complications; still, no-one was sure what would happen next. By going away, Alex would always feel as if she were abandoning Ricka. The illness had already revealed its pernicious streak in other people and was completely unpredictable. Alex wanted to be there for her mother in case of emergency.

For months, Alex sat at home for five days a week in front of the computer, reading job descriptions and scouring the internet for the latest news about developments in the solar and robotics industries. Trends in this sphere generally had a very short half-life, and it was extremely important that she didn't lose touch. Evenings and weekends she spent with friends or at her parents' house. She found it harder and harder to be alone; the thing she missed most was having a strong, manly shoulder to lean on; to help her rediscover her self-confidence.

The more time elapsed without her having a defined task for the future, the greater the pressure on her, and the sleeping problems still weren't any better; if anything, the opposite was true. Doubts began to eat away at her more and more. She had said goodbye to all her contacts in an email circular, vaguely mentioning that she would be devoting herself to other activities in the future. Whether or not they would involve PsoraCom was something she had left open.

Increasingly, she began to ask herself if something had filtered through onto the market, and that was the reason she was having so little success. Had her colleagues mentioned something about her situation to former clients or third-party companies? It was more than possible that one or two people had asked what had happened to her and why she had disappeared so abruptly from sight. She certainly wouldn't have put it past George or Brian to phrase their answers ambiguously. But she could hardly ask – and besides, who would know. The only thing for it was to intensify her search. At least, that's what she thought.

Like a steam engine whose tank had been under too much pressure for too long, Alex's valve exploded after Christmas and caused her to break down. She fell headlong into a black hole of depression and remained in bed for days, shutters drawn and with no contact to the outside world. The daily phone call with her parents was the only exception. She didn't want to seriously worry the two of them. All other calls were fielded by her patient answering machine.

Appropriately enough, the turning point came at New Year. Tired of being put off, Renata had come by in person and refused to stop ringing the doorbell. A few hours later, Alex was dressed to the nines and ready to go. Renata had all-inclusive tickets for the New Year's Eve ball at her hotel.

After a five-course meal, they joined the rest of the guests to admire the fireworks from the balcony. As Alex turned to look for her friend in the crowd, her gaze was drawn to him like a magnet. She became immersed in the softness of his eyes, glistening like deep mountain lakes. Vulnerable and yet full of trust, she abandoned herself to the blissful warmth of his smile, losing all sense of time.

Captured by his spell.

Lightning Source UK Ltd.
Milton Keynes UK
172141UK00001B/15/P